Flood Waters Rising

A Novel

by

E.M.A Hirst

Other Printed Works by Elizabeth Hirst

Short Story Collections

Monsters and Mist: A Fantasy Short Story Collection

Visit Pop Seagull Publishing on the Web at:

http://www.popseagullpublishing.com

Copyright 2011 by Pop Seagull Publishing
All rights reserved. No part of this book may be used or reproduced in any manner whatsoever without the written permission of Pop Seagull Publishing. For reprint permissions, please contact Elizabeth Hirst at jinyu_shanlin@yahoo.ca.

All characters in this book are fictitious. Any resemblance to persons living or dead is strictly coincidental.

Cover Design Copyright 2011 by Robin McLean
Published by
Pop Seagull Publishing
Oakville, Ontario, Canada

Printed and bound in the USA

Table of Contents

Prologue	5
The Last of the Pack	9
Misunderstanding	23
Djarro and Wardan	35
Experiment	53
Over My Head	61
Spines	69
Dead Meat	81
Bauble	91
She Rises	99
Djarro's Contribution	109
Yellowfine	119
Afternoon	125
Evening	141
False Dawn	157
Darkest Night	167
The City That Glides On Air	193
Zahenna's Song	203
Head in the Sand	213
Flood Waters Rising	247
Rue The Day	255
Packing In	265
Hauling Out	273
Over and Done	289
The Pwarnaa	301
The Warden	317
The Way Nature Made Him	339
Sun and Son	357
Mixed Signals	371

Leethia's New Commission	381
The Cut-Maker	397
Burning Ground	415
The Lost Cause	433
Vaedra	445
JASIMOTH	459
Epilogue	469
Appendix: Glossary of Terms	475

Prologue

Citizens of Nova,

I, Toraus Flood, am your only salvation.
With every day that passes, the Metriskan army is gathering its strength, planning to march on us while we are still helpless. Do not be fooled by their diplomatic façade—the Metriskans cast us out because they hate us and our way of life. Danorah Prel will not rest until every last resident of our fledgling colony, male, bitch or puppy, is drowned in their own blood, and all because of fear.

The Mettoa, the Bugbats, the Ziallon... these creatures are not our enemies, but Alpha Prel would have us bar them from our cities. She would have us hunt them down and kill them for meat when they stray onto our land. We seceded from Prel's council because she is a savage. We allowed ourselves to be exiled to Nova, at great cost to the trade of our clans, because we would not continue to exhibit such vicious behaviour. Now that our belly is showing, do you really believe that Prel's predators will hesitate to rip out our entrails?

The Elder family and their followers would have you stay here, between the mountains, waiting to be slaughtered by the Metriskans, citing the law of the pack. They argue that we are no more than a year gone from Prel's pack, and so to strike at her now would be to break the very truce bonds which prevent our society from descending into chaos. House Flood feels differently. We, the greatest of all the Novan clans, care only for the protection of you, the populace. For it is you who make us great, who fuel the economy so that we can survive here in this barren wilderness. House Flood is the populace's only ally against Alynnia Elder's assembly of naysayers and petty lawmakers, who, despite our petitions, remain disconnected from the real concerns of the colony. I say: What good is a pack, if it cannot defend its members against treachery? Despite the best intentions of Alynnia's assembly, we are engaged in a conflict in which our opponent cannot be trusted to adhere to the rules of good conduct. Shall we, then, die upholding the law, leaving only a race of Geedar who care nothing for common decency?

Friends, fellow dissenters, we must not allow our way of life to pass quietly into oblivion. We must strike the Metriskans first, doing to them what they are planning to do to us. Until every Metriskan city burns, we will never be safe.

Part One: Ferion

8 Flood Waters Rising

The Last of the Pack

I burned them all... I watched the cities, one by one, go up in flames. We were so close to accomplishing what seemed, at first, an impossible goal. The swamps were my only weakness, on the borders of the flatlands. They led their troops there, gradually, pulling them out of the cities just before my arrival. My scouts reported them as fleeing civilians. But they ambushed us on the Fortbine Hill, as we readied ourselves to take Pellor.

Now we die, one by one, outside the gates of the home we set out to defend, starving, freezing, so far from the warmth of our victory fires. My voice is weak from howling over the dead.

Toraus Flood, Unfinished Memoirs

Sithon watched Vaedra shiver from his darkened corner of the kitchen, listening to rain pattering against stone. The sound reminded him of his grandfather's faltering breath.

Under the tenuous shelter of a great fire place, Sithon's mother stirred at a small but heavy pot hanging over a pile of embers. She raised the stirring stick up, and Sithon noticed that the broth within dripped off of the spoon in gelatinous strings. Between the rancid odor of their lunch and the bitter smell of the mold climbing the walls, Sithon found the air thick with smell, difficult to breathe.

Above their heads, water pooled on the remainder of a ceiling support before gradually dripping down the slope where the roof had broken in two. From there it bubbled down a set of stairs and out a frame missing a door.

"Sithon," Vaedra raised a skeletal finger and beckoned him to the cauldron, "come here and try this. I want to make sure that it won't make Toraus sick."

Sithon rolled himself into a standing position by shoving the corner of the wall with his elbow.

"Don't test the walls that way. You're getting too big to think that they won't crumble under your weight."

Sithon checked the wall for any signs of damage. He stood about six feet tall, not yet fully grown, but his slouch concealed much of his actual height. Over years of crouching to fit into half-collapsed ruins, his posture had naturally developed that way. He knew that he had developed some stringy muscle over his chest since his last birthday, but he didn't know why Vaedra would make such a fuss about it. The wall looked fine... well, as fine as anything looked at Flood Waters.

Sithon padded over to where Vaedra was cooking. He accepted the spoon from her and took a cursory slurp of the liquid, ignoring its vile taste. It was delightfully fatty and coated his throat in a shield of warmth. He swung his tail back and forth and closed his eyes.

"I don't know who left that piece of carrion all the way up here," Vaedra tilted her head up at him, "but maybe it will help Toraus to stay alive for one more day. . ."

I'm glad the old bastard isn't toddering about any more, Sithon thought, *The only good thing about him is that he seems to know where to find food.*

Sithon thought these things, but never spoke of them to Vaedra. Vaedra had enough worries. Short, balding and brittle as deadwood from years of wasting under the M deficiency, his mother had wiry grey fur, where it grew at all, and the skin underneath was browned and tough as leather. Sithon wanted to pull her into his arms, but held back, afraid to hit her bad shoulder.

Sithon, in spite of all the hardships he had suffered as a child, had grown into a fine specimen of an adolescent Geedar. Long of torso and strong in the legs, his arms reached down past his knees, a trait which allowed him to run on all fours or, more usually, on his digitigrade hind legs. His thin, muscular arms ended in hands with thick, black paw pads on the undersides of his fingers, and short, dark claws. He had a fine face, as well, although it was a Flood face, and it disturbed him to see how much he resembled his grandfather when he looked in the well. He had tall, pointed ears, a long snout with a square black nose at the end which stayed wet and shiny unless he was sick or too dry, and blue-grey eyes like his mother's. The fur covering Sithon's body was a light grey, like the rest of his family.

Sithon's healthy physique would be a great help finding food, if he knew where any was.

Unfortunately, Vaedra wasn't any help with finding meat, either. All that Sithon or Vaedra had been permitted to see, during their life trapped in the ruins, was the ever-constant disappearance of the possessions that were left in their family home, followed by the delivery of partial carcasses to the border of the estate. The bodies of the beasts were always badly mangled, but they found the meat intact and edible.

Vaedra sighed, and Sithon could feel her breath brush past his belly.

"Ahhh, Sithon, there certainly have been better times for the Flood family."

Sithon shifted his weight. "I've collected more rainwater, mother. It's safely covered over in the root cellar."

Taking a dingy bowl made of a large beast's skull in her hand, Vaedra scooped a portion of the steaming broth out of the pot. She was about to leave the kitchen for Toraus' room.

"Wait! Mother! I've earned my portion of supper, haven't I?"

Vaedra's response blended with a clap of thunder, and sounded louder for it.

"You eat after Toraus is finished."

Vaedra headed further toward the rotting doorway, and Sithon decided to slink after her.

Toraus has been turning his food away lately. If I stay around long enough, I might get that first bowl after all.

Sithon stayed behind Vaedra as she ascended a short set of stairs to the master bedroom. Her ears made rough triangular silhouettes in front of him in the light that seeped out from under the doorway, and he followed those silhouettes. His footsteps were almost indistinguishable from the beating of the rain.

"I had meant to see Toraus before dinner anyway," he said.

"Mind you don't wake him," Vaedra replied as she pushed aside what remained of the rotted door to Toraus' apartment, "He was just telling me yesterday that he detests your attitude; he thinks that you smell too presumptuous, whatever that means, and he doesn't care much for your resemblance to your father, either."

Sithon brushed a palm along the wall and rubbed the mildew between his fingers. "Good old Grandfather..."

They both entered a square room with smooth stone walls painted with faded murals. An interior room with no windows, Toraus's chamber glowed with the flickering light of a rough oil lamp harassed by the drafts. Toraus, only visible as a lump under some sheets, began to stir. Vaedra moved into the room as though there were glass shards on the floor.

"And don't call him grandfather, either," she whispered, "You'll have him screaming for hours about racial purity."

Sithon padded over to the crate in the far corner that he liked to sit on. Once there, He slouched down and tried to concentrate on the faded frescoes adorning the walls.

Toraus had chosen this room during their last move because it was one of the few remaining rooms in the estate with its battle art intact. If Sithon remembered correctly, this one depicted the retreat from Metriska. On the left side of the room were the citizens of Nova, their masses fleeing for safety in the mountains of the North, and Toraus, young and bold and in a halo of light, at the head of the army defending their flight. On the right were the nameless hordes boiling over the plains of Metriska to purge the Novites from existence. Most of the figures had faded to outlines, and many were choked with moss, but Sithon remembered the stories well enough to fill in the edges.

Stories were much more exhilarating than Sithon's actual life. Vaedra's bony back was hunched over what was left of her father, with three of the family's five remaining blankets piled on top of him to make up for the wealth of holes that they all had acquired over the course of fifty years. He didn't have to suffer the indignity of sleeping on the cold, damp floor. His bed was made of a slab of salvaged metal from the city ruins, held up on wooden stumps. The original had disappeared long ago to be replaced by a pile of carcasses. Vaedra kept vigil here during the day and routinely placed pans of coals from the fire underneath the slab to keep Toraus at a comfortable temperature. If nothing else, at least they had wood to burn, smoky and damp though it usually was.

Sithon just sat, as Vaedra seemed to get more done on days when he kept her company. She would spend most days sitting there waiting by the bedside for a movement to indicate that Toraus was still alive. On the odd occasion that he did wake up in a lucid enough state to talk, Vaedra would rub her hands together and groom her face as though the breath coming from Toraus'foul lips warmed her. When Sithon compared them, side by side, he saw far too much resemblance. It was as if Toraus dragged her down somehow, his sickness adding to hers. She always looked older by the bedside.

Why are you still hanging on to your life, old mange? Give my mother a chance to enjoy the time that she has left to live.

Toraus' jaw dropped open, and his head flopped to the side. Sithon pulled his crate over to the bedside to protect Vaedra when he woke up. Any movement from Toraus, now that Sithon knew his own strength, sent the irrational part of Sithon's mind drifting back to that day when Toraus had destroyed Vaedra's shoulder. Sithon had been too young to help then, and his grandfather too healthy.

The smell of Toraus's foul breath became unavoidably sharp at this range. Sithon looked at Toraus's vicious fangs, and wished that his mother would find something to brush them with. Toraus's muzzle was becoming bony along the top ridge, and where it had once been straight from the forehead down to the nose, it was bumped with veins and leftover cartilage. The blankets looked as if they were draped over a tiny mountain range of sharp peaks and valleys. Vaedra reached out to touch Toraus's cheek and some of his stunted, stubbly fur fell out with her caress. Toraus' eyes opened like cracks in an earthquake. The irises were acid green laced with red, their gaze still sharp.

"Vaedra," he croaked, "what's that smell?"

"A broth, father," she held out the bowl to him, "I found a carcass on the borders of our land."

He laughed, or perhaps coughed. "A gift from my friends outside. But don't waste this precious gift on me. I don't need food to survive any more... I'm Toraus Flood! Eat, eat, and share some with the boy. He may not be pure Flood, but you'll need him when I'm gone."

Sithon scowled, and made sure that Vaedra noticed. He wondered why he bothered to hang around Toraus' bed all day.

I used to run around the valley and play. Now I just work and watch and try to comfort mother as best I can. I miss my uncles. Why did they have to die first and leave the Old Mange?

Vaedra held Toraus while he struggled with a fit of hacking coughs. Pulling him up by the armpits, Sithon helped Vaedra sit him against the wall. She then had a seat on the bed with her broth still in hand. It was feeding time, the most miserable time of the day. She filled a spoonful and held it out to him.

"We won't eat until you eat. You're the eldest, and you need to make yourself strong again so that we can stay here."

"Enough of this." he choked and coughed louder.

"Can't you see that I'm never going to recover? Stupid litterling, you're wasting your time here with me, when you should be fleeing to the city!"

Coughs consumed Toraus for a few moments. Sithon moved forward, as if to get in between them, but stopped when he realized what was happening.

You tail-chaser. He hasn't been strong enough to beat her in years.

When Toraus spoke to Vaedra again, he hunched over and so he had to look up to see her eyes. "If you don't leave the Northlands soon, you'll have no way to defend yourself from the kinds of things that will want to inhabit this territory after I'm gone. There will be bugbats... and mettoa. I didn't think that I'd brought you up to be so naïve."

Sithon got up and threw his crate aside to get the Old Mange's attention. By now, Toraus's insults were about as penetrating as puppy's teeth when directed at him, but he would not allow Toraus to abuse Vaedra that way. She had been too patient, too faithful to be treated as if she were worthless.

If I were mother, I would have killed him as soon as Uncle Mardon died and taken off for the outside world.

"So this is the thanks that my mother gets, after taking care of you, while you've been sick all these weeks? Why didn't we just slit your throat and throw you out as a peace offering to the bugbats, you old bastard!"

Toraus' old eyes burned. He pointed a knobby finger.

"Insubordination! In my army, you would have

been shot on sight for that remark, you half breed, insolent whelp!"

The hair on Sithon's back raised, and his eyes welled.

He barked. "At least we feel the same way about each other. I wouldn't want to think that you'd die without knowing what I thought of you, old mange!"

Sithon picked up his crate, and with one hammer blow of his arm, shattered it to pieces on the wall. "If you mistreat my mother any more, I'll crush you like this splintered wood!"

"You will not!" Vaedra stood up, her knees shaking. She winced at her old injury when she squared her shoulders.

Sithon stared at her, breathing hard and full of restless anger. Vaedra bared her proud Flood family fangs.

"I love Toraus, and you should give him the respect that he deserves! He kept us alive in this wilderness for fifty years, and he saved my life after your grandmother died. Without Toraus, you would not exist. Now get out of here before I throw *you* to the bugbats, you ignorant, impudent pup!"

Sithon stared at Vaedra for a moment. He felt another surge of anger, felt it fill his muscles with the urge to strike at something, anything, and make the blow more devastating than just smashing crates. A bolt of fear stabbed through him that he might lose control, and hurt her. He raised his tail up and ran down a corridor that led to the interior of the estate, feeling the cool air hit him at intervals from the doorways of ruined rooms.

Toraus' cough had sounded worse than ever, and the sudden wave of energy that overtook him filled Sithon with a heavy mix of dread and relief. The vitamin deficiency that they all suffered from, known as Virus M, caused those symptoms just before death. Uncle Mardon had even gotten up and tried to sharpen his favourite knife before he keeled over with a trail of blood dripping from his mouth.

Sithon burst through an open archway into a moss-lined hall which had lain unused for fifty years or more. In the old paintings concealed in Sithon's secret place, this hall was all shining marble and gleaming torch brackets, but for all of his life, it had looked more like a forest clearing with a spiral staircase. Young trees sprouted up at intervals from the debris-strewn floor, and ferns swayed with his passing as he made his way toward the stairs. He hopped up the staircase with a long-practised grace, despite the fact that many of the steps were missing or covered in chunks of mouldering plaster.

I want to be anywhere but here. Anywhere but here.

He had tried to escape the Northlands, once. If only he hadn't hit his head on the invisible barrier and passed out, he would be out there, living the good life. No Virus M, no Old Mange, no rotting meat drippings for breakfast. They dragged him back. They convinced him that he couldn't do it. But soon, Toraus would be dead, and the barrier would evaporate, like so much air. He wanted to run, that very minute, and never look back... but Vaedra needed his help, and

Vaedra couldn't run.

After conquering the stairway, Sithon inched along the wall of a second-floor hallway, his ears swivelling to detect any new creaks in the flooring. The sight of the bottom floor beneath, strewn with stones, dizzied him at times, but he pressed on, until he came to a place where the wall had crumbled, near the ceiling, to reveal a hole that was just big enough for him to wiggle through, and just low enough that he could pull himself into it by the tips of his fingers.

This he did, his feet scrabbling on the plaster, until he emerged, through several more layers of wall, into a small attic, relatively untouched by the decay of years. A rare window with its Glastik still intact, sheltered under a long overhang, let in a narrow beam of grey light by which Sithon could see a small collection of paintings, which he had arranged to good advantage on the opposite wall.

Sithon pulled in a heavy sigh, and released it. No one could reach him here. His relatives had long been too feeble to climb anywhere so high or so small, and the true door to this attic had caved in long ago. Even the ever-present mildew smelled better here, because the space was his, the warm beam of sunlight like a hidden treasure of which nobody knew.

Of all the multitude of ruined rooms in the estate, this place was the only one he would regret leaving; not because of its privacy, or its tranquility, but because *she* still existed there. The only vestige of love and warmth this place had ever known: his grandmother, Darna.

Of the many pictures of her that had hung in the estate at the beginning, only these six remained, and yet, even in such a small sampling of images, her goodness shone through, like a light from her eyes. Here, she was standing in formal regalia in the warmly lit great hall, welcoming all to the estate. In another, she held Uncle Mardon in her arms, beaming at his tiny face and blissfully unaware that in time he would come to be known as Mardon the Murderer.

Vaedra had told him stories about her, in the old days, about how she could make something delicious from the worst cuts of meat, and how she calmed Toraus's rages and instilled him with compassion. According to Vaedra, Darna had possessed the ability to make any miserable hovel a home, simply by her loving presence. To an outsider, used to the comforts of friends and family, she might sound like an exemplary mother, and no more. To Sithon, she became no less than a legendary hero of old, someone able to soothe wounds at a touch, and right all of the wrongs of the world with love.

Toraus had put a stop to the stories, forbidding all mention of Darna, and he had destroyed all of the images of her that he could find as he slowly descended into madness and grief. For all Sithon knew, Vaedra had forgotten her too, after years of beatings and cruel manipulation at the hands of the old mange... but nothing could make him forget.

Sithon noticed that one of the paintings (Darna sitting on a stool before an open window, sunlight streaming over her upturned face) had developed a green streak from leaking rainwater. With nothing handy to plug the hole in the low-lying roof, Sithon picked up the frame and moved it to the other side of the arrangement.

He leaned forward and rubbed his cheek against the canvas, whining softly.

"Someday, I'll leave the world with good memories of me, like you did. I'll stay with her, because that's what you would do. Farewell, Grandmother," he said.

When he was almost out of the hole again, Sithon heard a wail that cracked every few seconds. He immediately recognized that Vaedra had been crying for a long time. Sithon saw her long before she could have seen him. She stumbled into the atrium, arms outstretched in the growing darkness.

"Sithon," she squawked, "come out here, you wretched beast! You've killed your grandfather, and now you're going to get what you've earned. Come out and receive your inheritance, Sithon..."

Sithon watched her for a while until she gave up on trying to find him and collapsed into a tuft of moss at the base of the stairs. There she made soft sniffling noises, and finally fell asleep.

Convinced that she wouldn't be getting up until morning, Sithon started back toward Toraus's bedroom. Someone had to bury the Old Bastard and try to salvage the soup.

Misunderstanding

... and I, as the last true upholder of pack law, was left with a conundrum: how was I to dispose of the beast? Barely a month had passed since our two packs had split apart, he embarking on his gruesome errand and we, left to wait. If my government killed him, we could no longer claim the legal high ground. The answer came in the form of Halra, a young servant of mine whose Talent had only just blossomed. You see, Halra could make shields out of nothing more than air...

Queen Alynnia Elder, from 'A Treatise on the Implementation of Pack Law: Case Studies from the State'

Sithon licked at his fingertips. They tasted metallic like scab tissue and stung. His feet weren't much better, but he had a hard time reaching the tips of his toes with his tongue. After first digging Toraus' grave and then filling it in, his back had all of the flexibility of a dry twig.

Vaedra strode toward him the tall grass. The heads of the stalks waved back and forth, and eventually her ears poked up among them. Sithon crouched a little bit lower behind the tree where he had made his bed. Vaedra sniffed the air, swivelling her ears to take in ambient noise. Sithon cringed as his heel dug into a stick and caused it to snap. Vaedra's head turned toward him. She took another few sniffs to confirm his whereabouts, and called out.

"I know that you're in there, Sithon. You might as well show yourself."

Sithon didn't move.

Vaedra paused. "I won't beat you. Father was the one who favoured beating you. You're my last living relative now."

Vaedra's ears drooped and she sighed. Sithon noticed that she hadn't stopped to smooth her tail, and her wrap was skewed as though she hadn't re-tied it this morning.

Sithon moved out from behind the tree. His mother ran to him as soon as she saw him, and they met at the tree line. She threw her arms around him and Sithon jumped back a little. He relaxed when she made no move toward the soft spots on his wrists or stomach.

"I need your help," she said, "to move Toraus' body. I can't do it alone."

Sithon's tail wagged. "You don't need to worry about that, Mother. I've already buried him for you, in the clearing by the rock fall."

Vaedra let her arms drop to her sides. She blinked, and her jaw grew slack.

"You disgraceful excuse for a son! I never, ever gave you permission to dispose of Toraus' body that way. Do you have any idea what you've just done? No, no you wouldn't, would you?" She grabbed Sithon's wrist faster than he would have expected, and let her nails penetrate through the thin fur to skin. "Come with me." Sithon went with her, at first. He didn't want to cause any more pain in his hands by struggling. She led him through the forest on paths that he thought only he knew about, the ones that would get them there the fastest.

"Mother, would you slow down?"

"Not until we get there. Keep walking."

"What is your problem, are you crazy? Let me go." He twisted around and finally got free.

Vaedra glared at him, but kept walking. Her tail stuck out at a slight angle, every hair on it pulled straight back.

"What's my problem? I need to take Toraus to the edge of our land, and I'm too weak to dig him up. That's my problem. Now march, puppy, you are digging up his corpse and that's final."

Sithon followed her, eager to resolve the argument.

"I thought you'd be happy with me. I was paying my last respects."

"Respect!" Vaedra's fur bristled all over, "What would you know about showing respect to your elders? The last thing you said to him was that you were going to smash him like rotting wood! If you want to prove to me that you're sorry, you'll do as I say."

"Fine," Sithon crossed his arms, "but first I want to know why you want this so badly."

Vaedra's tail relaxed a little. They were drawing near to the clearing by the rock fall. Up ahead, Sithon could see the little mound where he had laboured overnight.

He had even found a nice, flat rock to stick in the ground as a headstone.

His mother stopped at the edge of the sunlight. The tip of her nose was covered in golden highlights, and the rest of her stayed in the gloom.

"I want you to retrieve Toraus' body," she said quietly, "because there is a chance that we may be able to bring him back to life."

Sithon snorted. "Then I'm most certainly not doing it. You've been grieving too heavily, mother. Go back to bed until you accept that he's really gone."

"No," Vaedra cried, "My son, you have to believe me!"

She stepped forward and grabbed Sithon's chest ruff.

"Toraus told me before he died. He has allies. . . they have the technology to do it. He can live on forever!"

Sithon made sure to be gentle as he pried his mother's fingers away from his fur.

That old mange was always claiming to be immortal. I'm sure that he would only assert it more heavily on his death bed. Mother needs rest, and some hard evidence that he's gone for good. Maybe then she'll start grieving for him.

"Very well, mother," Sithon conceded, "I suppose I'll just have to dig him up."

Sithon held up his right hand as he walked over to the burial mound. As he went, he peeled off one of the scabs on his fingers, revealing new, healthy skin. His wounds healed that way sometimes. The pain could be much larger than the extent of the injury. He immediately went to his knees upon reaching the grave. The sooner that he got working, the sooner Vaedra would be ready to travel. She followed him over to the grave.

"Dig deep, now. We haven't got that much longer until your grandfather's allies get here. I won't have you floundering about in the dirt when they arrive." Sithon grunted and dug his nails into the earth. It had settled since being filled into the hole, and that made it harder to dig out. The rain had also made it heavy. He grabbed one handful and flung it out behind him, then another, and soon a little pile of dirt had accumulated behind the grave.

When a pair of feet landed square between his shoulders, he cursed his weary senses for not alerting him sooner. Sithon fell forward, his ribcage bruising on the uneven ground. Sithon tried to use his arms to push himself up, but found his opponent too heavy to throw off. The attacker used Sithon's movement to catch his arms and force them behind his back. This action sent Sithon thumping onto the uneven dirt again, the ache in his ribs and back pulsating with every heartbeat. While he groaned, the Geedar on his back clamped a pair of restraints over his wrists.

Sithon tried to find his mother. At the edge of the forest she dodged around a tree in an attempt to avoid a short orange male dressed in gray.

"Mother, run," Sithon yelled.

Vaedra peeked at him around the tree, and in that moment of unsteadiness another Geedar, tall with auburn fur, snatched her up like a small child, her arms pinned to her sides. She kicked, but her legs flung forward in a useless flail. She snapped, but could not reach anywhere on her attacker's body to bite. Without any further recourse, Vaedra howled, a high and desperate tone that denoted the need for immediate aid. Sithon whined in harmony.

The tall Geedar holding Vaedra brought his muzzle indecorously close to her right ear, so Sithon could see.

When he spoke, she flinched away slightly. "Shhhh, calm down, lady. This isn't the way we're going to get through this. Now, we've come a long way *just* to talk to you, so answer our questions and things will go a lot more smoothly." He said.

Vaedra bristled.

"First, you answer me a question. Who sent you all this way to talk to a couple of worthless outborns?" she croaked.

"Oh, dear," said Vaedra's captor, assuming an expression of mock disappointment, "It seems that the M deficiency has made this one go feeble-minded already. Not only is she unaware of her, um, illustrious heritage, she has already forgotten that I am the one asking the questions. Dacc, get out your spear."

The short Geedar who had originally accosted Vaedra ran over to the rock fall and returned with a barbed spear of about the same height as himself. He levelled it at Vaedra's throat.

"Don't hurt her!" Sithon growled.

The Geedar holding Vaedra set her down, and in a leisurely fashion drew a pair of leg restraints from his knapsack and clamped them onto Vaedra. The guard holding Sithon down pulled him to his feet.

"Now, sit," said Dacc. Vaedra did so, scowling. The tip of Dacc's spear followed her throat as she went. The taller Geedar, now free of his burden, approached Sithon.

"I will hurt her. Unless... you tell me some basic information about how you scum have managed to survive out here for so long. The Royal Rakarian Empire wanted you to suffer and die in the Northlands, with the lack of vitamin M in the soil. Indeed, all scientific fact would dictate that your upper vilobes should have worn out long before now. Where have you been getting your food?"

Sithon considered lying. He hung his head, brows shadowing his eyes.

"I don't know. My grandfather kept it a secret from us." He stammered. Visions of Vaedra being beaten by Toraus flashed through his head, making his hands start to curl into fists on reflex.

The interrogator flashed an insincere smile. Sithon noticed that his teeth were dull at the tips, ugly. He continued.

"Okay, I'm not unreasonable. I'll give you one more chance to save your mother a great deal of pain. It has to do with an internal matter of the Rakarian

Army Special Forces. Now, we don't let civilians near this area. It belongs to our government and we have been using it, at considerable expense to ourselves, to try and kill your family quietly. Naturally we were shocked and alarmed when we learned that your mother had become pregnant with you. Your father could only have come from one of two places: our military station on the edge of this land, or, unfortunately, your own family. So tell me this: who was your father, really?"

Sithon flinched a little. His lips drew back.

"My uncle Mardon was also my father. Toraus wanted an heir badly enough to force my mother and my uncle together for the purpose." Across the clearing, Vaedra's eyes and ears displayed disgust, but the more prominent posture of her back displayed pride.

The auburn interrogator sneered.

"Ah, it's just as I suspected. You still have the audacity to lie to me after a show of superior force. Stupid Flood; Stupid, but not inbred. You see, your Uncle was much older than your mother, meaning that his illness was much more pronounced at the time she became pregnant. That also means that your grandfather is out of the question. I only left you that option to try and establish good faith, as it were. Oh well. We'll do things the hard way, now." He said, turning toward Vaedra.

Sithon's biceps tensed. He applied a subtle but noticeable pressure on the grip of the Geedar holding him from behind. The soldier (Sithon assumed he was a soldier, anyway, as he wore the same jumpsuit as the others, tan with a blue stylized paw on the breast) stayed rigid. Sithon kept on flexing his muscles, but held still, his teeth clenched. Perhaps the interrogator did not know the location of Vaedra's injuries. In a swift, smooth motion, the auburn Geedar simultaneously seized Vaedra's weak arm and thrust her shoulder forward with his palm. At first her muscles tensed in resistance, but the exertion of the interrogator's weight on her already injured joint won out after a moment of gritted teeth and clenched biceps.

Vaedra's torso ground forward. With his ears pricked forward, Sithon could only just hear the click and pop of broken cartilage under the hoarse outpouring of her breath.

A sweat broke out on the tip of his nose. Some larger force inside him wanted to go to her, escape the confines of the body trapped by soldiers and pour out his rage upon them all. Hatred, smouldering resentment and frustrated loyalty expanded beneath his ribs. With every breath he felt as though he grew a little bit larger, a little bit stronger. Blood pounded at the confines of his skin, swirling with the ebb and flow of luminescent power. Sithon twitched his right forearm. The soldier's grip slackened a little, then he struggled to regain it, pinching Sithon's skin in the process.

Vaedra, still prone, uttered a whine. The auburn Geedar grinned at Sithon and applied more pressure. Sithon bared every tooth in his mouth. The hair along his back bristled.

He yelled, "Out-born parasite! I'll kill you for

this!"

The interrogator spat out a witty reply from behind his ugly, dull teeth, but Sithon heard only the roar of his blood, pounding behind his ears, through his brain. He took a step forward, then another, the guard dragging behind him like a bundle of deadwood for the fire. Sithon shook him off and used the few seconds of freedom to pull outward on his wrist restraints. He felt them bend, twist and finally snap apart. His ears twinged; the guard was running up behind him, forcing his heavy boots into the soft earth. Sithon could feel the vibrations from the guard's footfalls, the crack of a twig, smell the aggression-triggered hormones in the air. His consciousness felt large enough that he could track each motion of the leaves in the trees and still step aside to catch the arm of the guard as he charged by. Sithon used the momentum of the guard's run to shove him in the direction of the interrogator, who had let go of Vaedra in favour of pointing a small weapon in Sithon's direction. The guard lost his footing and stumbled into the interrogator.

Both Geedar toppled to the ground, causing the interrogator's weapon to go off. A shower of miniature lightning bolts crackled above Vaedra's head, knocking loose a large dead branch extending from the lower part of the tree that she leaned on.

Sithon lunged forward to protect his mother, arriving just in time to grip the branch and hurl it away. It rolled toward Toraus' half-dug grave and stopped when it hit the pile of disturbed earth along the edge. Sithon attempted to locate Vaedra. Now a few feet away, she struggled with Dacc, the spear-bearer. Sithon put a foot forward to go to her, but he flinched after a small shock like the sting of a fire-warmed needle coursed through his back muscles.

"Don't move, unless you want another. I warn you now, tree branches may not fend very well in the face of an energy weapon, but you will do even worse. It'll cook you from the inside out," hissed the interrogator.

Sithon whined. The other guard stood at his right side with another stinging energy weapon trained on his head. He pushed his nose forward, trying to get just a bit nearer to Vaedra. With her back to the grave, she gripped Dacc's spear, her hands spaced wider than his, trying to gain control of the weapon. Sithon wondered why soldiers who carried fearful, energy-based weaponry would use something as crude as a spear—then he noticed that Dacc wore thick protective gloves. Under Vaedra's tiny right hand at the end of the spear was a pivot switch.

He yelped, "Mother, let go of the spear!" Vaedra pulled back for only half a second but it caused her grip to slip. The switch turned, sending a wave of blue electricity down the shaft of the spear. Sithon pulled back his lips in horror, his eyes going wide.

Vaedra hurtled backward, and for a moment Sithon captured her in his memory, arced over in mid-air with her thin hair streaming like a malleable metal caught in the sun.

Her arms floated forward, embracing the ghost of an imaginary lover. When her feet touched ground she was still not in control of her bodily movements. Moving at incredible speed with no one to catch her, she landed on the discarded branch by Toraus's grave, its broken edge piercing her chest. Sithon smelled her blood, his blood and the pungent pheromones expelled by the shock of Vaedra's impact all together in one noxious cocktail.

Vaedra shivered once. She pulled herself up just enough to lock eyes with Sithon. He heard her last, shuddering breath as she leaned back and her body pulsed out its final heartbeats onto the earth.

Djarro and Wardan

Although any conjecture about Toraus's longevity in an environment free of Vitamin M would ultimately remain conjecture, Halra's shield optimized the chances that Toraus would die free of heirs. His mate was, indeed, pregnant at the time of the exile, but an infant pup can only last a week at most without a source of M. A grown male, on the other hand, whose reserves have built in the Upper Vilobe over time, can last for many years. Thus, we tied the shield to Toraus's life force, causing it to dissipate only after his death.

Queen Alynnia Elder, cont'd

Sithon's nerves stabbed him. He smelled the exact location of the guards, heard the pulse of their blood at all of the vital points in their bodies. His jaw clenched. While the guards still stared at the corpse of his mother, Sithon reached back with both hands at once, ripping their energy weapons from their hands. He made sure to look directly into the interrogator's eyes as he crushed the metallic oval capsules in his hands. Hot bolts of the same energy that felled the tree limb seared his palms, arcing out around his fists for a few seconds before dissipating into an ill-smelling smoke. He held on to the burning debris until he could no longer stand the pain. After dropping the broken weapons on the ground, he held up his charred palms to the interrogator.

"If you know as much about the Floods as you claim, then you'll know that we always commemorate our first kill. This ought to scar, wouldn't you say?" Sithon said.

The tip of the interrogator's tail showed between his knees. He grimaced, pulling his ears back.

The interrogator said "I wouldn't become too confident. We... still have... a spear..."

Sithon grinned, and advanced on them.

A flash of light and a wicked sound like the solid crack of two rocks colliding stopped Sithon's advance, and left the soldiers looking to the east. There, in the harsh light of the morning sun, stood a Geedar larger than Sithon thought Geedar grew to be. His fur was ruddy brown with black, splashy stripes that rippled down his back. He had relatively short legs, a long, bulky torso, and shoulders that looked as though they could crush a rock in one armpit. His bent posture made the fur along his spine stand straight. Although Sithon could not imagine who made the clothes to fit such a creature, he wore a deep blue tabard that hung around his neck like a cravat and a cream linen loincloth.

The large interloper held a long staff with blades shaped like curving leaves on either end. His stance, feet apart and weapon forward, communicated a distinct lack of tolerance for trickery.

The interrogator, once so full of bombast, oozed a

chorus of nervous smells. He raised his hands, nudging Sithon in the ribs as he did so.

"Raise your hands, boy. Have the sense to know when you're outclassed." He hissed imperiously.

Sithon did so, palms outward. The new stranger wore the same livery as the soldiers, and so Sithon grudgingly admitted to himself that they probably knew what to do in the presence of this monster.

Using a nose the width of Sithon's hand, the monster tested the air.

"Queen's Special Forces, I see," he grimaced at the three soldiers, "Well, you've made a royal botch of this expedition, haven't you? Let's just drop that spear, now. We're on the same side so there aint nothing to fear."

On the count of three, Dacc opened his hands and let the spear clatter to the ground. The red hulk slowly placed his staff on the grass, as well.

The giant addressed Sithon, saying "Now, I trust there won't be any funny business out of you, Mister Flood. I don't mean you no harm neither."

Sithon noticed with some surprise the conspiratory arch of the agent's eyebrow, the mischievous prick of his ears when he promised him no harm. It reminded him of the way that his Uncle Mardon used to look at him after lying about Vaedra's whereabouts to Toraus.

Sithon let himself exhale. His ears lowered, his fur flattened. The charge in his blood became a weight in his veins, then goose-bumps, then a chill. He shivered, twitched his tail, and the chill dissipated.

The giant nodded.

He said, "Now then, allow me to introduce myself. Lieutenant Djarro Baero, Queen's special operatives."

He started rummaging through a pocket sewn into the back of his tabard.

"I believe that I've got a badge here somewhere... Ah, here we are." Lt. Djarro said, producing a small piece of crystal formed in the shape of a stylized paw ringed in flame.

Dacc perked his ears up. He asked, "What do you want with us, uh, sir?"

"Get out of our air space, that's what we want from you. Tell Nikira he's been overridden by the Queen's men. The Northland border guard answers only to Queen Leethia, so even your illustrious High Commander lacks the power to control us. You'll be handin' these two over to me, unless you want to take up the contents of the new constitution personally with your Queen," Djarro said, arms crossed.

The interrogator tried to argue. "But... but we..."

"Go on, get," Djarro said, waving a meaty paw,

"Easiest mission you'll ever run. Now hand over the body, before I start to get impatient."

"What do we tell the General?"

"Nothin' I'd say to him, that's for sure." The Lieutenant snorted, unclasping a wide piece of cloth from his back and laying it out on the ground. After making sure the sheet lay flat, Djarro trudged over to Vaedra's body. He studied her from one side, then the other. Then he picked her up almost gently, if someone of his size ever really looked gentle. When a trickle of blood touched Djarro's fingers, Sithon saw the hair on the back of his neck raise in a nearly invisible shiver.

"They don't teach you recruits the same respect we learned going into the service. My basic training commander would have had you lot tied to a post with your eyes to the afternoon sun for harming a captive with noble blood." The Lieutenant muttered.

The interrogator spat back, "Pah! Noble blood... Floods are only worth slightly more than small game where I come from."

Djarro laid Vaedra on the sheet from his back. The ridge of his spine bowed upward. He gave a ghost of a chuckle, baring teeth the width of garden spades.

"Well, if she were an animal, she were a wretched thing. We watched her all her life in the border guard. She was born to this waste, and, as you saw to yourself, here she died. You've accrued all the honour of shooting a caged animal," He said, giving a dismissive flick of his left ear.

The three soldiers stood still while Djarro wrapped Vaedra in the white linen, buckling it between her legs and securing it around her fragile torso. When he finished, only her head and legs showed from underneath the sheet.

Sithon gestured to the interrogator with his head, indicating that the soldiers should leave. The interrogator sneered at him, and the orange-furred guard made a rude gesture.

The guard's motion caught Djarro's attention.

"What do you want, a kiss?" Djarro bellowed, "Shove off!"

The three soldiers turned tail and ran, and their ship slid out of sight along the horizon within ten minutes.

Sithon called out to the Lieutenant. "I could have escaped by now, you know."

"You'd be a bloody fool to try," he called back over his shoulder, "Where you plan on going, eh? How're you going to get there? Who's going to take you in? If you've got half a brain you'll stay right where you are."

Sithon's response froze in his lungs. He sunk into his trademark slouch.

Djarro wrapped his arms around Vaedra and hefted her over his shoulder. From there he carefully extended her over his back until a pair of metal loops on her shroud connected with a pair of hooks on the back of his tabard. When Djarro finished, Vaedra sat upright with her back to his, leaning over the way she did when she fell asleep sitting up. Djarro swung back and forth. Vaedra swung too, but did not fall.

With a satisfied posture Djarro said to Sithon, "Are you coming, or aren't you?"

"That depends where you're going, and what you plan on doing about Toraus. My mother said some pretty crazy things before those soldiers came. Said there was someone who could bring Toraus back, of all things." Sithon said, crossing his arms.

Djarro motioned to the sky and said, "Well, I can tell you that I'm headed someplace better than where *they* were going to take you. And with all due respect to the old guy in the ground, we got to see what we can do about your mother first."

Sithon stepped forward a little. "Do...? She's dead too, isn't she?"

"Dead as a doornail; but that don't matter to Wardan. Follow me if you want to know more about it. I got to get back soon." Djarro said. He started to walk away into the forest. The shadows played in the stripes on his arms and legs, extending them into camouflage.

"Wait," he called. Picking his way around Vaedra's blood and Toraus's burial mound, Sithon ran toward the place where Djarro merged with the shadows.

Sithon refrained from speaking for much of the journey.

Eventually, he heard Djarro say, "We just passed the border of the Northlands, young Flood. You're free now."

"You don't quite understand my situation do you, Duh-Jar-o? I've had a rough day. I'm all out of pleasantries. Just take me wherever you plan on taking me and spare me the tour. I know where I am." Sithon grumbled, bearing a single fang.

A bird screeched overhead. Sithon crouched down, protecting his head with his hands while tucking his tail between his legs.

"Euh! What in Bleirah's Pool* was that?"

Djarro chuckled, although his face looked kind of scary when he did. "That was a bird. You might've seen them, but you'd never of heard them, eh? Noisy little buggers, birds. Shit all over the sentries at the HQ, too. Out here in the South o' the North, as we like to call it, we got all sorts o' things."

Sithon rolled his eyes, saying, "There's something that you can answer for me. . . why didn't my family have those sorts of things? There was never anything in the ruins but the Floods and the trees. What happened to the other creatures? The old mange could remember when we had them, and so could Uncle Mardon. They all just sort of... went away after the exile, they said."

"Ah," the Lieutenant said, testing the wind, "That was the Royal families. They drove the animals out and then erected a barrier in the hope that you'd all die of Vitamin M deficiency. So much for that, eh?"

Sithon mumbled to hide the quaver in his voice. "I didn't see any barriers..."

Djarro stopped to sniff at a tree trunk. After pausing for a moment, brows furrowed, he made a turn to the south-west.

"You won't," he replied, "It's not the kind of thing that you see with your eyes."

When Djarro went ahead at the turning point, Sithon watched for a moment before continuing on. Vaedra's head mirrored the Lieutenant's head from behind, giving him the aspect of a demigod with one head in the world of the living and one in the world of the dead. Her vacant gaze pointed past Sithon, past the forest and back into a place that no one ever returned from.

Sithon jogged to catch up with Djarro.

When he reached the Lieutenant, he asked, "Can only the dead see the barrier? Can my mother see it, or Toraus? That's a bitter punishment. . . to be able to see your prison only after you're unable to escape it."

Djarro shook his head, answering, "How should I know? I'm not dead. I wouldn't be surprised if that were the case, though. The Rakarian senate would probably support just about any punishment for a Flood, in this world or the next."

Sithon kicked a bushy plant in front of him, making detached fronds fly into the air.

"But you're helping me! Why would you work for the rotting out-born Rakarians if you want to help me," He growled.

Djarro reached over unexpectedly and rumpled Sithon's hair, making him cringe. Sithon almost gave in to the urge that told him to bite the lieutenant's hand, but then he remembered the size of the hand and thought better of it.

"Aw, lad, don't think badly of us yet. Sometimes the best way to avoid notice is to place yourself right in the thick o' things." Djarro said, with a wink.

Sithon didn't answer.

A building loomed up ahead, imposing its rigid outline onto the soft curves of the shifting canopy. Moss and brown rust stains coated the sides of the gritty cube, making it look like a rotten piece of cake.

Djarro walked up to a dark rectangular area on the side of the building closest to them and brushed some moss from its edges. The resulting dust cloud made him cough, then sneeze, then wave his paw in the air, pronouncing the day to be too hot.

Sithon shifted his weight from one foot to the other. Spores tickled his nostrils, but he willed himself not to sneeze.

"So this is the place where my mother is to be kept; a mouldy old bunker crumbling under its own weight? Yes, Djarro, I'm liking this plan better and better. It's too bad we couldn't include Toraus in all the *fun*." He said, crossing his arms.

Djarro thrust a hand into his tabard pocket. He emerged with a black bit of metal, grooves set at the end. He fitted the grooved end of the metal into the dark patch on the wall, then jiggled it back and forth a few times. Sithon heard a metal squeal and a click. Djarro replaced the trinket back in his tabard pocket and proceeded to roll the dark patch in the wall up into the ceiling.

Sithon crept, nose forward, to the new doorway. Beyond Djarro he could smell lichen, rotting vegetation and cool air coming from deep within the earth. Somewhere far below, something rumbled.

Djarro loomed down on Sithon. The afternoon sun obscured all but his gargantuan, shifting jaw.

He said, "This here's the tunnel to The Burrow. Follow me on the way down or you might not like where you end up. Now, you've got a pretty smart mouth for someone I could break in half, so heed me on this: When we meet Wardan, don't be testing out that wit 'o yours on him. He may decide you're not as useful whole as in pieces."

As the Lieutenant ambled forward into the tunnel, his footfalls changed from the robust crunch of a heavy predator moving along the forest floor to the uniform scrabble of claws on gravel. Sithon pushed forward into the dark behind Djarro, hoping to keep enough distance between them that he would not have to smell his mother's congealing blood in the still air.

No sooner had Sithon's eyes adjusted to the darkness to the point that he could track Djarro's movement than the door behind them slid shut. He shivered as a gust of gritty air swept past them.

For a moment, Sithon felt walled in by darkness, as though the blackness of the tunnel was so complete as to enter his mouth and lungs, to creep behind his eyes and forever blind him to the outside world. Worse yet he smelled Vaedra's blood mingled with the damp.

Sithon heard a click, and saw Djarro's hand descending from a pin on the shoulder of his tabard which emitted a round, focussed beam of light.

"How did you do that? Why isn't that little torch burning you?" Sithon asked, his words pinging from the walls.

Djarro grunted, "Science," and went on.

Sithon tried to forget where he was while they descended through a set of pathways arranged in a gradually inclined spiral. While Sithon languished in claustrophobia, Djarro sang a very lengthy song about hunting.

Ooooooh,
The bugbat's spine
Don't waste the tines
They're mighty good for roastin'

Bring on the ale
And a slice of tail
Our leader I'll be toastin'

We'll hunt the mighty forest down
To every mouse and then,
"Wardan," we'll shout,
Oh, call him out!
He'll bring them back again

Just when Sithon thought that he'd rather venture back up the tunnel in the dark than listen to another verse of Djarro's drinking song, the Lieutenant's footfalls stopped.

Up ahead the tunnel opened out without any apparent light sources. Djarro motioned for Sithon to stay put. He and his patch of mysterious light migrated over to a box on the left-hand wall.

Sithon shielded his face as white light, like the light from Djarro's pin amplified a hundred times stung his eyes. Up above, beyond a mess of rafters painted a grey-white shone long tubes of contained sunlight. Sithon's tail pushed on the back of his legs, and his knees trembled. They were in a huge, flat pavilion with a floor of polished brown stone.

Djarro opened his arms, saying, "Welcome to the Burrow. You'll be staying here for a couple 'o weeks while we fix up your mother."

The Lieutenant stepped aside, to reveal a mattress and some blankets, held up by a frame of metal tubing.

"This is yours," he said, "Put it wherever you'd like, you've got the run of the place."

Sithon skipped across to Djarro, scrupulously avoiding the reflections the lights made on the floor. He tensed inwardly when he heard Djarro stifle a chuckle.

Using both hands, Sithon tested the bed. To his surprise, it gave underneath his weight.

"This is nicer than what Toraus kept for himself. Why are you giving me this? For that matter, why is this place so howling clean? I could sweep all day and not make a floor shine like this." He said.

Djarro took a deep breath and exhaled slowly, his eyes closed. Sithon trembled, imagining Djarro struggling not to hit him for his impertinent questions. Instead, when Djarro opened his eyes again, he reached a hand out and placed it gently on Sithon's shoulder. He had a sad face, for all that its blockiness would seem to guarantee menace.

He pointed across the room and said, "If you go in there and turn left, there's a wash basin and a toilet. In an emergency, like a ventilation shut-down or a cave-in, the service elevator— uh, platform that will raise you up to the level of the rest of the base-- is behind this wall and to your left. Be careful, though. Always ask for permission to enter the base while you're coming up. I'll show you how to use the voice sender later. The men here are all loyal, but if we've got an unexpected visitor it could mean your life if you're seen."

"So... this isn't the whole place?" Sithon asked, flexing his ears incredulously.

"No way," Djarro replied, "We've got a whole complex upstairs full of gadgets and military doodads... but it's under surveillance— er, other Geedar that we don't know can watch it from far away. This is just an old storage basement that we've converted."

Djarro sunk into a whisper, "The higher-ups think that it's been caved in to cut costs. That's just the way we like it."

In a sudden wave, Sithon's limbs felt heavy, his head felt light. Now that he stood still, hearing nothing but the distant whir of machinery, he realized that the sound of the wind through the trees was gone. In this blank room, with Djarro, a bed, and her corpse, Vaedra was impossible to ignore.

"What will happen to my mother now? Where will she go?" Sithon said, concentrating on the ground and trying to take shallow breaths to avoid the dreaded death smell.

Djarro pulled something small, shiny and grey out of his pinafore and flipped it open.

"I'm on that right now. Just a sec," he held up a finger and spoke into the grey thing, "Plok, this is Djarro. Tell Wardan that the target is safely within the Burrow, and have him come down when all is clear."

"Right away, Lieutenant," the grey thing said. Sithon assumed that the voice belonged to someone in the surface level of the base. Djarro waved a hand, saying, "Alright, lad, you have a seat and then in a few minutes Wardan'll come down for your mother. He'll get her all fixed up... if it's possible."

Sithon plopped himself down on the cot and felt the springs dig into his leg muscles.

He sat there on the cot without saying anything for quite some time. He started when the elevator doors opened and a young, gangly Geedar in a long white smock hopped out. Long sections of mane framed his face and ran down the length of his back, where a leather thong secured them in a loose ponytail. Strange, shiny glass discs covered his eyes, secured by a strap around his head. Upon reaching Sithon, he immediately grasped hands with him and sniffed him behind the ears. Sithon mirrored his actions, bewildered. Wardan smelled like musky fur and sharp chemical spray.

Wardan wavered as though he could not contain his excitement, saying "You must be the Flood boy. It's a pleasure to meet you. I'm Wardan, Head of the Burrow Laboratories." Sithon noted his wide-eyed gaze and sincere smile.

"Sithon. I'm not really a Flood, you know... I'm a bastard." He replied. Wardan curled his upper lip.

"Yes... well, contrary to what your family might have told you, you have Flood genetics. In the eyes of science, you are the rightful heir."

Sithon hesitated, "I... I don't understand..."

Wardan waved a hand at Sithon, and once again he stifled the urge to bite.

"You don't have to understand. It's the truth. It's science," Wardan said, "Djarro, unhook the body and hold it up for inspection."

"Yes, Wardan." The Lieutenant said, pulling Vaedra from behind his back.

Wardan entered the shadow of Djarro's bulk and ran his hands over Vaedra's frame. Sithon crept over, and listened as Wardan talked to himself.

"Hmmm... Significant M deficiency damage to the nervous system, wasted muscles, demolished rib cage, one two three four rib bones destroyed entirely and if I'm not mistaken, one two three badly healed fractures to the rib cage and shoulders. That'll be Toraus' work, I'm sure." He took his hands off of her back and caressed her face. "Let's see about the skull now... not much wrong here, although she could use some ocular implants to sharpen her vision. Moving downward under the ribs she has significant damage to the heart, lungs and stomach, any one of which could have given the cause of death." Wardan went silent for a minute, letting his hands drop to his sides.

"Take her to the suspension tanks. We'll start work in the morning."

Wardan turned on his heel and started walking back to the elevator, mumbling, "I don't know what we're going to do about that upper vilobe, though, it's almost completely consumed. We'll have to find a live donor somewhere, and then synchronize it with the rest of the organs' healing cycles. This is going to be risky."

"Uh, Mr. . . Wardan?" Sithon called.

Wardan pulled his ears back.

"Yes?" He said.

"How did you figure out what was wrong with her? You just put your hands on her and you knew."

Wardan closed his eyes and sighed, "Oh, I forgot that you don't know about my Talent. I can raise the dead."

Great, Sithon thought, *another maniac.*

Experiment

Truly, it was a punishment worse than death, to watch everyone he loved die before him. I knew his mate, Darna. I watched her continue begging us for mercy as we flew away toward Rakaria without her. But the law forbade us from killing Toraus, and Alpha Prel had agreed to the cessation of hostilities between our societies only on the condition that he was never allowed to produce heirs. We decided to leave him at Nova, certain that the barren land would perform the task for us.

Queen Alynnia Elder, cont'd

Djarro left, telling Sithon it was night. First, Sithon laid down on the soft fancy bed along the wall. In the dark he felt himself being swallowed by the cushions and springs, pulled ever downward at the onset of sleep into a burrow beyond the Burrow. After starting up for the fiftieth time from the horrible sensation of falling, he tested the floor with his nails and laid down there.

On the slick tile his bruised ribs twinged at every inhalation. Sithon rolled over onto his back, but the disembodied slit-eyes of the light generating things hanging from the ceiling stared like predators in the thicket of grey rafters.

After locking gazes with the lights for a while, he forgot about trying to sleep. Perhaps Geedar living in a place without real sun had no need of sleep. What did Djarro say about sir-veil-ants? They all expected him to stay alert. This was a test, to see if he was worthy of having his mother resurrected.

So, with his new revelation in mind, Sithon got up and ran back and forth along the length of the bunker. He stopped to catch his breath, then traced a path along the outer wall. He passed by the hallway leading to Wardan's lab without stopping.

Sithon walked loops without counting, without estimating the time. Sometimes, when he grew tired of the rhythm of his feet tapping against the tile, he let himself fall forward and roll shoulder-first. Every time he passed the lab he looked a little deeper into it. A square of deep blue glow delineated a small window in the door. He imagined Vaedra, engulfed in the blue light, not dead but dreaming.

Sithon finished his thirtieth lap in front of the hallway to the lab. He half expected to see his mother's hand, her face flash by the window to beckon him inside. His muscles tensed, but his mind swirled when he tried to recall the way she looked now. He couldn't remember any details, just the blood, the bandages and her closed eyes.

I have to face her, he thought after a particularly slow pass by the small window, *She would want me to be with her the entire time she's here.*

Sithon pulled in a deep breath, then strode to the door. He touched it, trying to find the way in. The door swung inward with very little effort. A brush on the bottom swished against the floor.

A row of tubes confronted Sithon on either side of the door. He moved between them, marvelling that he could see warped impressions of the things behind the tubes through their shiny surfaces.

In all of the tubes, at Sithon's shoulder height, things breathed. He bent down a little to study them.

Heart-shaped, grey-purple and pulsing, they floated in mid-air with scaly purple valves facing him.

On impulse, Sithon tapped the side of the tube. The heart-shaped thing popped, flattened, then fell to the floor. Where it had been, a ring of condensation decorated the inside of the tube.

Sithon tucked his tail between his legs and scurried away from heart-shaped things and the door, looking back at them all the while. He stopped when his shoulder collided with something cool and solid.

Turning around, he found himself staring into his mother's face. She floated in a semi-circular tank inundated with the deep blue light Sithon had seen through the door. The source of the light was not readily apparent, but Sithon noted how it silhouetted her, making her look for a moment as if she were alive and well fed. With her body coated in different shades of blue, the gory hole in Vaedra's chest blended into the rest of the contours of her figure. Her arms pushed upward in a rising burst of fluid causing her thin hair to halo her head.

Sithon noticed that Vaedra was not wearing any clothes. Despite his better inclinations, he bristled at the thought of two strangers seeing her naked without permission. He leaned a forearm on the front of Vaedra's tank, covering her exposed breasts. Leaning on the tank brought the pain in his ribs back to the forefront, but this time instead of deriving energy from the stabbing sensation it radiated outward, to his legs and neck.

Slowly Sithon bent forward until his forehead rested on his outstretched arm. The glass tank wall felt cool on the tip of his nose.

He groaned from the depths of his aching gut.

"Mother, you once told me that Floods should never show weakness. I can protect you, but who will protect me?"

Vaedra's hair swayed a little, but her body remained still.

Sithon sat down with his back to her tank to await the morning.

Sithon opened his eyes when a sudden, bright light intruded upon his sleep. For a moment, he panicked. Vaedra only pulled the skins off the windows when he slept in and neglected his chores. With his eyes fully open and his mind alert, he wished for his mother standing there in front of him, ready to scold. Instead, Wardan loomed over him, his white jacket and scruffy hair offset by the opposite wall which consisted of a shelving unit filled with all sorts of containers. Most of the containers held things that, while varying widely in size, colour and shape, all looked as though they had been ripped from a larger body. One organ just above Wardan's right shoulder was brown, gnarled and knotted like tree wood. Every few seconds, its blackened whorls would shift position. Sithon stared at it rather than look into Wardan's face.

"I hope I wasn't intruding, I just wanted to stay near my mother and... watch you work. I'm not sure exactly how you plan to bring her back and, well, I guess I wanted to see what it is that you do." Sithon said, hunching over a little.

Wardan smirked, holding out a hand to Sithon.

He said, "If I had anticipated you being a problem in the lab, I would have locked the door. What is it that you wanted to know, exactly?"

Sithon considered the row of tanks that stretched along the wall where he spent the remainder of the night.

He counted fourteen of them in all. Except for Vaedra's tank, they were empty.

"I want to know about Toraus. Why aren't you trying to resurrect him, too? My mother was convinced that you wanted him. Djarro wouldn't tell me anything, but I'm sure that you must know." Sithon asked, the tendons in his hands tightening.

Wardan took off his glasses and polished them on his coat. He smiled. With an air of nostalgia, he said, "Your grandfather and I were quite close, you know. I wouldn't dream of endangering the legacy of his family."

Sithon perked his ears in confusion.

"So. . . you're willing to do anything for Toraus's

family, but Toraus himself has to stay in the ground to rot? Forgive me, but I lived my whole life with Toraus, and that doesn't sound like any kind of contract that he'd design. What exactly *was* your relationship to my grandfather?"

Wardan's smile faded for the space of a blink. Then he laughed, slapping Sithon across the shoulder. Sithon felt a growl rise in his throat, until he realized that it was not an act of violence but camaraderie.

"Ah, Toraus's grandson for sure!" he said, "Even after growing up in the wilderness, you have a keen nose for intrigue. Seeing as I can't fool you, I'll ask you something that I like to call a hypothetical question. It will help you to understand my line of thinking. Say that I did resurrect Toraus: what do you think he would do first?"

Sithon did not think about his answer for long.

"He would kill all the Metriskans in the building and then beat my mother for good measure while his blood was still hot. I'm not sure whether he would leave me alive, or not." Sithon said, his words trembling.

Wardan lifted a relaxed hand to his mouth.

"So, I would be using my power to strengthen someone who would murder most of my soldiers, abuse his heirs, and refuse to share power with me. I don't understand why you think that Toraus's return would be good for either of us." Wardan said.

Sithon sighed. An ache settled into the pit of his stomach as he pictured his mother's second life. Would she be better off with Toraus as her tyrannical God-sire, or with only Sithon and her own conscience to keep her company?

I can't let Toraus live again to hurt Vaedra.

Sithon moved toward the door, the hair on his neck rising as he passed the rows of heart-shaped things suspended in their tubes.

"I don't favour digging Toraus up," Sithon said over his shoulder, "but at least I never pretended to like him."

Wardan's reflection in the window locked eyes with Sithon. He exposed all of his rounded, ugly teeth.

"So I'm an oath-breaker, am I? In that case, this is the last time that you should turn your back on me," He said.

Flood Waters Rising

Over My Head

I have survived long enough to learn that even the most elite guard force contains at least one member who is susceptible to bribes. However, in my old age, I have finally met someone who cares more about the treachery than the treasure. Of course, that has never stopped him from accepting the last few scraps of wealth that I could offer him.

Toraus Flood, Unfinished Memoirs

Sithon took his hand off the door to the lab. He jumped back just in time to avoid being hit as it swung inward. Lt. Djarro stood on the other side, his arm outstretched. He beckoned three others inside.

"After you kids," Djarro said, nodding.

Sithon waved a hand. Djarro's ears perked.

"Oh, didn't see you there, young pup! Must've almost knocked you down, eh?" He boomed.

Sithon shrugged his shoulders.

The reek of dried rot filled the room suddenly, and he struggled not to make a face. Three figures hooded in green entered the lab. Their eyes hidden under the folds of their cowls, they strode smoothly toward Sithon and the smell grew stronger.

Sithon backed up against the tubes to let them

pass. The first figure ignored him. The second leaned out of his way. The third hooded one, by far the largest leaned toward Sithon as he passed, his scarred muzzle extending to sniff Sithon's neck. He inhaled once, snarled and turned away. Sithon felt as though he had just been spared summary execution.

Djarro let go of the door. Sithon tried to catch it before it closed, to sneak out and breathe some fresh air, but Djarro touched his shoulder and steered him back toward the center of the lab.

"C'mon now, you should be here for this meeting. We're going to be deciding how to fix your mum." Djarro coaxed.

With every sense alert and humming like a freshly-plucked string, Sithon allowed himself to be led back toward Wardan.

The three figures arranged themselves in a half-circle around Wardan. They crouched down, arms folded around their midsections, leaning their noses down almost to the ground. Wardan stretched out his arms, raising them into the air. The three figures stood up in unison.

"Kids, may I introduce Sithon Flood." Wardan said, extending a hand in Sithon's direction.

Djarro gave Sithon a slight shove forward. He stumbled, then straightened. The dead-smelling ones circled around him, at once examining him and scrupulously avoiding any bodily contact. Sithon hunched over and struggled not to let his tail slip between his legs.

A charcoal grey female with white double-stripes

on her nose came within inches of Sithon's face, pulling her hood back as she did so. Her black, fearful eyes hung on Sithon's visage, then fell away. She exhaled sharply, as though *he* smelled bad.

A tall, thin male pushed her away from Sithon with one hand. He turned toward Wardan with one lip drawn back.

"*This* is the Flood heir? He's nothing more than a mangled heap of bones!" He spat.

The last one, the large-muzzled fiend chuckled into Sithon's right ear. "I like to crush bones," he said.

Sithon felt his stomach tighten after inhaling a puff of moist, putrid breath.

Wardan cut into their circle, "Now, kids, that's enough playing around. Sithon's going to be with us for a very long time, and we don't want him to be uncomfortable."

Wardan shuffled the three 'kids' into a line before Sithon.

"Just call them by my nicknames for them. The thin one is Slash, The shy female is Stab, and the feral individual, over here licking himself is Hack. They shouldn't give you too much trouble," Wardan instructed.

Sithon looked to Djarro for a clue as to what to do next. The Lieutenant raised his eyebrows and wagged the tip of his tail. Sithon felt a withering sensation in his shoulders as he realized that Djarro expected him to be polite. He forced himself to wag the tip of his tail and puff up his chest ruff.

"I'm pleased to meet you," he mumbled.

Djarro burst into the group.

"That's just wonderful, lad! Now that we're all acquainted, let's see what Wardan's order of business is for today. What'll it be, Cap'n? Lab work? Hauling? Hunting?"

Wardan shook his head.

"No, I'm afraid that after spending most of last night studying the preliminary chemical analyses of Vaedra's body, we have very little choice but to enact the Spines Contingency. Her upper vilobe is almost completely consumed." Wardan said, nudging his glasses further up the bridge of his nose.

The roll of flesh on Djarro's brow wrinkled. His lower lip contracted.

"I never liked the Spines Contingency, Wardan. We jawed about it for days, but I still don't think the final plan is secure enough. There's no way to ensure that we don't sustain a heavy loss o' personnel." Djarro mused.

Sithon addressed Djarro and Wardan together.

"Excuse me, but what's a kem-kull? And... a contingency? Are those parts of my mother?"

Stab and Slash snickered. Wardan sighed loudly.

"Sithon, you can stay at this meeting provided that you *keep quiet*." Wardan said.

Sithon bristled along his back. Djarro placed a hand there.

Leaning down to Sithon's right ear, he whispered, "I'll explain later."

Wardan continued on with his argument.

"Now, Djarro, we don't have to expend Rakarian

troops on this. We've got all the weaponry that we need right in this room." Wardan coaxed, gesturing toward the three 'kids'. They all perked their ears at his suggestion, looking back and forth between Wardan and Djarro for some sign of an answer.

Djarro made a rumbling noise in his throat, a signal of reluctance, before he answered.

"But you are the only one who can control the three of them. Any other commanders would be... would be..."

"Murdered," Hack said, grinning.

Djarro swallowed, then continued, "In order to mobilize the three, you would have to put yourself, and the leadership of this base in danger."

"Father, you outrank Djarro! Just take us to the target and we'll get the job done without him," Slash interjected, raising a fist.

Wardan raised a hand, making a signal with his fingers for Slash to shut his mouth. After a moment of indignant silence Slash stepped back into an attentive posture, his feet shoulder width apart and his tail forming a question mark.

Wardan leaned forward, making himself look vulnerable to Djarro. He widened his expansive blue eyes.

"Djarro, I refuse to move without you. You know that if any other plan would work, I would use it rather than risking all of our most valuable research, but right now the future of Vaedra Flood depends on our ability to harvest a working Upper Vilobe. The *only* available live donors are the Mettoa."

Sithon moved out of the way for Djarro, who stepped toward Vaedra's tank. His severe features smoothed for a moment as he looked at her. Sithon noticed that one of her arms floated outstretched, bent at the elbow. Djarro reached out a fleshy paw, in line with hers.

Sithon tilted his head, confused. When Djarro noticed Sithon's expression he quickly moved his paw to his face, drawing it slowly downward over his features.

Djarro tugged on the fur below his jaw, saying to Wardan, "I'd hardly call the Mettoa donors, but if you're sure this is the only way we're going to get Vaedra put to rights, I'll get on board. The other senior staff members aren't going to like this, though."

"That's why we leave immediately, through the rear entrance to the burrow," Wardan replied, "No intelligence, no objections." He held up both hands and shrugged.

The kids celebrated Djarro and Wardan's newfound resolution by rushing to several cupboards around the room.

Wardan directed them while they filled several pack sacks with equipment and what Sithon assumed were weapons. Djarro picked out his own supplies from the things that the kids threw into the sacks. He collected the links of his leaf-ended staff from the confusion, screwed them together and tucked the whole thing under one arm. Sithon waited until Hack was distracted by the shiny plate armour Stab fitted onto his wrist, then scampered up to Djarro.

"What do you want me to do?" Sithon asked.

Djarro swung around, the arm of his staff stopping just short of Sithon's cheek.

"Sorry, lad, but you're pretty much doing it right now. You're strong, but you're not experienced enough to hunt a Mettoa." Djarro said.

Sithon's chest tensed at Djarro's bleak assessment of his abilities.

"If my mother's fate relies on this mission, then I have to help. I could've handled those soldiers in the clearing without you; what makes you think that one animal will pose a threat when we all work as a team?"

Djarro tossed his head.

"Soldiers don't have hundreds of spines as long as my staff, or long sharp teeth that can cut wood and puncture metal armour. You're still just a pup. Take my advice and *stay home*." He urged, his snout raised.

Sithon took in Djarro's scent. He smelled... genuinely afraid, his hormonal print a cocktail of body odour, flight-signal pheromones and aggressive posture. Sithon narrowed his eyes at Djarro.

He said, "Why do you care so much about what happens to me? If you get the part you need for Vaedra, then you'll have *her* to carry on the Flood family name. She's got purer blood than I do."

Djarro drew back from Sithon as though he had just been snapped at. His nervous pheromones mingled with a new set of scents. Wardan's subtle aroma of bombast mixed with blood imposed on the scene. Sithon braced himself for another frightening confrontation.

"If the boy wants to come, let him come," Wardan said, tossing Sithon a pack-sack with straps that made an x across the chest, "Sometimes the only way to teach pups anything is to let them barge into dangerous situations, especially if they're as annoyingly persistent as this one. This way, Hack will only have to carry one pack."

Sithon looked down at the pack, then at Wardan. Wardan grinned, but not nicely.

I know that you're just trying to teach me a lesson by letting me come, Wardan. Still, this is what I want, right? I'll prove them wrong on the hunting trail.

After a few seconds of fumbling, Sithon managed to sling his pack over his back. The tension that the added weight caused in his stomach and shoulders reminded him of his quiet time, hauling firewood for the family. He took the familiarity of that feeling and used it to form a confident smile.

Sithon caught Wardan before he went back to directing the kids.

"I've never seen an animal before, Wardan. What are they like?" He asked.

Wardan wrinkled his nose.

"They're smelly, dangerous and unpredictable. You'll get used to it quickly after having lived with Toraus."

Spines

Together, he and I will transcend mortality... that cursed punishment handed down to us by the Elders! Death is the weapon of my enemies, used to enforce their authority. If I can resist it, I will become the only authority! I'll live to see Vaedra bear me true-blooded grandpups, and then great-grandpups, down a hundred generations. The Flood family will rise again, with me as its immortal patriarch!

Toraus Flood, Unfinished Memoirs

Stinging pain plunged into the back of Sithon's neck. He writhed in place, slapping the site of the sensation.

The tall grass around him rustled in the wind as the source of the pain, a tiny insect, buzzed away across the waving seed fans.

Wardan stopped the line. The hunched, loping posture that he used for travelling made him look like Hack wearing a white coat.

"Sithon," he hissed, "Stop making so much noise."

Sithon grimaced and rubbed his neck. At least crouching so close to the ground felt familiar after spending most of his young life skulking around Flood Waters. The afternoon sun beating on his back, the extreme dryness of the field and his bumpy, over-exposed tongue felt distinctly less friendly.

Wardan started the line moving again. Behind and downwind of the kids, Sithon suppressed a gag as a fresh puff of dry rot floated his way. He raised his head a little closer to the waving grass heads to try and forget the experience.

All around the party, scattered over the fields beyond the base and occasionally in their path, pieces of carved stone jutted from the ground like the remains of creatures stuck in deep mud. Sithon knew ruins when he saw them: these remnants of Geedar architecture contained the pock marks and deep gashes indicative of sudden, severe damage.

Sithon collided with one such stone in mid-stride while trying to keep his nose in the air. He shook his head, feeling a bruise forming on his left cheek. This particular stone still had carved eyes which stared at him, but its long Geedari nose was missing. Creeping ground cover worked its way up the broken portion of the face, a torn veil.

Sithon felt a familiar pair of hefty hands grip him under the armpits and lift.

"Get on, now, lad. We're almost there." Djarro said, planting him on top of the overgrown half-head.

Sithon flashed Djarro a pointedly pleasant non-smile.

He proceeded over the curved surface stone, careful this time to watch where he put his feet. On the other side of the stone the others waited for them. The grass thinned beyond the head, receding into shade and the tangle of forest underbrush. Beyond a fallen archway trees spiralled into the blue sky, their vine-strewn trunks wider around than Toraus's old bedroom.

Sithon eagerly breathed in a few lungfuls of fresh, leafy air before approaching the kids. When they all stood in a semicircle by the toppled arch, Wardan addressed them.

"Now, just inside the forest is our target, a giant tree growing out of the ruins of a large warehouse. Mettoa are extremely territorial about their trees, so stay on your guard. When the Mettoa shows itself, we'll stay out of the way and wait for it to retreat back into the canopy. Once it has, kids, you'll need to get out the net and have it spread by the next attack. We'll try to hobble the Mettoa so that we can reach its vital points. Oh, and watch out for the spines. If they get into you, they stick there." Wardan said.

The others nodded, but Sithon knew that Wardan really only spoke for his benefit. All morning, he had been the one jumping at rustles in the grass, running into others when he missed the signal to halt and generally missing Wardan's sub-verbal cues.

I never thought of hunting as a social skill before. No wonder Djarro didn't want me to come.

The hunting party reformed and entered the trees. All around them, giant trunks creaked in the breeze. Mossy rocks and drifts of green sprouts gave in under Sithon's weight. He did his best to ignore the sensation of small, scuttling things dashing to safety from the undersides of his feet. The things that Djarro called birds flitted about everywhere, filling the air with high trilling sounds. Sithon still ducked a little lower whenever one glided overhead.

The ruins continued through the forest, manifesting themselves as lone, sloped walls hobbled against old growth or statue legs groped by twists of flowering vine.

As the trees grew larger, the ruins grew stranger.

Soon the party approached a large, flat area partially walled in by a stone partition with many gaping windows. They entered the area at the place where the partition crumbled into nothing.

Sithon smelled a strange scent, animal but not Geedar. Remembering Wardan's description of the target area, he watched intensely for any body-instruction. Wardan perked his ears, swivelling them to catch ambient noise. His tail curled into the alert position.

A tree as big around as half of the burrow hangar bay grew out of a floor of heavy stone tile. Squares of former flooring stretched up a quarter of the trunk, embedded in moss, vines and shaggy bark. Sithon tried to spot a patch of sky beyond the tree's outstretched leaves, but he only saw glowing green.

Wardan called the party to a halt halfway between the giant tree and an arch with its keystone dislodged in the crotch of an overgrown sucker root. Wardan moved to the back of the line, speaking over Sithon's shoulder.

"Ok, Djarro, I need you to... Djarro?" Wardan yelped. Djarro's pack sack and spear lay on the ground behind them. Wardan ran up to the sack, lifted it to his nose and twitched an eyebrow.

"Kids, spread out the net; Now!" He said, his voice rising in pitch.

Stab ran to the pack on Hack's back and picked at the knotted ropes holding it closed. Slash came over to assist. Sithon looked upward when a small pebble rapped him on the nose from above. On a branch halfway to the sky, Djarro inched along with arms outstretched to keep his balance. Between Djarro and the trunk crouched a monstrosity, a giant ball of spines with small, round ears and thin legs. It opened a mouth filled with chisel-like teeth and advanced on the Lieutenant.

"Wardan," Sithon gulped, pointing, "Djarro's up there! It must've grabbed him!"

Wardan steadied his glasses.

"And why do you think we're hauling out the net, Sithon?" He growled.

Sithon thought of helping with the net, but instead he kept watching Djarro, unable to look away. Djarro inched back another few paces, but the mettoa came forward much further. The creature adjusted its hindquarters and leapt for Djarro. Its hands landed square in the middle of his chest, knocking him off-balance. The creature rolled several times, Djarro in its clutches, until both of them bobbed up and down on the end of the branch. Sithon checked on the others, but to his dismay they still struggled to untangle the net.

The mettoa stood on its hind legs, lifted Djarro over its head and hurled him toward the ground.

Djarro let out a cry of terror. His arms flailed through the air, trying to gain purchase anywhere that might slow his fall. Sithon noticed a thick vine located about halfway down from the branch.

Sithon hollered, "Djarro, grab onto the vine! Hurry!"

Djarro tumbled end over end for several more seconds before his armpit caught the vine. He flipped over once, his own momentum propelling him down the vine despite his gripping it with all the claws on both hands. Splinters of wood drifted down after him as he descended. The vine sagged and bent.

Sithon heard a crack. The sucker root tree swayed violently as the keystone to the arch shifted. Sithon's eyes widened: the vine's roots ran through the pock marks in the stone! The branch holding the stone in place bent downward with a groan. Djarro descended to within a few feet of the keystone, causing the whole vine, roots, stone and all to dislodge from the sucker tree.

Wardan left his folds of net.

"Incoming," He bellowed, forcing Hack down to the ground with his own body. The other two kids and Sithon dove onto the mossy tiles. As the stone swung overhead, clods of dirt spattered them. Sithon held his breath until the shadow of the stone passed them by completely. At the apex of its swing, the vine snapped, sending Djarro and the liberated keystone sailing toward earth. The Lieutenant flattened himself, limbs outstretched to grip the corners of the stone as tightly as possible.

Djarro, stone and vine crashed down onto the old warehouse floor with a rumble that shook the ground under Sithon's feet. Tiles shifted. The falling block carved a swathe of broken and upturned stones as it dug deeper into the ground. When it finally stopped moving, Djarro wobbled to his feet and staggered out of a cloud of dust and disturbed greenery.

He called out to Sithon and the others. "Well, that's one way to climb a tree, but not one I'd recommend."

Djarro ran immediately to where he left his pack and staff. Sithon exhaled for the first time in what felt like half an hour.

Returning his anxiety to the treetops, Sithon hurried over to where Wardan and the kids still struggled to spread out the net. He found Stab fiddling with the knot tying the whole net together, her long fingers entwined in a series of loops and twists. She pulled one loop over another, passed a section of string in between her index finger and thumb, then pulled her hands out of the knot entirely. The net collapsed, free from its bindings.

The others grabbed hold of globular weights attached to the edge of the net. Sithon found the one nearest to him and held it tight.

Wardan swivelled his head in a circular motion, his eyes rolling back. Everyone started moving outward in a rough circle. Sithon checked the ground behind him, made sure all of the kids had done the same thing, then backed up at a jog. His section of net was the last to lift off the ground.

Wardan jerked his nose toward the sky and audibly tested the air. The kids turned their senses toward the canopy as well. Sithon scanned the upper branches of the mettoa tree, swivelling his ears to follow any sudden noises.

From the shadow of the great trunk the mettoa jumped, landing in the middle of one smaller tree, then another. It spring-boarded from tree to tree, using the backlash from its jumps to propel it forward and steadily down. Sithon held his end of the net steady even when the creature came so close that he could see the light sheen in its black eyes. It reached the bottom of a tree across from Sithon and clung there upside down, studying them all.

Spines overlapped on the mettoa's back like flattened reeds in a river bed. The mettoa spread out its front and back paws, fleshy-fingered appendages that resembled stretched out hands. With a slight waggle of its tail, its beady eyes locked on Sithon's.

The mettoa launched off the tree toward Sithon. Without looking toward Wardan he knew what to do. Taking the net weight in his right hand, he hurled it over the mettoa's head as hard as he could. On his right and left, Slash and Hack did the same thing. Wardan and Stab, positioned under the flying mettoa stayed put to anchor the net. The creature collided with the middle of the net. The flying weights returned to earth behind it.

Djarro ran forward with his spear.

He called, "Wardan, it's trapped. Want me to finish it off now?"

Wardan said nothing, holding up a hand. His attention never left the creature. The mettoa's hands gathered folds of netting together, until the net stretched taut over its back. It flexed its back muscles and the flattened spines extended. Cords ripped, ropes frayed, the mettoa shook out its spines and the net was no more. Wardan's expression sickened.

Djarro, meanwhile, drew a rope from his pack sack with a loop on the end.

"Let's see you use your spines to get out o' this one, pointy!" He grumbled.

Djarro closed the distance between himself and the mettoa in a matter of seconds. Holding the rope in his right hand and twirling the looped end, he dove toward the creature while its spines still held erect, deftly casting the rope over its head, between its spines. He cast himself toward the ground shoulder-first, his weight immediately tightening the rope against the creature's throat. The great beast cried out in a chattering scream that echoed Geedar profanity. While Djarro was still off-balance it tossed its head and shoulders, flinging him toward its deadly tail.

Djarro let go of the rope. He hit the ground in a roll on the same side of the Mettoa as the others. He got a few steps away from the creature, but not far enough. Its tail whipped around, spines erect, spearing Djarro's right side in a spray of blood. Djarro bellowed and arched his back. When the mettoa pulled its tail away, one spine stood out of Djarro's shoulder at an upward angle, the other pierced his side.

"Slash," Djarro said, his voice tinged with pain, "Help me pull these out, quickly!"

Sithon smelled the blood in the air. Anger at Djarro's injury and the mettoa's brutality tightened in his chest.

Blood pounded in his ears, at the confines of his skin, expanding him. The more he breathed, the more heavily he felt the urge to plunge his teeth into the mettoa's underside, to tear its throat out with his own mouth. As the others danced around the mettoa, trying to confuse it and regain control of the rope, Sithon tasted its warm insides over and over in his mind. Filled with violent energy, he lunged forward, feral on all fours. When the mettoa turned its head to threaten Stab, Sithon sprang for its throat.

His claws barely caught in the skin before the mettoa noticed him. Using a paw the width of Sithon's head it smacked him away onto the ground. Before Sithon could get to his feet, it rounded on him and charged. The mettoa's front paws landed on Sithon's shoulders with a force that scraped his back along the ground, causing pain to rip at him from most of his chest. Its weight on his shoulders ached like a deep bruise to the shin. He cried out.

The mettoa bared its chisel-fangs, foam flecks hitting Sithon in the face. It leaned forward, trying to bite him, but something held it back.

"I knew you'd come in handy, Sithon," Wardan yelled, clearly out of breath, "You distracted it long enough with your foolery that we could get the rope."

Sithon craned his neck over to the left enough to see Wardan, Stab and Hack pulling on the rope. Their claws dug at the ground and every muscle in

Hack's neck stood out. Even with their combined efforts, the mettoa still managed to come a little closer to Sithon's face and neck with every new attempt. Its tongue stood out beyond it lips. Its eyes glittered with malice. It lunged again, its claws digging into Sithon's shoulders as it tried to pull itself closer.

Sithon screamed, pushing upward on the Mettoa's paws. He felt his strength growing with the pain and terror, but no amount of strength seemed to be enough; the mettoa was too heavy to budge.

From somewhere far off, Sithon heard a roar. Something came whistling through the air, dropping bits of soil in his eye and casting a shadow over everything. The weight of the mettoa on Sithon's shoulder's lifted suddenly. He rolled over and rubbed his face while a crash and a squeal echoed in his ears. When he looked up, the mettoa lay slumped at the base of a fairly large tree, its head obscured by the keystone that Djarro had dislodged earlier. A smear of dark, sticky matter extended down part of the trunk.

Sithon looked behind him, trying to follow the trajectory of the stone. Djarro sat on his knees in the depression from his impact, bleeding profusely. Slash tried to staunch the bleeding and apply bandages. Djarro let him do his work, but kept stiff, staring at the tree and the bloody mess he had created.

Sithon ran to Djarro, shaking his hands in front of him.

"Slash," he puffed, "What can I do to help him?"

Slash addressed Sithon without adjusting the arc of his spine as he pushed wads of material into Djarro's shoulder wound.

"Talk to him. Maybe he'll stop tensing up," he instructed.

Sithon slapped his sides, pacing in front of the wounded Lieutenant.

He croaked a little, before asking, "So, um, Djarro, how did you manage to lift that stone? I knew you were a heavy guy, but that thing must weigh ten of you, at least."

Djarro groaned a little as Slash used a foot for leverage against his arm.

"When I get scared, I can do lots o' things you wouldn't expect." He grunted.

Sithon raised one eyebrow, his ears pushing forward.

"Scared... you? I've seen you intimidate three hardened soldiers with barely a look! Why do you care so much about a bastard like me?"

Djarro closed his eyes tight and raised his chin, pulling away from Slash as he knotted the last piece of linen on his shoulder.

"Because I'm your father."

Dead Meat

They have lived too long. Someone is funneling the Floods M supplements, and the answer can only be that there is a security leak in our forces. The personnel files have been tampered with. I know that much, but the rest happened during my mother's reign. We of the Rakarian assembly now face a difficult decision—compromise the security of our operations on Ferion further by replacing all of our troops, who were previously appointed for life, or risk letting two of the Floods escape at Toraus's death.

Queen Leethia Elder, Address to the Rakarian Security Council

Wardan gestured emphatically, his silhouette periodically merging with the trees in the orange of twilight. Stab and Slash's figures formed a lump crouched near the earth with four erect ears. The vertical sheen of a cylindrical container glinted between them. Sithon listened to their conversation above the crackle of Hack's campfire.

"Get to the base as fast as possible, and flatten anything in your way. That vilobe can't survive more than about a half a day outside of the containment equip-

ment at the labs. As it is, I've convinced it that it's still inside the host. Mettoa are stubborn. . . it won't stay fooled forever."

The log underneath Sithon shifted, tilting him toward the ground. Sithon extended his legs and gripped his seat to avoid falling off.

Djarro used his left hand to shuffle himself into a comfortable position. His right hand bounced in its sling. Firelight licked over him, diminishing his overwhelming size with shadow.

Sithon wagged his tail, staring at the coals at the base of the fire. His skin prickled and his stomach clenched deep within him. He opened his nostrils wide to try and detect Djarro's mood, but smelled only smoke.

"My mother never spoke about you," Sithon said, "Only about the burden of giving birth to me. I assumed she was raped."

Djarro's eyes widened. He held out both hands, palms forward.

His teeth showed when he said, "No, lad, it weren't like that at all, I swear. I know I'm big and all, but most of the time I don't feel it."

Sithon narrowed his eyes. His lips pressed together, and his fingers drummed the log.

Djarro continued, "When I was young, just a little older than you, I went on my first border patrol. I saw your mother for the first time then. She walked the woods in a poor excuse for a cloth, calling out for someone. Over the coming weeks and months, I started to look forward to the times that I would catch a glimpse of her. She seemed like such a caring young thing, despite what we were taught about the Floods before accepting our posts.

You see, back in those days, we didn't have Wardan around. We believed what the government handed us about your bloodline—had to in order to get assigned in the first place. You've probably heard it all before anyway: Floods are born without a conscience, the Flood family will inherit Toraus's lust for blood, all that rubbish.

From the time I started watching Vaedra, I knew that all those slogans were untrue. She would come out in any weather, at any amount of personal danger just to make sure your old mange of a grandfather had a roof over his head and a scrap of cloth on his back. More often than not, she'd get a fist to the jaw as her reward. I'm not sure whether she spotted me first, or whether I let myself be seen. Sure, I wanted to make love to her, but more than that I wanted to speak to her, to let her know that I was there, that others were there. I wanted to tell her not to give up. Seems like that's what she wanted to hear, deep down. She took my hands in hers and... well... we followed our instincts."

Sithon felt weaker than when the mettoa pinned his shoulders. He dug his claws into the bark beneath him to hide his trembling. A breeze rustled the leaves in the canopy above, and Sithon wished that he could blow away with it.

He flinched as he said, "If the two of you had such a great understanding of one another, why did she never mention you? You must have hurt her somehow that night."

Djarro's good arm remained still. No kicks darted at Sithon from the lieutenant's side of the log. Instead, Djarro's face scrunched up at the temples as though Sithon had delivered a blow. He hummed a low note, a whine from deep within his chest and leaned back, nose toward the stars.

"Aye, that I did. I burdened her with a child. I never got to see her after that. They caught me, locked me up and held a trial that I didn't get to attend. Because they thought that I had raped Vaedra, I got to stay here, but they forbade me ever to patrol the border again. I begged my commander to take you away from your family so that we could treat your M deficiency and place you in army custody, but he had done all that he could just to spare my life."

Sithon's skin burned. He could feel his mane beginning to stand on end.

"So," he said shakily, "my mother never wanted me?"

Djarro raised a hand, closing his eyes.

"No, pup, I'm sure she wanted you. I think it was the prospect of carrying you only to watch you die that she hated. As for me, I don't blame her for trying to forget. I meant well when I went to her that night but I only brought more trouble." He said.

A snarl erupted from behind Djarro, in the shadows of the tent. Hack caught a piece of bloody flesh in his jaws from mid-air and gulped it down.

Wardan, garish in the firelight waited for Hack to

lick the red flecks from his muzzle before picking out a larger piece to toss. He acknowledged Djarro and Sithon's sudden silence with a wide grin.

"Dinner time. Will you be taking your meat cooked, or raw?" He sing-songed.

Sithon continued to stare at Hack, mouth agape. He gripped the slab of meat with both his front and back paws, tearing at it with his front teeth. Blood dyed the backs of his fingers.

Djarro answered for both of them, saying, "Er, just set a couple of cuts down here with us, Wardan. We'll tend to them in a minute. I'm not sure the pup is feeling hungry."

Sithon placed a hand over his stomach. The whole area felt hollow. He remembered the longing he had felt while watching the kids butcher the remains of the mettoa.

Sithon interjected, "No, I'm hungry. I'd like mine raw, please."

Wardan strode over with the sack of meat in hand. Upon reaching the log, he sat down in between Djarro and Sithon. He opened up the top of the leather sack and held it out in front of him. Sithon thrust a hand into the brown-stained interior, feeling the give of the warm tissue as it rose up to meet him. His hand emerged clutching a grey-purple hunk of organ, tubes sprouting out of one side.

"Ahh," smiled Wardan, "You got the heart. That's good luck, you know."

Sithon brought the heart close. He closed his eyes and relished the smell of untainted meat before allowing his jaws to press down into muscle. A rush of rich, salty flavour burst over his tongue. He sucked on the first piece of heart for at least a minute before chewing and swallowing it. He had never tasted meat this good—never.

Wardan, Djarro and Sithon ate without speaking for some time, the grunts and growls of Hack's exertions by the tent punctuating the silence of the forest. When all that remained of the mettoa meat was a stained sack and wet muzzles, Sithon sat looking at the fire, thinking.

"Wardan," he said, "Why didn't I die like the guards said I would?"

Wardan rubbed the corner of his white jacket to clean his hands.

He said, "You take after your father. You might not have noticed, but Lt. Djarro can stand up to a lot more damage than the average Geedar. To anyone else, the spines that pierced your father today would have been near fatal. Djarro, on the other hand, was able to get back up and keep fighting the mettoa. He has a special Talent, a unique supernatural ability called Smart Blood. It allows him to heal at an accelerated rate. You inherited the same trait, and it healed all the effects of M deficiency faster than they could affect you."

Sithon glared at Wardan.

"Quit nipping my tail. I'm uneducated, not stupid." He growled.

Wardan giggled, an unwholesome low warble.

"So... you don't believe that I have the Talent to

raise the dead, either?" He teased.

Sithon snorted, "To be honest, no, not in the least. I don't know what's wrong with Stab, Slash and Hack, but there must be some other explanation. They probably just eat too much rotten meat."

Wardan snickered twice, then tilted his head back and howled with laughter. His hands clutched his belly, and his feet lifted off the ground. On the other side of the log, Djarro's ears flattened and his lips stretched in mild embarrassment. Hack, now on the last few bites of his meal, chuckled deeply. Pieces of food dropped from his teeth as his laughter grew into an echo like the shrieks of a demented bird.

As Sithon watched, Hack's laughter morphed into gurgling coughs, and he started to clutch his neck. His tongue slid out. The ends of his lips curled back, and his eyes bulged, beckoning for help.

Wardan remained quite calm, seated on the log. When Djarro started up, Wardan pushed him back with a hand on his shoulder.

Wardan purred, "No, leave him be. I couldn't have asked for a better way to deliver an object lesson to an obstinate pup."

Hack's face contracted in horror as Wardan's pronouncement reached him. His chest convulsed over and over as he tried to pull in some air.

Sithon got up and tried to run to Hack, but a steel-hard grip encircled his wrist. Before he could struggle, Wardan jerked him back and off his feet.

"Don't even think about it, Outborn mongrel. I want this death to remain on your head. You'll think twice before doubting me again, so help me." Wardan whispered into Sithon's ear.

Hack flailed his legs in the air, writhing on the ground. Finally, after over a minute of struggle, Hack's eyes rolled back in his head and he went limp.

Wardan waited yet a few more seconds before letting go of Sithon's wrist.

Sithon ran immediately to Hack's side, Djarro following at a distance.

"Go ahead, feel his wrist for a pulse. I can assure you he's quite dead." Wardan taunted him, still perched on the log with a self-satisfied smile on his face.

Sithon lifted Hack's right hand. He felt limp muscle, solid bone, but no heartbeat.

Sithon bared his fangs.

"You killed him. He trusted you with his life, and you just let him die!"

Wardan stood up, dusting the last crumbs of dinner off of his clothes.

He replied, "Oh, Hack will be obedient enough as long as I bring him back again. He probably won't be too pleased with you for provoking me, though. Dying is a very uncomfortable process... or so I've heard."

Sithon raised his hackles and growled. As Wardan approached Hack's body, he crouched low to the ground, determined not to let him near.

Djarro's thick arms reached around Sithon's waist and hoisted him away from Hack. He held Sithon just above ground level, murmuring in his ear,

"Stay back, Sithon. Don't do anything you'll regret later."

Wardan's glasses flashed in the firelight as he knelt over Hack's awkwardly sprawled corpse. Sithon watched as Wardan gently reached his hand, forefingers first, down Hack's windpipe. He came back quickly with the obstruction and threw it off into the grass beyond the fire pit. After drying his hands, he put them on either side of Hack's head.

Taking his mouth to Hack's ear, Wardan whispered, "I can feel you dreaming. . . dream of me."

Wardan whispered again, louder. "I can feel you dreaming... dream of me."

Sithon started, causing Djarro's grip on him to slip enough that his feet touched the ground. He blinked, and blinked again, but the scene before him stayed the same. Hack's limbs drooped downward, but his body floated just above the ground.

"Djarro..." Sithon gasped, gripping his father's forearm. Djarro set him down fully and placed a hand on Sithon's head.

Wardan's voice was authoritative during his next pronouncement of, "I can feel you dreaming! Dream of me!"

Hack's body rose further into the air, his limbs floating out beside him, pulling straight.

Wardan's final call shook the ground and vibrated the air in Sithon's lungs.

"I can feel you dreaming! Awake!"

Hack gasped. A sound filled the air like wind sounding off through an empty chasm. Hack's eyes fluttered open, and he lowered to the ground, where he took to his feet. Wardan took his glasses off and stared directly at Sithon. His wide blue eyes radiated light.

"Don't doubt that we have powers, Sithon. That road leads to madness." Wardan said.

Sithon covered his eyes with his hands. He leaned closer to Djarro, farther from Wardan.

He shuddered, "I don't think I'm going to get any sleep tonight."

Bauble

Truly, we fear an heir to the Floods more than Toraus himself. For what would a lone Geedar, divorced of any pack affiliation, not do to avenge the wrongs done to the only connection that they have in the world?

Queen Alynnia Elder, 'Notes to the future Queen'

Djarro swung an arm around Sithon's shoulders. Sithon felt a nervous thrill in his stomach, but held back the urge to flinch.

"Good job, son," he boomed, "I'd say you're almost fit for high society now, you are."

For the past few weeks, Djarro had been bringing Sithon with him wherever he could, attempting to teach him small amounts of reading, writing and the finer points of pack communication. Sithon had felt like an embarrassment at first, as certainly he would be to any but Djarro, who seemed not to notice any of his clumsy little transgressions, but slowly he was learning to get along with those he encountered at the base. Well, everyone except the Kids, that is. They still sniggered at him openly and made thinly veiled death threats, but considering that on the day before this, Sithon had seen them threaten, in no particular order, a cafeteria worker, a lab technician and the janitor responsible for cleaning their rooms, he didn't feel too singled out.

Today, on Djarro's lunch break, they sat on a sunny hill just behind the barracks, reviewing etiquette.

"Okay, that's enough of ceremony rules," said Djarro, "I hate sitting still, so I can't blame you if you fidget. Just don't let Wardan catch you squirmin' tonight at the assembly, or he'll wonder what I've been teachin' you."

Sithon pulled some grass out of the earth and ground it between his fingers.

"Are you sure I'm ready? I just... don't want to do anything wrong. I already feel like I've jeopardized my mother's future by upsetting Wardan too many times. What if I ruin her resurrection ceremony, too? There just seem to be so many things I don't know, and everyone reproaches me for them," he said.

Djarro lowered his ears. He seemed sad again, even regretful for a moment, then he perked up again, wagging his tail and flashing Sithon an optimistic grin.

"Take it from a hard-headed old tail-chaser... the more you study the hard stuff, the more it slips away from you when you need it. Best to pace yourself, lad. Don't take it all so hard. You'll come along. Now... how would you greet a group of old friends if you saw them coming toward you on the street?"

Sithon laughed, a bitter laugh.

"Friends? Spending time with other Geedar in public? When is this actually going to happen to me?

I bet even you have only ever had one or two friends in your life," he said, "Good Geedar are rare, and I bet the ones that would associate with me are even rarer."

Djarro frowned. A long silence drifted in between them, and as Sithon watched, his father's expression never changed. At length, fearing he had offended Djarro, he touched his arm.

"Did I say something wrong?" he asked.

"No, no," Djarro said, and Sithon realized that he was struggling to control his voice to hide tears, "'Twarn't your fault, not really... I just wish I could have taken you out of that place, and shown you some of the places where I grew up. Good Geedar aren't rare, lad, they're just rare in here. There are some places, many places, where whole towns are packs unto themselves, where they live as a happy community and enjoy their lives. When things... when they're the way they're supposed to be, Geedar have as many friends as they could ever need, hundreds of them. And you will too. And when you greet them, when (not if), you will lift your tail and howl."

Sithon nodded. Djarro still looked troubled, staring out into the forest with his arms crossed over his knees, and so he broke the silence.

"Not all of what I learnt as a pup was bad. Mother used to tell me stories about Darna, my Grandmother. Whenever things were at their worst, when Toraus was yelling and Vaedra was crying and my uncles were retching by their bedsides, I would go and look at her portraits, and remember that she was my family too. I didn't have to be like them. I could be caring and brave in the face of hardship, like her," he said.

Suddenly he felt a shock go through his body, making him tremble. He had never told anyone about Darna before. What if Djarro thought him weak? Toraus certainly would have, and even his uncles would have scoffed.

Djarro simply stood up on the hill, the afternoon light gilding his coarse fur.

"Where I come from, we have a saying: A child of the night is fully grown by dawn. It means that only through hardship can children become stronger than their parents. I thought it was a load of tripe, until I found you. Funny how life works sometimes, eh?"

Djarro ushered Sithon back into the base. Beyond the threshold of the outer doors the air felt cooler, and cleaner.

Strange, alien shapes, shiny bracketed vines and funny bricks with keyholes lined the walls. Most of the base looked this way, a dirty facsimile of nature. As Sithon followed his father down the hall he let his fingers slide along one of the metal cylinders. It felt cool to the touch like a real vine, but something underneath its outer shell hummed and vibrated. Djarro ignored all of the pseudo-natural things lining the walls. Djarro always ignored them.

A minute or so of walking brought Djarro and Sithon to a stairwell. Windows along the far wall highlighted dust specks in the air and made the handrails glow. Sithon remembered the other times that Djarro brought him here in the past two weeks.

"Will this be goodbye for today, Father? I think

I can find my own way back to the Burrow." Sithon asked, tail up.

Djarro raised his left hand, and rummaged through his tabard pocket with his right.

He said, "No, wait a second, lad. In all our meanderings, I forgot I have a present for you. You can have it if you prove to me that you've been studying hard. Answer me this."

Djarro tossed Sithon a shiny, rounded piece of metal. Sithon recognized it as a bauble, a golden rank marker worn by the denizens of The Base. He caught the bauble in cupped hands and studied it.

"What rank is this?" Djarro demanded.

Sithon breathed deep, then answered, "The gold braid around the rim means that the wearer is important, on par with an officer, but the white opaque center means that they are also not officially part of the military. None of the merchants are this important, so it must belong to a noble."

The Lieutenant grinned with his rows of knife teeth.

"Good job, pup. A noble it is. Now turn it over, read me the inscription and it's yours to keep." Djarro boomed.

Sithon held the back of the bauble up to the light. Behind the façade of precious materials, it was hollow. Swirling Ferian characters glinted in the sun, etched into the gold outer band just beneath the clip. He looked into the spirals and dots, trying to decipher the letters, hear the sounds in his head.

"It says. . . Seh- thu- on, Fuh- luh- duh." Sithon

ground out, then, "Sith- Sithon Flood! Wait, this was *made* for me?"

Djarro winked, saying, "I might've had it put together, yeah."

Sithon studied Djarro, searching for any sign of an ulterior motive in his countenance. The Lieutenant's scent remained steady, although somewhat tinged with excitement, and his posture dictated only goodwill.

Sithon felt excitement rise up within himself but fought it with the assertion, "I'm not a noble. Maybe Mother still is, but to dress *me* up in finery would be a lie. You have to change this." He tapped the face of the bauble with his forefinger.

Djarro pursed his lips and raised his eyebrows.

"So, you mean to tell you father to his face that he's not good enough to be a noble? In that case, I'll have that bauble back from you."

Sithon's tail lowered. His fur tingled in alarm. Without thinking about it, he closed his hands over the bauble and drew it closer to himself. Djarro blew air out between his pursed lips, then broke into a laugh. Sithon smiled in response. The excitement he tried to squash earlier came shining out of his eyes.

Sithon looked back down the hall. No one approached. He checked the stairs, but no one was on them. Sithon approached Djarro warily at first, parting the dust motes in the air in rough spurts. His father stopped laughing, almost stopped breathing.

When the two of them were only inches apart, Sithon whispered so low that only Djarro could hear,

"Father... I love you."

Sithon jumped up, throwing his arms around Djarro's mountainous shoulders. Djarro stooped down to accommodate his embrace. Sithon pushed his cheek into Djarro's, giving an affectionate upward rub. Sithon knew that he should feel awkward: Uncle Mardon and Toraus despised foreign touch. No matter how deeply he searched his heart for shame, however, he could find none in his father's embrace. Djarro lifted Sithon into the air in a bear hug, like a child.

"Wear your rank with pride, son. There'll come a time when you're recognized again." He said, giving Sithon's cheek a nudge.

For one instant, Sithon thought the single most blasphemous thought that he had ever conceived. He quickly tried to bury the emotion, but it remained burned on his consciousness from the single moment in which he had acknowledged it.

I would rather live with Djarro than as a Flood heir. I would rather stay with Djarro than go back to Mother.

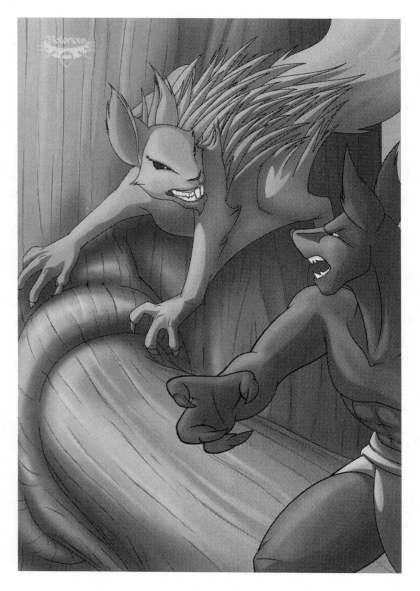

Djarro Faces the Mettoa

She Rises

Indeed, Wardan knows that my family name is the only thing that could lend political sway to a large-scale rebellion amongst the Rakarians. He has no choice but to resurrect me, because I alone can give him the legitimacy he so sorely needs within the clan system. Despite his powerful Talent, he is a friendless former street urchin, drafted into the army at a young age. Without my power, he will remain nothing to the generals.

Toraus Flood, Unfinished Memoirs

Sithon affixed his bauble to the bottom edge of his cowl after seeing Djarro's rank marker there. When his hands came away from the white dome he tugged at the edge of his hood, making sure it covered his eyes. The tips of his right forefinger and thumb stayed gripping the dark fabric while he followed Djarro and the kids down a maze of unrecognizable hallways.

Sithon's tongue tasted acidic and swollen. His teeth felt coated in velvet. He swallowed, hoping that the abrasive flavour would keep him standing upright during the ceremony.

The line stopped. Sithon's stomach clenched. He peeked out from behind the expanse of Djarro's back to see Slash rapping on a dented metal door. The clangs of his knuckles reverberated down the pipe-lined hallway.

The door opened a crack. A brief exchange of words opened it wide. Djarro placed a hand on the small of Sithon's back and ushered him in behind the kids. Freed from the shadow of Djarro's wall-like form, Sithon could orient himself better.

Beyond the door, Sithon and the others entered a dark room. The ceiling above them held none of the bars that released concentrated sunlight, only criss-crossed slats of wood and metal. The space in front of them was very limited because someone had set up rows of stands with long wooden benches along three sides of the room. Thousands of black-robed figures moved up and down the stands, visible through the open framework.

Sithon followed the kids through a break in the stands. While he passed the figures, he listened.

"Hoi, Melli, how long you think it'll take the Flood heiress to choose a mate?" One queried.

"As long as it takes for me to sneak into her dressing room, am I right? Am I right?" Answered Melli.

Djarro cleared his throat.

"Private Melli, Private Gora, good to see you up to your old antics." He boomed in his growling baritone.

The two inferiors returned strained smiles.

Melli, a dappled black and grey Geedar with a

spot over one eye, chuckled tightly, "Well, you know what *jokers* we are, Lieutenant, always laughing the day away..."

Djarro rolled his eyes and urged Sithon onward. Past the stands, the room lay open in the middle, illuminated by a single spotlight. Sithon's skin crawled as the kids led him across the open expanse of floor between the bleachers.

In the corner of his eye, figures hooded to the middle of the nose craned their necks to see more of him than their neighbour. Until a few weeks ago, the entire world could have contained this many Geedar and he would never have known. Now he stumbled across this gauntlet of gazes, this burning expanse of unwanted attention.

Sithon breathed better once Slash showed them all to their seats. Beside Djarro, his left elbow touched his father's. The point of contact between them allowed Sithon to concentrate on something other than the masses of robed figures and the distracting levels of unintelligible conversation humming in his ears.

The conversation, at least, ebbed down to nothing as another sound permeated the room. Sithon followed the sound, a scraping squeal and realized that a square metal door as tall as two Geedar and just as wide receded into the fourth wall of the dark room, making the sound as it went.

"I love that door," Slash intoned, "It always shuts the crowd up."

Sithon said nothing, but agreed with a swivel of his ears.

Behind the door waited a silhouette, silent and lit from behind by an ambient red glow. Sithon leaned forward to try and discern if he knew the figure: one thing was for certain, it had Wardan's confident pricked ears and glasses-sheen.

Sithon confirmed his first impression when Wardan strode forward out of the square door. Ahead of him, he pushed a table with wheels. A sheet covered the table and the peaks and valleys of the figure hidden beneath. Sithon flared his nostrils and scrunched his eyebrows.

"Shouldn't Mother have some sort of medical equipment along with her? She had so many tubes threaded under her skin when she was in the lab." He whispered to Djarro.

Slash answered before Djarro could say anything.

"What would you have Wardan do? She's dead." He rejoined, his white grin showing even in the dim light.

Sithon hunched over, the fur on his back prickling. He scowled and fiddled with his cowl some more.

Behind Wardan, slender figures robed in red marched two by two, each holding a strange round object in their hands. The spheres glowed a deep, bloody red that swirled and coalesced inside them. Sithon tugged on Djarro's sleeve.

"We saw Wardan raise the dead with no equipment or anything. What are all these Geedar doing here?" He whispered, feeling the acidic flavour rise in his mouth again.

Djarro grunted under his breath.

"Theatrical trickery from the city. He wants the soldiers to see your Mother as powerful, so he's making a big to-do where a small one would bring her back just as quickly. I don't care for it, myself."

Slash leaned over. Sithon had the urge to bite his overactive nose.

"Well," he breathed, "It's a good thing you're not in charge of the ceremony, then, isn't it?"

Sithon and Djarro flattened their ears in a remarkably similar way.

When Wardan reached the center of the auditorium with Vaedra, the single spotlight went out. With the burnished glow of the bloody spheres in a circle around him, he addressed the crowd.

"My followers," he began, "Tonight I will ask of you only one thing: be silent, be still. For if you approach the area in which I am working, I cannot guarantee your safety. You could be caught up in the inter-dimensional crossfire and (forgive the expression) spirited away by the energy currents which my Talent stirs up. Stay seated, and you will be safe."

"Yeah, unless Hack gets bored and starts his limb collection up again," Stab quipped. Slash elbowed her in the side, prompting a small yelp and then silence.

Wardan gestured to the red-robed figures.

"All is ready. Release the spheres." He said, raising his arms in the air.

In unison, the sphere-bearers released their cargo. The orbs floated up into the air until they hovered higher than the stands then burst, releasing a glowing red smoke that undulated in the air like blood in still water. The smoke floated around the operation area, illuminating everything.

Once the glowing red tendrils had settled over Wardan's workplace, the Geedar ringing the resurrector began an eerie, thrashing dance. Without making any sound except for footsteps, they threw their hands in the air, twirled and then bent down to the earth. The dancers rotated around Wardan and Vaedra, making the red smoke swirl and eddy as though alive.

Sithon's heart constricted when Wardan pulled the cloth off of Vaedra's body. Her tiny frame had been pieced back together with metal and bits of machine. Her eyes were gone, goggles in their place and a jointed plate covered her chest where the tree had pierced. White cloth wrappings covered her breasts and loin.

Sithon saw Wardan's lips move, and barely heard his whisper in Vaedra's ear.

I can feel you dreaming. Dream of me.

The dancers sped up, spinning more fervently and reaching to the sky as if to pluck Vaedra out of the ether.

The second time, Sithon knew that he was meant to hear it. He felt the familiar horror as his mother rose off the slab with her limbs dangling. A snarl rose in his throat because Wardan could control her like this, like a doll.

"I can feel you dreaming. Dream of me." Wardan said.

The dancers replied, "Save the lost! We're lost in dreams!" Their voices filled with fervour.

Wardan let his arms fly out in different directions.

"I can feel you dreeeeeaming, dream of meeeeee!" He half-yelled, half-howled into the red ribbons of light swirling around him. The dancers yowled in answer.

Sithon leaned forward, lending his energies to Wardan for the final push. The resurrector raised his hands, fingers clawed, to the level where Vaedra's body floated.

"I can feel you dreaming... Awake!" He called, drawing out the last syllable in a harsh growl.

All the dancers stopped. Wardan stopped. Sithon felt nothing beyond what he sent to the body of his mother, the prayers he said for her safety. Vaedra's body drifted down onto the table and for a moment she lay still.

Then, Vaedra's chest convulsed. Her back arched, and her lips stretched tight over her teeth. Her hands scrabbled for the sides of the table, and when they gripped onto the metal they clung there, while she writhed with the pain of being brought back into a severely damaged mortal body.

When the tremors died down, Vaedra turned onto her side facing Sithon. A mixture of blood and froth poured from her mouth and onto the operating slab. Once her stomach and lungs emptied, she sat upright, her arms still clinging to the sides of the table.

"Where's Toraus?" She demanded, as sickly yellow fluid laced with blood pattered onto the stone floor, "What have you done with my father?"

Vaedra's head tilted downward, and she saw her knees, jointed metal caps extruding from the flesh.

"Great Bleirah's Pool*. . . what have you done to *me*?"

She gasped, then bared her fangs at Wardan.

"You'll never get away with experimenting on me like this, you monster! Why, when my son Sithon catches up with you you'll be sorry you were ever born."

Sithon eluded the grasps of both Djarro and Slash and ran toward the center of the room. One of the red-robed dancers stepped into his path, but Sithon shouldered right through him. The dancer stumbled aside with an injured cough. A shocked murmur ringed Sithon from the stands.

"Mother! You're safe here. They brought you back from the dead. Don't you remember what happened with the shock staff, in the clearing?" He pleaded, hands out.

Vaedra's face crumpled, and her fists shook in front of her.

"You left Toraus in the grave. . . didn't you? *Didn't you!* He was supposed to be the one resurrected, and now *I'm* back, and what's more, I find you wearing Royal Rakarian insignia!" She howled.

Sithon's knees bent, and his tail curled between his legs. He struggled to keep the acidic slime in his throat from reaching his mouth.

"I only did what I could, Mother. Toraus was beyond repair." He said quietly.

Vaedra clutched her midsection, something piercing her again in memory. Her breath became more laboured, and she exhaled through her mouth.

"With Toraus gone, this new life is pointless," she cried, "Without him to overthrow the ruling clans, we will never be free to live our lives. How could you, Sithon? How could you..."

Sithon let a thin whine escape through his nose. Everything on his body felt heavy, from the robes he wore to each single strand of fur. He could feel the attention of every spectator in the hall, and it only served to weigh him down further.

Wardan's white teeth cut through the dim reddish glow. He affected a deep, disappointed grimace.

"My Lady Vaedra, I should stand by Sithon in his assertion that we mean you no harm. This is a secret station and we obey the Rakarians only nominally. Please, let me take you to your quarters so you can see that we are truly acting in your favour." He purred.

Vaedra tilted her head.

"Are you the 'Wardan' that my Father spoke about?" She asked.

Wardan bowed, saying, "That I am, my Lady."

Vaedra narrowed her eyes.

"Then we have much to discuss. I will need to be carried, I think."

"If you wish. Hack!" Wardan called to the perimeter of the hall.

Sithon stayed entirely still while Hack lifted Vaedra over his outstretched arms, and Wardan took off for the square door after addressing a few parting words to the crowd. He cursed the back of Wardan's head as he walked from the room, leaving only Sithon, an operating table and a cooling puddle of spume for the crowd to focus on.

That Out-born bastard knew exactly what I would do.

Djarro's Contribution

And so, the clan leaders exiled the Flood family because they were incurably insane down to the last member. Floods are incapable of common decency, mercy, love or loyalty. They think only of blood, and how they can next shed it.

Recitation Five of the Royal Rakarian History Primer

Sithon's legs went numb after about an hour of sitting on the wooden risers, head in hands. Djarro stayed with him, periodically administering a pat on the back or a sympathetic grunt. The dark-robed watchers left the auditorium in large, enthusiastic clouds at first, then died down to the odd Private rummaging through the debris under the stands and the out-service cleaners swishing their brooms along the floor.

The spotlight came back on over Wardan's operating table. Sithon tilted his head upward, away from his stiffening fingers. He shot to his feet, his arms hammering the air down at his sides.

"Mange and tooth rot, this auditorium reeks! Why haven't they cleaned that up yet? No, I know, Wardan wants to rub my mother's leavings in my face as well." Sithon growled, the fur on his spine standing on end. He paced back and forth in front of Djarro.

Sithon pushed his hood back, rumpling his hair as he went. He grabbed two handfuls of mane, pulling on them until they stood out. Djarro sat, watching him with disappointment playing across his features.

"Say something Djarro," Sithon begged, "Tell me you saw what he did to me during the ceremony. Tell me you want to make him pay."

Djarro put his square palms out, resting them on his thighs.

"What would you have me do, pup? He's my commanding officer, and without him I'll never get my military career back. The Rakarian special forces wouldn't trust me with anything important again, not after your Mother." He explained.

Sithon snapped, "My Mother... yes, what about my Mother? She could be in danger under Wardan's care. I know *I* am. But, I guess she and I aren't as important as your precious career."

Djarro shut his eyes, pinching his forehead with a thumb and forefinger. He exhaled loudly, the breath shaking for a moment and then smoothing out. He rose and headed for the square door. His voice echoed as he got further away.

"Wardan made a promise to me, son, a solid promise that if I helped him with his plans, he would give me Vaedra. We're going to see her now and make good on the bargain. I reckon that will settle your fur." Djarro rumbled.

Sithon jogged to catch up with him. "She's not a possession, Father. You'll still have to win her back."

Djarro hunched over a little, his ears flattening as he walked on. Sithon trailed him down a hallway equally as square as the door that led to it. Somewhere ahead, he heard muffled voices.

Wardan waited for them at an open door. His hair hung wet over his shoulders, where he dabbed at it with a white fluffy towel. In the hour interim he had changed back into his usual uniform of a loincloth and white smock.

Vaedra's voice, abraded with tears, issued out from the room behind him. A loud groan coincided with the sound of clattering equipment.

Djarro pointed to Wardan, all the while looking over him to catch a glimpse of Vaedra.

"We're here to see Vaedra. Sithon wanted to see if she was all right." He lied.

Wardan grimaced, saying, "She's not well at the moment. Blood kin only past this point."

Djarro stuck his chest out.

"Come, now, we both know I could break in past you quick enough. Be serious." He blustered.

Wardan scrunched a handful of golden brown hair.

"Oh, I'm plenty serious. Sithon can see her now, you can see her later."

"How much later?" Djarro asked, a growl forming at the back of his throat.

Wardan shrugged. "When she admits you."

Djarro quietened.

He flicked his nose toward the sound of Vaedra's wailing as he said, "You know she'd never admit me. I need to talk to her to straighten things out."

Wardan skewed his mouth to one side. He let the towel hang across his neck, using his hands to stroke his chin fur. He moved to one side of the door, tilting his head to instruct Djarro to do the same.

"Sithon," Wardan said while still facing Djarro, "There's no reason for you to stay here while your Father and I have this discussion. Go on ahead and I'll be with you in just a moment."

Sithon passed Wardan, heading through the doorway and down a narrow hallway lined with arched openings. He followed the sound of Vaedra's keening with his right ear, and Djarro and Wardan's argument with the left.

Djarro's voice strained to stay quiet.

We might as well be blood kin, Vaedra and I. I supplied the transfusions of smart blood what fixed her organs. She has my blood running through her veins.

Wardan's voice remained calm.

Be serious, Djarro. We both know that the smart blood will have morphed to match her blood type at this stage in the healing process. She's no more your blood kin than I am.

Djarro made no effort to disguise a loud snort.

Blood kin? I'm not even sure we're friends anymore.

Sithon heard a set of heavy footsteps recede down the square hallway.

No sooner had the steps faded in the distance than Wardan was at Sithon's elbow. Sithon jumped at his touch.

"I... I didn't mean to stop walking," Sithon blurted.

Wardan pulled the towel from his shoulders and folded it over his right forearm.

He purred, "If you didn't mean to stop, then by all means, keep moving. You'll find her up here on the left."

Vaedra's quarters emitted a smoky scent which Sithon struggled to identify. As he passed the threshold, he noticed the air growing thicker. In the far left-hand corner of the grey-walled room, Stab watched over a small dish full of smouldering plant matter. Using a yellow pleated fan, she forced smoke into all of the room's negative spaces.

Sithon placed three fingers over his invaded nose. Wardan raised an eyebrow at Sithon, following his gaze over to the corner.

With a nod of the head in recognition, Wardan explained, "Yellowfine. It's a plant grown in the grasslands to the southeast of here. Locals use it in a variety of folk remedies, but its main purpose is to cover up the distinctive scent of my work."

Sithon nodded and lowered his fingers, his lip curling unintentionally.

On the other side of the room, Sithon heard Vaedra groan. Slash was on top of her, on a bed of mottled blue and white sheets set into the floor. Without his shirt, Slash's forearms squeezed and released visibly as he applied pressure in short pulses to Vaedra's prone form.

Sithon's chest expanded in an instant, his arms

forming an aggressive C around his torso. Wardan grabbed at Sithon as he bolted for the bed, but Sithon anticipated him and ducked out of the way. Sithon sunk his fingers deep into the ruff at the back of Slash's neck, making sure to pinch the skin together as tightly as possible. He yanked Slash up and away from the bed.

Slash stumbled backward where Wardan caught him. Some fur from his neck ripped off into Sithon's hand, the ends frosted with red.

Slash regained his footing. He grimaced, rubbed the back of his neck and winced when his hand came away wet.

"Bite it, Sithon, learn to control yourself," He snarled, "I wasn't hurting her."

Sithon's spine remained arched and his teeth remained visible.

"Don't touch my mother," He warned in a cold rumble, "She doesn't belong to you."

"I don't belong to you either, Sithon," Croaked a familiar voice.

Vaedra supported herself by leaning on both arms and turning on her side to face them. Sithon saw her with a wavy distortion in her midsection from a tube in the center of her bed. The recently-healed trench down the middle of her chest folded in with every exhalation.

Vaedra continued, "Young Slash here was helping to ease my pain by applying pressure to my joints. I doubt you could do as well."

Sithon wiped his furry palm off on the front of his

loincloth.

"I'm sorry, mother," he mumbled, ears low.

"Well don't be sorry to me," Vaedra sighed as though she weighed as much as a large paving stone, "Although you've got plenty of explaining to do, I must say."

Sithon scratched his side twitchily.

"Can I do that without all of the others here?" He asked.

Wardan answered immediately, "No. Vaedra, I must insist that you let us monitor you at all times. A relapse into death at this point in your recovery could mean several more precious weeks spent in the suspension tanks."

Vaedra let her arms fold beneath her. Her right arm extended above her head, cradling her cheek while her left tarried bent on her hip.

Vaedra's voice slurred as she said, "Well, son, there's your answer. Wardan says I'm vulnerable, and I'm in no condition to shoo him out of the room."

Sithon glanced at Wardan and Slash before approaching Vaedra. Wardan pressed his towel into Slash's bloody spot as he crouched on the ground. Slash's master looked like the catch of some great trap, holding the deadly spring at bay. Sithon could smell the aggression hormones radiating off of Slash despite the overbearing smell of Yellowfine smoke permeating the room. Slash's elegantly tapered nose twitched, his eyes shiny with extra moisture.

Sithon backed up to Vaedra's bed, darting visually back and forth between his mother and the two monsters. Upon reaching the edge, he consciously stopped himself from flinging himself on her. Instead, he lowered himself gently onto all-fours and crawled. When he could smell her real smell over the Yellowfine smoke and feel her breath on his fur, all without disturbing her position on the mattress, he stopped and lowered his hind end to the bed.

Vaedra smiled with glassy eyes.

"They tell me that I smell like death. You might not want to get too close," she said.

Sithon took her tiny hand in both of his. He recalled a time, not so long ago really, when his hands had been the tiny ones.

"The others smell like death. You could never..."

"Never be what I am?" She chuckled wetly, "Oh, Sithon, I think I may have brought you up to be too much like me, loyal to a fault."

Sithon squeezed her little hand tighter.

"What other choice did I have but to be like you, mother?" He soothed.

Vaedra pursed her lips.

She lectured, "Well, you could have been like Toraus. Your grandfather was no Old Mange in his prime, you know. He was a great and illustrious commander of armies."

Sithon groaned, "Yes, mother, armies that burned cities full of innocent Geedar and enforced lies and hate. Toraus's 'career' is why we're here in the first place."

"Toraus's career is what saved us, whelp! Do you think that Wardan would have bothered to resurrect me if I was the daughter of some peasant farmer?" Vaedra pushed herself up, her chest contracting to the point of folding over on itself.

Sithon's ears flattened. He had not realized until now how much he enjoyed the lack of lectures on Toraus's greatness with Djarro. He kept silent, determined to overcome his mother's stint of harsh feeling. Then Wardan's voice entered the conversation.

"She's right, you know. If Vaedra hadn't been the daughter of such a great, illustrious and misunderstood genius, I never would have sought her out. Soon you will learn just what an asset your grandfather was to Geedar society, and, truly, the rest of the two worlds." He said.

Wardan lounged with his weight on one foot, his hands in his pockets. His face displayed a too-perfect mask of intelligence, reverence, even the facsimile of love. Behind him, Slash loomed with his right hand pressed to the towel on the back of his neck. Slash held a pole with something sharp-looking on the end.

"Liar!" Sithon spat, lunging at Wardan with every muscle at the ready to tear his throat from his body. While still in mid-air, he felt something strike the back of his head, making everything go black.

Sithon's eyes opened on blackness, as well. Up above, he could see the familiar eye-slit lighting of The Burrow ceiling. From somewhere unintelligible, he heard Slash's voice.

"We decided in your, um, embarrassing absence that you're too dangerous to see Vaedra alone. I'm her new bodyguard. Burst out like that again, and I'll kill you on the spot."

Sithon clutched his throbbing head. He heard Slash grumbling as he headed for the elevator, the butt of his newly given halberd banging the floor every few steps.

"*Nobody* ruins my hair..."

Yellowfine

Intelligence tells me that Darna died yesterday, on the lawn of the Flood Waters estate. She was guiltless of any crime... what must she have thought of me, her former friend? Sometimes I am glad to be near death myself.

Classified Personal Diaries of Queen Alynnia Elder, Property of the Royal Rakarian Secret Service

Djarro came to visit Sithon in The Burrow the next morning. He carried a pitcher of cold water, a cloth and a hunk of meat cut from what was probably his own breakfast. The clanging of the elevator doors at the top of the shaft woke Sithon long before Djarro actually entered the room. After the head injury and the intense quiet of keeping underground quarters, every extraneous noise accompanying Djarro's entry clanged twice over in Sithon's head, leaving his consciousness buzzing like the ceiling lights in a thunderstorm.

Djarro himself rang in and out of focus in Sithon's vision. He approached by dangling his feet out in front of him one at a time, then placing them toe first on the floor. Sithon chuckled inwardly at the thought of Djarro moving the same way in front of the others.

"Hey, lad," Djarro said in a whisper, halfway across the room. His neck swooped, and his ears stood at attention.

Sithon propped himself up on one elbow. He struggled not to retch when he admitted, "Wardan's loudest goon hit me over the head."

Djarro nodded.

"I brought something that might help, plus some breakfast." Djarro replied, half-smiling. As he came closer Sithon noticed that his father's normally well-licked fur stuck out at odd angles around his cheeks and elbows. The dark stripes lining Djarro's chest, neck and face were blurred.

Sithon narrowed his eyes. The pressure on his eyelids added a new layer of pressure in his head. His eyeballs felt like they were struggling to escape his raging brain.

Sithon asked, "Father, what's wrong with you? Did you even go to bed last night?"

Djarro reached Sithon's cot, lowering himself to his knees.

"I got a few hours. Don't mind me, pup," he said, dangling the cloth from his massive paw and dunking it in the pitcher.

Sithon laid back and pointed his nose to the ceiling. The friendly smell of fresh water drifted into his nostrils, easing some of the tension in his neck and forehead.

"You're worried about mother, too. I know you

are. You're worried about what Wardan has planned. . . not just for her, but for all of us. You don't have to hide it from me."

With a grimace, Djarro wrung out the cloth. He raised a knee and used it as a flat surface, carefully folding the damp cloth into a rectangle.

"Don't matter what I think. You'll only worry about it if I tell you. I heard about what happened last night, and it only proves to me that you've let worry and frustration get to you too much already. Worry aint worth anything in a fight." Djarro said, reaching out with the cloth in his hand.

Sithon accepted having the cloth laid on his forehead before replying, "He was lying again, Djarro, about my grandfather. He tried to force me to honour Toraus because... because I think that he's trying to trick my mother into believing his lies."

Djarro adjusted the cloth with two fingers.

"I know, pup, but how are we going to keep her safe if you can't get her alone and I'm not allowed to see her? You need to control your temper so we'll still have a way in." He admonished.

Sithon took a deep breath then let it out. With the cool cloth applied, his head throbbed less than before.

"Father," he said, "Does the Smart Blood Talent cause you to get really powerful when you're angry?"

Djarro chuckled, "Yeah, that it does. When I'm over my rages, though, I can't ever justify the amount of skulls I've crushed. That's why I've learned to control my temper. We're more than the sum total of our urges, son. You're going to get bigger, and the bigger you get, the more you'll be responsible for. At least, that's my reckoning."

Sithon sat for a moment, pondering Djarro's words.

"Thanks," he said, "I know Vaedra will want to see you, eventually. Let Wardan block your entry all he likes, I know she'll keep asking to see *me*. I'll tell her about you, let her know that you still care."

Djarro's ears sank, causing him to look even more tired.

"I hope that's enough, lad. I've missed her so much over the years you've been imprisoned, and then to have her presence denied me now..." Djarro confessed, his voice breaking at the end of the last sentence.

Sithon spied a thick, flat tear wending its way down Djarro's mammoth snout. He cast the cold cloth aside and threw his arms around his father's neck. Djarro pulled Sithon close. His huge, flat nose pressed against Sithon's neck, then the undersides of his ears, dragging in large, ragged breaths.

"Yellowfine," Djarro said, his hands shaking against Sithon's arms, "Son, why do you smell like Yellowfine?"

Sithon drew back and studied his father's face. Pain played in the creases of his eyes, the tension around his mouth.

"Wardan was burning it in Vaedra's quarters. He said he needed the strong smell, to cover up the stench of death." Sithon replied.

Djarro picked up the pitcher by the bed, swung

it around once and hurled it into the far wall of the Burrow auditorium. Water burst out of the mouth of the pitcher and hit the floor in fat splashes. His hands then formed fists, and he roared, a deafening, primal sound that made Sithon grab his blankets and pull them up over himself. When Djarro finished, panting hard, he answered the question clearly visible on Sithon's face.

"Yellowfine is not used for incense. There are thousands of plants that can do that. Yellowfine is used to prevent pregnancy. He is planning to seduce her. That's why he won't let me see her. That's why he won't let you alone with her. Tail raping, out-born son of a mange monger! I should have known all along."

Flood Waters Rising

Afternoon

In the aftermath of the failed colony at Nova, seeking a glorious new life for their faithful elite, the clan leaders led the settlers to the barren planet Rakaria, carving out an empire between the territories of the alien Hyatcha and the Tothari, who had already been there for centuries. The Tothari, after seeing the moral virtue of the clans, joined the Empire soon after.

Recitation Ten of the Royal Rakarian History Primer

Djarro barked, and the first Private in line lunged forward. On all fours, the Private scrambled up an inclined ramp with wooden ridges the height of two Geedar. He reached the top edge and leapt with his body stretched out to the limit, determined to reach the ramp set in mirror image a few yards away. After a short time in the air, the Private's hands caught the edge of the second ramp and he hauled himself up. He continued on toward a line of poles used for agility drills, his bushy brown tail flowing up and down with his steps.

Sithon felt the pulse in his head beat faster. The frenetic motion of the Private racing by, combined with the swaying of the trees beyond the obstacle course threatened to set his head into an irreversible spin.

"Ugh," Sithon groaned, placing his hands on either side of his bandaged temples. He crouched down and tried to focus on the grass.

Djarro, a distended dark sun blocker, spoke to Sithon without taking his eyes off the obstacle course. His usually hearty voice sounded dry and thin.

"You okay, lad?"

Sithon waited for the ground to come into focus. When he could distinguish individual grass blades again, he said, "Yeah, I'll be fine," and got to his feet.

The Private had crawled under a vine-covered lattice placed close to the ground while Sithon recovered. Now he shimmied up a pole the size of a large tree trunk for the balance exercise.

Sithon leaned toward Djarro.

"Are you sure a full-grown Geedar can cross a railing that small? It's only about the width of my palm," He said.

Djarro leaned in too.

"Well, I don't know that any Geedar hang around up in the canopy, if they can help it, but never doubt the power of good training and the balance of a long Rakarian tail." Djarro replied.

Sithon scrunched up his nose.

"Just watch him if you don't believe me," Djarro said, pointing to the balance apparatus.

The brown Private gained his footing atop the pole. Sithon's tail raised, his ears perked.

The Private balanced himself, leaned over for stability and scuttled across the thin strip of metal with his tail compensating for any shifting of weight. He quickly spanned the two poles and slid down a rope on the other side, completing the course.

Sithon flicked an ear, saying, "On second thought, I guess it wasn't all *that* impossible."

Djarro said, "I would've let you try today if you hadn't gotten that nasty bump on the noggin."

Sithon bared a tooth.

"That's just another thing that we can thank Wardan for later."

Djarro's neck and shoulders twitched. He coughed into his fist, then barked twice to bring the troops at the starting line to attention. Over by the grey wall of The Base, the troops shuffled themselves about until all of them stood in a straight line, feet shoulder-width apart and tails placed deliberately between their legs.

Djarro rummaged through the back of his tabard, reminding Sithon of the day they first met. Instead of producing a crystal ID badge, this time he pulled out the small, shiny grey thing that he used to tell time and speak to the other officers over long distances. Placing his thumb over a raised button, he spoke into it.

"Obstacle course control, start up the stinger."

Sithon swivelled his ears forward.

"Stinger?" He said.

Djarro pointed to the middle of the obstacle course where a cylindrical shape spiralled out of the ground, stopping at knee height. A black, shiny glass eye rotated around to face them.

"All right, Troops, today we, erm, intensify your exposure to realistic combat," Djarro called, "Private Bentroa, be ready on the bark."

Private Bentroa, a grey long-hair at the front of the line shook perceptibly as he shifted into battle stance with his arms guarding his torso and his feet shoulder-width apart. Sithon noticed that without meaning to, Private Bentroa stood facing Djarro. Even at a distance the whites of his eyes stood out in contrast to his face.

Djarro's eyes lacked expression. His lips wrinkled at the edges and Sithon could see the very tips of his front teeth. Djarro took his time replacing the remote in his tabard pocket. He brought his hand slowly down to his side, exhaling loudly for the benefit of the troops. Then, with a controlled spasm of the face and neck, he barked.

Private Bentroa kicked off of the starting area hard enough to displace a large tuft of grass. When he moved, the eye on the stinger cylinder followed him. He scampered up the first ramp, launched himself toward the second, but came up short by several feet. Crouched on the ground, Bentroa jerked his head toward the cylinder and then quickly looked away. His chest heaved despite the minimal exertion required to jump off the ramp.

Sithon smelled Bentroa's fear but didn't understand until the Private started scaling the flat side of the ramp. His fingers jammed and his wrists strained to pull himself over the lip. The eye on the stinger cylinder flashed red and ball of energy similar to the ones used in the battle at the clearing shot out of it, striking the Private in his thigh.

Bentroa yelped and slid, but eventually managed to pull himself up over the lip. As he scuttled down the ramp, another ball of energy fire shot out and singed his tail.

He hopped, running harder toward the crawling apparatus. Djarro kept watching the obstacle course, his face unflinching. Sithon tugged on Djarro's tabard.

"Father... why are you doing this to the troops," Sithon asked, "I've never seen you inflict pain in training before."

Djarro's nose stayed to the obstacle course. He breathed in a long sniff of the air.

"All the officers use this kind of training, lad," He said, voice straining. Sithon wondered how long Djarro had howled after his first outburst in The Burrow. He remembered the way his father's ears had drooped as he kneeled on the floor, water from the pitcher spreading, soaking into the knees of his uniform.

Sithon said, "But *you've* never done this before. What's wrong?"

Djarro raised his muzzle.

His lower jaw jutted out as he said, "Nothing's wrong, son, it's just that I've had a slight change of heart."

Over on the balance apparatus, Private Bentroa limped across the metal strut on all-fours. He moved hand-over-hand, energy bolts to his side punishing him periodically for his lack of swiftness. With every bolt, Bentroa moved slower.

Sithon whined softly through his nose. He searched Djarro's face, trying to identify any of the emotions he associated with his father.

Djarro finally met Sithon's gaze.

"Look, lad, I've just realized that in this line of work, you can't keep any soft emotions to yourself. I waited twenty years for your mother, and I would have waited twenty more because... because I was a terrible fool for her. I near ruined my career for Vaedra and now, if I don't learn, I'll 'x' myself out for good. Career soldiers have to be lonely, lad, it's the only way for them to survive."

Sithon faced straight ahead, out toward the obstacle course, but he saw before him many events that he thought Djarro's kindness had buried. He remembered Vaedra after a beating, contracted in on herself and sobbing.

"You're wrong, father." Sithon said, jaw set and tail erect.

Djarro's mouth stretched, his head jerked back a little.

He said, "No I'm not. I've been thinkin' it through for days."

Sithon shrugged.

"Doesn't matter how long you've been thinking about it. I know you're wrong," Sithon said, "You may think loneliness is a good thing, because it's taken a part of your life. You're prepared to give up the rest of your life, too, because you're scared that you'll keep trying to reach out to others and fail. Well, father, I lived my whole life lonely up until I met you. I watched as Toraus dealt with my mother using a heart twisted by isolation and hatred. He loved her, and yet he still beat her bloody. From him I learned that you can never cut yourself off completely from others. All you can do is choose whether to lash out with a fist, or reach out with an open hand. I know you don't want to be another fist."

Djarro's aspect darkened.

"You don't know what it's like to love someone the way I love Vaedra. You've never even mated with anyone before."

Sithon shook his head slowly as he said, "I don't have to understand your feelings. I want you to be together, too. And... I think I might still be able to help you."

"I'm listening," Djarro said, his features softening.

Sithon continued, "Well, the other officers are all attending a meeting tonight in Vaedra's new quarters off of the auditorium. Wardan said I can come as long as Slash watches me. I think he just likes watching me squirm. Anyway, the room is small and there will be lots of guests. I'm sure that I can lose Slash for a few minutes sometime during the evening."

Djarro's ears drooped.

"You said the meeting was for officers. I never heard anything about it," he sighed, "and if you're planning to try talking to Vaedra again, I have my doubts. What makes you think you'll be able to reach her while Slash is distracted?"

Sithon smiled, shutting his eyes.

"I know my mother. After our first meeting, she'll be more anxious to talk to me than ever." He replied.

"I still don't know what you think you're going to do once you have her."

"I'm going to tell her what you've done for me over the past few weeks. You saved my life. It only makes sense that she'll be grateful to you for all your help." Sithon said, palms up.

Djarro rumbled deep in his throat. He exhaled loudly through his nose.

"Gratitude... Well, it's a start," He said, hands fiddling with his tabard. After a moment of silence, he reached into his inside pocket again. He produced the grey controller and straightened out his arm, aiming for the center of the field.

The next Private in line had yet to start the course.

He faced Djarro, waiting for a decision. Djarro pressed the button, and with a beep and the whir of machinery the stinger column spiralled into the turf again.

"What are you waiting for," he growled at the Private, *"Arf! Arf!"*

* * *

Sithon's fur stood up a little higher than usual at being surrounded by so many strangers. He could feel the patch of mane at the nape of his neck tingle every time someone said his mother's name. He also jumped a little every time Slash nudged him from behind with his knuckles and the shaft of his spear.

Across the room, ringed by Geedar with many insignia pinned to their tabards, Vaedra smiled in

Hack's arms. Sithon glanced at her once, and again, noting how her little hands flipped back and forth when she talked.

Sithon smelled the trace of Yellowfine in the air and it parched him. Without a word to Slash, he started wedging his way through the packed room to the table with the pile of snacks and drinking fountain. Officers shifted out of his way as he went, with murmurs of "Flood heir…" and "Vaedra's bastard" among other less frank assertions following him long after he passed. Several officers studied his face directly, ignoring the taboo of making direct eye contact before introduction. Sithon placed his hands on the snack table when he reached it the way that a drowning victim grabs a floating board.

He leaned over into the mushroom-shaped stream of fresh water and lapped it up greedily. Before he could really feel the cool of it in his mouth, a familiar set of knuckles nudged him in the lower back.

"Hoi, this is a fancy party. Reign in the tongue and leave some for everybody else, will you?" Slash heckled.

Sithon repressed the urge to reach back and crush his Gonads.

"I'll just be a minute, and then you can go back to parading me around at the end of your spear." He hissed, then continued lapping.

In Sithon's peripheral vision, he saw Slash pick up a tidbit of tripe from the table.

He then swallowed it whole, saying, "You know, I'd rather parade you around *on* my spear. Why don't we try that?"

Sithon pulled away from the water fountain and walked a few paces back toward the bulk of the crowd.

"Let's not," he replied, his footsteps resounding on the hollow planking that covered Vaedra's bed for the party.

Slash bumped a fist into the small of Sithon's back. Sithon felt the skin along his spine tingle at the hiss of Slash's breath in his ear.

"Quit looking at the ground, Dung Heap. The guest of honour approaches, and you'd better be on your best behaviour."

Vaedra's ring of followers opened up. Sithon saw that she wore a blindingly white shift with many layers which simultaneously increased her presence and diminished her size. Hack held her under the arms, locking his hands around her midsection.

Vaedra nodded toward Sithon. Hack pushed his way through the parting crowd, Vaedra's gown flowing backward around his legs. Sithon adjusted his posture and brushed down his tabard.

Vaedra took very little time to reach him despite the density of the crowd and the inconvenience of having to be carried. Wardan and Stab followed her along with several high ranking officers.

When she reached him, Vaedra held out both arms. They trembled in the air.

"Sithon, I've missed you," she sighed.

Sithon hesitated to embrace her, noting the musculature of Hack's jaw jutting up against her sparse mane.

"I... I've missed you, too mother." He said, rubbing cheeks with her.

Vaedra gripped his head on either side, keeping Sithon close to her- and to Hack. She rubbed his cheek several more times before letting him go.

Sithon drew back, a bashful smile on his lips. He straightened his cheek scruff with the back of his right hand.

Vaedra wagged her tail against Hack's leg.

Extending a hand to Wardan, she said, "Sweetmarrow, may I have a word with my son in private please?"

Wardan hunched over, his ears pulling back.

"That's not possible, my Lady. Sithon has been assigned an armed guard for the evening, and you are not yet well enough to walk without Hack's help."

Vaedra flashed her fangs.

"I do not need an escort to talk to my own son. Set me down on the refreshment table. I should be able to hold myself up for a while." She said.

Wardan drew back his lips, appearing sick. One of the officers surrounding them crossed his arms and another female officer fixed him with an unimpressed stare.

"But... my Lady..." Wardan wheedled, "As your physician and guardian, I alone know the precise details of your condition. Any excitement, and you might... regress."

Vaedra snapped, "I've been sick all my life. I know my own limitations. Now let me alone with Sithon before I begin to suspect you of hiding something from me."

Wardan's upper lip trembled.

"Very well, Lady, Hack will drop you off at the table. Expect me back in twenty minutes." He said, clipping the ends off of his words.

Wardan walked away, Stab and the officers in tow. As the female officer who glared at Wardan passed Vaedra, she leaned forward to speak in her ear. Sithon edged close enough to overhear.

"Well played, Lady," she murmured, "I believe I'm going to enjoy serving you."

Vaedra touched the officer's shoulder.

"Thank you, Sashi. Your loyalty will be rewarded."

Sithon waited for Vaedra to balance herself on the edge of the refreshment table before saying anything more.

With his eyes focussed on Hack's back receding into the crowd, he said, "I don't understand any of this, mother. They call you Lady. They pledge you servitude.

They..." Sithon noticed Slash still lurking along the edge of the empty area.

"I thought you were supposed to clear out with the rest of them." Sithon called to him.

Slash responded without looking up from the shaft of his spear.

"Shut it, Dung Heap. Would you rather other Geedar drifted over here while you're trying to hold a private conversation?"

Sithon snorted, forcing himself not to look at Slash. He leaned closer to Vaedra, saying, "We are *geedari refuse.* They shouldn't be serving us. And you... you look so... so..."

"Proud?" Vaedra asked. The way she held her head since the resurrection reminded Sithon of the painting of his grandmother that used to hang in Toraus's bedroom at Flood Waters. When he used to run his fingers along the image of Darna's curly mane he would think to himself that she looked nothing like his mother, the crippled and emaciated female shadow of Toraus. Now, with her ears raised and her nose in the air Vaedra exemplified the dignity of the old Floods.

Sithon's stomach felt uneasy. The room swayed in his vision, causing him to lean on the table and focus more closely on Vaedra's face.

"You look like Toraus," he said as quickly as he could.

Sithon cringed, but Vaedra's hands stayed still and her expression calm.

"Naturally I look like Toraus. The resemblance can only strengthen the loyalty of our followers. Soon, those with weak or nonexistent Talents will flock to Wardan's new order because they know that I truly am the heir to Toraus's legacy, and enemy to the Rakarians. Wardan explained everything to me." She said, flipping her right hand.

Sithon groaned, "New order? Just what is he planning?"

Vaedra gripped Sithon's long, lean hands in her tiny ones. His fingers spilled out over most of her wrists.

"Something marvellous, Dear One. He is enacting Toraus's revenge on the Rakarians. By this time next year, he plans to have overthrown the Rakarian monarchy. He is going to engineer an Empire where Geedar like me have powers... all with the help of his incredible science."

Vaedra said, grinning.

Sithon scowled.

"Mother, forget about the Old Mange's ravings. Now that we have a second chance at making a life for ourselves, we should forget about the ideas he tried to force on us. I need you more than ever. Please, tell Wardan that we're not interested in the Rakarians anymore." He pleaded.

Vaedra's mouth turned down, her ears flattened.

"The Rakarians are still interested in *us*, Sithon. Wardan told me that my murderers were the Rakarian General, Nikira's task force. Because of Toraus the government will pursue us until we die. The only way to ensure that we live free is to ensure that the monarchy is destroyed."

"That can't be the only way." Sithon said, shaking his head.

Vaedra let her hands slip from Sithon's. They slapped against her thighs and made her dress billow up around her legs.

"We're in no position to negotiate, Sithon," She said through gritted teeth, "Wardan has us here, and that's where we have to stay."

She smiled.

"Besides, I wouldn't leave even if I knew where to

go. Wardan has been very kind to me."

Sithon pressed two fingers to his forehead. He grunted.

"Please tell me you two haven't coupled. Please."

Vaedra narrowed her eyes and leaned closer to Sithon.

"And what if I have? What would you do about it, pup? Remember who is the elder here. I may be weak, but you owe me more respect than to go poking into my private life,"

She spat.

Sithon pursed his lips, nodding.

"I knew it. You know, Djarro still loves you. Did you even think about him when you decided to pack in with Wardan?" He said.

"I see Djarro has been lying to you then," Vaedra replied, looking off in the direction that Wardan had gone, "I hate to spoil your newfound affection for him, but if he really loved me, he would have come to see me by now."

Sithon took a deep breath before beginning.

Here goes, Dad.

He said, "You're wrong about Djarro, mother. While you were in the stasis tank, he provided the Smart Blood that healed your organs. When we went after a replacement for your upper vilobe, he saved my life from this horrible spiny monster called a Mettoa. Now he's been teaching me to read, write and decipher ranks. He's been kinder to me than anyone ever has been."

Sithon choked on his last words. The look of profound hurt in Vaedra's eyes stopped him from saying any more. She raised a frail hand to her mouth.

"I... I did the best I could for you, Sithon. I'm sorry I couldn't give you what you wanted."

Vaedra waved to Slash. He swooped in, cradled her in his arms and set off toward the crowd, scowling at Sithon all the way.

"Wait," Sithon called to her, "That's not what I meant. Mother I love you."

Sithon heard Vaedra instructing Slash. Her voice broke at intervals, reminding Sithon of the way that she had bitten back sobs to keep him calm during Toraus's fits.

She said, "Take me to Wardan. Tell him the party is over and I want to be alone."

Sithon covered his eyes with one hand. In his mind, he was Djarro, hurling the pitcher and howling at the top of his lungs.

Evening

There are some radical groups within my trusted circle of parliamentarians who have been putting pressure on us lately to free Vaedra Flood and her son. I will refuse these demands, and continue to refuse them at all future dates.

Queen Leethia Elder—Rebuttal to the Proposed Bill Pardoning the Floods

Sithon went back to the Burrow alone, looking behind him every few steps. In the longer hallways, the pipes lining the walls looked big enough to swallow him. Cable casings wormed over the periphery of Sithon's vision. Every once in a while, he would catch snippets of loud talk or laughter from officers drifting back to their quarters from Vaedra's reception. The cold of the floor on his paws matched the cold of the knot tightening his stomach and spine.

He collapsed on his cot in the corner as soon as he reached the large, empty Burrow. With the blankets at his back and darkness invading his senses, Sithon relived his conversation with Vaedra. When he finished the first imaginary conversation, he imagined more things, things he could have said and things that he never would have said. Sithon pulled the blankets over himself, then kicked them off. He sat up, flopped over and lay on the cot like a breathing dead body.

He woke up to the Burrow lights turning on without ever having realized he fell asleep. Sithon rolled out of bed onto his hands and knees. He paused there, blinking back sleep and feeling the slickness of the floor.

I should have told her that I still love her more—I don't know if that's true, but I should have said it.

Sithon reached under his bed and pulled a folded fresh loincloth from the stack there. He balled up his old bottoms and tossed them on the cot, then tied the new linen sheeting around his waist. After tucking up his tail and pulling it through the holes, he made for the elevator, shaking out his fur as he went. His bones ground together at the joints. When he stopped to summon the elevator, Sithon felt strain drooping his arms and shoulders.

He boarded the platform. Standing in the darkness of the lift shaft, he imagined a new conversation, this one in the future.

She'll never love me, lad, Djarro cried, *I knew we could never be a whole family again.*

Sithon said, *No, she'll realize that I need you, and that will be the first step to reconciliation. Just give her time.*

Dream Djarro wiped his eyes with a muscular arm. He protested, then Dream Sithon prepared another rejoinder.

Sithon continued arguing with himself until he

arrived at the exit to the outdoor obstacle course. With his hand on the dented handle, he paused for a moment and forced himself to focus. He could feel the blood pulsing quickly beneath the palms of his hands, pushing against the door handle.

Sithon licked his lips, closed his eyes and pushed open the door. The scent of sweet new grass combined with the many-faceted breeze slowed his pulse.

Another Lieutenant led Djarro's troops. All of the usual Privates stood in line awaiting their turn on the course: Sithon recognized Private Bentroa standing fourth in line, a bandage plastered to his right thigh.

A thin female surveyed the course with her back to Sithon. She wore the same Royal Rakarian blue striped livery as Djarro, the only difference being that the shirt wrapped around her chest to conceal her breasts and tied behind the neck.

Sithon strode across the field toward the Lieutenant. She stood with her shoulders pulled back and her arms crossed. As he got closer Sithon realized she was the same officer that Vaedra had talked to at the reception.

What had his mother called her... Sandi? Lakshi?

Sithon approached the Lieutenant on a polite diagonal path. She swivelled an ear in Sithon's direction as he approached but kept her eyes on the course. Sithon considered reaching out to tap her, but at three quarters of his height her posture still forbade it.

"Excuse me," Sithon said, "but where is Lieutenant Djarro?"

The Lieutenant waited for a moment, her wavy

yellow fur a pawn of the breeze.

She pouted a little while saying, "I don't believe we've been introduced."

"You don't know who I am?" Sithon asked.

She tossed back her forelock.

"No, I know exactly who you are. We still haven't been introduced."

She uncrossed one arm and offered her hand to Sithon.

"I'm Lieutenant Plok. Everyone calls me Sashi."

Sithon shivered as his hand rubbed against the soft leather of Sashi's gloves. He felt his groin tighten in spite of the previous night's fatigue.

"Sithon," he said, then checked himself, saying, "But, you already knew that. You said so. I should have..."

Sashi started talking in the middle of Sithon's sentence.

"No problem. What did you come here for, Sithon?" she said.

"Wait, don't answer that just yet," Sashi added, holding up a finger. She turned to face the troops. Sashi drew a long, flexible wand about the length of his forearm from the waistband of her loincloth. He caught a brief glimpse of the curve of her hip as it came out.

Sashi thumbed a switch on the base of the wand, causing an arc of blue lightning to jump from her hand to the tip. The hiss of energy interference stung Sithon's ears. She whipped the palm of her left hand with the wand.

"Alright, troops, let's get the mud off our paws! On the bark!"

Once the first Private started the course, Sashi returned to her discourse with Sithon.

"Apologies," she smiled, still holding the wand at either end, "Now what was it that you wanted?"

Sithon stared at the wand.

"I... I uh... Where's Lieutenant Djarro?" He blurted.

Sashi rolled her eyes.

"Oh. I should've known. Geedar have been asking me about that like I have all day to discuss it. He's been handed a special assignment and I have to take over his usual rounds on *top* of all my regular duties."

Sithon asked, "Where do I have to go to see him?"

Sashi flicked the wand back and forth.

"You won't be allowed to see him. Not when he's sequestered with the project crews. Djarro ought to be free sometime this evening, though, and he'll know where to find you." She said.

Sithon scuffed the dirt with his paw. He flicked his tail back and forth.

"Well what am I supposed to do until then?" he complained.

"Even if I wanted to nip at the heels of Wardan and the kids, *which I don't*, they're not in the Burrow labs right now and I'm positive that they don't want me around. And I don't even want to start explaining why talking to my mother is a bad idea."

Sithon flattened his ears as he realized Sashi was staring at him with her arms crossed and her eyebrows raised.

"I'm sorry, that was, uh, too much information." He said.

"No, actually it's not enough. With a master manipulator like Wardan running the base, I can't afford to wander off the hunting path." Sashi replied, pinching the end of her wand. Little circular ripples of energy pulsated out between her thumb and forefinger.

Sithon swivelled his ears to catch ambient sound. He heard the thump-thump-thump of feet passing through the obstacle course, the hiss of tree branches rubbing together and the low hum of Sashi's weapon, but no approaching sounds from the direction of the base. The only pheromones on the air smelled distinctly female.

He still spoke more quietly when he said, "Are you suggesting that you want something from me?"

"I was hoping for a donation of sorts, yes. As a token of my esteem for such a donation, I might be willing to entertain you for the day."

Sithon frowned.

"A minute ago you said you were too busy to talk to the other officers." He said.

Sashi smiled and shrugged, saying, "Okay, so I'd let you follow me on my rounds. That's entertaining, right?"

Sithon paused for a moment, admiring the way Sashi's hips curved.

"What did you want to know?"

Sashi smiled again. Sithon admired her clean, sharp teeth.

"Well," she said, "I know that you made Vaedra very upset last night, and then this morning we all woke up to a radical change in high-level assignments. I would feel a lot more secure if I knew what, exactly you fought about."

Sithon's eared pricked.

"That's personal!"

"If it wasn't personal, I'd know it by now." Sashi said, shifting her feet into a determined stance.

"You promise to take me with you?"

Sashi laughed, a single pulse of deep sarcasm.

She said, "I never promise anything. All I can tell you is that I'll do my best to keep you away from Wardan and the kids. Slash especially seems to have a problem with you. That bump on your head must have been sore for quite a while."

Sithon scratched behind his head as he said, "Mother and I were arguing over Djarro. She's very jealous of the way he treats me."

Sashi's eyes widened in apprehension. Her lips formed an 'o', then she sucked them in, one under the other. Sithon tilted his head, pushing his ears forward.

Sashi motioned across her body with the wand.

"Come on up here beside me, Sithon. You're my assistant today," She said, flicking her head to the side.

"Not unless you turn off that weapon," Sithon replied.

Sashi laughed with her teeth parted this time, a penetrating guffaw.

"I like you," she said, "You're just wary enough to survive here."

Sithon soon found out that Sashi's rounds took them the same places as Djarro's had. Late morning saw them at training on the obstacle course. After a light lunch of stew and crunchy raw tubers, they spent the early afternoon inspecting the eastern block of weapons lockers and moved on to martial arts drills in the gymnasium until evening. As twilight glowed through the high row of windows ringing the gymnasium, Sashi shook out her mane and sighed.

Sithon felt an itch in his legs that told him to dash quickly away and find Djarro but he held himself in place, waiting to be formally dismissed. He shifted his weight from foot to foot.

Sashi said, "So, I guess you'll be running off to find Djarro now. Pity I couldn't tempt you to come back to my quarters and talk a while."

Sithon drooped his ears, saying, "Djarro won't know where to find me."

Sashi reached under her wrap top and pulled out one of the round grey things Djarro and Wardan always carried.

"This," she said, holding the grey thing forward, "is a Guide. Most Geedar in the outside world have them. Using this, I can contact anyone at the base by pressing the right combination of these buttons around the rim. It tells me the time, lets me use most of the remote-control tools around the base, alerts me to any new orders... well, it does many things, but what you should know right now is that I can use it to contact your father."

Sithon reached out for the Guide.

"How does it work? Can I look at it for a moment?"

"Nope, not a chance," Sashi said, pulling one neck strap of her top out from the rest and dropping the Guide back into its pocket. "You're just going to have to trust me. You've seen Djarro use one before, right?"

"Yes..." Sithon said.

"Then you know I'm telling the truth," Sashi rejoined, slipping her arm through Sithon's at the elbow, "Let's go. I've got some dried meat stored in my foot locker we can share."

Sithon's stomach rumbled, and certain other parts of his body thrilled at the firm arm curled around his. He followed the tug of Sashi's weight, saying, "All right, I'll visit for a while, but the minute I contact Djarro, I have to go."

Sashi shook her head.

"Don't worry, I *understand*. Bleirah's Pool*, if you're this resistant to overtures of friendship, it's no wonder you don't know very many Geedar here."

Sithon scowled, but remained silent while Sashi led him down through the back door of the gymnasium, past the turn in the hallway that led to Vaedra's quarters and into a brighter, smaller set of hallways lined with wooden doors. Many of the menacing pipes and wires prevalent in the other hallways of the base were swept off of the walls here, in favour of stringing them unobtrusively along the ceiling. Control boxes sat at intervals along the halls, but even they were contained in neat white metal sheaths.

Sithon spotted a sign hanging from the ceiling as

they entered a long row of identical entrances.

"Fee-mayul... doh-ru-meh-toe-ree," he mouthed.

Sashi shrugged, "We think it's nicer than the male dorms."

Sithon felt that the two sets of dormitories were exactly the same. As Sashi ushered him into her quarters, he looked around to find that beyond individual decorating taste, all of the officers' quarters were built according to a uniform plan. Like Djarro, Sashi lived in a single room about the length of three of his cots on any given side with a small washroom adjacent. Tan paint covered the walls and ran in streaks where the builders had used too much. Braided rugs covered the floor because it was both the colour and texture of the walls.

Sithon deduced that Sashi's furniture must have come with her to the base, because it was different from Djarro's. Along the back wall stood a long rack hung with uniforms and a set of shelves filled with colourful boxes labelled with the titles of stories. A pile of cushions sat below the bookshelves, looking inviting. Sithon walked in and flopped onto them.

Sashi finished locking the door, then approached her bed, a flat, wide affair raised off of the ground on wooden pegs. When she sat down on the edge of the mattress she bounced up and down several times. Sithon watched Sashi's breasts with interest as she did so.

Sashi tossed her insignia pin into a bin sticking out from under the bed.

"So, I see you've nipped the most comfortable

seat already," she teased.

Sithon fiddled with the corner of a large, red cushion.

"I'm sorry, I, uh, I didn't think before I sat." He stammered.

Sashi reached into the bin under her bed. Sithon caught the enchanting shadow of her cleavage. Sashi tossed him a hunk of dried meat, Ziallon from the smell of it.

"Here, eat some of this. It ought to hold us over until tomorrow morning, at least," she said.

Sithon tore off a chunk with his teeth. The meat tasted a little salty but still satisfying. As he chewed, he remembered Sashi's Guide.

"Are you going to do that thing where you call Djarro now?" He said with his mouth still full.

"Sure," Sashi said, producing the Guide from her bosom, "Once we have a time set up for you to meet Djarro, you'll be able to relax."

Sashi used three fingers to key in commands on the Guide. She fiddled with it for a moment, then it beeped.

Contacting Lt. Djarro Baero via Base Network. Please wait. Said a calm, nearly Geedari voice. A pulse of warbling noises started up which Sithon assumed to be the sounds of the connection process. The warbling stopped, and the nearly-Geedari voice came back.

Apologies, Lt. Plok. Lt. Baero is unavailable at this time. Base Network asserts that his Guide is not operational. I encourage you to try again later.

Sashi tossed her Guide on the bed.

"You heard the Guide, Puppy. He must still be working." She said.

Sithon frowned. He struggled to swallow the last mouthful of dried meat. When he succeeded in forcing the over-chewed lump down his throat, he placed his hands underneath him and pushed himself up.

Sashi tilted her head and crossed her arms.

"Pull my tail, you can't be thinking of leaving so soon!" She cried.

Sithon stood all the way up, but waited to head for the door.

He said, "I can't stay here when Djarro might be out in the base looking for me. And... don't call me Puppy."

Sashi stood up to face him.

"I'm going to be honest with you now, and you need to understand that I'm not *always* this charitable. You might as well make yourself comfortable here because you won't be able to see Lt. Djarro," she said, her breath hitting him in the chest.

Sithon started. His eyes widened as Sashi untied the knot holding her top together. She turned around deliberately so that Sithon could see her tail was pushed invitingly to one side. When her top unravelled completely, the tantalizing rounds of her breasts peeked out from behind her shapely back.

Fingers trailing through her mane, she said, "My bed is much more comfortable than that little cot of yours. Djarro may be gone for a while, but I can make you feel very, very good in the mean time." Sithon shook his head.

Through his rational thoughts danced images of Sashi and the things he wanted to do to her. His anger at her attempt to distract him mingled with an uncomfortable desire to reach out for her breasts, to squeeze them hard as he plunged first his fingers into her, and then something much more intimate.

He scratched at his face to regain some hold on reality. The thoughts filled his mind until he had difficulty even remembering what to say in response to Sashi's effrontery.

Sithon fell to his knees.

"What are you doing to me? Get out of my head!" He groaned.

Sashi let her loincloth slip onto the floor. She placed a hand on Sithon's shivering shoulder.

"Seduction is my Talent. You'll enjoy it more if you stop fighting."

A surge of anger welled up in Sithon, making his skin tingle in a familiar, unsettling way. He breathed, he expanded and within seconds he felt a new consciousness opening outside the confines of his body. Taking refuge in his Smart Blood-induced awareness, he got to his feet and towered over Sashi.

Sashi trembled beneath him. With one hand, Sithon swooped in, grabbed her by the neck and thrust her against the wall. He pulled his ears back and bared all of his teeth.

"Dirty little cheat," he growled, making sure to put his face as close to hers as possible, "Wardan sent you to keep me away from Djarro, didn't he?"

Sashi pressed herself into the wall in an attempt to avoid his gaze. Another surge of impatient rage passed through Sithon. He lunged at Sashi's neck, nipping her hard without breaking skin.

She yelped.

"No! No, Wardan didn't send me anywhere. I knew Djarro would be gone so I thought it would be easy to seduce you in his absence. Do you have any idea how a new Flood heir would upset the balance of power here? Wardan and your mother would have a challenger for supremacy, and youth nearly always triumphs over frailty in leadership disputes."

"You have a nasty way of endearing yourself," Sithon snarled, "Planning to force me to mate with you, deprive my mother of her position and exploit the absence of my Father."

Sashi swallowed, and the muscles in her throat contracted against Sithon's palm. Sithon felt the motion of her fist leaving her side. He reached out, caught it and twisted her wrist. She grimaced.

Through gritted teeth, she said, "You don't want Wardan in power any more than I do."

Sithon blew hot breath from his nostrils into Sashi's eyes.

"I don't want you in power, either. Wardan manipulated you without you even guessing what he was doing. Play games with him and you'll be dead." He said.

Sashi furrowed her brow.

"Manipulated. . .?" She murmured.

Sithon tilted his head to one side, saying quietly,

"He set you up to meet me, knowing you would have plans to seduce me. He knew exactly what you would do and *he used you.*"

Sashi closed her eyes. Her lips curled back, revealing one ivory-coloured tooth.

"Your father is in the east wing right now, behind so many security barriers that you would need an earthquake to break them all."

"Tell me a time when I can reach him," Sithon urged.

"Early tomorrow morning he'll be eating breakfast in the east wing's cafeteria compound. Take the entrance closest to the outside wall. That's your best chance to avoid running into any guards because they tend to place more personnel around internal entrances for things like this. Make sure you get there before sunup. They don't expect you to be awake that early."

Sithon released his grip on Sashi's neck and wrist. She coughed, glaring at him. With the flat of her palm, she gave him a sharp push to the chest. Sithon stepped back from her, a dull ache spreading along his ribs.

"You've got the information you wanted, now get out," she said, her voice unsteady.

Counter to the urging of his Talent and the restlessness in his body, Sithon backed out of Sashi's range of attack but stayed in the room. Crouched against the wall and trembling, Sashi reminded him of Vaedra in the old days.

I will not become my Grandfather.

"I know it hurts to be manipulated. Wardan does it to all of us. Will you be all right?" He asked.

"*Get out!*" Sashi barked, hurling a pillow in Sithon's direction.

Sithon closed the door tightly as he left, stepping loudly down the hall to cover any sound behind him. When he reached the lift entrance to the Burrow, he leaned against the grey control box in the wall and inhaled deeply. The tingle in his blood flowed out with his next breath.

The lift door opened. With legs like bags of sand, he shuffled in.

I only have a few hours of night left to plan.

False Dawn

These admittedly soft-hearted individuals have lost sight of the fact that in order to have survived in exile for this long, the Flood female and her son would have had to have accepted shipments of M vaccine—and used them—without the express permission of government officials.

Queen Leethia Elder—Rebuttal to the Proposed Bill Pardoning the Floods, cont'd

Sithon sat on a metal-framed chair outside Vaedra's chambers, pretending to be asleep. While he rested his eyes he listened to the whispers of the Geedar behind him in the receiving line.

"*Is he really asleep?*"

The shadow of someone waving passed in front of Sithon's eyelids.

"*Yep, he's gone,*" said the waver. Sithon gave a heavy snort to further cement the ruse.

No one said anything for a few minutes. Sithon resisted the urge to swivel his ears, to track their movements by sound.

Finally, one of them said, very quietly, "*Can you*

imagine having to make an appointment to see your own mother? He must really be out of pack with her."

"Don't ask me about mothers," grumbled the other one, "*I'm an army orphan. If I could see* my *mother again, I'd gladly make the appointment.*"

Someone grabbed Sithon's left shoulder and shoved. He jostled into the Geedar next to him and opened his eyes, forgetting to pretend to wake up.

Slash loomed over him, making the dim light of the hallway even dimmer.

"Light sleeper, Sithon?"

Sithon arched his back, saying, "I always keep one eye open."

"Well in that case, let's pluck out the other one," he said with a conspiratory grin to those behind Sithon in line, "Lady Vaedra will see you now."

Sithon rose to follow Slash.

"See you later, sorry about your mother," he said to the two Geedar beside him. They growled.

Vaedra's room still smelled of Yellowfine and bathed in an ambient yellow light. Sithon switched to breathing through his mouth immediately after passing the threshold.

Vaedra sat at the back of the room, observing Sithon's entrance from a pile of red cushions on a raised block. She lounged on her back, legs bent in front of her and arms out to the sides. The black drapery she wore emphasized the scarring on her chest. It cast shadows into the trench between her ribs.

Sithon reached a polite distance from the block. Slash stopped Sithon's forward motion by putting an arm in front of him.

"Kneel before the Lady," he grunted.

"Don't bother," Vaedra countered.

Sithon said, "Thank you, mother."

Vaedra uncovered a smile that showed all of her teeth.

She reached out both hands to Sithon.

"My son, I'm so flattered that you've come to see me. Whatever can I do for you this fine morning?" she said.

Sithon ducked a little while saying, "Weren't you angry with me at the party?"

Vaedra placed a hand under her chin.

She said, "I was, but now I'm better. There are so many more important things to worry about right now, wouldn't you say?"

Sithon drew back. Her easy manner made him distinctly uneasy, especially in its similarity to Wardan.

"Floods hold grudges. This isn't like you." Sithon said.

Vaedra held her grin up at the edges with visible difficulty.

After a period of silence, she said, "Is this really all you came to see me about?"

Sithon took a deep breath before saying, "No, I've come here to ask you about Lt. Djarro."

Vaedra's smile shrunk into a vague sliver moon of the lips.

"Lt. Djarro?"

"Yes," Sithon replied, "He's been too busy to see

me for several days. I want to see him again so that I can continue my education."

"You can learn from Slash from now on. Lt. Djarro is a high-ranking officer in Wardan's army and he can't afford the time it would take to teach you." Vaedra said quickly.

Sithon frowned.

"Slash and I don't get along. You know that. I want to learn from Djarro." He said.

Vaedra raised her nose.

"Lt. Djarro has been promoted to a top secret assignment. I thought you would be happy for him. I'm certainly a lot happier knowing that he is occupied with his job and not with... personal distractions."

Sithon trembled, anger rising up within him. He struggled to remain calm, but the smug, satisfied look on Vaedra's face overwhelmed his sense of decorum.

"You did this!" He exclaimed, pointing at Vaedra, "All the time that Djarro has been missing I thought that Wardan must be the one keeping us apart, but it was you all along."

"Lt. Djarro is of questionable moral character, and I won't have him near you," Vaedra snapped, the tendons in her jaw flexing visibly. She leaned forward on the cushions, pushing out her chest in a futile instinctual attempt to look bigger. From the trench in her ribcage, Sithon saw his mother's heart beating.

"You can't keep us apart," he said.

Vaedra scowled, her bony brows contracting over hollowed eye sockets. The fingers of her right hand flexed menacingly.

"Oh, I *can* keep you apart, Sithon. Not even the most determined son can follow his father to the grave."

Sithon's vision blurred. His face crumpled like a watery root thrown into a fire.

"You're not my mother," He whispered, shaking his head, "*What happened to my mother!*" Sithon's hands formed fists, which shook at his sides.

Slash swooped in to restrain him. Sithon tried to push him away, but Slash caught his wrists and flipped them behind his back. Sithon tested Slash's grip but the twisting hold sent pain shooting through his forearms.

Slash tugged him backwards by the wrists and Sithon moved, his elbows close to popping out of alignment.

"Wait, I'm not finished here," Sithon grunted.

Vaedra waved a lazy hand.

"I'll brook no more discussion on this matter. You are dismissed."

"You can't dismiss your family this way, mother. You owe more respect to a fellow Flood." Sithon called as Slash dragged him further backward.

Slash manoeuvred Sithon almost to the door by the time Vaedra replied.

She said, "Flood. . . hah! You're nothing but a bastard child, half Flood at best. You can't seem to decide whether you're a Flood or a Baero, filthy peasant name that it is. Cut ties with Djarro, and I might reconsider your inheritance."

Sithon spoke clearly as Slash shoved him out the

door, leaning back through the door frame. His nose pointed down and his ears flattened.

"Never."

* * *

Sithon pulled the black ceremonial hood over his face and eyes until he couldn't see properly.

If I can't see out, they can't see in.

He took a final peek out of the small, square window in the door, cementing Djarro's position in his mind. His father sat hunched over, a tiny white bowl in his hands, licking furtively at a little pool of morning vegetable mush. The row of tables he sat at was empty. Three rows over, a knot of other officers chatted away to one another, ignoring Djarro. A few outservers dashed back and forth with water pitchers.

Sithon opened the utility door and stepped through. He wanted to freeze, to analyze every aspect of the environment before continuing toward Djarro, but he forced himself to keep moving.

Refracted light drifted in from the outside and dappled the flat grey paint of the walls. The rain pattering on the high windows of the cafeteria masked the sound of Sithon's footsteps. He drifted across the floor, past the table full of chatting personnel and up to the end of the row where Djarro sat. Sithon flipped his cowl up just enough to confirm his position, then headed down the row.

Djarro's nose twitched once at Sithon's approach, then twice. He glanced in Sithon's direction, his ears stood up, then he looked down again just as quickly. He began talking as soon as Sithon came within earshot in a low lipless mumble.

"I was wondering when you'd find a way to get to me," Djarro said, purposefully omitting Sithon's name. Sithon pulled his cowl even closer to his face, feeling exposed.

"Don't do that, lad," Djarro said, waving his hand in a gesture that could be construed many ways from a distance, "Wardan's agents don't show insecurity in uniform."

Sithon said, "I'm sorry, father. I came to you to warn you..."

"That I'm in danger," Djarro said, cutting Sithon off, "Now listen closely because there are guards posted at all the other doors, and if we're lucky they haven't looked in on me yet."

Sithon jerked his nose toward the door, intending to look for the guards, but Djarro snapped, "Don't look over there. Your body language will give us away."

"So... you know Vaedra wants to kill you?" Sithon asked, leaning in closer.

Djarro slurped up a mouthful of mush and swallowed.

"No... I didn't know that. But I'm not surprised. Wardan is working me long days. I only get a few hours of sleep every night. He's using my experience to get all of his preparations made for the coup, and after that I can only guess what he is planning to do with me. I don't need to have a complete brain to be a source of Smart Blood, after all. Remember how he kept the Mettoa's upper vilobe alive long after we took it from the beast? He can do the same thing to me, only in reverse."

Sithon's throat contracted, making it hard to say, "But you had a plan. . . didn't you?"

Djarro licked his lips. He shifted his bowl a quarter-turn around.

"We're going to light out of here. Before Wardan knows anything. You meet me an hour after dusk at the southern perimeter. I've got a supper break then so it'll take 'em a while to realize anything's wrong. We'll run as long as we can, get out of their range and hide in the forest. Wardan's troops aren't supposed to set foot outside of Base land. Once we reach Ferian government territory, they won't be able to touch us without raising a lot of alarms with the Rakarians."

"That's right... what about the Rakarians? If Wardan's servants aren't protecting us, Rakarian agents will find us just as quickly as the last time I was out in the open," Sithon whispered.

Djarro glanced at Sithon once, sidelong. The edge of his lips curled up just a little.

"The Rakarians are *going* to find us, pup. We're going to seek them out, and when we find them we're going to tell them everything we know about Wardan's operation in return for your freedom, and my pardon." He said.

Sithon raised a hand then lowered it, remembering where he was.

"Father... I'm scared. I know we can't stay here, but the Rakarians? I can't live the rest of my life among the Geedar that imprisoned my family." He said, shaking his head.

Djarro snorted, saying, "Take it from an old outlaw: Living with the enemy is better than not living at all. Now get on. It's almost time for the guards to check in on me."

Sithon nodded, pursing his lips to keep them from trembling.

"An hour after dusk, at the southern perimeter," he said.

Flood Waters Rising

Darkest Night

My opponents also forget, conveniently indeed, that the very existence of a male Flood heir, not just a son, but a **grandson** *to Toraus Flood, indicates that the Flood female manipulated a member of our own guard to help her produce an heir. Make no mistake: she intends to escape, and if given the chance, this conniving piece of filth will attempt to use her son to make a bid for the power that we of the five clans have worked so hard to maintain. With this vote, we must send a strong message: The government of Rakaria will not tolerate lawbreakers, oath breakers or pack-breakers, and the Geedar in question represent all three.*

Queen Leethia Elder—Rebuttal to the Proposed Bill Pardoning the Floods, cont'd

Sithon waited until he reached an empty stretch of hallway, then pulled his ceremonial robes over his head. Once he had the robes balled up in his fists he stuffed them behind a large set of pipes lining the wall. Underneath his robes he wore a normal livery loincloth lined with a blue stripe.

When he arrived at his cot, in the corner of the Burrow's expansive main hall, he pulled the sheets off in one fluid motion. Then he overturned the mattress.

Lying against the metal frame were his only possessions: a pointy tooth he scavenged from the carcass of the Mettoa in memory of the day he found his father, and the white bauble rimmed with gold braid Djarro gave him before Vaedra's resurrection.

Sithon rolled the tooth into the fabric of his loincloth and pinned the bauble to the edge of his belt.

He began the afternoon wrapped in blankets, staring off at the walls and thinking of all the things that could happen after dusk. In the forests of his mind, he and Djarro fought Wardan a thousand times, each time with a new and terrifying weapon bearing down on them with more stealth than a Mettoa in a tree. Sometimes they won; most times they lost.

Sithon shook his fur out after a few hours of internal fighting. He stood up, dropped the blankets from his shoulders and headed for the small washing area adjacent to the laboratory.

The narrow room smelled like pooled water and the acrid tang of disinfectant solution. Wardan insisted that anyone working in the lab wash themselves all over with a slimy bar that left all the fur on their body smelling like fermented tree sap. Sithon had submitted to a washing with the slimy bar once before his mother's resurrection ceremony. When he had tried to straighten his fur out after the shower, the residue of the sap-smelling stuff had burned his tongue.

Sithon hung his loincloth on a peg at the door and padded over the white tiles lining the floor and walls. No moisture soaked into the fur between his toes, so he assumed that the showers had not been used for at least a day. Above him, little metal spigots stared at intervals from the ceiling. He never had gotten over his conviction that many technologies looked like malevolent eyes.

He pressed his palm to the slick surface of the wall. A black dial protruded from a rectangular hole cut into the tile. Sithon slid the dial to the left until cold water shot out of the nearest spigot, spattering on the floor.

He stepped under the stream. The water pounded against the top of his head, trickled around his long ears and then down his back. He shifted his weight a little so that the water would hit his shoulders first, then the crook in his spine just above his tail. With a constant stream of cold distracting part of his sensory perception, Sithon found he could think more clearly. The scenarios that bombarded him when he sat in the corner stayed on the periphery of his thoughts, while the core issues at stake in the night's plan moved to the forefront.

Sithon sat down on the floor, near a drainage grate.

We may fail tonight, but even if Djarro dies he's better off than if he were to stay here, waiting for death. I don't want to leave mother, but I can't knowingly let Djarro try to escape without helping him.

Sithon felt the conviction of his thoughts more strongly than he'd ever felt anything short of his hatred for Toraus. Still, he repeated the same few words of encouragement to himself for so long that his legs felt stiff and sore when he finally reached for the dial to turn off the shower.

He stretched on two legs and all fours, then used his tongue to straighten any fur that the water had washed out of place. Sithon's fur dried. He tied his loincloth well enough that it would not fall off during a chase, and then left the Burrow for the final time.

Sithon headed for the southern perimeter through the storage basements underneath the main hallways. Djarro often walked the basements with Sithon, as he could speak more plainly there and let down some of his officers' affectations. Sithon crept along beneath the dim lighting of sparse yellow lamps, between the hollowed-out shells of old artillery vehicles and piles of giant, worn fan belts.

He almost missed the staircase that would lead him up to the nearest door to the southern perimeter. The double row of strange armoured vehicles mounted with downward-facing cannons that usually marked the southernmost tip of the extensive network of storage basements had been replaced with stacks of partially stripped gears.

Sithon stepped up the grooved metal stairs, his feet sending reverberations through the framework attached to the basement wall. He worked his way up through three landings before reaching a beaten metal door. He pushed the release, shoved the door from its sticky jamb and stepped out into a main-level hallway. The squeals of the reluctant door echoed down the corridor. Sithon waited until the only sound was the distant whoosh of circulating air through the pipes before he crept into the hallway and pulled the door shut behind him.

Sithon closed the small distance between the basement and the outside door in very little time. He slipped with his torso facing sideways through the inner door, then beyond a small antechamber to the outer door.

Sithon flattened himself against the outer wall of the base as soon as he cleared the door. His ribcage flowed up and down with breath after tense breath. With his arms against rough brick, he surveyed the surrounding area. A slight breeze blew in from the west, carrying him a spectrum of information. A party of three individual scent patterns drifted in from a long distance away, becoming more faint with the passing minutes. Sithon assumed that the scents belonged to the closest party of perimeter guards. Straight ahead, he caught some movement along the tree line. A broad-shouldered, square silhouette appeared between two trees, then blended back into the shadows.

After sniffing the air one last time and finding it clean of approaching scents, Sithon crouched over and scurried across the stretch of manicured lawn surrounding the base into the protection of the forest. Some sticks crunched to his right. As Sithon's eyes adjusted to the forest gloom Djarro came into focus, looking in a brown camouflage tabard and loincloth like a tree trunk come alive. He swooped in on Sithon, scooping him up in his arms, pulling him in tight and lifting him up off the ground.

Sithon half-smiled, half-grimaced with the pain

of having his breath temporarily cut off.

"Father, you made it," he wheezed.

Djarro placed Sithon on the ground. He turned toward the south, jerking his head in the direction of their intended escape.

"No more talk after this. The next patrol is due along here in five minutes, and if we don't get going they'll catch our scent trail. Follow me and try not to disturb the underbrush," he whispered, beginning the march forward even before he finished speaking.

Sithon followed Djarro at a brisk trot, using scent and sound to follow him accurately over logs and holes while his night vision adjusted. Every few minutes, Djarro would hold out a hand to Sithon's chest and stop abruptly, his ears perked and swivelling for any sign of motion from behind. The character of the forest around them changed from the supple, tall, closely grown trees of the Northlands to a mixture of Northern trees and the more southerly, thick-trunked trees with branches reaching further down toward the ground. Rocks also started jutting out from the soil at far intervals, the rough kind of rocks that Sithon remembered from the Mettoa hunt. Night descended upon them, and Sithon watched the moon rise through the canopy of the trees. When the moon was almost directly above them, Sithon's chest collided with Djarro's palm. Djarro frowned.

Before them, the brush thinned and opened into a rocky clearing full of short grass, the moon above illuminating the boulders like a mouthful of ugly, rounded teeth. Djarro crouched low, and motioned in hunt-speak for Sithon to do the same. At his signal, they slunk into the moonlight, knowing that the lack of cover would betray them in the silvery moonlight, no matter what they did, if there were enemies present.

Sithon started to relax a little more as they reached the shadow of a great boulder, in the middle of the clearing. The darkness, and the cover it afforded, made him feel as if he were clinging to an island of stability in the middle of an ever-changing ocean of light.

Djarro pulled out a knife, and signalled with his ears that they should go now... the coast was clear for the last push. Just a few hundred feet farther, and they would be free.

He thought of his mother then, and resolved that he would come back for her, as soon as he possibly could.

Before Sithon knew what was happening a concealed figure pushed off the ground and kicked Djarro in the knees. Djarro dropped the knife, and in the split second of confusion that caused the robed figure flew to Sithon's side and punched him in the stomach.

Sithon doubled over, pain arcing through his midsection and bringing the taste of his supper up into his throat. The scout hefted him up over the back of his shoulders and bolted for the other side of the clearing.

Sithon kicked and squirmed in the scout's grip.

"Djarro," he called out, "Djarro!"

Djarro bellowed and came after the scout on all

fours. When he started to catch up, Sithon pummelled the scout with his fists, trying to get him to run slower. After a few blows, the scout slowed down a bit. Djarro ran even faster trying to reach them.

Something large and cylindrical flew out of the night toward Djarro, hitting him in the neck. He stumbled and fell to the ground, then looked toward Sithon and tried to regain his balance. He crawled a few paces, then fell on his side, breathing hard.

Sithon's eyes went wide as he realized what direction the projectile had come from. He breathed harder, and struggled harder.

Sithon's captor scrambled up the side of a large, steep rock face, then dropped him like a bag of sand. His head struck the grainy material of the plateau, simultaneously making a new epicentre of injury and re-awakening the old one from Slash. Cloudy orbs of light rose into the air around him, stinging his bleary eyes.

Two robed figures leaned over Sithon. Cold blue light orbs hovered behind them, causing their features to recede into darkness. The two figures grabbed Sithon's arms and hauled him to his feet. Sithon twisted in their grip, trying to catch them with a kick or a bite. He snarled, foam flecking his lips.

"You mange mongers! Let me go! *Let me go!*" He said.

An unseen foot knocked Sithon's knees out from behind, giving his captors the opening they needed to begin dragging him. The ridge of rock that he had been hoisted onto was a flat topped, slope-sided plateau running along the back of the clearing. Over its edge, still in the center of the grass, Djarro struggled to stay conscious.

"Father," Sithon called, "Listen to the sound of my voice. Stay--"

The figure on his right hammered a fist into Sithon's muzzle. The crack of his teeth resounded in his ears and sent a trickle of blood down his throat. Sithon felt the familiar rush of energy that accompanied his battle rage. He arched his back, pulled on the arms of the two guards and nearly sent them off balance.

Just a few more seconds and I'll be able to pound them together! Hang on Djarro.

Sithon felt himself grow a little taller. The guards did too.

"Wardan, we need reinforcements. His Talent is about to peak," called the guard on the left.

Robed figures swarmed in on Sithon from all sides. He wondered how many of the base's inhabitants Wardan had dragged from their beds to deal with two solitary deserters. Hands grabbed him all over, concentrating on his limbs and head. When they lifted Sithon off the ground, he bared his teeth and barked at them.

"Barking won't do you much good, Sithon," Wardan's voice nagged from further down the rock. Sithon heard the kids snickering at his predicament.

The group of guards slammed Sithon onto a hard, cold piece of metal. His spine struck first and sent collisions echoing out to all of his joints. Yet more robed guards appeared with thick metal shackles. They secured the shackles to the slab, then locked them, one by one, around Sithon's wrists, shoulders, neck, knees and ankles.

One of the guards' hoods slipped back as she snapped the lock into place around Sithon's neck. Her hands felt surprisingly familiar on his body. A piece of wavy yellow mane turned an unsettling green by the light of the floating orbs hung out of her cowl.

"Sashi," Sithon said, his face contorted with fear, "Sashi you have to help me. Think about what you're doing... with Djarro and I gone, you'll be stuck under Wardan's power forever."

Sashi's supple hands pulled away from his neck. She said, "I'm sorry, Puppy, but you were right. I'm no match for Wardan. I'd rather be safe under his control than be in the position that you two are in."

Sashi avoided contact with Sithon as she locked the neck restraint. Off to his left, he heard a familiar whistle, and the guards scattered. Sithon struggled to distinguish Sashi's outline from anyone else in the retreating crowd.

"You can't be safe with Wardan, Sashi. No one is safe, do you hear me? No one!"

Out on the grass, Djarro lay on his side, breathing heavily. His tongue lolled out of his open mouth. Sithon whined, high and desperate. Groups of three and four soldiers ringed the clearing, accompanied by pilots curled up in the control spheres of their two-wheeled battle vehicles like clothed fetuses.

A cloaked figure blocked Sithon's view of his father. No, not a cloak, a white lab coat.

"No one is safe, are they," Wardan growled. He glided forward, until Sithon could feel the breath from Wardan's nose parting over his muzzle.

He murmured, "You've been very disappointing, Sithon. I thought that you would be like Toraus, but young enough that I could teach you, enlist you into my service. Instead, you've tried to make your mother hate me, fought my every edict and worst of all, turned my best officer into an enemy and a deserter."

Sithon spat at Wardan. He shut his right eye and bared his disgusting, dull teeth.

"I didn't turn Djarro into an enemy, you did." Sithon said.

Wardan lunged at Sithon, digging his claws into the tender flesh of Sithon's ear lining. He pulled down on Sithon's ear and placed his muzzle into it.

"I-don't-think-you're-in-any-position-to-*argue*," he yelled. Sithon's ears hurt deep inside, and he whined.

Wardan pulled back to within a nose-length of Sithon's face.

"Now let's see if the sedatives I shot into Djarro are wearing off yet. If my estimates are correct, the Smart Blood..."

Sithon watched Djarro stagger to his feet out in the clearing, then fall to one knee.

"Wardan, your quarrel is with me. Leave the pup alone," he called.

Wardan raised a finger.

"As I was saying, the Smart Blood should be overtaking the effects of the drugs right now." He said, grinning.

Wardan walked to the front of the platform to address Djarro. Sithon felt the hair on the back of his neck stand up straight.

"Don't you turn your back on me, Wardan. I'll kill you," he said.

Wardan did not respond to Sithon's threats. He brushed a lock of mane from in front of his glasses.

"You've made a terrible mistake, Djarro," Wardan called out in the voice he used for ceremonies and formal addresses, "I was hoping perhaps you would reconsider at the last minute and we wouldn't have to go through any of this. It's an awful waste of resources when I've got a coup to plan."

With all the contempt he could muster, Djarro replied, "You knew all along, and you still let us try to get away?"

Wardan said, "Naturally. If I punish you for something you haven't done yet, I have no proof. If I wait for you to commit the crime and catch you escaping, the whole base can watch the traitors come to justice."

Djarro's lips spread into a sarcastic grin.

"Ah, but I know you better than that, Wardan. You could get proof of my treason with a listening device in my soup bowl. There's another reason why you wanted me out here, surrounded by artillery." He said.

Wardan laughed in two sarcastic yips.

"You do know me well, Lieutenant. It's surprising that you overlooked my sociopathic tendencies for so long, actually. You see, I always felt that your feelings would eventually hinder your work as a soldier."

Djarro arched his back, the ridge of his spine bristling.

He said, "What?"

"I'm a scientist, Djarro, I experiment. So here are the rules to this particular investigation. If you surrender now, I'll let Sithon go. He may not be very happy with what I do to *you*, but he won't be harmed. He'll stay on at the base and work for me." Wardan said.

Sithon cried, "No, Djarro! He's lying! I won't work for him! I'd never..."

Djarro held up a hand. He called, "No, son, it's all right. I know he's lying. We're still going to hear him out."

Wardan frowned, but continued on, saying, "Your first option is to surrender. Your second option, Djarro, is to try to escape without your son. I'll admit that the second option is more fun for me."

Djarro raised an eyebrow.

"And what if I decide to take the pup, kill you and break through your reinforcements on the way out?"

Wardan tilted his head to one side, making his long mane dangle down over his shoulder. He grinned.

"If that's your choice, then I get the extreme pleasure of watching you die. Oh, and I almost forgot something."

Wardan reached into his pocket, and Sithon watched him draw out something tubular, about the length of his hand. Sithon strained against the shackles binding him to the table as Wardan approached. He held up the tube, and as it glinted in the orb light Sithon could see that it was hollow, with a pointed tip.

Wardan raised his hand and swung it downward in a quick arc. The pointed end of the tube struck Sithon's exposed side, plunging in under his ribs in a burning explosion of pain.

Sithon screamed, long and loud. The scream then morphed into a howl, which died off in a trail of whimpers. A spurt of red emptied out of his side. Along the edge of the slab, blood trickled down a recessed indentation into a decanter underneath.

While Sithon screamed, Wardan yelled over him, "You have until his blood runs out. Good luck."

Djarro howled along with Sithon, a sound rough with the anguish of years. Wardan grinned and grinned.

Djarro finished his howl and panted hard, breathing the last vestiges of the tranquilizers from his system. His senses expanded outward until he could feel the vibrations of the attack vehicle engines, map the location of every stone on the field at once and still have enough consciousness left to focus in on one or two conversations.

His muscles tensed and he ached to use them: on the vehicles, those vile assistants of Wardan's, then on the fiend himself. He swivelled an ear toward the plateau where Wardan commanded the others.

Djarro swore aloud. Wardan was speaking in body-code. He couldn't hide the approach of the attack engines, though. Djarro heard them approaching now, ten of Wardan's model 2200 Screamers.

He ducked behind a large outcropping. Two Screamers came at once toward the rock, slowing down before sweeping in on Djarro from either side. He sprung forward, tackling the clear spherical cockpit of the vehicle to his left. The twin gun turrets of the other Screamer trained on him but stayed on standby, balls of energy pulsating at the tips of their elements. Djarro clambered up onto the top of the cockpit of his vehicle and used both hands to rip one energy cannon from its casing. He threw the cannon at the other Screamer, smashing its cockpit bubble. The pilot struggled to undo his safety harness as Djarro leapt into his command center. Djarro reached him quickly, and with one savage bite ripped his throat from his body.

Djarro turned to the other Screamer, his muzzle still decorated with beads of red condensation. He emitted a feral growl. The sounds of five more engines were closing in quickly.

He dashed to the ground just as the other vehicle's remaining energy cannon fired. His muscles ached for a challenge.

The pilot tried to back away from Djarro, but he bounded along too quickly to be outmanoeuvred. He grabbed one of the large spokes in the center of the Screamer's right wheel, pulling it to a stop. The Screamer spun around Djarro as its other wheel tried to compensate, and he used the momentum to start pulling it through the air like a weight tied to a rope. As the other five vehicles closed in on him, he swung the incapacitated vehicle in his hands toward them. He hit the first vehicle: the impact jarred his elbows.

The enemy Screamer careened backward into a rocky outcropping and exploded on impact. The heat of the explosion warmed Djarro's face and sent a fresh rush of Smart Blood to his extremities. He gripped the Screamer's wheel harder, listening to the pilot banging his fists on the wall of his crippled cockpit. A half-turn around, two more Screamers made contact with his weapon. They flipped onto the side of one of their gigantic wheels and spun around madly until their pilots ejected. Djarro glanced back at the cockpit. The Geedar banged his fists no more.

One more Screamer approached him—but that only made four of the five engines he'd heard. The last one hung back, just out of his swing radius.

Screamer number four attempted to fire on Djarro. Energy shots glanced off of the hull of his vehicle/weapon, slowing down his swing. He pushed harder to keep the Screamer in the air. After a turn and a half he let go of the wheel and sent it directly into the firing vehicle.

As both vehicles exploded, he felt a satisfying burn in his biceps and shoulders. He dashed through the smoke and fire surrounding the last wreck to gain some reprieve before the next round of carnage.

He listened to the fifth Screamer as it followed him, gaining speed. He heard the conversations of the two ejected pilots, as well. They trailed behind him at a distance, their voices echoing out from behind boulders and running quickly down wreck-less corridors. Djarro dashed behind a rock and doubled back. The vehicle tailing him sped up and followed, but the ejected pilots stayed their course. Djarro broke into a run.

He heard the pilots directly up ahead.

"Here he comes. . . now when he runs by, shoot him."

Djarro vaulted over the boulder they used for cover and tackled them both at once. Dragging the pilots up by their necks, one in each hand, he pulled them screaming into the lane where the vehicle sped down towards them. He hurled one into the cockpit shield. The pilot decomposed into a red smear on the window, blinding the driver. Djarro calculated the perfect distance from the boulder and then, with Smart blood-driven precision, hurled the second screaming pilot into the spokes of the vehicle's left wheel. The pilot fell into two ragged pieces on the ground. The vehicle veered off course and smashed into the boulder Djarro had vaulted over to ambush the pilots.

Djarro located a tall rock nearby and clambered to the top. He faced the plateau. Beyond the yellow haze of fire and the rising smoke, Sithon lay strapped to Wardan's slab. Djarro focussed in on his son. The whites of Sithon's eyes stood out against the night, meaning he was still awake, if not definitely alert. Djarro wiped the blood from his muzzle and sighed.

Something flew into Djarro's neck and stuck there. He felt a plunger release as a painful draught of liquid forced its way into his veins. He reached behind his head and wrenched the tranquilizer dart out. A wave of dizziness washed over him, and he dropped the dart. It fell down the side of the rock, bouncing on the way down. The glass body of the dart shattered in slow motion on the wheel of another vehicle. Three of them surrounded the base of the lookout rock, not two-wheeled Screamers but single-wheeled, silent Assassins.

Slash shielded himself from the shards of glass as they rained down on him. He sat in an unshielded command chair mounted on the axle of the Assassin's single wide wheel, and a dart launcher balanced him on the other side.

The other two kids grinned up at Djarro.

Djarro roared.

"These darts won't stop me," He bellowed.

"Well," Stab replied, her charcoal-grey mane hiding her eyes, "Maybe one dart won't stop you, but we've got hundreds."

Djarro roared, flying from the top of the outcrop toward Stab's pilot seat. Another dart plunged into his ribs from Stab's launcher, and he ripped it out in a spray of blood. He landed on Stab, knocking her Assassin off-balance. The giant wheel fell on top of both of them.

Djarro shrugged it off, and it spun to the ground like an oversized dinner plate. He squeezed his arm around Stab's neck as the other two vehicles closed in on him. Stab bit his arm: he ignored the pain. Stab pulled a knife out from the inside of her robe and slashed his forearm. Djarro bit his lip, but kept his grip. He pulled out his own knife and plunged it into

Stab's heart.

The other two kids fired on Djarro immediately. Slash barked over the sound of his dart cannons.

"You tail rapist! I'll dismember you while your filthy son watches!"

Djarro dodged most of the flying syringes. One pierced his side, but he left it there while he picked up Stab's Assassin. He peered through the clear, blast-resistant center of the vehicle's wheel while using it to shield himself from Slash and Hack's incoming darts. The Assassin started to feel slightly heavier as more tranquilizer entered Djarro's system.

He shifted the weight of the vehicle as he heard Slash and Hack rev up their engines. Slash charged Djarro first, the wheel of his Assassin churning the dirt up behind it.

Djarro held Stab's vehicle behind his back, arms spread. He braced his knees.

Slash's Assassin connected with the edge of Djarro's makeshift shield. Djarro waited until he could feel the full weight of both his vehicle and Stab's. He bowed for a moment, struggling against the extreme load on his back, then shoved himself backward as hard as he could. Slash's vehicle flew backward through the air into Hack's wheel. Slash bailed out, his pilot seat smashing against the treads. He uttered a string of swear words as he fell into a shoulder roll.

Hack's Assassin vehicle wobbled off balance and dumped him out before spinning away and landing on its command chair.

Hack roared in frustration some distance away.

Djarro swivelled his ears to determine Slash's location. He heard the snap of fire, Hack's heavy footfalls. He sniffed the air. Smoke permeated the area, making it hard to catch any other smells.

Three needles pierced Djarro's spine in quick succession. He arched his back and roared. Djarro reached behind himself, but the width of his back prevented him from pulling the syringes from his spine. A wave of dizziness and nausea passed over him, and though he fought the recession of the shimmer in his blood Djarro felt his senses dulling. He lost track of the positioning of the rocks around him, forgot where the explosion fires were spreading to.

Slash's voice reverberated through Djarro's skull. A slender shadow with shimmering edges, he approached through the smoke with Hack by his side. "You're always using your size as a weapon, Djarro, always jamming those brute fists into some problem or other for an instant solution. I know better than to think of size as an asset. I can shoot you in your upper spine as many times as I want, and you'll have to take the payload of the darts." Slash taunted.

Djarro bristled along his spine. His eyes focussed again, but his Smart Blood strength had dissipated. He shivered for a moment as the last of it left through the tips of his ears. He kept pretending to be disoriented and allowed Hack to kick him in the ribs. Djarro tensed his abdominal muscles and it didn't hurt as much as it normally would. He made a show of doubling over even further and whining pitiably.

Slash grinned, an impressive copy of Wardan's

most prized expression.

"I'm going to torture Sithon when you're gone, Djarro. Oh yes, I'm going to cut him a different way every day. I'll see where he bleeds, where he begs, and where he cries out for you until I'm tired of listening to him. I might even kill him a few times, if Wardan lets me." Slash said, approaching Djarro until the Lieutenant could see the laces of his boots.

Djarro opened his jaws and grabbed Slash by his right boot. He closed his teeth around the leather, pushing down until he felt the crunch of bone, the soft give of skin and the salt of blood. Then he grabbed Slash's thigh and pulled away, part of the boot and most of Slash's muscle and arterial tissue coming with him.

Slash arched his back and let out a shrill wail, his fingers curling like dried flower husks. Djarro thrust him to the ground, where he trembled in a heap, his life fast bleeding out into the grass.

Hack tackled Djarro from behind. Djarro slammed him into the rocky outcropping, back first, and felt the grip of his left hand release. Djarro swung Hack around to face him. He elbowed Hack in the jaw, then hooked his arm around his neck. Using his leg as a trip, he flipped Hack onto the ground. Djarro drew his knife. Hack lunged for his throat.

Before Hack could connect, Djarro stabbed him in his stomach, then pulled sharply upward. Hack froze in the guise of a lunging monster, blood pouring from his mouth, then flopped to his side dead.

Djarro fell to his knees, panting hard. The tranquilizer darts were gaining a foothold in his system. The steam rising off of Hack's body wavered, assumed new shapes.

Djarro heard a weak voice on the periphery of his blurry consciousness. Slash dragged himself along the grass, his mutilated leg leaving a trail behind him.

His voice quavered with convulsions as he said, "I'll be back, outborn. Will you?"

Slash propped himself up on one elbow and aimed his dart gun. He squeezed the trigger once, twice, then collapsed.

One of the darts hit Djarro in the leg, the other in the shoulder. He tried to feel where they were, but the darkness blocked his way. Mist closed in on him from all sides. He lurched to one knee, then fell to the earth.

Wardan ripped the shunt from Sithon's side to wake him up. Too weak to struggle, he moaned as the ache in his side sharpened. Wardan looked like two Geedar, but he only had one voice. Some soldiers climbed onto the plateau in front of him and dropped a giant, limp figure at Wardan's feet.

No... NO!

Sithon must have started yelling his thoughts without knowing it, because double-Wardan struck him over the nose with a hammer fist.

"Silence, insect. You're lucky he's still alive after all the destruction he's caused tonight. I think that we're going to get along much better from now on though, Sithon, oh yes. You see, the precious, irreplaceable Lt. Djarro is going to be put in stasis, in a place you'll never be able to find. You'll work for me, slave for me, serve my every whim (and the kids' every whim, once I fix them up), and the minute you do anything that I don't like, he gets a lethal injection in the neck instead of a tranquilizer dart. I think it sounds very fair, and as I said before, you're in no position to argue." Wardan said. Sithon couldn't focus well enough to see the grin, but he imagined it anyway. He felt bile rise up in his throat. Sithon turned his head to one side and spurted brown foam onto his good tabard.

Welcome to hell, Sithon.

End Part One

Flood Waters Rising

Part Two: Rakaria

Flood Waters Rising

The City that Glides On Air

The Koro-Dah warned me that my path in life would be hard. They also warned me against forming attachments to others. What good is a wandering warrior whose heart keeps him from wandering?

Tyrius (Tai-Riahs) Spineheart, "Kattari-Rah Mah"

Sithon lurched to his feet in the dark space beyond his eyes.

Large, yellow lights snapped on one by one, a dotted line between himself and Vaedra's throne. They made the echoing boom of a large switch being thrown each time they illuminated. Or at least, the Second Skin, the system of neuro-connectors implanted into Sithon's brain made the noise for him to hear.

Sithon felt a sob of panic well up in his throat, but the Second Skin system had no expression for panic. He glitched instead, becoming blurry for a moment around the edges and stalling in his subtler body movements.

Vaedra's avatar shifted her non-existent weight on an imaginary throne of gold spires. She chose to appear naked.

"Stop struggling, Sithon. You'll only damage your 'Skin and make yourself blurry." She said.

Sithon commanded his avatar to fold its hands.

He tried to avoid uncomfortable glances at Vaedra's breasts as he said, "Maybe if we could meet face to face, we wouldn't have this problem. Real life doesn't have 'Skin glitches."

"Nonsense," Vaedra laughed, "What is 'real life'? In your 'real life', I'm a feeble old stick. Here, I am the controlling consciousness of Rakaria's most feared hover-city. The Second Skin system lets me go anywhere I want, with only the power of my mind. Why, just last night I was carrying on a conversation with your grandfather."

"You mean you were carrying on a conversation with something that the ship created that looks like Toraus. I'm sure he's still begging your forgiveness for all the trouble he caused you?"

Sithon couldn't keep the jack in his head from registering the sarcasm he felt. He cringed for Vaedra's reaction.

Right on time, she snapped, "This is precisely why I'm too busy to entertain you in my quarters. All I ever hear from you is sarcasm, disapproval, insubordination!"

Sithon narrowed his eyes and crossed his arms.

"That's an interesting choice of words, mother. As I recall, there was someone else who was fond of the word 'insubordination'. It was one of his last words, in fact." He said.

Vaedra's 'Skin smiled.

"I told you we've been talking. I've decided to forgive him, provided that he helps me with our campaign. We need his tactical genius."

Sithon clamped down on his mind to avoid having the jack pick up on any of the thoughts that budded there. Memories of Wardan, the lab and some very uncomfortable conversations played out beneath the jack's level of notice. Sithon's 'Skin stuttered, but nothing concrete came out of its mouth.

Vaedra nodded, taking Sithon's silence as acquiescence.

"I'm glad you've come to your senses early today, Sithon. With the arrival of Wardan's captive, the ship and I have more business to take care of than usual." She said.

Around her throne, the great hover ship *Death's End* personified itself as a crowd of eyeless male Geedar with red Flood livery loincloths who lounged with the air of philosophers. When Vaedra mentioned them, they turned their noses toward her. One ship's avatar, then another piped up in a simulated voice designed to be inoffensive.

Vaedra, Engine Block B is heating up.

Vaedra, someone is scribbling on the divisional rampart in Sector 12D.

Vaedra...

Vaedra shook her head the way she used to when Sithon spilled something on himself.

"Ship, be quiet. *Just* because I mention you in conversation does not mean I am inviting you into the conversation." She sighed.

Duly noted, Vaedra. I will save this recommendation to better serve you in future.

The ship's avatars settled back into their statuesque lounging. Vaedra waved a hand. Her throne disappeared, leaving her floating with her toes pointed at the ground.

She glided toward Sithon.

Sithon slouched backward, away from her.

"I can't be this close to you… not when I can't smell you," He whimpered.

Vaedra opened her arms. Sithon backed away further.

She dropped her hands to her sides.

Her 'Skin sighed, "Every time you refuse to touch me, it solidifies my suspicions about you, Sithon. You're still your father's son, despite everything that Wardan has tried so hard to teach you about the dangers of living Djarro's lifestyle. Do you want to end up in stasis as well?" Sithon bared his teeth.

Vaedra raised a hand and held it shaking in the air.

"You dare to bare your teeth at me?"

"These aren't really my teeth," Sithon said.

Vaedra turned her open palm into a fist, curling one finger up at a time. She held the fist under her chin.

"I can't *wait* until Wardan learns to record these conversations. Show up at the main lab on the tenth floor of the command bubble sometime before midday, but not a minute past. Dawdle in any capacity and the next three doors you have to walk through will smack you squarely on the nose. That is all." Vaedra said.

Vaedra separated into particles, then the particles funneled upward into an invisible hole above her head and she disappeared. The ring of *Death's End* drones faded out of Sithon's vision like a sun spot.

The contents of the room swirled back into position as Sithon doubled over on himself, panting and holding his sides. Soon he could feel the vibration of the engines beneath him and the strange, pulling feeling of being fast in motion without being able to see any immediate evidence of travel. Everywhere, noise flooded in on him. Doors opened and shut, engines hummed, processors whirred, air vents whooshed. Deep down below, always, the whine of the hover ship's jet thrusters sang a hymn to Wardan's glorious achievements.

Sithon pictured himself on a warm summer evening, lying splayed out on a flat ruin rock still hot from an afternoon of direct sunlight. Djarro lay there alongside him, his gargantuan chest rising and falling with deep, relaxed breaths. No sound assaulted them but the wind through the treetops and the beating of their own pulses.

When the noise of the *Death's End* faded into the background and Sithon could determine up from down again, he turned the lights off in the maintenance cabinet he had stumbled into upon Vaedra's arrival and headed out the door.

I wonder what would happen if any of the crew

found me like that?

The Kids had already found him blacked out once or twice in the short time since Wardan had forcibly installed the Second Skin jack: they seemed to make a game of it.

Sithon now had a nick out of one ear and a patch of fur burned off in the middle of his tail as souvenirs of their discovery. He checked for new wounds as he exited the cabinet, but found none.

Sithon continued along the catwalk that spanned the space between the dormitory building and the lavatory building. Around him, more catwalks, bridges and glassed-in pathways stretched between the great gulf separating the two buildings.

Although now a functioning whole hovercraft the size of a small city, the *Death's End* had been pieced together during the conquest from four Royal Rakarian vessels. Personnel traversed the gaps between ships by using a network of flimsy connections improvised by Wardan's engineers. Above, Sithon could see the grey sky of the vast ocean continent of Asarium, and below, the metal mesh of the catwalk followed by a gradually obscuring haze of walls, pipelines and slouching wires. The ship had been on the borderlands for days, and today they would cross into the desert continent of Inner Rakaria.

Sithon's stomach, now secure in its own equilibrium, growled for food. He exited the catwalk at the lavatory building and entered a stairwell to the second floor.

He arrived at the cafeteria checkpoint and joined

a long line of personnel dressed in Wardan's livery: black with a silver plume of smoke in the center. When he got to the front of the line, he moved forward to press his chest against a tube set into the wall. The tube sucked in some air, making the hair on his chest stand on end.

Scent Identity Confirmed: Sithon Flood. Proceed, Said the ship's smooth, polite voice. A door slid open to the cafeteria and Sithon stepped through it.

Once inside, all he had to do was sit down and someone small and nameless came to serve him a bowl of raw muscle meat.

Sithon pinched a tidbit between his thumb and forefinger and dropped it onto his tongue. As he savoured the way that his teeth sank into the chewy meat, he heard a voice say, "You know, it's impolite to pass by your friends without even a tail wag."

Sithon leaned over his bowl as though someone was about to steal from it.

"I have no friends here, Tyrius. I thought I told you to leave me alone." Sithon replied.

Tyrius, a mottled desert brown, came to the other side of the table and slung one leg over the bench. The Geedar on either side of him shifted away. He brushed a lock of grey mane behind one of the horns that jutted out of his forehead. Tyrius had horns grafted all over his body: on his knuckles, his head, his arms, and he always seemed to be acquiring more.

"Why do you keep bothering me?" Sithon asked after swallowing his mouthful of food.

Tyrius tossed his own bowl onto the table and

scooped up a handful of meat.

"You're not afraid of the way I look," Tyrius said, stuffing the handful of meat into his mouth and downing it in seconds, "Even if you weren't Toraus Flood's grandson, that alone would make you interesting. Besides, you don't see anybody else clambering for my attention, do you, eh? They know my reputation."

Sithon poked at his food. He scowled, but allowed himself to be drawn into the conversation.

"The staff may not talk to me but I can listen to them just the same. You're an exotic minority black op that one of Wardan's cronies gave him as a tribute gift. Tothari, aren't you? Stab said that Tothari come from the ice plains above the Rakarian capital." Sithon said.

"So what's the problem with talking to me? You already know what I can do, and you don't seem to be afraid," Tyrius coaxed, wagging his tail.

Sithon continued eating. He tried to ignore Tyrius by keeping his head down, but the Tothari reached over and pinched his nose. Sithon curled his upper lip.

"Take off. You work for Wardan," Sithon snarled.

"So do you," Tyrius said, hands flying up in the air, "That's a crazy thing to say! No wonder nobody talks to you."

Sithon grumbled, "You work for Wardan voluntarily. There's a difference."

"I think Djarro would forgive you for talking to me," Tyrius said, standing up with his bowl.

Sithon's ears flicked upward.

"What?"

"I meant exactly what I just said, Sithon. I'd also be careful around Wardan's new captive if I were you. They say she's near immortal."

Tyrius took his dish, now empty, and headed off in the direction of the bus trays. Sithon stood too, bowl in hand.

"Wait, what do you know about my father?" He called after Tyrius.

Tyrius turned his back on Sithon, showcasing the line of ponytails cascading down his back.

He said, "What do you care what I know about Djarro? I work for Wardan."

Sithon slammed his dish back on the table. He sat back down heavily, then dug his hand into the pile of meat in his bowl. As he watched Tyrius leave the cafeteria through the theft detectors, he ripped a large chunk off of the muscle slab in his hand and swallowed it hard.

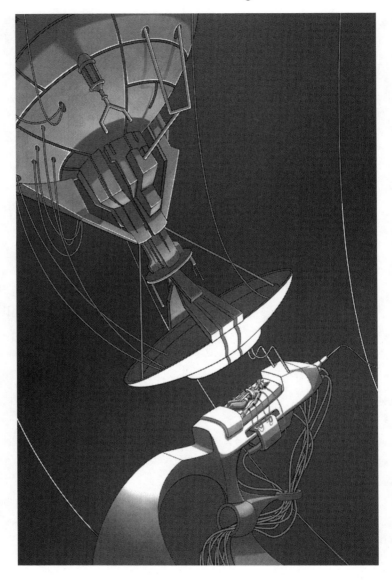

Vaedra in the Death's End

Zahenna's Song

Like every young male, sure of himself and his independence, I thought that keeping aloof from society would be the easiest part of my duties. Then, in the service of Alalias Skye, I met Chanir, and from that moment on, detaching myself from others became close to impossible.

Tyrius (Tai-Riahs) Spineheart, "Kattari-Rah Mah"

Sithon gobbled the rest of his meal without even tasting it and left the cafeteria with tension in his neck.

He went back through the stairwell to the upper floors of the lavatory building, entering his assigned shower block. The large, painted metal room had nozzles extending from the ceiling like Wardan's laboratory annex back at the old base. At least fifty Geedar bathed there in the steam.

Sithon positioned himself under the nearest jet, straightening his fur and licking under his arms. Then he left the showers, shook off and headed for the Command Bubble.

Sithon followed the hallways south, through humid corridors with peeling paint and condensation on the ceiling. Eventually, he came to an exit door with a small window flooded by natural light. He pushed through it into the area known as the Command Bubble.

Sithon crossed the curved pathway ringing the atrium and leaned over the waist-high railing. Up above, and stretching on over a section of the ship the size of the entire Flood Waters compound, a clear dome let in the sunlight. Underneath, paths curved around the edge of the dome for twenty floors. Sithon rested his elbows on the railing and watched the shadows of the rain pattering down the dome's panes.

Someone grabbed Sithon around the waist and hoisted him over the railing, head first. He froze with his fingers splayed out in front of his face.

Familiar laughter mocked him from the pathway.

"You shouldn't hang around the railings, Dung Heap. You could fall over," Slash said.

Stab chimed in too, saying, "When Wardan gets his new captive working for us, he won't need you anymore. Maybe we should just let you go."

Hack just chuckled, a disgusting, gurgling sound. He let Sithon slip through his grip until he hung by his knees over the vast hole underneath the dome. Down below, on the bottom floor of the Command Bubble, uniformed officers milled about. They looked tiny from the tenth floor railing.

Sithon yelped, tightened his lips and closed his eyes.

The kids laughed even harder.

Another voice joined the group. Disorientation and the feeling of having something thrust into a bodily orifice unexpectedly accompanied Vaedra's arrival through the jack.

"*Sithon, what are you doing hanging over the railings like that? You should know better,*" she said as a disembodied voice in Sithon's head.

Sithon tried to concentrate, to send something intelligible back through the jack. All he managed was a mental retch.

"Time to fly, Sithon, get ready," Slash sing-songed.

Hack swung Sithon upward, letting go of his legs.

Sithon screamed. Then, he hit the coarsely carpeted floor of the hallway tail-first. His back slumped with embarrassment when he realized Hack had swung him back over the railing.

Sithon got to his feet while rubbing his behind. The kids ringed him, with Slash in front. Sithon felt a growl rising up in his throat.

"I... have to go to the labs now. It's only an hour to mid-day," he said, pushing past Slash.

Sithon heard their footsteps following him.

"Look at his spine," Stab whispered to the others, "The hair is standing straight up! He wants to turn around and hurt us, but he's too weak to go through with it! He knows we'd kill him, and Djarro too."

"Where are you going, Sithon? You've got a whole hour. Let's settle this in a fight, here and now. Try and rip my throat out, Sithon. You know you want to kill me." Slash called.

Sithon walked stiffly onward. His tail bristled along with his spine. The muscles tensed across his chest and in his stomach.

Slash's verbal assault continued.

"Smart Blood... Hey Smart Blood carrier. You seem pretty biting stupid to me. Wardan has conquered the Rakarians. If might makes right, he's a God. You might as well swear allegiance to him formally: you'll be working for him until the day you die, whether you like it or not."

Sithon saw the doors to the tenth floor labs up ahead, and ran for them lest he lose any more control over himself. Already he felt the tingle of blood power in his extremities.

He dashed inside the double doors and threw the interior lock. One of the kids banged a fist on the other side. Their silhouettes melded together through the milky panes of the door glass.

Vaedra shoved her way into his mind again.

"Sithon, what in the world are you running around locking doors manually for? Don't you trust me to keep the ship safe on my own?"

Sithon managed a short reply this time.

He said, *"Please don't unlock the door."*

Sithon held his breath, expecting to hear the click of the lock undoing itself. Instead, the door stayed closed through another flurry of pounding from the kids.

Vaedra said, *"I won't unlock it... now. Don't expect to stay in there all afternoon, though. I have to let Wardan's guests in later."*

Sithon slumped against the door. The next knock sent extra tremors down his shaking back. The kids stopped knocking when Sithon stayed quiet.

"He's probably run down the back stairwell. Either that or he's gone further in to see Wardan's new capture. We'll catch up to him at the ceremony," Slash said.

"Ooh, I hope he touches her," Slash said, her voice a little further down the hall, "Remember the show we got when that stupid pup from Crystalline got too close? And this time, the bio-imagers in the lab would catch every detail!"

Hack groaned as though anticipating a sexual experience. Sithon tuned them out at that point and imagined his rock in the forest.

At least Djarro is still safe.

Sithon sat in the shadows under the entrance to the laboratory for a few minutes, resting his back on the crease between the doors. A line of daylight from the atrium started above where the shadow of his head ended and stretched into the blue gloom of the lab. The light line climbed up the side of a huge, dark tube two thirds of the way into the room, then ended at the ceiling. Pink muscular tissue undulated against the side of the tube where the light touched. Sithon's skin dimpled up and his tail hugged his leg.

He sensed motion all around him, just beyond the edge of his vision. Flat panels lined the ceiling at angles designed to face spectators on the floor. On every single one, the same image played out from different vantage points. A female Geedar hung suspended in a large cylindrical enclosure lined with slitted eyeballs on stalks. Her chin rested on her chest. Sithon felt a pang of shame for staring at the round, full breasts that hung there, and her thick red mane flowed over her shoulders and clung to her cheeks. Fleshy, slick ropes of muscle snaked around her thighs, waist and wrists.

She groaned and opened her eyes. Her face contracted like someone remembering a head injury and the groan turned into a despairing whine.

Sithon got to one knee and pressed his hand to the release for the door lock. He could head in the opposite direction from the kids, and probably still avoid them until the ceremony.

The female began to sing. Sithon stopped, transfixed by deep, wretched notes that resonated with grief.

Abandon your homes, now
Abandon your wares,
A city glides to us on air.

My failing heart gutters and dies like a flame,
But they'll pick me up and use me just the same,
I'm sure that I'll never see my love again,
When I'm shipped off to see the Death's End.

Across the horizon
It blocks red dawn's glare
The city that glides on the air.

Our pitted old soldiers they fight till the death,
And the mothers of young pups can scarcely draw breath,
'Neath the pillars of hot air that waiver and bend,
The last heralds of the Death's End.

Abandon your minds now,
Abandon all cares,
A city glides to us on air.

Sithon let his hand drop from the door handle. Images of Djarro's body being hauled up from the battlefield flooded his mind and the floor beneath him started to bend.

He pictured his mother the last time he had seen her, reclining in a chair with a cold, smooth visor over her eyes, while all over her body tubes and wires violated the paper-thin barrier of her skin. He gulped hard for air. The air burst out again as a single, silent sob no louder than the emptying of his lungs.

The female on the screens whipped her head about.

"Who's been there listening to me? Is this another one of your sick experiments? Answer me!" she demanded.

The screens on the ceiling projected sound, but Sithon heard a muffled duplicate of the female's voice coming from the tube with the pink muscles. He took a few steps toward that end of the room.

"I'm... not Wardan, if that's what you were thinking." Sithon replied, feeling the muscles in his throat tighten.

The female wiggled her shoulders against her bonds. Her neck contorted as she tried to wrench her wrists away from the tentacles unsuccessfully.

She grimaced, saying, "I'm sure you're a *huge* improvement. Which are you, a mindless resurrected goon or a null* traitor?"

Sithon circled the tube, trying to find another way to see her. All around, the twitching muscle wall blocked his way.

"Actually, I'm the bastard grandson of Toraus Flood," he said to the screens.

The female growled. The heat of her breath caused one of the eyes to blink. Over in the corner, one of the screens went dark.

"A Flood! The worst scum of all… why if it weren't for your flea-ridden grandfather, we wouldn't be in this mess! When I escape, you're going to be the first one I hunt down," she said, her nose pointed upward and away from the disconcerting gaze of the eyeballs.

Sithon said, "Who told you my grandfather was responsible for this? He died before Wardan even launched his coup."

"Wardan has been spreading messages all over the countryside. He says his mission is to fulfil your mother's mandate to control Rakaria, as dictated by Toraus." Her forceful voice softened a little.

Sithon's ears drooped.

He sighed, "My mother… is only interested in controlling the *Death's End* and living out her own fantasies, none of which involve ruling Rakaria. I'm not even sure she can leave her room, now."

"Furthermore," Sithon continued, "why would you believe anything Wardan says in a propaganda message, when everything else he pretended to be before the coup was a carefully constructed lie?"

Up on the screens, Sithon saw the female's brows contract. She winced again, shaking her head.

"I don't know... the rebel forces don't have any other information to go on," she said.

Her eyes widened and she looked around, forgetting that no one could see her.

"Wait, why are you telling me all this?" she asked.

A shock ran through Sithon. For a brief moment, he felt as vulnerable as if he had no fur.

Why am *I telling her all this?*

He turned to go, hoping that she wouldn't miss him until he had slipped out the door. She heard him, and he could see her twisting frantically in the tube.

Sithon was halfway to the door when she said, "Please don't go. I'm sorry I threatened you. My name is Zahenna."

He stopped.

"I'm Sithon," he said, "and I told you all of that because I don't want to be here any more than you do."

Sithon caught her next words more as a motion on the screen than a sound in his ears. Zahenna looked straight into one of the larger eyeballs as she said, "If you want to escape, then get me out."

Flood Waters Rising

Head in the Sand

Chanir inspired me to fight better, to think faster, and to keep myself in top physical condition—but my aim was never to outdo him. In a contest of skill, I would win every time. I wanted to improve so that I would be worthy of him, so that he would love me the way I loved him.

Tyrius (Tai-Riahs) Spineheart, "Kattari-Rah Mah"

Once the last of the guests cleared out of the lab, Wardan left Sithon at the door to the back stairwell. He slouched in the space where yellow light poured into the dark blue room.

Wardan's claws scratched the floor on the way to Zahenna's tube. His hands, half-hidden underneath the sleeves of his laboratory robe, twitched.

Sithon crouched low, trying to make himself invisible. He knew what was coming but Zahenna didn't. Up on the panels, the eyeball imagers showed her resting with her head tilted downward and ears drooped.

Wardan crouched in front of the tube. His

hunched shoulders and curved back accented his heavy breathing. The blue light from the image panels arced down the back of his robe like a decorative stripe of paint.

He bellowed at Zahenna, hands clawing at the air. Sithon heard him mumble some words to himself, words like the ones he used to raise dead bodies.

He raised a hand, and Zahenna's voice was everywhere, screaming. Sithon shivered, hugging himself close to the wall.

"You scheming, biting little pool of pus! I won't kill you... I'll never kill you. Oh, I might have let you die eventually, if you had been too weak to really be an asset to me," Wardan hissed. He made a pulling motion in the air and one of the tentacles twisted Zahenna's arm backward, then yanked it down. She gritted her teeth and hollered through them. Sithon heard the distinctive crunch of breaking bone.

"But you," Wardan continued, quieter this time, "You made a fool of me."

Another tentacle snaked past the eyeball trained on Zahenna's knees. As it hovered a few inches from the hair on her lower back, she twisted her head around to try and see. Wardan grinned. He opened the palm of his hand, and Sithon saw the spade-shaped pad at the end of the tentacle grow slick. The air above the pad wavered in the eyeball feed.

Zahenna sniffed at the air. She widened her eyes until Sithon could see the whites on screen. When she tried to twist around again, Wardan said, "You're not going to see. I don't want you to see until I'm done."

The muscles along Zahenna's back tightened. She held her chin up high, where it trembled.

Sithon remembered the first time Wardan had strapped him to the chair where he drained his blood. He had looked away from the needle, tensed his jaw and tried not to make a sound. Djarro would not want him to give Wardan the satisfaction of seeing him suffer.

Wardan clenched a fist, making the tentacle pad grasp the base of Zahenna's tail. She hissed through her front teeth, but refused to scream. Wardan moved his clenched fist in a slow downward swoop, and the tentacle slid down Zahenna's tail. The area behind it smoked as the fur burned away. Sithon cringed at the sight of skin burned to a patchwork of crimson, purple and black. Even with the air filtration system draining the tube, he could smell acrid smoke and cooking flesh.

When Wardan opened his fist the tentacle released Zahenna's tail. Only a tuft of her original fur remained. She slumped over, her stomach stretching in and out with slow, heavy breaths.

Wardan stuck out his lower lip. He swivelled one ear and narrowed his eyes.

With one swift up-and-down pinching motion, Wardan ripped a piece out of the side of Zahenna's left ear flap in a ragged crescent. Blood spurted from the wound and down her face. Zahenna shut her left eye. Her right eye glistened in the feed.

Wardan dropped his arms to his sides, ending the incantation.

He stalked toward Sithon.

"I'm going to make you into something you won't even recognize," he muttered.

Sithon stayed crouched in the shadows when Wardan reached the doorway to the back stairs.

"Come on," Wardan said, his voice betraying a hint of weariness, "Let's get this over with. I want to get back to the Soldier Labs."

Sithon's stomach lurched as he followed Wardan through the yellow-lit door. Watching Wardan's back descending down the stairs, he imagined himself lunging down after him, sinking his teeth into the place where his spine met his brain and shaking the life out of him.

Right now, I could paint myself in his blood.

Wardan stopped on the stairs. A wave of calm scent wafted off of him.

"It's only natural for you to fantasize about killing me when my back is turned, but I'd appreciate it if you accompanied your fantasies with a little more forward motion. I have a schedule to keep up, you know," he postulated.

Sithon ran his hand along the banister to keep it from shaking as he started behind Wardan down the winding staircase to the lower labs.

They passed two landings before Wardan said, "She's going to give in, you know. She's going to give in because she's a liar."

Sithon perked his ears, but said nothing.

Wardan pointed up at Sithon from the staircase below. He was still a flight ahead.

Wardan said, "Ah, I know you, Sithon. You disagree with me, or else you would have grunted. Or sighed. Or tossed your head. There's a doubt floating around in that bastard brain of yours and I want to know what it is."

Sithon paused on his current step, raised his head, then lowered it again and kept descending. Wardan reached the dinged metal floor at the bottom of the stairs and turned to face him. Even without the advantage of the steps, Sithon stood a head higher than Wardan. Sithon left the final step and hung over him, careful not to touch him.

"I want to know what you're thinking, and I'm not in the mood to be denied," Wardan said, "Tell me what you think of her or Djarro loses a hand."

"You gave her a choice. You said she could join you, or stay in the tube until she died. She only chose one of the options that you gave her," Sithon replied.

Wardan frowned, looked Sithon up and down, then went to open the lab door. Before he opened up his Guide to talk to Vaedra and the security system, he remarked, "Death isn't a real choice. Everyone is afraid of death."

Sithon said, "No, everyone is afraid of you. From what I've seen, many Geedar would welcome death... *lasting death*, to avoid coming here."

Wardan lowered his brows and turned his back on Sithon to unlock the lab door. Sithon caught a whiff of uncomfortable smell before Wardan commanded Vaedra to turn on the air purifiers.

The first tremor shook the ground floor labs as Wardan lifted a hollow needle out of his tool drawer. Wardan's fingers, balanced delicately on either end of the needle, contracted as the specimens lining the walls of the lab sloshed around in their tubular jars. Sithon heard the faint tinkle of the needle hitting the floor.

Wardan bit his finger.

"Son of a stinking Pwarnaa," he exclaimed, then shook out his hand, "I've really got to have those rear thrusters looked at."

Sithon allowed himself a half-grin. From his vantage point on a cold metal countertop, he could see the bead of blood welling up on Wardan's fingertip.

Wardan bent down to pick up the needle. Sithon lifted his left foot and closed one eye, imagining how it would feel to kick him over and stomp on his spine.

Sithon's leg was still in the air when the lab lurched to the left. He slipped down the polished metal of the countertop. A set of glastik tubes gave way against his left hip and crashed to the floor. The lights buried in the wires and struts of the low ceiling vibrated in Sithon's vision as the labs shook like a struck bell.

Wardan lurched to his feet. Sithon knew he was talking to Vaedra because he had two fingers in his right ear. His left hand rubbed spastically at a frizzy patch of mane. He paced in irregular circles punctuated by the occasional straight line. As Wardan paced, he talked with increasing intensity, his glassy eyes not focussed on much of anything in the immediate area.

"Calm down, calm down CALM DOWN! BE

QUIET. Just be quiet. No no no no shh stop screaming at me. I can't stand it. Tell me what's wrong with the ship," He begged, his voice edging on a whine.

Sithon knew this kind of behaviour all too well: Vaedra was afraid. Vaedra was yelling. Wardan had opened communications with her and now he couldn't muster enough presence of mind to push her out or slow her down. Wardan's self-absorbed muttering turned to a whisper, then a vague contortion of the lips. He continued to pace.

Sithon slid down to the floor, leaning most of his weight on the edge of the counter. He put his right foot forward, but quickly retracted it when he felt the edge of a shard of glastik dig into his paw pad. He scanned the floor to find a safe place to step and spotted an empty space behind the end of the counter. Resting most of his weight on his arms, he shuffled down to safety.

Wardan was standing right behind Sithon when he turned around, waiting for him. He raised his eyebrows, and Sithon noticed that his eyes were sharp and clear again.

Wardan crossed his arms.

"And where were you headed off to on this fine, tremor-filled day? Looking to escape your weekly Smart Blood donation? I hardly think Djarro would approve," Wardan said, shaking his head slowly.

Sithon scowled, saying, "I saw how upset Vaedra was just now. She hijacked your reasoning center. Shouldn't your *vast intellect* be working to save the ship? I hardly think my blood is the most important priority."

Wardan narrowed his eyes.

"Your blood is my only priority," he said with flat, threatening ears.

The glastik shards on the floor tinkled as everything vibrated. After a few seconds of clinking debris and humming girders, what could only have been a giant slam to the side of the ship knocked Sithon into the corner of the countertop stomach-first. The breath sailed out of his lungs and aching pain replaced it.

Wardan struggled to keep an even footing, legs spread and arms out. Halfway through the lurch, a jar containing a spongy, many-pronged brown organ jostled off a nearby shelf and struck him on the shoulder before spilling its contents out in front of Sithon. Cold, acrid-smelling liquid washed up around Sithon's toes as he gasped several painful breaths.

Wardan's back formed a tense arc. He shivered once, then pointed at Sithon.

He said, "I should dock Djarro's tail for the way you just spoke to me. You're lucky that I'm in a hurry. Get out to the south hallway and meet with my agent. He'll make sure you get to a secure location. Stay here... and I'll get to add your organs to my collection when you get smashed on all this glastik."

Sithon looked down the lab: the ground floor labs covered a wide arc around the edge of the command bubble.

On one end of the labs, Wardan operated. On the other end, he experimented. Voices drifted down from the experimentation wing, beyond the curve of the wall.

Wardan lurched into motion, his left arm covering his injured shoulder. A clear stain splattered the entire right arm of his lab jacket. The scruff on the right side of his face also dripped with preservation fluid.

"That's my liaison team you're hearing. Get out to the south hallway," he said, stepping over the remains of the pronged organ on the floor. Wardan walked away with a lopsided gait, his claws scratching on the metal floor as he went.

A low-level rumble vibrated the floors but failed to materialize into a major shock. The bits of the broken vials drifted right. The pronged organ jiggled up and down as its articulated limbs curled in on themselves. It shivered, then froze in a ball of alien rigor mortis. Some brownish fluid leaked out of the space between its tentacles.

Sithon forced himself to stop watching the organ die. He stuck out a foot and then jumped, toe first, onto an area with less broken glastik. The ache in his stomach lessened with motion. He opened the door to the south hallway, a squat white maintenance hatch, and left the darkness of the lab behind him.

As Sithon made his way down a bright corridor that his shoulders barely fit into without rubbing against the walls, he talked to himself.

"For once, I think Wardan actually came out of one of our confrontations a little worse off than me. I wish Djarro could have seen that."

At the end of the narrow corridor, a short ladder

stretched up to the open mouth of a doorway. Sithon noticed the figure crouched there only when it moved.

"Don't you talk to yourself enough without doing it in front of an audience?" Chided a familiar voice. Sithon reached the bottom of the ladder and peered up into the doorway.

He called up, "Tyrius? You're the agent Wardan sent for me?"

A hand with rough paw pads and horned knuckles reached down out of the darkness.

"Don't sound so surprised. I *am* the best at what I do," he said as he hoisted Sithon up out of the corridor.

Sithon smoothed out the front of his loincloth. "But you're not supposed to kill me... or at least not as I understood the arrangement," Sithon said.

Tyrius rolled his shoulders forward slightly and swivelled his ears frontward, the gesture for 'let's go' in hunting language. Sithon fell into step behind him as they travelled down the south hallway toward the command bubble. Tyrius continued to talk without looking back at Sithon.

He said, "I am Kattari-Rah. We do not make a living of killing. We kill for our masters, just as we guard prisoners for our masters and any number of other things."

Tyrius looked back then, his smile white and visible even in the dim lighting.

"Of course, we are rather good at killing."

Sithon tripped over a piece of ceiling that had fallen in a previous tremor. He put his hand to the wall, and noticed that the steady vibration of the walls and floor was still happening.

Tyrius held a door open up ahead.

"Here we are. First door, first floor. After you," he said.

Sithon passed through the open door with a puzzled look at Tyrius. He wondered how someone with so many spiky protrusions on their face and exposed body parts could manage to look so cheerful. He wondered how anybody could be cheerful living on the *Death's End*.

Sithon squinted at Tyrius as if he could understand him just by seeing him better. He stopped walking at the edge of the light let in by the command bubble dome. Behind them, figures in officers' insignia scurried back and forth over the floor of the bubble, some hunched together and conversing in hushed tones, and some conversing with no one at all. All of them stole furtive glances out of the window, as if afraid to acknowledge the vista.

Outside the domed window, a cloud of ships stormed over the yellow desert of Inner Rakaria. The four satellite ships to the *Death's End* had left their defensive positions and balls of high-intensity energy fire rolled between them and a hodge-podge line of half-dismantled Royal Rakarian vessels and retrofitted freighters. A cloud of Wardan's Swoophawk fighters hovered at either end of the fight, chasing down any fleeing enemy vessels that the satellite ships had managed to cripple.

Sithon gaped out the window.

"Tyrius, the rebels are attacking us," Sithon said before realizing how obvious his statement sounded.

Tyrius stepped in front of Sithon and pushed him back toward the edge of the Command Bubble, where the path began that led to the interior of the ship.

"Get on. This isn't story time at Camp Fluff! We're in potential danger here."

Sithon moved a step or two backward, but his eyes stayed focussed on the battle.

"Why are they attacking us," he asked, "If they don't have enough ships remaining to destroy us? It must be a distraction. They're after Zahenna."

Tyrius bared a fang. A grey piece of forelock fell over his scarred eye, and he brushed it back. He advanced on Sithon.

"I don't know about Zahenna, but if you don't move on your own, right now, I'm going to knock you out and carry you because I'm sick of your barking."

A distant boom echoed in Sithon's ears, a deep noise like the clearing of water from his ear canal. He noticed the round shadow on the Command Bubble floor just before he caught sight of the giant, spherical object hurtling toward them in a celestial arc.

Sithon ran, Tyrius leapt as glastik shards fell and rebounded against the matting on the floor. Sithon dove for the South Hall doorway, where he grabbed bottom of the raised doorframe and held on tight.

The crash of the shattering dome and the screams of fleeing officers gave way to a painful melange of cracking, squealing, groaning beams as a sphere of dark metal two storeys tall slammed into the command bubble interior like a rock lobbed into soft mud. *Death's End* listed forward, down and down until Sithon's feet slipped out from under him and he dangled by his fingertips from the doorframe.

Wind howled into the atrium from outside, but it could not prevent things from sliding down the floor and out of the broken bubble window.

A female wearing the white of an Outcrafter slid down the matting on the floor, her claws digging ruts into the matting. As the ship tilted, she slid faster and faster until Sithon saw her slam into a ragged slice of window along the atrium edge. The glastik shattered as she hit it.

Out into the desert-coloured blur she sailed, surrounded by a constellation of glastik and blood spray in the split second before she disappeared under the ship.

Sithon gritted his teeth and locked his fingers. Through the open gash in the bubble window, he saw the ground rising up at the front of the *Death's End*. Sithon flopped outward, and then back hard against the floor as the listing end of the ship struck ground. Sand sprayed into the atrium, encrusting Sithon's eyes with burning brands. When the sand went up Sithon's nose, he coughed and lost his hold on the South Hall door.

Sithon fell free for a moment, his eyes dark and his breathing all but stilled. Then his shoulder hit the floor and he skidded, gliding round and round in near-fetal position before colliding with a wall.

He sat up, wincing at the renewed pain in his ribcage. He tested his shoulder by rolling it forward and back. He felt a twinge, but nothing more.

It was then that Sithon felt the quiet. The floor was still, nothing whirred, and nothing whined. Far away, he heard engines with the muffled distinction of an approaching thunderstorm. Sithon stuck a finger in his ear canal and wiggled it around. When he finished, he still heard silence.

Harsh daylight poured into the atrium. It highlighted the top ridge of a wave of sand tossed into the ship by the first impact. The jagged pieces of glastik still clinging to the bottom edge of the bubble window jutted up from the sand, their edges white with sun sheen.

The black sphere reflected light only dully. Sithon saw that it was made of pieces of scrap, burnished and dented.

The black sphere started ticking. Sithon put his hands underneath him and fumbled along the wall, toward the South Hall exit.

"Tyrius," he called out, wanting at once to whisper and to shout, "*Tyrius!*"

Hissing filled the Atrium. Sithon swivelled his ears toward the noise. A breeze brushed his cheek ruffs.

Phoom

A square hatch burst out of the side of the dark sphere facing Sithon. At least two other hatches blew out at the same time as the first, denting the floor on impact.

Sithon shuffled along the wall faster than before.

His hand hit the empty space of the doorframe and he ducked inside. He peeked at the sphere with his nose sticking out from behind the door.

Light defined the square hole in the side of the sphere. A crowd of Geedar stood in the hatchway, lined up with the telltale rigidity of career soldiers. A Geedar in an armoured vest, short loincloth and shin guards coloured deep Rakarian blue hopped down from the lip of the hatch and gestured to the others. He swayed his head back and forth, bearing his teeth.

Fan out. Leave no survivors.

Sithon flattened himself against the wall again, his chest heaving.

"Ah, so you do understand Hunt-Speak. I was beginning to wonder," said a familiar voice from down the hall.

Tyrius leaned on the same wall as Sithon, a few tail-lengths away. His right arm contracted over a lump on his side, wrapped in his tabard like a bandage. Sithon moved in front of him and gestured out toward the atrium. Flashes of blue energy fire made rolling shadows in the doorway as they rocketed past. The sizzling sound of energy balls cooking things on impact punctuated the cries of combat.

Tyrius lurched away from the wall, grunting. Then he broke into a jog heading back toward the labs. With every other step, Tyrius leaned a little too far over on the side with the lump. Sithon kept pace with him. His legs prickled with the urge to bolt down the nearest hallway and find a safe place to hide, but he remembered what Tyrius had said about Djarro in the cafeteria and resisted his instincts.

Tyrius panted, "The safest way out of this area now is to move up a few levels and take the back hallways. We have to get there before they do."

Sithon spotted the low-placed door to the ground floor labs. He bent over and pulled the door open for Tyrius.

"Can you get down the ladder all right?" Sithon asked.

Tyrius positioned himself jerkily onto the first rung.

"I'll be fine. Just keep an eye out. Those rebels can't be far," he said with a last glance toward the atrium.

Sithon crouched toward the wall to protect Tyrius and minimize his own visibility. At the same time he leaned backward to peer through the atrium doorway about fifty tail-lengths away.

Tyrius had barely cleared half the ladder when a hand curled around the edge of the atrium door, then another, flickering with the blue pilot light of a strapped-on energy gun. The pilot light made a circle of blue on the wall, through which Sithon first saw the silhouette of a nose and ears.

The soldier ran his nose up and down the doorframe. He turned, gestured to some invisible others, and entered the hallway with his nose held high. The blue circle of gun light sliced down the walls, just shaving past Sithon's position behind a bend in the hall.

Sithon pushed his legs into the passageway, despite the fact that his knees almost collided with Tyrius's nose. Tyrius glared and flicked his ear.

Just calm down. You're not helping things.

Sithon's vision swirled in an unnatural way. His niche in the hallway became a dark patch of colour, the opening to the lab passage a smudge of light. He lifted his hands to his face and slapped his own cheeks. The sting barely registered.

No, no, no, not now. Not Now!

Vaedra yelled into his head without even trying to form an avatar. Sithon's consciousness vibrated with every word.

"Sithon, they're tearing me apart! Outborns take you, answer me!" Vaedra shrilled, her voice travelling down through Sithon's throat, punching him in the stomach and then slithering out through his trembling legs. Sithon tried to gather enough concentration to shove himself further into the hole, but his limbs moved like they were buried in mud. Tyrius leaned over him, the tips of his horn grafts leaving brown streaks on Sithon's retinas. Tyrius's mouth moved, but the only sound that Sithon heard was a bubbling stream of distant murmurs.

"Mother," he formed in his mind, "Stop yelling at me. Soldiers are after us and I can't move!"

Once Sithon concentrated on the words, he felt himself lift a little out of the thick air-soup around him. He quickly used that clarity to prop himself up on his arms and slide himself into the hole. Once he slipped into the indistinct light blur of the hallway, Tyrius caught him and tried to haul him to his feet. Sithon slipped through Tyrius's weakened grip and fell to his knees, then onto his side. He tried to regain his balance but found that getting 'up' was directional. His head swirled like a broken compass needle.

"Not enough, not enough! Get out of my head!"

Vaedra thrummed between his ears, "The guards Wardan sent have been intercepted. There's damage to Zahenna's containment system. Go and guard her, or I come back screaming."

Finally, blessedly, the room pulled back into focus and Sithon could feel his own weight pressing downward on the sheet metal floor.

He found Tyrius with his good shoulder pressed against the hatch door at the top of the ladder. He grimaced, audible breath coming through his bared teeth. Sithon heard the soldier pushing on the other side, calling for reinforcements. He wobble-ran to the door and leaned against it. His added weight tipped the balance, and the door barely clicked into the latch.

Tyrius spun the airlock wheel with one hand, locking the door for good. "Let's get out of here. They're bound to find another way."

Sithon walked into the lead this time. "Right. Up the back stairs."

Sithon felt Tyrius's hand grip his shoulder. He yanked Sithon back even with him as they reached the exit to the ground floor labs. The floor in front of them was now slick with preservation fluid salted with shards of glastik and flipping, flopping, writhing organs of various descriptions waiting to die.

"No, we head through the labs and out into the dorm blocks. From there, we catch a shuttle at the docking station that will take us to a secure location. *That's* the plan." Tyrius said.

"Plans changed. Mother said we have to get to Zahenna. Her containment system is damaged."

Sithon extended a foot onto the slick floor, finding a place where there was relatively little glastik. Tyrius grabbed his wrist and twisted, not enough to hurt, but enough to promise hurt.

"Don't gnaw my bones, pup. We both know who's in charge here."

Sithon flicked his tail. "Can't leave me, can't carry me. You'll have to do one or the other if Mother comes back."

Tyrius grunted. He let go of Sithon's wrist, came forward and shoved Sithon along toward the door to the back stairs. Sithon skidded on the slick flooring, then skipped quickly out of the range of the glastik. Tyrius made it across the floor without tripping or bleeding but scratched his paw pads a couple of times. He jogged out in front of Sithon and up the back stairs two by two, as if it were his idea to go to the labs in the first place.

"Come on, set fire to your tail! They're on their way!"

Sithon followed Tyrius up the stairs, trying to take them two by two. He scraped his shins every few steps when he miscalculated the distance between stairs. The bluish tube lights along the walls flickered on and off, sometimes pulsating end to end with waves of dim glow.

Sithon overtook Tyrius at the landing below Zahenna's holding cell. He stood doubled over, hands on his knees. A few small drops of blood rat-tatted on the grate floor before dripping through.

Sithon started to take off his tabard. "Do you need another bandage?"

"No, I just took the stairs too fast. Stretched the wound. Keep going."

Sithon padded along the landing, skirting Tyrius, and his blood, as best he could. He took the stairs one at a time, and looked back at Tyrius often. He moved faster after Tyrius got to one knee and hoisted himself up.

When Sithon reached the landing with the locked door to Zahenna's holding tube, he felt the air above him suck in slightly—a vent in the ceiling opened to confirm his identity. The door pushed itself open with eerie grace. Vaedra the omnipresent was welcoming him to the danger zone.

The door caught on something just inside the room: a bench perhaps, something thrown against the wall when the ship hit ground. Sithon had to wedge himself through the door, then step over a pile of—yes, it was benches—to enter the holding area. He sniffed the air. No foreign scent patterns.

Tyrius wiggled through the doorway. He bumped the wound on his side and hissed in a breath.

Sithon listened to Tyrius's hiss as it blended into the other sounds in the room. With the engines silent, Zahenna's amplified breathing swelled and released in soft waves. Black screens peppered the wall of monitors lining the ceiling but the ones trained on

Zahenna's face still operated—her mangled ear had clotted and a dark, sticky stain ran down the left side of her face. Her eyes were open, and she smirked like someone who knew an embarrassing secret of their enemy. Sithon cringed.

Outside, he could hear booms, cracks and shouts muffled by the sealed doors. Blue energy pulses sailed by the crack under the door, casting long flashes that swept over the floor like searchlights, then disappeared. From far off in the back corner of the lab, something crackled. Sithon had spent enough time in the bowels of Wardan's robotic nightmares to recognize the hiss and pop of energy interference. White light flickered in time with the sound. It bounced off Zahenna's tube, highlighting the writhing horrors lining the glass.

Tyrius clambered past an overturned bench and walked back out into the lead.

"I don't like the sound of that," he said, swivelling his ears toward the crackling sound.

"Oh, but *I* do," Zahenna's voice was everywhere at once, smooth and confident, "They're coming for me."

Tyrius shook his back as if he had just been in the water. He jerked his head in the direction of the flickering lights and energy interference.

Ignore her. Follow me.

They reached the place where the shadow of the tube fell, flickering, in the intermittent light.

Probable damage to the sound system caused Zahenna's voice to sound like multiple, malevolent versions of the same promise.

"Just a hairline crack in this tube, and you'll wish you'd never been born."

Sithon and Tyrius paused. When Tyrius kept on walking, Sithon forced himself to move as well.

He jogged up to Tyrius and leaned in, whispering, "What, exactly can she do if she gets out of there?" Tyrius ignored him.

They reached a bank of control panels, big metal boxes lined up along the wall in a crescent behind Zahenna's tube filled with peaks and valleys of various colours and shapes. One box looked like a wide washbasin glittering with tiny, white lights beneath a black veneer. On another, a little white ball hovered over the peak of a little conical metal mountain, looking as if it were held there by a constant up-gusting of wind. On another, a smaller version of the screen on the ceiling displayed scribbles of green on a black background, accompanied by a distant 'whee-urr' at the highest swell of green.

The damaged panel sat at the intersection of two walls. A great rectangular sheet of metal ceiling tile sliced it near in two, undoubtedly dislodged by the force of the *Death's End's* foray into desert exploration.

"I'll need your tabard now," Tyrius said, holding out a hand.

Sithon crossed his arms. "You never answered me."

Tyrius came to within a few inches of Sithon's muzzle and spoke through his teeth, quietly.

"She absorbs... other... Talents. If she gets out of

there, we're yesterday's tripe. Now get on, we have to assess the damage."

Sithon pulled his tabard over his head and held it out to Tyrius in a ball. Tyrius shook his head.

"No. Rip it apart at the shoulder straps and wrap one side around each hand. You're going to need some insulation if you want to pull that ceiling tile out of the panel."

Sithon yanked on either side of one shoulder strap, and felt the seams, then the cloth itself give way beneath his grip. Soon all that was left of the join between the halves of his tabard were a few long, straggling threads of black linen.

Good riddance to Wardan's livery. I hope he runs out of these before I can get another one.

Sithon wrapped the two sides of the tabard tightly over the palms of his hands, leaving only the tips of his fingers to poke out. He examined the ceiling piece for a good hand-hold. The sides of the tile were as smooth as a baking tray, with a small lip on the edge. He grabbed the tile with his fingers over the lip, pressed his grip down as hard as his paw pads would allow, and pulled.

The slab stayed lodged in the control panel. Sithon shifted his weight onto his heels and arched his back. He just felt the initial flow of Smart Blood begin to tingle through his forearms when the slab came whistling out of the control panel. Sithon let go of the ceiling tile almost immediately. He dropped to the floor to avoid being beheaded by the massive metal slab.

Sithon watched in horror as the slab of metal flew

across the control platform toward Zahenna's tube.

Just one hairline crack and we're yesterday's tripe...

The slab spun past the tube, over the control platform steps and into the pile of benches surrounding the back stairs door. They erupted into a chorus of clangs and scrapes, bunching closer to the exit then ever before.

"Well, I guess we don't take that way out," Sithon said as he got to his feet.

Tyrius was already nose-first inside the damaged control panel. It had stopped sparking once the slab was gone.

"Call your Mother. I can't figure this out on my own."

Sithon shivered. For a moment, he weighed in his mind the feeling that he got when Vaedra invaded him with the feeling he got after hearing Zahenna promise to make him rue his birth, and decided that Vaedra was only a marginally better choice. He closed his eyes and receded back into the part of his brain that Wardan had hooked up to her, the obscured part where dreams came from at night and irrational fears lurked like hunters waiting to cripple rather than kill. He pictured the words in that black place before sending them whizzing out of his brain and into hers.

"Tyrius is not a technician. We need your help."

Vaedra's voice jabbed out of a black mound of speaker on the control panel to Tyrius's right. Sithon relaxed when he realized that Vaedra would not be speaking through him.

"I must hurry... the rebel forces are creeping farther into me as we speak and I can only do so much to squash, slice or shoot them on my own. Tyrius, do you see the thick blue wire at the back of the control panel?"

Tyrius nodded, then realized that Vaedra probably wouldn't register a nod from her current vantage point.

"Yes, I see it," he said, "It's cut in half."

"That is the main power conduit which sends life support to the tentacles lining Zahenna's tank. If the power levels dip much lower, the tentacles will begin to die and will release Zahenna. You must reconnect that conduit."

Sithon stepped toward the speaker.

"But Mother, he already told you... it's split in two!"

Vaedra's reply sounded even sharper in the harsh treble of the little speaker. "Hold the two ends together, tape them, use your tongue for all I care. Just reconnect that conduit before we all end up a smear under the rebels' paw pads!"

The black mound went silent. Sithon tapped the speaker. No reproach sounded back at him.

Another female voice replaced Vaedra's. Sithon watched on the monitor as Zahenna half-hooded her eyes. He could practically see the flood of thoughts flowing behind those hunter's eyes, or rather, as it turned out, the thoughts of Floods.

"Sithon! I thought it was you. Whatever you do, don't let him reconnect that conduit," she said.

Sithon first felt a rush of adrenaline—she remembered him. Maybe she was serious about taking him with her when she escaped.

Then again, he remembered the threats she had hurled at him at their first meeting: *When I get out, you're going to be the first one I hunt down.* Sithon happened to be in a rather convenient place, if that was indeed Zahenna's intention. She hadn't exactly welcomed Sithon the second time, either.

"What," he yelled at the tube, "So I can rue the day I was born? I've done enough of that already, thank you. I have no desire to think the same thing while I die."

Below Sithon, Tyrius yanked on the two ends of the blue life-support conduit. The broken ends met, and a shower of sparks flowed outward from their joining. Tyrius scrunched up the base of his nose at Sithon. The white sparks accentuated the wrinkles in his facial skin.

Are you with her?

Sithon put both his hands up, palms out.

I don't know what she's talking about.

Zahenna continued, "I'm giving you a chance, Sithon. If you're not really a Flood, if the Floods aren't really responsible for any of this, then stand up for me! You're the only ally I have."

This time, Tyrius barked, "Is she telling the truth, Sithon? I can still take you down with my back turned."

Sithon flattened his ears. "No, no. She's just trying to delay us."

Tyrius said, "Good," in a clipped sigh, but Sithon noticed something queer about the set of his back, the twitch running through the tip of his tail. He sniffed the air. The smells running off Tyrius's body made a strange mix; unique, in fact, fear mixed with anticipation and a large dose of sadness. Sithon scrunched his nose.

Maybe assassins knew how to send off every chemical signal at once.

Zahenna let out a long, shuddering breath that sounded as though she were freezing to death in cold water. The monitors showed her from many angles closing her eyes and baring a thin sliver of her teeth.

"Very well, Sithon Flood, I see that you're a coward, just like the rest of them."

Sithon shook his head back and forth slowly. He backed away from Tyrius, into the center of the room. Zahenna continued speaking words that cut into him like the spout Wardan had once shoved into his side.

"I know how you got here and I know why you continue to be here: you lack the strength to stand against those who wrong you, and the conviction to stand *with* those you love."

Sithon put his hands on either side of his head. He fell into the trademark slouch of his youth.

"Stop it. You barely know me!" He said, while Djarro fell again in the clearing in his mind, and Wardan grinned at him through a bled-out haze. Tyrius said something from his place at the control panel, likely some encouragement or other to ignore Zahenna, but Sithon could no more block her out than he could block out Vaedra's commands.

"I know your type, Sithon Flood. Oh yes, I've seen

thousands of you. Traitors, equivocators, weak all of you. I kill the weak out of mercy."

Sithon felt his blood spike with the surge of his Talent. His hunched shoulders filled with the twitching, aggression-laden shimmer that made him want to strike out everywhere at once. His rational mind barely held him back from striking Zahenna's tube with a pair of hammer fists. He panted and snarled, his hands almost touching the ground.

"If you're so perfect, then come out here and kill me right now, you out-born rebel pack whore. But you can't, can you? No, you're trapped in here like the rest of us. And I have a feeling that you've got even less chance of getting out than me." Sithon picked up a bolt on the floor and hurled it at the tube. It clanged against the glastik, then bounced away into the shadows.

"Don't do that, Sithon, that's exactly what she wants," Tyrius warned, still holding the conduit together.

Sithon took a breath and kept yelling at the tube.

"Tell me, out-born, what's the difference between someone with no permanent Talent and no Talent at all? Not much, I'd say. Miss tail-in-the-air, stuck in her tube, the next best thing to a Null. Oh, I can tell that you've got a lot to feel superior about."

Sithon almost ignored the flash of movement that he saw on the steps as a trick of the flickering light from the conduit. Tyrius's back tensed, raising the fur on his spine slightly. He swivelled an ear in the direction of the movement. He spoke on the subtlest level of body-code, but Sithon understood.

Enemies. Over there.

Sithon put his back to Zahenna's tube and shuffled along it for a few paces. His palm squeaked along the glastik, and he withdrew it. He kept the memory of his fight with Zahenna fresh in his mind, the anger he had felt when she called him weak. The name had hurt because part of Sithon felt that it was untrue, but even more so because another, deeper part of him said the same thing every day when he failed to find a way to get to Djarro. The shame that ached deep in his gut kept his Smart Blood activated.

Sithon felt a strange mixture of guilt and pleasure that he had discovered a way to control his Talent.

Sithon peeked around the edge of the tube. One of them stood in the middle of the lab where the benches had been set up before the crash and another dangled from the ceiling on a long piece of rope. Somehow they had managed to get in above the ceiling tiles and drop down through one of the holes left by the crash. Sithon wondered how many more were left up there, but no more came down the rope after the second one. He watched them, hoping they would come closer for an easy ambush.

The second operative disengaged himself from the rope and crept toward his partner. The first operative, a black male touched with brown on his limbs and nose pushed his ears forward and tilted his head while looking at the tube.

What in Bleirah's Pool* is that?

The second operative, a white shorthair dappled

with grey splotches, shrugged. He sniffed the air and then pointed with his whole frame at Tyrius's location. The black-and-brown sniffed, too, then they leaned over into tracking posture in unison, hands almost to the ground. Their noses and eyes glinted in the sporadic energy light as they approached.

Sithon quickly snuck around the other side of the tube. As the operatives approached the steps to the control platform, he crept up behind them. When he was almost close enough to smell all of their combined scents, he scanned the bands of their loincloths for weapons. The black-and-brown's waistband stretched around a small paunch, too tight to conceal anything. The hilt of a knife protruded from the white-and-grey's belt.

Sithon remembered Zahenna's voice: *Weak, weak, weak,* and his blood shimmered, then burned, then pushed outward on his skin, expanding him.

The white-and-grey noticed Sithon first. He wheeled around with his nose in the air and his hand on the hilt of his knife. A length of wavy white mane flipped from one shoulder to the other. He slapped his companion's arm.

"Guard, guard!"

Sithon dropped to all fours and charged the two operatives. The white Geedar pulled his knife from his waistband and held it out in front of him. He moved with Sithon, blocking his way up the platform steps while the black Geedar ran for Tyrius.

Sithon, forced to pause, stared at the white operative with deliberate and unsettling intensity. He felt his muscles build, tense, and then he sprung for the white Geedar's neck. His hand shot out and struck the hand holding the knife. The other pulled his shoulders forward. Sithon bit hard enough that he could taste blood welling up below the points of his teeth, but he did not rip away and take the operative's jugular with him. Instead he gripped the wrist holding the knife, harder and harder. When the operative insisted on keeping his grip on the knife, Sithon dug his teeth into the Geedar's neck just a little more.

Finally, the white-and-grey yelped and let go. Sithon took his teeth out of the white's neck and straightened up. He pressed a palm into the wound to make sure White wouldn't struggle too much. He grabbed the knife and held it in the air.

Up on the platform, glaring energy light and a shower of sparks arced out of the control panel. Tyrius blocked blow after blow from the black-and-brown operative with his forearms, high then low, kicks and hammer fists raining down almost faster than Tyrius could block. Tyrius's back took on the growing aspect of a Mettoa, with a sea of spines protruding out from his spinal column. The spines grew slowly bigger, thicker and more deadly. The largest ones developed curved tips.

The Black Geedar continued with his rain of blows, seemingly oblivious to the growing danger on Tyrius's back.

The White tried to yell out a warning to his partner. Sithon pressed harder on his windpipe so that only a gurgling squeal came out. The Black Geedar looked toward Sithon just long enough to give him a chance to aim.

Sithon hurled the knife as hard as he could toward the lower half of the Black operative's body. The knife struck home in the operative's upper thigh. He bellowed, then bent over to pull the knife free. Tyrius reached behind his back and yanked out a spine the length of Sithon's shin. A spray of fluid that looked in the light to be a mixture of blood and clear mucous misted out of the hole left in Tyrius's back. The Black operative raised his head just in time to see Tyrius raise the spine up with both arms and jam it once, twice, three times into his upper chest.

Tyrius left the spine in the operative after the third stab. He flopped over, his blood spreading in an irregularly shaped pool.

The White underneath Sithon tried to scream. Sithon pressed down on his throat again.

"Quiet. You want to follow your friend into the afterlife?"

Zahenna sobbed over the speakers.

"I can hear you killing them Sithon and I hate you. *I hate you!*"

Sithon flipped the White operative over and pressed his knee into his back. He unwrapped the bindings on his hands and used them to tie the Geedar's hands and feet behind him.

"I see, he grunted, "So you expect me to let them kill *me*? Well, I suppose I'd die with the honour of knowing that I fulfilled my destiny by being trampled under the feet of Princess tail-in-the-air."

Tyrius motioned for Sithon to come closer.

"Help me drag this body over to the control panel," he said.

Sithon thought for a moment, then realized what Tyrius intended to do.

"Tyrius, we can't... can't you just... I can hold the ends. You'd do better on guard if more rebels came in."

The spines on Tyrius's back receded beneath the tips of his fur.

"Who's to say that there won't be more of them next time? I need my hands free and we need those tentacles alive."

Sithon looked down at the dead body of the Black operative. Zahenna had heard them talking—she knew what they intended to do.

This is the last straw. If she ever gets out of there, I'm dead. But Tyrius is right. What choice do we have? The rebels won't ask questions before biting our throats out. Mites and Mange, I wish I'd never talked to her.

Sithon grabbed the corpse by its feet, the driest place on the body. The stripe of blood it left along the platform glistened like a swatch of new paint. When he reached the control panel, he hoisted the corpse up under its armpits and thrust it into the rend in the box. The body struck the side of the rend, then fell onto the broken conduit. The legs jittered, the arms flapped for a moment like it was still alive. Its claws tapped on the floor. Soon the smell of burning flesh permeated the air, carried along by puffs of smoke rising off of the corpse's clothes.

At that point, Sithon turned toward Zahenna's tube with a hand over his mouth. He felt his throat spasm in a gag.

He looked up at the screens. Zahenna's mouth turned down at the edges. She lifted her nose up, trying to get away from the smell seeping into her tentacled prison.

"M-m-murderer!" she screeched, then broke into an inarticulate squeal of frustration and rage.

Sithon covered his ears and hunched over again. His head swirled, but not from exertion or the smell. Vaedra's consciousness pushed itself into his, shoving his rational thought processes aside.

"Sithon, I've managed to subdue most of the invaders staked out near the labs, but I've lost track of two males: a black-and-brown and a white-and-grey. Keep an eye out."

Sithon's blood still burned with the urge to swipe at something with his claws, rip into it with his teeth.

He growled out loud and in the speech they shared in Second Skin, "No need mother, they've already been taken care of."

Flood Waters Rising

> *Time passed, and the occupation swept over the land like the shadow of Wardan's dreaded hover city. Alalias was one of the first to ally himself with Wardan's new regime, selling the services of his assassins to Wardan indefinitely. Chanir and I moved to the Death's End, but our relationship remained the same.*
>
> **Tyrius (Tai-Riahs) Spineheart, "Kattari-Rah Mah"**

Sithon felt blurry. He shook out his virtual fur to dispel the feeling, but the fact that he couldn't feel any fur shifting on his body only added to his sense of disembodiment. The fur on his arm ruffled back and forth in an implied breeze, but it looked too soft to be his. It blended too regularly with the play of light and shadow. It felt almost like being underwater, only without the pressure in his ears.

Vaedra trailed along a railing of carved white stone, coming toward him. She looked... more substantial, her bony corners rounded just enough to add an air of health to her appearance. The trench in her chest had disappeared entirely. She wore a cream-coloured drapery that attached at the shoulders with stylized golden clasps shaped like foamy waves. All Flood insignia had been destroyed at Toraus's banishment as a symbol of his fall from honour, but Vaedra had drawn the Flood crest for Sithon many a time, and made sure that he knew how to draw it in turn.

Behind Vaedra curved a terrace lined with many soaring white arches. The keystones sported upturned wave motifs, the columns jumping fish with their tails curled around and their mouths open in wide o's. Sithon remembered dangling from this very terrace as a young pup when the last of the railing gave way. It had been a jolly play area until Uncle Mardon had been forced to fish him back over the ledge. By that time, the stone had mouldered to a dingy, salt-and-pepper grey and all of the ornamentation had been knocked off of the walls by the banishment authorities. Sithon had always climbed up there for the view.

In the Second Skin, the green and black of the forest contrasted in new and striking ways. Clean, bright leaves with curvatures too perfect for nature stood against flat black shadows that cut along their edges with the precision of finely sharpened knives. The sky, of course, was blinding bright blue. The forest, a crowd of twisted growth curled around on itself, listed toward the compound. Vaedra had even recreated the gnarled old tree, barely more than an abnormally braided trunk with a few straggling leaves, that grew around the block of stone announcing the perimeter of Flood Waters. In this version of reality, no carved graffiti obscured the name.

Sithon leaned over the rail. Vaedra had added ornamental gardens to the lawn below.

"Since I haven't needed to control the ship's navigational functions for quite some time, I've been able to work on this little side project. What do you think, Sithon? Is it beautiful?" she said, leaning back to let the non-sunshine warm her face.

Sithon paused for a moment, before saying, "It really isn't like anywhere I've ever been before."

Vaedra had two faces for a moment—another skin glitch.

The system had a hard time figuring out complicated emotions. One face froze in a startled snarl, the other continued talking in a pleasant, chiding tone.

"Nonsense, Sithon, you've lived here your whole life up until that whole unpleasant business two years ago. I just restored it to its former glory."

Sithon put his head on his folded arms. A wave of unease passed over him—the weight of his head didn't feel quite right, and it reminded him of where he really was, lying in a stairwell somewhere between the room where he slept and the cafeteria.

"This—this is perfect. My Flood Waters was about to cave in on itself. That's why I'd never go back there. I thought you felt the same way."

Vaedra leaned out over the rail and surveyed her created vista. A few puffy clouds swirled into existence and moulded themselves back and forth before settling into aesthetically pleasing courses of drift across the horizon. A bumpy freighter ship appeared in the distance, travelling in a straight line for the outer atmosphere. Not going anywhere, really, but looking for all the world like it was.

Vaedra jutted out her lower jaw a little.

"Oh, I wouldn't go back to the *old* Flood Waters either. Think of this one as what might have been, what it *should* have been."

Sithon, head still on his arms, sent a puff of non-breath sailing out of his nostrils.

"At least you're comfortable here, Mother. I didn't like the black space." *Speaking of the black space...*

"Mother," Sithon asked, "How are you keeping track of the ship? Where are the drones?"

No crimson robed figures paced the terrace, or the Garden, or the shadows behind the arches.

Vaedra's eyes widened. She smiled in a tight knot at the front of her mouth, like someone trying to contain a small, live animal behind their teeth.

"That's the surprise I've been saving for last, Sithon. I consolidated the drones into a single personality, one that is above mere diagnostic readings and error reports. I have managed to create an entirely distinct personality within the confines of the Second Skin."

Sithon coughed hard. He hoped that his physical body, trapped in the stairwell, could stave off the nausea until he could re-awaken. His avatar's eyes widened. His focus snapped to Vaedra, then over her shoulder, where a middle-aged male limped toward them. Grey hands, shaggy at the knuckles grasped the head of a cane that Sithon had seen the back end of too many times. The hard lines of the newcomer's nose and the proud set of his ears at once scared

Sithon and reminded him of his own reflection.

Sithon braced for the moment when Toraus would run up and strike Vaedra with his cane, kick her on the ground and make her cry out for mercy. The new version of Toraus limped along as fast as his cane would allow him and when he reached Vaedra, he threw his arm around her, cane and all, and licked her avatar's cheek. Vaedra looked at him out of the corners of her eyes and smiled a self-satisfied smile.

Sithon's mouth gaped open in an upside-down 'u' of horror and disgust. He backed away from the Vaedra, while the acid-green eyes of his grandfather fixed on him, flecked with red as though the blood of his kills had splashed up into them. This Toraus was at least thirty years younger than the Toraus that Sithon had known. Which meant he was mobile—and dangerous.

"Get him away from me," Sithon said, pointing at the thing hanging off Vaedra's shoulder, "He's your creation, isn't he? Tell him to go away. Never bring him back in my presence. Please, if you love me..."

Vaedra touched the arm draped over her shoulder.

"I can no more dismiss your grandfather than you can dismiss me. He is my elder and my better."

"He's you! You made him," Sithon exclaimed, the volume of his voice making the Second Skin system click at the high point of 'you'.

Toraus disentangled himself from Vaedra and stepped toward Sithon, his cane preceding him. A non-existent wind agitated the grey shag on the sides of his face. Vaedra turned the sunshine up behind Toraus until a halo of light surrounded him.

"On the contrary," Toraus said in a gravely, careworn voice, "I created Vaedra, and now I'm here to advise her on how to squash the Rakarians forever. I think Wardan will find my experience in war to be an asset to his plans."

"You don't share power. You beat my mother. You don't *talk* to me without calling me whelp or half-breed or some other name first. You're... not... Toraus!"

Sithon punctuated the assertions with little neurotic shakes of his hands, pointing the tips of his claws toward the avatar with his grandfather's face. He backed further down the terrace as Toraus approached.

Toraus reached out to embrace Sithon.

"I am Toraus. I am not part of her. I do, however, want to claim a part of you."

Sithon scrunched his neck up. He felt his mane rise. He whined a little, in spite of himself.

Toraus continued, "Look at you... the spitting image of me at the age when I bathed in the blood of my oppressors and rallied armies to my hand. And so wary... you don't even trust your own mother. You're a survivor, Sithon. Just like me."

"Wrong," Sithon said, pointing, "I *survived* you. You're *dead*! And you deserve to be dead."

Toraus dropped his arms to his sides. Sithon felt his stomach lurch as Toraus's blood-flecked green eyes did something that the real Toraus's never did:

they softened along the edges, becoming gentle, almost kind.

"You must forgive me. I only acted the way I did to make you strong, Sithon."

"That's a lie. You beat us because you were weak. Mother, I'm begging you, come to your senses and destroy this... this thing!"

Vaedra walked the other way back down the terrace. Sithon felt his avatar wavering, the Second Skin world dissolving around him. Toraus's silhouette in the unnatural halo of sunlight was the last thing to stay with Sithon as he drifted back into his own head. The shape of Toraus's rigid ears and hard-ruled nose wavered just behind his eyes like something underwater.

"I'd sooner destroy myself," Vaedra's voice floated to him out of the ether.

Sithon pulled himself off of the grate floor of the stair landing. The bumpy pattern of the grating imprinted itself on the edge of his nose where the fur was thinnest.

He ran his hands over his ribs and felt a bump there. Probably a kick, maybe a blunt instrument.

He pulled himself into the dingy corner and curled over on the lump on his side, which started to throb as his consciousness seeped back. Sithon emptied his lungs through his nose. He drew the breath back in as a gasping sob. He missed lunch there, lying in the stairwell. Finally, in the midst of the ache of his hunger and the lump on his side, beneath the despair of living linked to Vaedra and the horror of the resurrected Toraus, he came to the second shocking realization of his young life.

I might hate that tail-in-the-air Zahenna, but I have a feeling I'll need her just the same. I'm leaving through that hole in the command bubble, and I'm taking her with me.

Rue the Day

I loved him, and he knew I loved him, but I had learned long ago that it was not in Chanir's nature to mate with another male. But could that stop me from loving him? Never. Chanir, I knew, fed a part of me that had starved for all of my life before him. If we couldn't be mates, I would serve him as a friend until the day I died.

Tyrius (Tai-Riahs) Spineheart, "Kattari-Rah Mah"

The kids found Sithon in the stairwell, as he lifted his tail off the ground to stretch his cramped back. Slash and Hack each grabbed one of his arms and hauled him to his feet. Stab pushed the center of his back to prod him up the stairs.

"Hurry up, Dung Heap. Wardan needs you for a new experiment," Stab warbled in her grating alto.

Sithon made the usual protestations, but kept his feet moving along. They pushed him through the cluster of cafeterias. His stomach hurt even more than before when he smelled the leavings of lunch wafting through the halls.

Wardan leaned on Zahenna's tube, waiting for

them as Sithon came stumbling over the threshold. Wardan held a vial filled with a long purple organism that never seemed to stop twisting around in endless corkscrews no matter how long Sithon looked at it. As he got closer, Sithon saw that the purple thing had little lacy tentacles that wiggled it along through its holding fluid.

"Sithon," Wardan said, grinning, "I almost thought you'd disappeared out the hole."

"You posted too many guards."

"Well, they keep the Rebel harriers out, and everyone else in. When you're this far out in the desert, you learn to put things to more than one use."

Wardan opened a hatch in the bottom of the tube which led to a cylindrical pipe. He dumped the contents of the vial into the pipe.

Sithon looked up at Zahenna on the screens. She hung from the tentacles rather than bracing against them. Crisp streaks of blood darkened sections of her mane below the ears. Sithon couldn't smell her, but even in the limited, bluish feed from the eyeballs in Zahenna's tube he saw that her torn ear was more ragged than before, and swollen around the edges. Fur grew only in patches on her mangled right arm, and the bare patches were an unhealthy dark brown. Ugly flakes of skin curled off her blackened tail. Sithon still found her dignified, even with yellow crusts lining her closed eyes.

Wardan clamped the hatch closed. He muttered, "It's been a week. I'm sick of waiting. She joins me now, or she dies."

Wardan stepped back from the tube, spread his arms and murmured the unintelligible words he used to activate the tentacles. Sithon watched the purple twisting thing migrate up the space in between the muscles and the glastik tube, being pushed along in a gruesome facsimile of the way his stomach muscles clenched while bringing up bad food.

On the monitors up above, a tentacle tip lined with concentric circles of hollow teeth inched toward Zahenna. When the purple twisting thing reached the level of the tentacle, it disappeared, sucked into a miniscule hole in the back of the musculature.

Sithon grimaced. He understood Wardan's immediate plan, at least. Wardan thrust a palm forward in the air, the way one would strike a tree to get it to drop fruit.

Zahenna's left breast, like a ripe fruit, squashed up against the edge of the tentacle tip as it drove its hollow teeth under her ribs. No howls escaped her now, not even anything as exuberant as the grunt that came out of her when Wardan broke her arm. She called out with a sharp "A-ha," then issued a series of gulps that sounded like a cross between defeated laughter and a sob.

Wardan flexed the tips of his outstretched fingers. A lump (Sithon assumed it was the purple twisting thing) travelled quickly down the arm of the tentacle. He knew when it entered Zahenna's chest cavity, because then she started bellowing like she did the first day. Only this time, her cries grew sharper on the ends, like whatever Wardan had inserted into her body attacked the very core of her being.

The tentacle pulled out of Zahenna's chest, leaving a set of dotted rings dripping blood. Zahenna writhed and kicked, oblivious to the injury. She bared her teeth, flattened her ears and clawed her fingers.

Wardan assumed a normal posture. He called out to the kids, who watched the whole scene a few feet behind Sithon.

"All right, you three. Drop her down, then raise the tube."

A painful gasp echoed over the room as the tentacles holding Zahenna suspended in the tube released her all at once. She fell to her knees on the sticky floor, amidst a brown melange of her blood and mucous from the organs on the walls. She raised a hand like someone half-asleep. The substance trailed from her fingers like cobwebs.

One by one, a row of half-circular seals unlatched themselves along the bottom edge of the tube. The whole containment apparatus separated from a small platform base and slid, musculature and all into a mirror-image platform in the ceiling.

He saw her then for the first time, much smaller than her voice. Her slick, wet fur flattened her size down even more from the way Sithon pictured her after their verbal battles. Her eyes opened, blue eyes the colour of Vaedra's too-perfect sky. Those, Sithon recognized as belonging to the female he traded insults with back on the day of the crash. Even with trails of thick fluid running down from the corners of the lids, those were hunter's eyes.

Without any physical cues as warning, Zahenna leapt to her feet and made for Wardan, her arms bowed in an aggressive, size-enhancing posture. She reached the platform steps and fell backward, midsection first onto the bottom stair. She arched her back and coughed. A spray of blood spattered her chest ruff.

Sithon's knees shook, but he stood his ground.

You want to escape with her. Well, you'll never have a better chance than this.

Wardan tilted his head to one side in a mock gesture of pity. "Oh, Zahenna, did you really think it would be that easy to kill me? Poor pathetic rebel princess. Always thinking in noblest terms."

"What did you put in me?" She said with blood seeping through her teeth.

"The deadliest parasite I know of. It will kill you in half an hour."

Zahenna convulsed once, her body arcing backward like a trestle bridge.

"What's the catch?" She grinned, and Sithon could tell that it was bravado, not muscle spasms behind that smile.

Wardan picked some dirt from under his nail. "The catch... is that I'll only bring you back again. And when you come back, you won't be yourself at all. You may have heard that my resurrections return with an uncanny filial loyalty to me."

"Unnatural...more like..."

"Well regardless, your choice is this: Do me a favour and stay alive so that I can prove to my minions that we've won the moral victory over the rebels without the use of my Talent, and earn the right to keep your individuality, or end this now and come back later as my child in death. Either way, the rebels are going to hear you're a traitor."

Zahenna rolled over onto her side and more blood dripped from her muzzle. She glared at Wardan with all the hatred of a mortally wounded predator.

"I will die now in honour, and from where I go, no one will be able to resurrect me! I will not allow it!"

A mixture of emotions welled in Sithon's chest. He hated Zahenna for what she said to him on the day of the crash, but watching her now, holding herself up on the steps like a brittle piece of coal under a hammer, convinced it was a diamond, he also respected her. He also had another, very uncomfortable feeling. He wanted her for himself. In her defiant pose, in all the things she had made him feel even from a position of extreme vulnerability, he saw an unrelenting force of purpose that matched his own. She would battle Wardan to the death.

That was why he ran to her then, stopping just short of her area of reach.

"Zahenna, no!" he pleaded, "You can't stop him from resurrecting you. Think about all the good soldiers that have died loyal rebels and returned serving Wardan. I know the Rakarians have seen it… you sang of it when you first came here."

Zahenna's reply was softer than normal, but whether it was by extreme injury or tenderness Sithon couldn't tell.

"Stay out of this, mange-mongering Flood. I'd recognize your stinking voice anywhere."

Despite his keener survival instincts, Sithon knelt down by Zahenna. He held out his hand to her. She flinched back, then blinked at him like someone taking in the harsh rays of noonday. Sithon's hand trembled despite his best efforts to clench his upper arm.

"I thought my mother would be mine again when she was resurrected. I was wrong. She returned as something strange: neither the Geedar she was, nor someone completely different. Her memories of her past life became self-serving and her old loyalties slowly faded away into what was most convenient for him," he said, pointing at Wardan.

"I know you don't want to let him have those things."

Wardan shrugged. "A treasonous argument, but a valid one. The resurrection process scrambles all sorts of things around. Why not keep your consciousness *and* your life? All you have to do is absorb Sithon's Talent. It will heal you, and keep the parasite from affecting your vital organs. Sure, you won't be able to change Talents without being ripped to shreds inside, but if this deal held nothing in it for me, why would I make it?"

Zahenna hissed, "There are more important things than saving your own life." She breathed heavily now, her stomach trembling with each swell of her abdomen.

Sithon needed to get her attention off of Wardan. If she stayed fixated on Wardan, he knew that her pride would never allow her to save herself. He shrieked inwardly as he reached out and grabbed her hand.

She whirled back around on Sithon with a speed that surprised him.

"You dare touch me..."

"It's worse than that, miss tail-in-the-air. I'm daring to care about you. Pretty sad for an out-born piece of yesterday's tripe. Go ahead, make me rue the day I was born."

She stayed still.

"Don't listen to Wardan. Listen to me. Nobody knows what will happen today, or tomorrow, and I think that deep down, when Wardan's day really does come, you'll want to be there, fully yourself. Dying is taking the easy way out and I can tell that you're way too proud—and stubborn—to do what's easy."

Sithon hunkered down further and looked Zahenna in her intense blue eyes.

"Take my Talent before it's too late. Prove to me that you're the hard-tailed, neck-biting lead bitch that I think you are."

Zahenna convulsed now the way that Vaedra had done when she was speared on the deadwood log. Sithon squeezed Zahenna's hand.

Sithon felt the Smart Blood shimmer rise up in his body unbidden for a moment, and his first instinct told him to pull away from Zahenna before he harmed her. Then he realized that the flow was leaving the core of his body, flowing into the hand that

Zahenna held. Zahenna tilted her head back, and the loose parts of her mane blew behind her in an unfelt wind.

She let Sithon go. He stumbled backward, eager to get away from the strange sensation of having his power at once activated and drained.

Sithon stayed nearby and watched as the swollen edge of Zahenna's ear scabbed up and returned to a normal colour. She reached over to her arm, gritted her teeth and twisted it back into place as the bruising faded. Dead skin fell off of the part of her tail that was exposed beneath her, revealing new, pink scars. Her convulsions stilled to shivers which faded out in the regular swell and fall of her breathing.

"Neck biter," she said, as if considering the slur for the first time, "I'll live to make you pay for that remark, Flood."

Slash and Hack soon swooped in on Zahenna with the kinds of shackles that they used on Sithon, resistant to all but the strongest of Smart Blood episodes. Zahenna scowled and struggled, but the Kids had learned too well from Sithon's outbursts to be dropped by a relative newcomer to the Talent. Wardan grinned, nodding thanks to Sithon as they hauled her away down the back stairway. Sithon turned his back on Wardan for the moment.

Live to make me pay for my remarks, Princess, just make sure that you live.

Flood Waters Rising

Packing In

I remember only snippets of that day. I remember the way Chanir's blood soaked into the sand, his hand clasped tightly around mine, and the fear I saw in his eyes. He told me he loved me before his heart stopped beating.

Wardan later threw his body to the Pwarnaa to throw them off our trail. He did not consider the love of my life valuable enough to resurrect.

Tyrius (Tai-Riahs) Spineheart, "Kattari-Rah Mah"

After meeting with Vaedra that day in the stairwell, Sithon used any excuse to wander along the hole in the ship.

The day after Zahenna came out of the tube, Sithon came up the white passageway on his way from giving Wardan blood. His arm ached where Wardan had jammed the needle in even harder than usual, while asking him pointed questions about his relationship with Zahenna. *When were you talking to her? What end did you have in mind for helping her? Did you re-*

ally think you could talk that way about me without some sort of repercussion?

On the very brink of the hole, work crews had cut power to Vaedra's surveillance systems during repairs. Sithon enjoyed... not the silence, certainly. Tools clanged and banged and crewmen hollered from every direction. He more enjoyed the implied silence where Vaedra could not watch his every move. So far, no one had shooed him out of the area, but he knew that most Geedar on the ship would be quietly forbidden from entering the repair zone. As a result of this knowledge Sithon never stayed in one place too long and switched positions when he felt like someone might be watching him.

The dry air from the desert drifted into what was left of the atrium, and despite a series of impromptu canvas awnings attached to the top of the hole and extending out for the length of another atrium, so did the sun. Errant rays of scorching desert sun penetrated holes and cracks in the canvas roofing and illuminated motes of sand that the workers kicked up. So far, they had cleaned up the glastik, deconstructed the troop carrier and worked their way down through the broken flooring as an access point to the damaged hover engines. As for the hole itself, Sithon wondered if they'd have to take off without replacing the panelling. Glastik was a manufactured material, and Wardan would have to get to a city to find more. As for the hover engines, Sithon overheard Wardan saying to Vaedra that they'd have to wait and see what the workers turned up. If the ship didn't have the necessary parts on hand, Wardan would have to send out one of the satellite ships, the Battlecry or the Pwarnaa to get the parts they needed.

Out past the tunnel of awnings, Sithon saw the movement of the guards Wardan had placed around the perimeter of the ship. So many of Wardan's crew paced the sands surrounding the ship that very few of them stayed inside to do their original jobs. The amount of working cafeterias in the ship had dwindled over the previous week until the remaining few were so crowded that the food became carry-out only. Forget about the plates.

Sithon felt a tap on his shoulder as he looked out toward the desert. He jerked away. Tyrius stood behind him, his fearsome horned face softened by the muted light coming in from outside.

Sithon rolled his eyes and held out his hand.

"Fine, take me to wherever the 'safe location' is this time. You're better than the Kids, at least."

"At the moment, there is no safer location. And I'm here as a friend," Tyrius said.

Sithon avoided eye contact with him. "You have a funny way of assuming things."

"Not this time. I know you had a pact with Zahenna."

Sithon raised his voice before realizing that voices echoed in the atrium without the engines to muffle them.

"You can't prove that! She'll say anything to get her own way."

"I disagree. You hurt Zahenna's pride, and when

that much pride gets stepped on, it makes a noise." Tyrius said.

Sithon narrowed his eyes and flattened his ears.

"Well, apparently it's a noise only you can hear." He answered pertly.

Tyrius craned his neck around to make sure that no one on the work crews hovered nearby. The voices of a few out-crafter mechanics echoed up from the hole in the floor along with the clunks and bangs of their tools, and up overhead some workers suspended on ropes cut off the last shards of glastik clinging to the edge of the command bubble and caught them in large tubular sacks. No one approached Tyrius and Sithon from any direction.

"Listen," Tyrius said, "I'm going to clench right down on the bone here. If you want revenge on Wardan, if you want freedom, then meet me here tonight, after the moon rises. I've got a plan to get us a ship."

"Why should I trust you?"

Tyrius sighed and rubbed the place where his nose met his forehead.

"You... you'll just have to trust me. That is, if you actually want to leave this place. If you're really just like Zahenna said, another Geedar who talks about acting but never does, then I guess I've wasted my time, and risked my neck for nothing."

Again, like the incident with Zahenna, Sithon knew that Tyrius goaded him on purpose, to force his own agenda. Sithon decided to add a little of *his* agenda to the mix.

"All right, I'll meet you. But I'm bringing Zahenna with me."

Tyrius's tail gave a funny little squiggle as he tried to continue acting casual while clearly agitated.

"No you're not. You've seen it for yourself. She's crazy. Besides, she's under guard and taking her would trigger some major alarms. I'm not even sure if she would go anywhere with you. She seems like the type to refuse just on principle."

Sithon's calm radiated from within, to his great surprise. Even he would expect himself to be more nervous talking about something like this.

"She may be dangerous, she may be stubborn, but we need her. You can't tell me that a Talent like hers won't be useful to whatever you're planning next."

"Talents are great. It's the Geedar they're attached to that are the problem. My mother had a saying: Judge by Talent and trade water for dung." Tyrius held out his hands like he had just imparted a phrase of great meaning to Sithon. Tyrius tilted his head, and Sithon wondered how he avoided spearing himself on his own horns when he did so. Sithon tilted his head too, out of confusion.

"I don't get it. Water and dung are both very common," he said.

Tyrius emitted another exasperated sigh.

"Not in a rock desert. Water is the most precious commodity there. And the Tothari are herders. We've always got too much dung."

"Well, regardless, how many Geedar do you need to work this plan of yours?"

"Just two."

"Then you'll be missing a vital half of your team unless you let me bring Zahenna."

Tyrius wrinkled his nose, an expression that Sithon was getting more and more used to seeing on him. He bared a fang.

"Well who says that you're one of the two?"

Sithon walked past Tyrius and made for the back of the Atrium.

"Time to line up for lunch," he said, "We'll see you when the moon is high."

Tyrius moved, stopped, then moved again, grabbing Sithon by the elbow before he could go. "Wait, fine. You're just like your father, you know that? Always pulling impossible stunts. Well, you saw firsthand where that landed Djarro in the end. Just be careful, and..."

"I know it's dangerous. Is this going somewhere?" Sithon replied, tugging his elbow free.

"Yes. They're going to drain her blood this evening after supper."

"That mange monger," Sithon growled, "He sure didn't waste any time sniffing tails, did he?"

Tyrius held up a hand.

"To drain her, the Kids have to take her out of her holding cell in The Box, you know, over top of the engine rooms. If they're ambushed near the ground floor labs, chances are Vaedra won't hear about it in time to shut the doors on you before you can get her out the hole."

"But I would need..."

"That's your best chance. I'll be waiting for you

outside the ship. Watch for me."

Tyrius strode over to the edge of the hole in the atrium floor and peered down into it. He flicked an ear at Sithon: *Get out of here*, and then called, "Hey down there. Progress report. And while you're at it, explain to me why two of you are just sitting around when it's ten past your lunch hour."

Sithon left to line up for lunch. Djarro had barely survived *his* run-in with the kids: Sithon would need all his energies intact to deal with them this evening.

Flood Waters Rising

Hauling Out

If I had been the lesser-ranked member of that patrol, I would have been the one Wardan threw in front of that assault. If I had known what he had been planning, I could have pulled Chanir back.

And if I had another ear, I suppose there's a chance I could hear into the future. One thing, and one thing only, dispelled the endless cycle of regret I felt when I thought about him: sending Wardan to burn in the endless, white hot sands of Underlife.

Tyrius (Tai-Riahs) Spineheart, "Kattari-Rah Mah"

Sithon never returned to his dorm room, and he didn't consider that a loss in the grand scheme of things. Wardan allowed him a sleeping pallet, a small water tap and a door which, while not locked from the outside was monitored by Vaedra. Attached to Sithon's tabard was the only important thing he owned, and he always wore it clipped onto the top of his left shoulder strap, the way Djarro taught him.

Sithon rubbed the tips of his fingers over the

white and gold status bauble engraved with his name, his only gift from his father. Wardan had let Sithon keep it in hopes that it would serve as a depressing reminder of Wardan's all-encompassing blackmail tactics... or something like that. Sithon was sure it sounded a lot more self-righteous when Wardan said it.

He had wandered around the hole in the atrium again later that afternoon, trying to find a loose, sharp piece of glastik or a bent bit of metal to use as a weapon when he ambushed the Kids. Unfortunately, (and perhaps fortunately as well, because a dangerous area may well have been better guarded) Sithon found the floors clean of debris and the lower parts of the walls stripped clean of glastik remnants. He continued on to the hallway where he and Tyrius had escaped when the troop carrier smashed through the command bubble. He passed the little door near the floor where the Kids would take Zahenna to the labs.

Beyond that door, another stairway led to the dormitories and, by another hallway and more stairs, the cells above the engine rooms.

These stairs were made of solid metal sheeting attached to the wall. Sithon crawled into the dark space underneath the final flight.

They'll hear me, and they'll smell me, but concealment isn't the kind of surprise I need anyway. Better they pull me out in the open, underestimate me if this plan is going to work.

Faced with no prospect of a weapon, Sithon had thought of different ways to attack the Kids using

Smart Blood. After the attack, when Zahenna had provoked him, he had managed to keep his battle rage active by revisiting the hurt she had caused him, by picturing it all in his mind. He wondered if he could do the same thing again, only instead of using painful memories to sustain a battle rage, he could use them to initiate that rage.

Sithon crouched in the dark space underneath the stairs and tried to concentrate. It was easier in this part of the ship because the machinery underneath was quiet for the time being. He went into the dark, behind part of his mind—being careful not to tweak the place that summoned Vaedra, of course, and pulled out the memory of Djarro's capture. He tried to summon every sense possible from that night: the eerie blue glow of the orb-lights, the smell of blood—his own and that of others, the reek of sweat off his guards and the horrible, unending whine of vehicle engines chasing Djarro to his doom. He remembered Wardan's grin, the last thing he saw before blacking out, and the limp mass that was his father's prone body.

No shimmer in Sithon's blood. He had pictured that one too many times already for it to have the freshness he needed. He had to hurry now. He had been sure that memory would work and now that he had wasted all this time failing to trigger the Kids would be very close. All of Zahenna's insults had gone stale. He rushed through the recent past for a new memory...

And he pictured himself on the reconstructed

terrace of Flood Waters, leaning on the handrail and slowly backing away from Vaedra's horrifying new version of Toraus.

Why, mother? Why would you ever bring him back? He's not real, he's just another part of you. You're going insane.

The word insane stuck in Sithon's muscles like an electrified dagger. Vaedra *was* going insane, splitting parts of her own personality off into self-serving, revisionist bits of things better left dead. It was all Wardan's fault.

The tip of Sithon's tail tingled, and the rush travelled up his spine and out to his extremities. He breathed more heavily, and his hunched posture became a threat rather than a slouch. He kept Vaedra in his mind, the strange, healthy-looking avatar of Vaedra that lied by her very existence. The shimmer in his blood raced around underneath his skin until finally, he heard four sets of footsteps coming down the stairs: three clomping along at regular intervals, and one stumbling down two or three stairs at a time.

He heard Zahenna's voice say, "I work for you now, right? Just tell me where you're taking me."

"Why bother?" Stab mocked her, "You won't like it anyway."

They got as far as the second flight of stairs from the bottom before they stopped and sniffed.

Slash's voice was next. "Hey, I smell Dung... do you?"

Stab agreed. Hack just chuckled, a gurgling, virulent sort of a chuckle.

"The Flood..." Zahenna whispered to herself while the others were occupied, but with his senses heightened, Sithon could hear her perfectly.

The kids fairly trotted down the stairs once they caught a whiff of Sithon's scent. He could see them now, shoving Zahenna before them like a handcart while Slash held the back tie of her wrap top.

Sithon lay flat on his back, doing his best to look like he had fallen there at random.

"Maybe he's passed out and we can decorate him a little," Slash said as they cleared the final step.

Stab stopped shoving Zahenna and swung around, holding the handrail. Sithon tensed his muscles as much as possible without giving away the ruse. Their intent to harm him was enough to keep the Smart Blood going now, without having to resort back to harsher images.

Sithon watched out of a mostly-closed eye as Slash tip-toed into the alcove. Slash drew a knife with notches at the base of the blade from the waistband of his loincloth.

"It's been a while since I tasted his blood. I think Djarro would be disappointed in us if I didn't make good on my promise to torture him, eh, Hack?" Slash leaned into the alcove.

"Oh Sitho-o-on," he sing-songed, "Mommy's calling..."

Slash tried to add 'you' to the end of that sentence, but it came out as a strangled 'urk' noise instead as Sithon sprung forward and shoulder-checked Slash into the opposite wall of the stairwell. He leapt onto

Slash's chest, grabbed his throat and dug his teeth in underneath the tense cords of his jugular veins.

He glanced quickly over to where he had last seen Zahenna. To his delight, she had used the disruption created by Sithon's entrance to elbow Stab in the face. Hack paced impatiently behind the two of them as they grappled, delayed for a few seconds by their bodies blocking the hallway.

With a surge of rage and relish Sithon pressed Slash into the ground and pulled his jaws back, ripping out Slash's throat. He spat out the flesh that had pulled away into his mouth, and as much of the blood as he could gather. The taste of rot assaulted his tongue and nose. Apparently, resurrected flesh tasted as bad as it smelled from the outside.

Sithon crouched on Slash's body, ready for more action. Hack approached him slowly, cautiously, like an animal handler gaining ground on an out-of-control beast. Or, more likely, Hack was the beast and stalking difficult prey.

Behind Hack, Sithon saw Zahenna knee Stab in the stomach three times, then hit her sharply in the back of the neck with the blade of her hand where the spine met the skull. Stab flopped to the ground on her knees, face-first, and Zahenna let her.

Sithon noticed Zahenna sneaking up behind Hack. He grabbed Slash's knife to keep Hack focussed forward and growled to cover the sound of her movement. Hack growled too, a deep, humming growl like badly aligned gears in some malevolent engine. Sithon felt a button on the rubberized hilt of the knife. He tossed the weapon from hand to hand once, twice, then pushed the button.

Purple energy sizzled along the length of the knife blade. Hack used Sithon's momentary distraction at the flash of light to lunge forward, one meaty, clawed hand swiping at him. Hack's long, sharp nails raked across Sithon's chest and over his left shoulder, pulling Djarro's bauble off in the process. It skidded away down the corridor, glinting in the artificial light.

Zahenna jumped up over Hack's back, both fists raised together, and slammed them as hard as she could into the back of Hack's head, using her own weight to gain more momentum. Hack bellowed and ducked down. With a quick sideways swipe, Sithon aimed a deep slash at Hack's eyes. His brow erupted into a fault line of cauterized flesh. He clawed at his face.

Zahenna waved Sithon on down the hallway.

"Get on before someone pulls an alarm!"

Sithon bolted past Zahenna, instinctually grabbing her hand as he went by. He spotted the bauble near the entrance to the recessed door, and he swooped down to scoop it up without even breaking step.

They ran down the length of the hall and into the command bubble atrium. With the power disconnected, only the orange rays of sunset held back the shadows creeping across the mangled floor. Light orbs glowed up in the scaffolding where the out-crafters still worked to repair the shattered window.

A voice drifted down from above.

"Hey, hey you, stop where you are!"

Sithon and Zahenna left the hallway behind them and dashed for the hole in the command bubble window. Figures scurried down the scaffolding, hand over hand and sliding down ropes. Lights rotating on mechanical posts flooded the atrium with their light. A siren honked out an incessant pulsation of 'Ree-urr, ree-urr'. Vents belched out the synthetic scent of alarm.

Four workers stood waiting for them at the rift in the flooring, scruffy-looking mechanics who smelled like they had been there all day. They formed a line along the hole to the outside. Sithon barrelled into one of the middle Geedar. They both lost their balance and tumbled back over the edge of the hole. For a moment, they grappled in the air, each vying for a better landing position.

Sithon swatted at the worker to keep him on the bottom. When they hit the sand, the worker landed first, his back to the dunes. Sithon landed on him a second later, his feet plunging square into the worker's torso. He still breathed when Sithon climbed off him, but he wouldn't be getting up for a while.

The realization that he was outside sent a shock of excitement up Sithon's spine. He checked behind him, down the line of linen awnings leading to the guarded perimeter. A party of guards had broken off from the main patrol and moved toward them, but the end of the awnings was at least a half-hour's walk from the ship. Running, it would take them ten minutes, unless they had one of the patrol vehicles.

Flood Waters Rising

Zahenna perched on the edge of the hole, about the height of four Geedar up from ground level. The lights inside the ship and the light of the sun just about matched in terms of intensity, and so she appeared as a greyish shadow in the twilight, distinguished from the others only by her breasts and her position in the fight. Her fur stood up, and she gained the aggressive posture Sithon associated with a Smart Blood spike. He recoiled a little—he had believed that she could absorb Talents (that much was obvious) but, especially regarding his own, he had not believed that she would necessarily be able to handle them well enough to use them.

Zahenna picked up one of the remaining workers and tossed him over the side of the ship. He struck the ground neck-first. Now that she faced outward, she peered down at him with a satisfied yet surprised smile on her face, like a young pup that has just caught a bird for its parent.

Several more workers approached her from behind. Almost lazily she raised a back-fist to the one nearest her right shoulder.

She sailed down from the edge of the broken window, her loincloth trailing behind her like an expanse of cloud trailing the sun. She landed in a crouch to compensate for the fall. Workers began climbing out of the hole after them, cautiously grabbing the edge, then dangling themselves over.

Zahenna picked up a piece of scrap metal half-buried in the sand. She swung it around behind her shoulder, ready to hurl it at the dangling workers.

Sithon grabbed the other end of the scrap. "No, no time! Patrol's coming in from the perimeter!"

Zahenna whirled around on him. Her hunter's eyes had morphed into something else, something that matched her primordial posture and the flecks of spittle escaping her snarling muzzle. They were mad eyes, over-wide and bathed in primal rage. Her hands curled into true claws and for a moment, she aimed them at Sithon.

"They tortured me... I'll kill them all!" she roared.

Sithon thought, quickly. "No," he said, "The ones that tortured you are still to come."

Zahenna snorted and dashed out into the desert beyond the canvas awnings before Sithon even realized that he had won her over. She ran on all fours, sand dusting out behind her as she followed the edge of the ship. Sithon came up alongside her, leaning over and panting for breath. In the twilight, the sand under their feet looked unnaturally orange. It felt like sand should, grainy and rough between their toes, but in the minimal light it flowed more like a strange, clinging solid, an entity unto itself. The *Death's End* seemed alive too, a dark tangle of blocks, bulbs and spires rising up on their immediate left, moving as they moved by the various outcroppings appearing and disappearing with the play of shadows. One minute a long, thin pole would be on the horizon and then, as they moved, Sithon would look back and see an uneven patchwork of blocky buildings in its place.

No wonder the Rakarians feared this ship enough to write songs about it. When it moves into a place, it must block the whole horizon with misshapen buildings, and satellite ships like a flock of metal insects.

Sithon tried to remember what Tyrius had said about a meeting place that morning, but as hard as he tried he could not remember being given any specific location. He and Zahenna just kept running, slowly working their way around the front arc of the ship. When they heard engines behind them, Sithon slowed to a stop while Zahenna just dug her paw pads into the sand.

Two hover vehicles approached from the perimeter, with thirty others visible by their bands of headlight about five minutes' ride away. Each hover vehicle carried two perimeter guards clothed in Wardan's livery and wearing wrist-mounted energy weapons, possibly nets, possibly ball throwers. Of the two immediately approaching vehicles, Sithon saw one guard driving the hover using a control glove, and the other levelling his weapon at them.

The hovers consisted of a small platform with a railing at the front and a tapered white nose. Yellow light glowed from underneath them where the heat-powered hover jets kept the vehicles aloft. The yellow light emitting from the bottoms of the vehicles highlighted the undersides of the guards' faces and threw their eyes into shadow.

Sithon raised both hands and put his tail visibly between his legs. Zahenna stayed on all-fours and barked at the hovers, spit spraying out from her muzzle.

"Don't move," called the hover operator on the

right, "Or we'll shoot!"

Sithon threw himself flat onto the slanted side of the dune they stood on when the energy gunman on the right-hand hover shot anyway. A ball of blue lightning burst up through the air, then dissipated about a hundred feet from the ground as someone leapt onto the back of the hover, imbalancing it for a brief, lurching second. The shadow, with a swift reaping motion jammed a large spike through the stomach of the gunman and into the driver's chest on the other side.

The shooter on the left-hand hover launched an energized net through the air and in the intermittent sparkle of energy Sithon saw Tyrius duck down below the railing.

Sithon turned to Zahenna to suggest that they help Tyrius, but discovered that she was already halfway toward the other hover, loping in that strange primal gait of hers. She leapt over the top edge of the hover's railing and knocked the pilot onto the ground. Whatever she did to him then resulted in a chilling scream and the final guard fleeing headlong toward the other patrol. Sithon avoided looking over there. He had no doubt that she would have blood on her muzzle when she returned.

Sithon pressed the release button on the net that now covered the first hover, stopping the flow of energy through it, then pulled it aside like the cover on a bed. Beneath, Tyrius grimaced up at him over the bodies of the two guards.

"I knew them. One's still twitching. Let's get out

of here," he said.

With Sithon's help, Tyrius dragged the bodies off the platform of the hover. Zahenna bounded up to them just as Tyrius peeled the control glove off of the pilot's curled fingers. She breathed hard in Sithon's face.

Tyrius stepped onto the hover. He slid the glove on.

"I'll drive. You pull lookout."

Sithon grabbed the side railing and hoisted himself up onto the hover. He offered a hand to Zahenna, but she leaped up on her own, landing again in a crouch. The hover took off at a speed that made Sithon's eyes feel like they couldn't quite keep up with everything that went by along the way. He had ridden in exactly two vehicles in his life: the *Death's End* and the transport that loaded him into the *Death's End*. With the wind tickling his fur and the cool night air bringing a mingled assortment of scents to his open nostrils, Sithon decided that he liked this mode of travel infinitely more than either of those. Tyrius sped them further along the outer curve of the ship, the headlamps of the hover brigade turning to twinkling ground-stars in the distance.

"Why aren't they catching up?" Sithon asked, holding the handrail and looking out over the hover's open rear.

"Because they've probably set up a blockade somewhere up ahead. In fact," he slowed the hover down for a moment, letting the drone of the engines fade to a purr, "I can hear them now. Sounds like Wardan's pulling out something big... something in the air. One of the satellite ships, no doubt. Listen."

Sithon swivelled his ears forward. A mechanical hum drifted out of the distance, similar to the noises he'd heard on the day of the crash when the engines had died and the only sound had been the fighter ships outside. It was a strange sound, a low drone that worked itself up into a high, intense pitch and then faded off again into low.

On the other side of the hover, Zahenna twitched. She cocked her head in the direction of the sounds.

"They'll blast us into flakes! Get us out of here," she husked, sounding like two versions of her own voice saying the same thing.

"There's only one way to keep that ship from firing on us," Tyrius said, "We have to climb to our destination over the body of the *Death's End*."

Sithon recoiled.

"But Vaedra has sensors all over the outside of the ship! She'll squash us!"

Tyrius vaulted over the front of the hover onto the ground. Zahenna clambered over the side.

"She won't squash you," he said, "We can use you as a shield. Maybe if she thinks you're a hostage, she'll hold off. We need to get to the docking bay on the far side of the ship. From there we can hijack the *Pwarnaa*, and..."

"Wait a minute. . . hijack the *Pwarnaa*? One of Wardan's personal transports? What made you think that we could do this with only two Geedar?"

Tyrius frowned and cocked his head. "Well, it

would have been a lot easier if someone hadn't sprung an alarm on the way out. The *Pwarnaa* got damaged in the last battle, and it's on the docks getting repaired. There are only about twelve personnel in it most of the time. Less at night."

"Oh, only twelve," Sithon breathed a mock sigh of relief as he headed for the blackened hull of the *Death's End*, "Then I guess breaking in and taking off with it will be easier than chewing sweet-root mush."

Tyrius pushed Sithon in the small of his back and grunted. Zahenna galloped up to jog by Sithon's side. They spanned the hundred tail-lengths or so between the hover and the *Death's End* just in time to see the arrow-shaped hull of *Nikira's Bane*, Wardan's largest satellite ship peek around the curve of its mother.

Flood Waters Rising

Over and Done

Sithon scrambled up the smooth, curved side of the *Death's End* single file at Tyrius's insistence. Tyrius reached the crown of the first curved lip jutting off the front of the ship and waited for Sithon and Zahenna to catch up. He waved them on, looking in the last rays of twilight like another part of the ship's jagged silhouette.

"Come on, you two, stay close together. They'll fire on *us* less if they think they'll hit Sithon in the process."

Sithon's foot struck something bony below him as he scrabbled up the last of the slope. Zahenna yelped, slapping his ankle.

"Ow, that was my nose, you tail-chaser!" she hissed.

Sithon followed along behind Tyrius without looking back, but he could tell from the sound of her voice that Zahenna was finally coming out of her Smart Blood rage. He had a feeling that if he'd done the same thing only a few minutes before, he would have ended up missing a foot.

Sithon thought about Zahenna's behaviour during their escape. Her rage had been much longer than his, and he had been fighting to keep his alive. Sithon believed what Tyrius had told him, that Zahenna could absorb any power she wanted, but he wondered if she could control them. After all, Sithon had lived with the Smart Blood Talent his whole life. He'd learned to control his temper. Zahenna wouldn't have the self-knowledge to understand that the Smart Blood made her more aggressive, that she would have to fight her urges in order to maintain civilized company.

Sithon did look back at her now, as they headed into the main tangle of bridges and utility ladders jutting out between the buildings on the *Death's End*'s back. She walked bent over a little, shivering as the first night breeze of the desert ruffled her tail. Or as the last of the Smart Blood finally left her veins. She held one hand up to her nose. Sithon opened his mouth to apologize, but Zahenna spoke before he could.

"You're clumsier than I thought at first."

"I was thinking the same about you."

The little growl that went along with Zahenna's bared fang was lost in the whoosh of airship engines as the horizon that was the edge of the *Death's End* experienced a second dawn. Bluish light swept across the metal hull like rays of sunlight on a partially cloudy day. *Nikira's Bane* flew up over the lip of its Mother Ship at low altitude with its targeting lights sweeping everything beneath. The ship, shaped like a giant arrowhead, created a swirling mix of wind, light and shadow as it swooped overhead at low speed. When it cleared them entirely, the *Bane* swung back around for another pass.

Ahead of them, Tyrius was already ascending a metal ladder on the side of the nearest building. At the top, a narrow catwalk stretched off down the side of the wall. Sithon jogged to catch up with Tyrius, and he could hear Zahenna following him—at a slightly larger distance, this time.

They scaled the ladder without incident, but Sithon paused at the catwalk. He remembered his many trips to the obstacle course back at The Base with Djarro, and regretted that he had never made it into training himself. The catwalk consisted of a thin strip of metal grating banded on either side by a very low railing, not much thicker than the slim pole that soldiers had shimmied across on the course.

Zahenna shoved Sithon from behind.

"Get moving, Flood, before that ship gets back."

Tyrius nodded at Sithon from his position in the lead. His horn grafts shifted when he said, "She's right. Get against the wall as they pass, or the *Bane* will blast this catwalk out of existence. Keep an eye out for Vaedra, too."

Sithon scuttled along behind Tyrius on the catwalk, unable to stop looking down as the space below them went from solid metal plating to a slope, into a black chasm that reached through the heart of the ship. In places the catwalk had tilted, probably due to the crash. Sithon missed the light sweeping in on them from the *Bane*'s targeting system the first time. Zahenna pulled him back against the wall just as a huge blue ball of energy hummed past them and down into the chasm under the catwalk. The heat from the ball burned in Sithon's eyes and nostrils and made the little hairs on his ears stand on end. The light spots on his eyes made it even harder to see the tracking lights the next time, but Sithon ducked out of the way just in time.

They continued on this way, ducking aside every minute or so until Tyrius swivelled his ears around. Sithon listened now, too, behind them. He could hear footsteps clanging off hollow metal sheeting, claws scraping on ladder rungs. More noises on the other side of the building, similar to the ones behind.

"I was afraid of this," Tyrius said while still moving along at a smart pace, "I can hear them all around. I'll bet they've set up slingshot snipers at the mouth of this crevice, waiting for us."

Sithon's tail curled between his legs.

"What do we do now?"

Tyrius kept going without answering. Sithon's mane prickled at the way Tyrius always went silent at the worst moments, as though telling him the plan wasn't worth his precious breath.

He's almost as arrogant as Princess Tail-in-the-air.

Zahenna seemed to read his thoughts as she chimed in after Tyrius. She put a hand on Sithon's shoulder.

"We just keep going and hope that something up ahead gives us a way to fight them. If we die, we die fighting."

"Right," Sithon managed to say.

After that Sithon pushed himself onward by listening to the patter of feet and the clunk of weapons against metal behind him. In these circumstances forward was as good a direction as any. At least forward held a slim chance of escape, and escape held an even slimmer chance of finding Djarro. He ignored the voice, growing constantly louder in his mind, that repeated *you're going to die up there*. He doubted that voice could take down a wall of snipers anyway.

Towards the end of the catwalk, where the new night sky made a 'v' of deep blue fading to purple and orange in the divot at the end of the trench, sat a large, squat machine with a box base and a long, bent arm. Sithon assumed that the arm was probably used to move materials around the outside of the ship. The teardrop-shaped appendage at the end of the arm, half lidded scoop, half claw suggested that perhaps the arm was used for large-scale installations, as well.

It slouched there on the opposite side of the trench, like an arm with only the tendons left around the bone.

Sithon tensed as he passed the shadow of the thing, but once he reached the section of catwalk beyond, he focussed again on the growing 'v' of night where they would meet their destiny.

A screech cut through the night air, along with the same sort of whoosh that the elevator from The Burrow used to make. All of a sudden the lift arm was in front of them again across the trench. It raised up its only appendage and slammed it down, scoop first, onto the catwalk.

Sithon rocked on his feet for a moment, wondering where he'd jump for safety if the whole thing crashed down into the crevice. Behind him, he heard Zahenna fall on her tail, and swear. Tyrius just waved his tail, bent his knees and braced himself.

The catwalk steadied after a few seconds of vibration. The scoop sat on the catwalk like the curled-under hand of a cripple, its two halves cocked open. The sand-blasted metal surface of the entire lift arm gave off a dull sheen with patterns like an oil slick running through it in the dim light.

It was then that Sithon noticed a tiny, round speaker on the neck of the arm.

"Hello, Mother," he said.

Her voice positively grated out of the old, unused speaker. It faded in with a low groan, and faded out that way too.

"Sithon... get in the scoop. I'm taking you to safety."

Sithon backed away from the speaker without even thinking about it. He collided gently with Zahenna, who pushed him away with a *whuff* of frustration.

"I'd be perfectly safe with Tyrius and Zahenna, if you'd call off the guard and let us go."

"Ah," Vaedra squealed the word as if she had just been stuck by a pin, "Let you go so that you can come back with the rebels and attack us? So that you can spend your last breath in a fruitless quest to find your father? I can't knowingly let you go to your death."

Sithon crossed his arms. He knew Vaedra was watching, somewhere. Probably up high.

"I *am* going to die. *You've* trapped me here, and soon the guards will catch up to us. I intend to fight them along with my friends."

The speaker clicked twice in quick succession. It sounded like Vaedra's electronic voice clearing its throat, but Sithon recognized it as a 'Skin glitch. He pressed his lips together to keep from grinning.

"You can't... I won't let you!"

Sithon tilted his head. "How will you stop me? I can move faster than this crane. You'd have to strike me down yourself."

"Then I'll scream into your head! I'll pull you into Second Skin while Wardan picks your body up!"

Sithon moved to the low railing along the catwalk and sat on it, his spinal fur standing on end as he watched his tail dangle into the chasm.

"He can't pick me up down there," He said, nodding toward the darkness.

The shouts and echoes of footfalls sounded louder now through the chasm between buildings, loud enough for them to reach Vaedra's speaker. Soon, Sithon thought, they would be too close for Vaedra to help with his plan.

"I know you hear them, mother. You have a choice: take me *and* my friends in the crane, to a point where we'll be safe from the guards, or let me die fighting. Either way, you can't stop me from leaving you."

Silence punctuated by clangs from behind, and underlined by the night breeze whistling through the chasm between buildings. Then, more quickly than Sithon would have expected from something so heavy-looking, the scoop lifted off of the catwalk and resettled with one of its halves open like a shallow bucket, large enough for them all to get into plus three more.

Vaedra spat words through the speaker now like bits of bad meat.

"Get in before they see you. I've shut off all the surveillance eyes from here to the loading dock, but this will have to be done quickly if Wardan is going to miss it."

Tyrius climbed into the scoop first. The horn graft on his knee caught the edge of the scoop, and Sithon could hear the echo of his next hissed-in breath as he crunched down in the back corner. Sithon came next, swinging one leg over, then the next. Inside the scoop, everything smelled like rust and desert dust, and the sloping floor was a wall ending in square teeth like battlements in a mirrored castle.

Zahenna landed beside him, more a breeze of smell and a brush of fur than a body in the darkness. Once she crouched down beside Sithon, the stars visible in the crack between the scoop halves smeared with motion as the arm lurched up and away from the catwalk. A brief squeal echoed over the chasm, but then they flew over it, beyond it, swinging in a horizontal arc left.

Tyrius nudged Sithon in the ribs.

"She's least likely to drop you... go to the edge and see where she's taking us."

Sithon waited. The arm stopped swinging left and bounced for a minute back and forth, making a coughing chunk-chunk sound. When the bouncing stopped, Sithon felt the crane begin to move forward, all as one unit.

He crawled to the edge of the scoop. Sithon's nostrils quickly filled with the kind of breeze that only comes with fast travel. He drew in a breath of cool night air, and surveyed the ship below. Vaedra had taken them in a wide left-hand swoop to the opposite side of the chasm. Sithon saw tracks recessed into the roof of the building beneath them, turning and circling in every direction. Up ahead, well before the mouth of the chasm between buildings, a bridge stretched over the gap in the direction of the loading docks. Sithon saw recessed tracks crossing the bridge, too. Vaedra continued on along the edge of the building until she got to the bridge, then she turned onto it quicker than Sithon was expecting. He grabbed the squared metal teeth on the top side of the scoop half to stay upright.

Sithon shifted over to the left-hand side of the scoop once the outside world had stabilized away from darkness and light-blur. He half-stepped on Tyrius's ankle, then drew back.

"Well, where's she taking us?" Zahenna asked. Her voice echoed off the walls.

Sithon turned back only for a moment. "I think she's telling the truth. We're heading further down the ship than the ambush, toward the loading docks."

The ambush... as Sithon passed the chasm in the mouth of the scoop, he spied the full extent of what Wardan had planned for them. The bright lights lining the rim of *Nikira's Bane* shone into the trench as it hovered by the exit. Beneath it, and lined up all along the top of the buildings near the trench, Sithon saw dark figures hunkered down, their only giveaway the tiny points of energy light from their active slingshots. Below the catwalk, and beyond the edge of the ship, more vehicles waited, a row of hover barges filled with soldiers, a row filled with Screamers (6500's, the sleeker descendants of the ones that Wardan had used on Djarro) and a row of bolt-packed Assassins. Wardan had rallied three times the personnel he had used for the forest ambush, and even then there had been no question that he was showing off. There would have been no fight, only a spectacle as Wardan revelled in the gore of their liquified corpses before carting them off to the lab to be salvaged.

Sithon put a hand to his chest. He closed his eyes tight, and breathed deeply to stifle the whine that so desperately wanted to come out. Like a sudden muscle ache that comes as quickly and inexplicably as it leaves, he felt a swell of forgotten love for his mother. It was a rusty feeling, a stretching of atrophied flesh, and it wrung him out just as relentlessly as any physical ache.

He stroked the rough side of the inner scoop, this extension of Vaedra's consciousness, imagining her long-ago hand helping him up after being knocked to the ground by Toraus.

Don't cry, she said, *That's what he wants. And then I'll cry too. You wouldn't want to see your old mother cry, would you?*

Maybe she never knew he saw her cry, that he wandered in when she sobbed and put his hand in hers, caressed her mane like he now caressed the side of this smelly metal bin. Maybe she was in too much pain then to notice. The knowledge that he had seen her cry never prevented little Sithon from straightening up, wiping his eyes and going about his business when Vaedra gave him that flimsy line. It was more the sound of her voice then, a softness that he never heard anywhere else until Djarro, that dried his tears. He hadn't even known he'd missed that softness until now.

The scoop lurched downward, causing Sithon to jog out of his reverie and grab the teeth for dear life. It stopped after a sickening half-minute with the same bounce and chunk-chunk-chunk as before.

Sithon crawled out of the mouth of the scoop, feeling like someone who had just physically walked out of the mouth of a vivid dream. Tyrius and Zahenna climbed out at the same time on either side.

They were at the edge of the right-hand building of the catwalk, too far down the ledge to be seen by the snipers at the chasm. A ladder curled down the corner of the roof in front of them. Below, Sithon could see the loading docks, stretching out into the desert like uneven fingers lit with orb-lights.

The others headed for the ladder immediately. Sithon could see the eagerness to get away from the monstrous crane in the curve of their backs, the low set of their tails. He hesitated, turned back to Vaedra, not knowing what to say. He felt tears building in his eyes. All at once he wanted to apologize, to howl at her all of the misfortunes she had visited upon him for Toraus's sake, to demand that she bring back that softness that he once loved and had only now remembered through the shroud of her later cruelty.

She spoke for him.

"Promise me you'll never return."

The speaker clicked off with another sickly groan, and Sithon knew Vaedra had left the body of the crane without hearing his answer.

He wanted to howl his grief at the moon, bark and holler until something echoed him back. He wanted to claw and bite and tear his clothing to pieces, tear Wardan's insignia to even smaller pieces and then piss on it all.

Sithon cast a glance down the edge of the rooftop toward the sniper line, then hunched over and scuttled to the ladder. As he climbed, he buried his nose in his tabard and wept.

The Pwarnaa

Sithon flattened himself against the wall with the others, pressed himself into the shadow of the great building that, until now, he had only seen the inside of as he ghosted himself to one place or another. On the outside of the building lay a great plain of metal sheeting, uneven at the ends. In great, light-delineated strips it jutted out into the night. Some of the strips were short, some too long to see the unlit ends.

More ships than Sithon had ever seen sat parked on the flat expanse of metal platform leading up to the launch ways, although he admitted to himself that it wasn't a hard record to break. He counted a few small, ovular transport pods, not meant for more than two or three passengers, but beyond that the ships ranged in size from the space of a few large rooms to enormous. The most enormous of these was the *Flood Vengeance*, the *Bane*'s sister ship. It rested on the dock to their left, looking as serene with all of its lights off and its turrets relaxed as a predatory animal lying in tall grass. Many of the other, smaller ships were freighters and ex-rebel transports, docked at *Death's End* to deliver supplies or be retrofitted with Wardan's technology. Like the *Death's End,* they mostly consisted of pieces of other ships, torn apart and then bolted back together again with varying degrees of efficacy.

Tyrius pointed with his nose at one such ship, a smaller-sized wad of garbage amidst a crowd of rusty turrets, bunched antennae and oddly-angled joints. The *Pwarnaa* started out low to the ground, its wedge-shaped nose covered in a banged brown plate that made it look like it was wearing a surgical mask. On the front of the ship, several grimy glastik pustules formed the windscreen, their edges encrusted with rust flakes and oily matter. From there the chaotic pile of scraps continued on, sweeping upward in irregular lumps and bumps, to a tail (and literally, it looked like a chewed tail) consisting of one long, flat antenna, drooping and crimped in several places.

The sudden rush of air from above flattened Sithon's fur: a patrol ship zoomed overhead toward the ambush zone, without even its spotlights trained on the ground. Even still, Sithon ducked a little lower. He noticed Tyrius's ears flatten.

A few more seconds went by with no more patrol ships. Sithon had time to feel the tightness in his chest, the difficulty of breathing while trying not to move at all. Finally, Tyrius swooped his head forward and scuttled toward the shelter of the shadow of the large ship, set on thick jointed legs, next to the *Pwarnaa*.

Follow me, and do what I do, he said in body-code.

Sithon and Zahenna followed, and soon they huddled in the chilly darkness below one of the giant feet of the great flying machine. Night was coming on in earnest now, and the desert would be cold enough to freeze Sithon's muzzle fur to his nose in less than an hour. He leaned against the ship's giant foot for a moment, but it was cold too.

Tyrius whispered to them, "I've got someone on the inside of that ship. Let's hope he hasn't been found out by now... he should have the scanners on, looking for us."

A few seconds of the chill breeze freezing the side of Sithon's muzzle, then a hatch began to open in the bottom of the *Pwarnaa*. It squealed on the way to the ground like a wounded Mettoa.

Tyrius took off for the opening hatch, with only a tug at Sithon and Zahenna's neck scruffs to warn them to get their feet moving. Sithon ran hunched over, his hands clawed and at the ready. A figure descended the gangway as the far end neared the ground. The figure, too, hunched over, gesturing to them in quick little motions. Sithon watched it for a moment. The hands weren't beckoning, but pushing away.

Stay away from here! Trap!

Sithon, Tyrius and Zahenna were almost there before the energy fire erupted. The figure on the gangplank resolved into a young male sliding down the ramp on his back, a large burn mark covering his chest. Another guard in Wardan's livery ran down the gang plank. Sithon saw another guard inside the square entrance to the ship push the button to raise the gangplank. The soldier still on the gangplank kicked the body of Tyrius's friend off the end of the steps and spat on him. He then raised his energy weapon and aimed for Zahenna.

A ball of energy sailed straight for her. She ducked, but not in time. The edge of the fizzing, swirling white mass struck the left side of her face under the chin. Her scream of pain mingled with the hiss of interference and searing flesh. Sithon coughed and covered his nose. He didn't want to smell her burns again after the first time in Wardan's tube chamber. Sithon lunged for the guard on the platform, but by the time he got there, the gangplank had raised to the level of his midsection. The edge pounded his ribs and stole his breath momentarily. The guard standing above him levelled his gun at Sithon's head.

Sithon felt a pair of arms around his chest. Tyrius pulled him back, off the gangplank and knocked him sideways, to the ground and out of the way of the incoming ball. Sithon crawled under the gangplank for cover. Tyrius followed.

A moment, and then a shadow passed over them, a leaping predator, a roaring, screaming, thrashing figure made of the dark. Tyrius and Sithon rolled out of the way of the gangplank just as it wrenched its way lopsidedly to the ground—Zahenna had grabbed it from the end and was holding it down as the machinery at its hinge squealed in protest. She strained and grimaced, making the lips on the blackened side of her face trickle blood.

Zahenna bellowed, "Kill the fools!"

The sudden downward motion of the ramp caused the guard to lose his balance: this time Sithon leapt for him and caught him right in the midsection, knocking him off the platform. He felt the usual Smart Blood rush as he smacked the guard's head against the ground and stole the energy gun from his limp hand.

Back at the gangplank, Zahenna still struggled to hold the way to the ship open. Tyrius had thrown the guard overboard already—he lay in a very unnatural position by one of the landing gear—but he was still pushing button after button on the panel controlling the opening.

"Sithon, get on," he called, "I can't re-open it from here."

Sithon scrambled onto the ramp and ran up on all-fours. Zahenna then swung her legs up onto the ramp to climb in as well. No sooner had she stopped pushing down on the ramp than it began to slam shut. Zahenna screamed, let go of the end of the ramp and slid quickly to the floor of the ship in a heap. Even sealed in the dim confines of the entryway, which seemed to have very little overhead lighting and really only the dim green glow of the control panel to light it, Sithon could see the manic sheen in Zahenna's eyes. She crawled to her feet like a reptile scaling a wall. The right side of her face looked scaled, too, in the dim light. Her eyes had escaped burning, but her neck, jaw, and most of her cheek were scabbed and red.

She wiped some blood from her face with the back of her hand, examined it for a second, then shrugged.

"Where are the rest of them?" she panted.

Tyrius swivelled his ears and sniffed the air.

"I'm working on that," he said.

"Where are the rest of them? I want blood!"

There was a doorway behind Tyrius, leading to the nexus of three dark corridors fanning out over the ship. Zahenna shoved past him. She stood at the end of the three hallways for a second, and sniffed the air. The sound of her breathing echoed in the chamber. Her nose snapped to the middle passageway and soon she was gone down it, past a corner.

Tyrius and Sithon stood staring at each other for a moment, heads tilted, eyes wide.

What do we do?

I don't know.

A loud crash coming from the direction in which Zahenna disappeared decided their course of action. They ran down the middle hallway, toward the source of the sound. Zahenna had found the cockpit. Sithon expected to smell blood before even entering, but he smelled only Zahenna's overbearing pheromones and traces of the others that they had already ejected. The room was surprisingly bare of control panels: one panel with speakers sat in front of a saddle seat with a narrow backing. Protruding from the back of the seat was a Second Skin jack which plugged into the back of the pilot's head. Sithon did not have one (he had the latest wireless model, unfortunately) but he doubted his ability to pilot a ship anyway. The padding of the Pilot's chair had claw marks ripped out of it. The stuffing protruded like Tyrius's spines. A toolbox lay spilled on the floor; Sithon assumed that must have been the crash they heard. Zahenna picked up another, stacked along the wall, held it over her head and then hurled it to the ground. Silver tools of all shapes and sizes skidded out from the toolbox in an expanding circle.

She bellowed, "They're all gone! All gone! You told me I could kill them!"

Tyrius flattened his ears and leaned away from Zahenna, toward the pilot's chair.

"I'm the only one of us with a head jack. I'll try and override the old pilot's commands and get this ship in the air... think you can handle her?"

Sithon frowned, saying, "What choice do I have?"

Zahenna drew back one fist and punched the wall. She then proceeded to bang on it with both fists like she had been mistakenly shut out of an airlock. She growled through clenched teeth.

"That's the spirit, Sithon," Tyrius gulped, his eyes trained on Zahenna as he edged over to the command chair.

By the time Tyrius made it into the command chair, Zahenna had stopped pummelling the wall. She leaned on the wall instead with her crossed arms over her head, panting audibly.

Sithon moved toward her.

"Z... Zahenna?" He said, reaching out a hand.

"What?" She snarled.

"Are you all right?" Sithon stopped about a tail length away from her. Under their feet, he could feel a rumbling. The air filled with the sounds of engines kicking over, vents whooshing and exterior panels sliding shut.

Inside himself, he still felt the Smart Blood humming in his veins.

Zahenna's next answer was more pant, less growl. Sithon noted that her scent hadn't changed from the violent, hormonal excretions of a Smart Blood episode, however.

"I'll be fine. Just get over here and help me clean all this up."

Sithon inched a little closer to Zahenna, making little side steps. With his attention still on her, he bent down to pick up a few of the tools on the ground. With his nose at a lower angle, he could smell a different pheromone... and all too late he remembered what the tail end of a particularly potent Smart Blood rush could do to someone not accustomed to bearing the Talent's emotional cost.

After smelling her, he also felt his blood begin to rise to the occasion.

Zahenna swooped down on Sithon, hauled him up by his armpits and pinned him to the wall she had previously been pounding. Metal studs dug into his ribs as she brought her face cheek to cheek with his. She brushed the good side of her face against him—hard. She whispered in his ear, "I hate you, Flood, but that doesn't stop me from wanting you. I've got an itch I need scratched, and it looks like you're the only one around with claws."

Sithon squirmed. Did he want to get out of this? With his heart pounding in his ears, and his Talent throbbing every part of him at her touch, he couldn't tell. Her breasts pressed against him, and he could feel himself growing hard in spite of his efforts to calm down.

"Zahenna, listen: I don't want to take advantage of you." He gulped.

"Good. I'll take advantage of you, then."

Over at the command chair, Tyrius stared forward, blank and unaware of anything beyond the Second Skin programming piloting the ship.

Zahenna undid her wrap top at the neck and unravelled the bindings covering her ample chest. Although her face was half-burnt, her breasts were still perfect, blanketed with a soft coating of the reddish fur which covered her entire body. In the divot between them, there was just a touch of cream. Her nipples stood erect and pink, facing every so slightly away from each other.

"Go ahead," she purred, throwing her wrap around Sithon's back and drawing him in, "Touch them."

Well, maybe this wouldn't hurt anyone. After all, the soldiers at the base used to say it felt really good.

Besides, Tyrius said to keep her occupied. Better than her throwing more toolboxes around.

Sithon raised a hand and touched her breast. It was warm, and he squeezed it, feeling it give under his grip just enough to make him even harder. He slid another hand up her belly to the other breast and gave it the same treatment. Zahenna leaned in and licked Sithon's neck, which made the hair stand on end all along his spine.

She then nibbled on his ear, whispering to him, "Get to the good stuff, Flood. You know where to find it."

Sithon hesitated a moment too long, because Zahenna grabbed him, swung him down onto the floor (among the other tools) and yanked her loincloth free of her waist. As she straddled him just below the hips, Sithon noticed that her cleft was covered by another tuft of delicate, creamy fur. Sithon moaned at the sight of it... he had forgotten how beautiful she was during all of the struggles between them. And yet, her strength of will made her even more desirable.

He pulled his loincloth off, revealing his own swollen member.

If we hadn't met in this here, this now, I might have chosen someone like her for my mate... if she would have the likes of me.

Zahenna grinned, then laughed a little.

"Oh, now we get to the fun part, my traitor pet." She said, slowly stroking the wet, pink underside of her cleft.

Sithon's penis exploded with sensation as Zahenna plunged herself down onto it. He felt something resist him, then give at the opening to her wet, warm vagina. Was she a virgin too?

Zahenna held him tight and pumped him with her body as she rocked back and forth on top of him. The firmness of her inner cavity told him that yes, she was a virgin. And it was good.

Her hands raked at his shoulders as she rocked back and forth. For several minutes Sithon felt that right there, on the floor of the *Pwarnaa*'s control room with debris scattered all around him and his head resting on the hard metal flooring, was the only place he wanted to be... ever. He thrust his hips up to meet Zahenna as she rocked, pushing ever deeper into that warm, wet place inside of her.

Zahenna cried out as he thrust deeper, rocking more vigorously.

"Oh, that feels so good... looks like Floods are good... for... something..." As Zahenna finished the sentence, her insides clenched up around Sithon's penis, then fluttered. She screamed with pleasure, grabbing a handful of Sithon's mane and tugging in a way that felt oh, so good.

Sithon couldn't hold on any longer; the pressure building inside of him since she started rocking built to a climax that made his back arch and his voice sing to the sky. He released his seed inside of her, and it felt warm and loving and... right, somehow.

Zahenna collapsed sideways off of him, and Sithon felt a familiar tingle; the Talent force draining from his body. Lying there on the floor, as the shimmer in his blood drained away, he felt cold, alone, and somehow misled.

Did I just do that? With her?

As soon as his wobbling knees would allow him, Sithon got into a crouch, then slowly straightened up. Zahenna's face was pointed toward the floor, but if he estimated correctly, it wouldn't be for long. If he had been acting rashly on a Smart Blood rush, then she would be coming down too...

Zahenna rubbed a hand over the burnt side of her

face. It came away brown with dried blood and scab tissue.

"My face... what's wrong with my face? It burns!" she said softly, with no trace of the frantic violence which had overtaken her before. She looked up at Sithon with wide eyes... his eyes after witnessing his mother's death... His eyes after witnessing Djarro's capture. Zahenna's hand went, slowly, to her mound, now sodden with bodily juices. Sithon put both hands out in front of him, as if that would do any good.

"Sithon, what did we just do?"

Sithon covered his head and slouched over, his tail between his legs.

"Bite it, Zahenna, you said you wanted to, and we—we were both on a Smart Blood high and sometimes that happens with Smart Blood, and... wasn't it good, though? Can't you remember how good it felt? And you wanted to!" Sithon looked to the side—anywhere to avoid that horrified, intense stare, and found himself looking out the windscreen. The black sky covered almost everything except for the faint lines of the dunes rolling underneath them and out of sight.

Zahenna's wail brought Sithon's attention back to the control room. She hadn't moved from her place sitting sprawled on the floor.

"I was a virgin, you out-born filth! What made you think that I would ever want to be with the likes of you?"

Sithon's mane rose a little at her insult. He felt his lip begin to snarl.

"Gee, I don't know who could have given me that

idea, Princess-Tail-in-the-Air. Oh, wait a minute, yes I do. It was you!" He said, "You propositioned me. *You* rode *me*. I suggest you remember *that* along with all of the rest of it."

Zahenna stood up, and brought one of the tools on the floor with her. She hurled it at Sithon's head.

Sithon ducked out of the way as she yelled, "Yeah, and I'm not in control of my own body since I took on this accursed Talent of yours! It's making me go crazy and I can't get rid of it!"

She slunk over into the farthest corner from Sithon and hunkered down facing the wall.

"And if you got a pup on me, don't think I don't know how to get rid of that, too," she grumbled.

Sithon's chest tensed up. For the first time since their infliction, he felt the deep scratches that Hack had dug into his back. He also felt nauseous. Very nauseous.

"You... would kill a pup?" He croaked.

Zahenna did not reply. Her back shivered and her tail curled around her legs for comfort.

A squealing sound echoed through the room. It sounded like it was coming from the control box in front of Tyrius slouched in the command chair.

The voice that came out of the speaker sounded like Tyrius, too, when it said, "Sithon, how are you managing with Zahenna? Has she calmed down yet?"

"Uhhh, in a way. You can hear me?"

"Now I can. Took me a while to find the controls, but there are audio receivers in the walls."

Zahenna looked up at the ceiling, although Sithon

wasn't sure that's where the audio receivers actually were. He was pretty sure Zahenna just didn't want to look at him.

"You want to know how he *managed* with me? Oh he *managed* quite a bit, the mangy son-of-a-Flood," she yelled, "Just wait until my mother gets her warships back, and then he'll be lucky if he isn't a big, grey burn mark on the dunes within a day and a half!"

Sithon's ears flattened.

"Warships? Why would your mother have warships?"

Zahenna assumed a mocking tone, exposing one incisor with her upper lip.

"Because, *Flood*, you just took the virginity of the Crown Princess of Rakaria! I must say, I thought you were a real *genius* not to figure it out sooner. My face was everywhere in the news before the conquest. The most honourable and warlike princess to be born in a century, they said, with the most formidable Talent. And beautiful, too... at least, I was before Wardan got hold of me. And you had the nerve to just... just..."

Sithon masked his shock, as he had masked so many other emotions around Toraus and Wardan.

He adopted his most sarcastic, hissing tone as he said, "*So* sorry, Princess tufty-tail. In case *you* didn't know, up until today, I didn't get out very much."

Tyrius let out a long "Uuuuuum" which crackled over the speaker.

"Have you two given any thought to where we might be going from here?" He asked.

"I didn't really think we'd even get out," Sithon replied.

"Well, we did, and we need to think of a plan. Wardan will have figured out where we went by now, and it's only a matter of time before we have clouds of ships coming to intercept us from where we came from, and from where we might be going."

Zahenna stood up and leaned on the wall for balance. She deliberately faced the front of the ship, not to the side where Sithon still stood.

"Tyrius, it sounds like you've already got someplace in mind," she said. Sithon didn't know how it was possible, but the narrowing of her eyes and the set of her ears seemed to imply that Zahenna followed the same train of thought as Tyrius—or at least she thought she did.

"Yes, I do have a target in mind," Tyrius replied, "But it's even more dangerous than the Death's End. The payoff for you two, if we succeed in the mission I have planned, is that you would both get your parents back."

A rush of energy shot through Sithon's tired frame.

"You do know where Djarro is! Take us to him!"

Zahenna's eyebrows raised—high.

"I thought so. You want to try and attack Takara? My mother's administration built that prison to contain Wardan's insurgents. It's madness to even consider..."

"And it did a fine job of keeping Wardan's crew in, didn't it? There are ways." Even filtered through a computer, Tyrius's retort sounded dry.

Tyrius continued before Zahenna could protest more.

"Takara *used* to be impenetrable. Since then, it's been in the middle of more than one battle and several serious riots. Wardan also doesn't have the resources at the moment to keep the entire building running. Your mother may not have been good at hiding from him, but she was good at hiding her resources, and so were a lot of her allies. I was stationed at the prison for quite some time. That's how I know Djarro and Leethia are in there."

Zahenna crossed her arms.

"Wardan is going to be able to figure out where we're going. We should head directly to the rebel stronghold, in Marrow Canyon. From there, maybe we could think about launching an assault..."

Sithon piped in with, "Yeah, but if Wardan can find us on our way to Takara, he can follow us all the way to *your* secret base. I agree with Tyrius. The only way we have a chance of escaping in the long term is by causing confusion... lots of it."

Zahenna frowned and said, "I don't like it, but it may well be worth the danger if we can release my mother. The rebels were becoming disheartened without her even when I was at Marrow Canyon—I can't even imagine what has happened since I was captured."

"Great," Tyrius said, "So gather around and I'll show you what I know."

The Warden

Three images, fading at the edges into the blackness of the outside sky and partially translucent appeared on the three middle-most bubbles of the wind screen. On the left, Sithon saw a black building on the horizon like a lounging beast, its back end crumbling into the earth and its front leaning ever so slightly over its center of balance. Around it was a wall, made out of cut-stone bricks, with battlements and watchtowers and sentries pacing back and forth. On top of that wall sprouted an unkempt forest of jagged metal spikes. A similar underbrush had been rolled into place below the wall. Sithon saw patrol vehicles circling the place, but mercifully, no sentry ships.

"Huh," Tyrius puffed, "I wasn't sure if I could do that here, but Second Skin is pretty flexible when you get to know it. These are my mental images of our targets, as they were when I last left them. Obviously, my memories can be wrong, but they're better than nothing. *Kattari-Rah* are trained to keep their minds sharp."

Sithon identified the first image easily as Takara Prison. He had an idea what the other two were, as well.

The middle image showed a dark room, almost black, lined with rows and rows of tall tubes. Geedar of all shapes and sizes floated in the tubes, cast in silhouette by the deep blue light which emanated from the liquid inside. The third image was the most blurry, distorted by the bubble shape of the small window which housed it and, most likely, Tyrius's fuzzy perception of the event which it belonged to. He saw a figure at a distance, lying on a reclined chair, strapped to the apparatus at the major points of motion. It was skinny, yellow and female. Sithon recognized the Second Skin hook-ups immediately: all the wires protruding from her skin, the tubes keeping her alive while she lived inside her brain. Whoever it was, she was also likely the prison's brain.

"So... it looks like, from what you're showing us, that the prison is controlled by another Geedar in permanent Second Skin, like my mother. And that other place... that must be where they are keeping Djarro," Sithon ventured.

Tyrius made a little noise of surprise.

"Well, you saved my having to explain it. These two points are the prison's main weaknesses. The most dangerous and hateful prisoners are kept in the stasis tanks. Let them out, and they start the hunt. The female—they just call her The Warden, controls everything, just like Vaedra. If you unplug her, you let the other prisoners out of their cells and cut power to all but the most basic systems. But we have to get the stasis victims out first. Once the power is cut, if they're not fully out of their sleep, they'll die."

Zahenna's brow furrowed.

"So, ideally, we would break into the stasis room first, hold off the guard until the victims woke up, and then find our way, somehow, to The Warden and unplug her."

One instant, while Zahenna was talking, there was nothing there, then the next, Sithon smelled them. He heard them breathing behind him. He smelled at least three, possibly as many as five other Geedar who had just appeared in the room—without a door, without anything.

Something struck Sithon from behind. He fell forward, so that he landed on his knees beside Tyrius in the command chair. A black, open-weave net unfolded over him from the point on his back where it had first struck. Heavy weights held it down at intervals. It reminded Sithon of the nets Wardan had used on the Mettoa hunt, and he knew that meant that if he moved, energy current would singe him through the cords.

There were three of them—one tangled with Zahenna. They wore strange livery, still with Wardan's grey smoke insignia on it, but the main colour was blue.

Zahenna bent down, as if the guard's weight was too much for her... but Sithon knew it wasn't. What was she doing? Trying not to use the Smart Blood? That wouldn't work, Sithon knew. No, he thought she might just have a plan, although he didn't know quite what.

Zahenna sank to her knees, the operative on her

back pushing her so that she looked folded at the hips and knees. Her eyes darted to Sithon for a second— only a second, but he knew that look by now. Zahenna had her own sort of body-code.

Be ready for me.

Sithon shifted his weight, just enough to have a hand free as he held himself up on all fours. He didn't know what Zahenna was planning, until he saw her breathe in a very distinctive way: one large pulsation of breath, in and out. And her mane... it flowed out ever so slightly as if a sphere of air had expanded beneath it and escaped.

Oh no, Zahenna, you wouldn't...

She would. Zahenna rose up, all of a sudden, the guard clinging to her back. She swung around, elbowing the guard off of her, and the force of her swing momentarily knocked him back into the other two guards. She dashed over to Sithon. He reached out through the weave of the net and grabbed her hand, and as he did a jolt of searing lightning went through the cords. He smelt the fur on his back singeing, his flesh burning. Zahenna grabbed Tyrius with her other hand and then... they were floating, then crashing onto a hard metal floor in a dark place, on what felt very much like solid land. No more engines whirred beneath them.

The net still cut into Sithon with blue arcs of fire. Someone pulled it off of him and sent it skidding into a corner of the dark place. He soon realized that it had been Zahenna. She ascertained that he was alive, then proceeded to face the floor and retch.

Around them, the blue glow of floor-to-ceiling stasis tubes tapered off into a thick darkness like a night without stars. They were in the middle of a row of them, and all around an array of Geedar, male and female, old and young, scruffy and proud-nosed, and the occasional reptile, Mettoa or other unidentifiable creature floated in the permanent limbo created by the tubes. Sithon noticed a male near them missing stripes of fur from his nose, like he had been struck repeatedly there with a weapon. He had many other scars, too, across his eye, down his chest and snaking along his thigh to his tail. He was old and skinny, but ropey with muscle at the same time. A veteran soldier, maybe even a commanding officer. Not all of the suspended figures *looked* dangerous, but this one did.

Sithon went to Zahenna. He touched her shoulder, but she shrugged him off and turned around to choke more.

"Zahenna, quickly," he held out his hand to her, "Take my hand. Take the Smart Blood back."

"No," she gulped, "that guard was a teleporter. Wardan said I had fifteen minutes before I die like this. Take him and finish the stasis tanks so I can take us to The Warden. They may also know where we've gone. Hurry."

Zahenna nodded toward Tyrius, who huddled in a foetal position on the floor, looking much more drained and skinny than he had on the ship. Maybe it was only the blue, ambient light of the tubes that made him look pale, but the skin of his nose and around his eyes stood out, white-tinged, against his fur.

Sithon bent down and shook him. Tyrius moved about like a sack of dead meat—no bones.

Tyrius pulled in a sudden, ragged breath, then a few more.

"Where am I? There's an error message where my eyes are supposed to be!"

He sniffed the air.

"Sithon, is that you?"

"Yeah, it's me Tyrius. We're in the stasis room. I need you to tell me how to drain the tanks before The Warden catches sight of us."

"Lift me up, and take me toward the line of lights at the front of the room. Can you see them?"

Sithon searched left, then right, forward and back down the endless aisles of tubes. He spotted the row of lights behind them.

Zahenna sat down, propped up on the base of one of the tubes. Sithon dragged Tyrius by her, with a chorus of her hacking coughs to bolster him. Luckily, after a short distance, Tyrius caught his own feet underneath him, and started to stagger along with Sithon's arm around his chest for support.

"Bleirah's Pool, you're not supposed to come out of Second Skin like that. It's dangerous. So, they sent a teleport. Bad idea. We'll be a few steps ahead of them, but not for long. That teleport will be back once they probe the Pwarnaa's memory."

Tyrius gave a savage grin, adding the points of his teeth to all the spikes outside him.

"That is, if they can hook in fast enough to avoid going into a death dive."

With Sithon's help, and the rising tide of Smart Blood in his system pushing them along, they soon reached the wall with the lights. A long panel of controls similar to those in Zahenna's prison room stretched along the wall. Sithon let Tyrius go, and he stood on his own.

Sithon paced pack and forth in front of the controls panels once, then twice, his hands out in front of him and tense.

"Ok, Tyrius, we're here. Tell me what to do."

Tyrius blinked heavily, as though he were trying to clear a lot of tears from his eyes. He leaned against the nearest control console.

He said, "I want you to find the console with the air intake vent on it. Bring me over to that console. Wardan won't have had time to change the programming by now, and I've got the highest security clearance."

Sithon spotted the intake vent, a squarish, upturned hook of pipe with a black intake hole facing him. Sithon brought Tyrius to it. When Tyrius felt the vent against his chest, he reached over, felt for a button on the side of the intake and pressed it. He shooed Sithon away with his other hand. Sithon imagined that if the smells got mixed, alarms would probably start going off.

A smooth, female voice issued out of the computer.

Sithon thought the voice sounded vaguely familiar. Maybe all console voices were meant to sound a little familiar, or maybe it was because his family lived in a console, but that voice itched at him.

Welcome, Agent Tyrius. Speak your command.

"Empty all stasis tanks, immediately," he said.

Passphrase?

"Baero is dead. We scooped out his head," Tyrius said in a clear voice, then, under his breath to Sithon, "Sorry."

Emptying Stasis Tanks, Agent Tyrius. I will notify The Warden.

A siren wailed from another, distant corner of the room, booming then fading in a constant cycle. Sithon smelled caution pheromone being pumped from the vents. The computer-voice spoke over top of it all, as well.

Warning, stasis tanks emptying. Controls on override.

Warning...

Sithon and Tyrius bolted for where Zahenna had been minutes earlier. When they got there, they found both the energy net and Zahenna gone.

"Over here!"

She called from somewhere over to their right. The sound cut off at the end of the sentence like she had been punched in the gut.

Sithon and Tyrius followed the sound of her voice to another wall, this one with a set of two doors in it. The doors were made of solid metal, without windows, and the handles, of the turning variety, were now wrapped in a rapidly sparking section of energy netting. Already, someone or something on the other side was pushing on the doors, making them bow inwards a little. Sithon knew it was only a matter of time before that pusher got friends together, and he hoped that the stasis victims were out of their tubes by then.

Sithon tried to push against the door with Zahenna, but his hand slipped. When he pulled back, his fingers were coated with blood. Zahenna coughed again, putting a fresh spray on the metal.

"Tyrius, we have to get out of here. She's going to die if she doesn't switch Talents soon."

Tyrius rubbed at his eyes with the inside of a forearm which wasn't quite as scaly as the rest of him.

"You two get out of here, then. Wait two minutes before unplugging The Warden, or else you'll kill all the residents of those tanks. Wait too long, and we'll all be fried. I'll find Djarro and meet you again, somehow."

"But you're blind! And they could burst through that door at any minute!"

Tyrius grinned, that savage grin that was only accentuated by his spiny nose.

"You're going to have to trust me."

Sithon got Zahenna's attention. She trembled badly as she moved away from the door, and made little involuntary grunting sounds during especially severe shakes. He took her hand, which by now was coated in blood and spit, and allowed her to lock fingers with him.

They floated for a second, a little longer this time, and then landed sprawled on the floor of a place that smelled like Vaedra's chamber back on the *Death's End*. The smell was of machine lubricants and the caked-on sweat of a body which hadn't moved for quite some time. The room was filled with a greyish light scarcely brighter than the faint glow of the stasis tubes, and in it Sithon found a long, sloping metal bed in front of his nose as he sat there for a few seconds, on one knee and still holding on to Zahenna. At his level, the body of the Warden was just beyond his line of sight, but he could hear her breathing.

The breaths of the one above him creaked in and out, belaboured sighs of an organic bellows. In counterpoint to the soughing sighs, Sithon could hear Zahenna's sharp, rhythmic coughing. Her hand had loosened around his fingers and she lay curled on the floor, tail between her legs and curving up over her belly. She shuddered hard and held her stomach.

Sithon squeezed her hand, clenching the fingers together.

"Zahenna," he said in a hoarse whisper, "Take back my Talent, quickly!"

Zahenna's eyes rolled back in her head. Sithon could see the whites peeking out under her fluttering eyelids. He looked around for a door, or any possible guards. One door at the back had shadows beside it, and when Sithon concentrated he could smell the faint odour of more than one Geedar beyond it. Another door at the back, to a stairwell it looked like had another guard. He had to be quiet at this, for it was only a matter of time until the Warden took a routine look at her security eyes in the control room... the scent detectors probably hadn't gotten a whiff of them yet because they had dropped in so suddenly.

Regardless, Sithon knew he didn't have much time, and noise was not an option. He slapped Zahenna across the bridge of the nose. When she continued to shiver and keep her eyes closed, he shook her.

She woke on the third shake, but not quietly. She uttered a single syllable, an inarticulate sob. Her hand tightened back around Sithon's, and he felt the drain through his fingers that he now associated with Zahenna's Talent. Immediately her breathing became more normal, but she collapsed into a heap again, clearly unable to aid Sithon in what he needed to do. He let her stay there on the floor for the moment and stood up to survey the attachments coming off of the Warden. If they were anything like the ones attached to Vaedra, he...

He was not expecting the figure that he saw laying on the slab, in that cold, circular room. The picture that Tyrius had given him was from a blurry memory, indistinct at best. He had been able to see the rounds of her breasts, the lines of tubing coming out of her in all directions, the strange machinery along the walls, looking like it had all been cut out to fit into and around itself, a wobbly, non-intuitive puzzle.

He hadn't seen her... no, not really. Now, standing before the Warden, he recognized her. Her yellow fur, that he once watched dance in the breeze with such fascination, hung in clumps coated by sweat and oil. Her long, wavy mane was gone, shaved off to make the maintenance of the wire jacks in her head easier. What was once a body covered in supple, sensual muscle puddled where it hit the slab, making many tiny wrinkles in her skin.

Sithon remembered Sashi's last words to him, on the night they had captured Djarro.

I'd rather be safe under Wardan's control than be in the position that you two are in.

"Oh Sashi, I warned you," he said, more to himself than to her.

She heard him. The rest of the lights dimmed, and a single, bright white light opened up over him. Sashi's voice, older and edged with interference at the edge of her words filled the air.

"Who's there? State your business." When she said this, Sithon imagined her still standing in front of him, brandishing her energy crop. As he opened his mouth to say something, anything that came to mind, really, to keep her occupied and the guards out at the doors, she spoke again.

"Wait... I know that smell. Let me get a look at you in the surveillance eyes... yes! It is! It's Sithon Flood! Well... you're not such a puppy anymore."

Sithon's mane tingled at the roots as she addressed him in familiar tones. He remembered whose side she had come down on in the last encounter.

"Wardan's cruelty has aged me. As I see it has aged you... the real you."

"I'll ignore that remark, and the fact that you have a guest who is clearly vulnerable, and keep the doors locked from the guards. I've ordered them to stand down, you know. You can't expect them not to notice something as noisy as the young female's exclamation back there." Her electronically tinged voice purred, like the hum of a badly insulated cable.

Sithon went to Zahenna and turned her over onto her side. She was breathing deeply, no doubt sleeping off her recent trauma with the help of the Smart Blood. If Sithon was correct about the extent of her injuries this time and the turnaround time of his Talent, she would be out for quite some time. No help from Zahenna's corner, then.

He spoke loudly this time, fairly certain that Sashi was telling the truth about the guards. He could smell a faint wash of aggravated pheromones under the normal smell of the room.

"And Djarro? What have you done with him and the other stasis victims?"

"I've sealed them in with the guards that had already headed into the area. The better group ought to win out, but if it's your friends in the tanks I'm afraid I'm eventually going to have to put them back where they belong."

Sithon flattened his ears. At least Djarro and Tyrius, assuming they had met up, and assuming Tyrius's eyesight had returned even a little, would probably not have let themselves be taken by the guard, yet. He wondered just how many guards had gotten into the stasis room before Sashi locked it off, and just how dangerous those high-security prisoners really were. With no real way of knowing those things, he shifted his concentration to Sashi. He knew it was, indeed, Sashi speaking right now, not the voice of the Warden that he had been so warned about. He was also fairly certain that Sashi had a reason for coming to him as

Sashi: the only reason that Sashi ever had for doing anything nice was because she wanted something.

"Why are you doing this for me?" He asked, but didn't really know where to look when he said it. Should he look at her body on the slab? Somewhere on the ceiling? Somewhere on the walls?

Sithon felt very dizzy, all of a sudden. A fuzzy figure coalesced in front of his eyes out of horizontal lines made of light. His eyes went out of focus as she blurred, then solidified again. It was another Sashi, more like her old self but still not as she had ever been. She had changed her Second Skin self (Sithon didn't as yet know how she was tapping into his jack but he knew what it was, for sure) to include round, heavy breasts that begged to be touched, an even fluffier, softer looking tail and long, long legs defined by a little bit of muscle. Her curly mane floated about her in a light-kissed halo.

"There, that's better," she said, her words skimming gently across the top of Sithon's mind, "We're not on the same frequency, but I can still get close enough to lick your muzzle."

"Please don't do this to me, Sashi, I hate Second Skin."

"You could get used to it, if you had the right incentives."

Sashi pulled the side of her wrap top over, revealing the globe of one breast and the pink hint of a nipple. Sithon angled his real body away from her and crossed his arms, despite the vertigo that threatened to floor him with each tiny movement.

"Sorry Sashi, Talents don't work in the 'Skin. Now what do you want from me?"

"I want you to stay here and keep me company. I don't know how *you* got here, but they never just let anyone interesting in. I never realized what a social creature I was until I took this post, this... jack." She sighed, and even through the programming Sithon thought he picked up a hint of genuine regret.

As Sithon responded to Sashi, he looked carefully through her to study the wires protruding from her head, while still maintaining the semblance of looking her in the face. A main bundle of cables stretched out from the back of Sashi's skull and draped between her slab and the wall.

If the setup was anything like Vaedra's chamber, those would be the control wires that Sithon would have to dislodge in order to shut down the Warden. He wondered, though, if crippling her mind was the only way. After all, she seemed unhappy. Maybe he could talk her into some sort of resolution.

"If you're so lonely, why don't you step down and return to the real world? Surely there are others waiting in line to try out Wardan's technology."

"Wardan wouldn't trust me to remain loyal, with the intimate knowledge that I have of the inner workings of the prison. I could turn the complex into a fortress against him and arm it with all of his most dangerous enemies,"

Sashi's wavering avatar said, sitting down to rest her non-existent behind on the slab. She slumped down until her translucent elbows were resting on her knees.

Sithon tilted his head.

"What would keep you from doing that right now?"

"It was that thought, finally gaining enough power to overtake Wardan, that drove me into this mess in the first place. You were right, though... no matter how far ahead of him I thought I was, he was always further. He has an override switch. The minute his main monitor back on the *Death's End* logs any hint of rebellion, he can press that switch and cut my mental life line. I would wake a gibbering wretch, never again aware of where I was or what was happening to me."

Sithon opened his mouth, but nothing came out. He had been expecting her to attack him, but now she seemed on the verge of...

Yes, tears came to Sashi's virtual eyes, and she pressed her hands to her face. She pulled in a long, deep breath, amplified by her cupped fingers. Her chest contracted in a burst of silent sobs.

"I've had so much time, sitting here, thinking alone, endlessly. I never managed to make any virtual friends that were as good as my real ones, and the real ones that were still there after I went on the slab drifted away from me over time. Who wants to sit for hours and talk to a blank screen, or a microphone? They moved on to creatures that they could smell and touch and see... I mean really see, not just imagine. I realized that I wanted power because I wanted to know everything, especially everyone around me.

Now all I do is watch them from screens. That's as far from really knowing them as a tree drawn in the dust is from a forest!"

Sithon didn't know if that word, forest, had echoed in the room at large—surely he thought it impossible—but it certainly echoed in his mind, with all the intensity of one of Toraus's tirades. He knew that he was only touching air, but he moved toward Sashi, with his real body, and put a hand on her shoulder. He wanted to feel her there, but nothing real met the pads of his fingers although he could see himself stroking her, wanting to comfort her. She reached up, left hand crossing her chest, and put her intermittent, fuzzing yellow hand over his.

"Oh Sithon... the forest. I should have stayed in the forest. Followed my instincts. Maybe died a real death at Wardan's hands that night. I know I should have taken the chance."

Sithon moved in front of Sashi, to look her straight in the eyes. He placed his hands out in front of him, on Sashi's shoulders. His muscles strained as he held them in midair, but he knew that if he ceased to treat her as a real entity, the fight might be lost in an instant.

"You can still show Wardan that he can't control you. You can still undo what you helped to do that night."

"No," she wailed, twisting her avatar in his grip, "I don't want to lose my mind! I'd rather die."

"But you know there's a chance that he won't find out until it's too late... you could start the disconnect process at the same time as the release of all the prisoners and maybe, just maybe you could get yourself out of the 'Skin far enough that his switch wouldn't end your mind. If you abandon me now, if you don't fix this thing, you'll spend the rest of your life talking only to yourself. And this time it will be a self that hates you."

Sashi's avatar eyes glowed with bluish light. She stood up from the slab, staring at a point above and beyond Sithon's left shoulder. Her avatar began to fade out of his vision from the center to the edges, like a light stain from the sun.

"I hope you can forgive me, Sithon."

Sithon froze in place. Was she apologizing for hurting Djarro, or for trapping them all to be fried by Wardan's goon squad?

In the odd, expectant quiet of that moment, he went to check on Zahenna and test her weight. He wanted to know just how quick an exit they could make if the doors flung open with guards waiting behind them. She could easily have summoned more guards during their chat.

In the distance, a siren wailed, then another. Sithon, crouched by Zahenna's body in the grey gloom, swivelled his ears and took on an alert posture. He listened around the sirens to try and hear any sign of what was going on... engines, energy weapons, doors, anything, but only the sirens sounded. New sets of them joined in every second, getting louder and closer. They pulsed, three shorts and a long.

Whip-whip-whip Wee-onk—
Whip-whip-whip Wee-onk!

Sithon started talking to Zahenna's unconscious form.

"Sorry Princess Ta—Princess. I think I just made the wrong deal, and we're all going back to where we started, if we're lucky."

Zahenna stirred, bringing a hand up to rub her scabbed face. She tried to turn over, but only really rocked a little back and forth.

"Don't call me Princess," she mumbled groggily.

Sithon's ears flattened. He slapped a palm to his forehead. Of all the times to insist on something so trivial…

"It's accurate, isn't it? You are, aren't you?"

The siren blared out of the speakers lining the Warden's chamber. A voice spoke above them. Sashi's voice sounded different as the Warden, solid, loud, authoritative, like a distillation of her bark during those far-away drills, that day when Sithon had followed her. Yes, although he hadn't realized it then, he had been rather like a puppy.

"This is the Warden," it said, "Commencing password-protected shutdown. Clear all cell doors. Personnel are advised to stow all weapons in the nearest security station until shutdown is complete."

"Haha, she did it!"

Sithon leapt into the air.

"Thank you, Sashi! When this is all over, we'll get you a pardon, I promise," he shouted, as a chorus of voices (all different versions of Sashi) placed around the circular wall of the room positively sang:

"Unlocking outer checkpoint doors in Cell Blocks zero through nine."

"Sealing off all surveillance posts."

"Locking off all weapon repositories."

And finally,

"Disconnecting from Warden server. Saving all changes."

Sithon heard hammering on the door, from several sets of fists. He also heard, down below, the stampeding, palpitating sound of thousands of feet beating against metal flooring. Shouts echoed up the stairwells beyond the doors, too indistinct and too many for Sithon to make out any words.

He also heard Sashi, over on the slab, choking. She coughed and an arc of phlegm shot out of her long-unused throat. Her back arched, an action which pulled her shackled arms taut as tent cables.

This time, the avatar shoved its way into Sithon's mind, and appeared in an instant. Sashi's form wavered. Sometimes she was tall, sometimes short. She stretched and bent like an image in water. Her face fluttered between the beautiful, creamy visage she had presented to him earlier and brief glimpses of something much more terrible, the haggard face of someone who has been fleeing on foot for many days, the terrified face of an exhausted and cornered animal.

"He's here... shutting down my functions one by one... Sithon, I'm starting to forget things... I'm holding him off as long as I can but I'm not going to be going with you..." She left off with an agonized keen, part howl, part whine.

Sithon lurched clumsily forward, holding out his hands, even though he knew in his heart that she would be gone before he reached her.

"Sashi, is there anything he hasn't taken from you yet? Anything important?"

"One last phrase. One last function. Goodbye Sithon."

Sithon regained his equilibrium as Sashi disappeared into a single line of light. Over on the slab, Sashi thrashed back and forth, her head shaking spastically back and forth and swinging the thick wires connected to the wall. She said her last words through her own clenched teeth, with her own voice and breath.

"Die Wardan..."

Her mind's final scream was accompanied by a huge explosion from lower down in the prison that rocked the command center and nearly knocked Sithon off of his feet. A wave of heat flowed into the room and stayed there, along with the smell of smoke and something else, like the sharp smell of chemical fire Sithon had sometimes smelled in the downstairs labs. Soon after the first explosion, another boom sounded from a wing of the building which sounded a lot further away.

The grey lights in the control room flickered once, then a second time, deeper. When they dimmed a third time, the light in the room died entirely. So much sound issued from below. Bumps, thumps, clangs and cries of all description battled with each other for dominance, sinking into a mire of confused noise. The control room, however, went silent as well as dark with the loss of power.

Sithon listened for Sashi's breathing. He heard nothing but Zahenna's snores from the floor beside him.

With her last ounce of control, Sashi overloaded the generators. I'd be willing to bet my tail on it. The resulting power surge fried her jacks.

Sithon felt his way to the slab. He found one of Sashi's restraints and pulled on it as hard as he could.

After a few moments Smart Blood enlarged the muscles in his arms and boosted his strength, but these were Wardan's signature holds... Sithon and Djarro proof, as their first order of business.

The door stood slightly ajar now, and a bittersweet breeze wafted to Sithon's nose. He smelled blood below, and lots of it. He had the sickly inkling that this whole prison was about to become as much a tomb as its command centre.

Sashi had implied that Djarro was safe. At least, he was while she had him locked down in the stasis room.

Sithon fumbled around near the floor until he found Zahenna. With the Smart Blood still coursing through his veins, he picked her up with ease and slung her over his shoulders.

He paused just before opening the door, whispering "I forgive you, Sashi. We both do."

The Way Nature Made Him

Sithon opened the door to Sashi's control center, and knew immediately why it had been propped open. A stack of Geedar bodies three high lay in the doorwell, mangled by teeth and claws. The jugular of the corpse on the top had been torn out, and several deep slashes criss-crossed its chest. Blood pooled on the floor, and Sithon had to step in it to get to the hallway beyond. It sank into his paw pads, still warm and very slippery. He closed his eyes and tried to concentrate on balancing, not dropping Zahenna... anything to keep his mind off of the gruesome feeling between his toes and the friend he was forced to leave behind.

I thought they were trying to get in to hurt me, or Sashi, but more likely these guards were just running for their lives.

Sithon realized, with a fresh burst of panic (and Smart Blood) that he was wearing Wardan's smoke livery, not the same colour scheme on his loincloth. Whoever (whatever) killed these guards would probably mistake him for prison personnel. He detached Djarro's bauble from his loincloth, and for the moment pinned it to Zahenna's top. He shifted Zahenna's weight to one side and used his free hand to pull off his only item of clothing. He then tossed the loincloth behind the pile of dead guards. Hopefully the blood that would inevitably soak the loincloth back there would mask his scent if anyone still lurked around.

Sithon paused, his undersides feeling rather too sensitive and exposed for his liking should physical grappling be the fighting style of the day. He tested the air. He smelled a strong scent trail leading away from the pile of guards, but heard very little except a slightly louder version of that same clunk-bang-rattle-shout that had echoed up to them in the control room.

He hadn't thought about where he might be in the building until now, but then again he had no real way of orienting himself with nothing but a few of Tyrius's vague memories to guide him.

A short hallway curved into a staircase which spiralled downward, and out of sight. On the wall coming up the stairs, Sithon saw a flickering, yellow-orange light.

The smell of smoke and heat wafted up into his face. He looked back at the other door leading from Sashi's chamber, locked and sealed still by some invisible mechanism that only the Warden controlled. He took a deep breath, perhaps the last for a good while if the signs of fire up ahead proved true, and carried on down the stairs.

The stairway, so narrow that Zahenna's feet scraped along the walls as they descended, twisted down for half of a long, thin spiral. Each subsequent stair that Sithon stepped on felt warmer against his paw pads, until the warmth turned into a burn and he trotted on tiptoe (a very uncomfortable exercise with Zahenna swaying on his back).

When Sithon reached the base of the stairs, the very air burned as it passed into his lungs. The room before him glowed orange, brown, orange as it pulsed like an ember at the side of a bonfire. The floor had eroded along the edges
of the room, the panels falling into an inferno below that Sithon knew only by its bright orange glare.

He also spotted a row of doors on the left-hand side of the room, three of them left open. One of the doors still had a couple of tiles left in front of it, but Sithon would have to be quick. He tested the narrow patch of unburnt floor still connected to the stairs. It held his weight, but the creaking sound beneath told him not for very long.

He scurried across the twisted section of good flooring, keeping his head and Zahenna's down as far as possible to keep their noses out of the clouds of smoke that hung in the air. Zahenna coughed lightly, and the temporary shift in weight caused the floor supports to let out a lengthy groan.

Heat belched up out of the holes around Sithon, and the flooring stung his paw pads to the point where the burn carried on long after he raised his foot. The whole thing felt like a more dire version of the obstacle course back at the base—but the stinger was nothing compared to the flames that were starting to lick up above floor level even as Sithon tiptoed across his makeshift bridge. He wished that he'd had time for Djarro's offer of training, for any more time with his father... now who knew where he was or if he was safe? Smart Blood or no Smart Blood, fire would make an end of things if Djarro had been caught in the wrong place when the generators blew.

The flooring lurched left as Sithon weaved around a bend in the floor toward the remaining door. He stood there for a moment balancing a single piece of tile with his feet on either side of the support beam below. He watched the other tiles fall down and down, into the inferno. A body lay down there, his head bashed in from being thrown back in the explosion, and he sizzled black, purple and red.

Jumping right now would be impossible with Zahenna's weight on his back, but perhaps he could throw her to safety first. He pulled her off his shoulders, into his arms, and stopped for a moment to regain balance. He tossed her as gently as possible into the hallway beyond, where she skidded along shortly before stopping curled up in a half-moon.

As Sithon threw her, he felt the floor support give way beneath him. Amid a hail of sparks that burned his back and tail, Sithon pushed off of the floor tile as it made one final collapse and he landed, clinging to the bottom of the doorframe. Now the wall burned his stomach and his arms, and his fingers started slipping backward toward the ledge. His legs scrabbled against the burning wall for a few seconds, feeling for many of them like he was losing the fight to stay out of the flames. Finally, after a moment of hanging over the pit with stiffened shoulders and a burning underside, his blood surged and he gained a few inches up the wall. After one more push of his aching shoulders, he managed to pull himself up to safety.

The air still felt very hot inside the doorway, but the flames hadn't touched this part of the building—yet.

The hall ahead was dark and ran off away from where Sithon assumed the worst of the generator fire was busy consuming the prison. Panting heavily, but not feeling very refreshed by it, he slung Zahenna over his shoulders and followed the hallway.

When they came to another intersection of hallways, Sithon used his nose. Wherever the air felt cooler, wherever the rioting noises echoed louder down the corridors and stairwells, he followed. Zahenna felt much lighter on this leg of the journey, more like a backpack than a limp body.

Gradually, the smoke along the ceiling dissipated and the air cooled. They moved toward what Sithon assumed to be the main bulk of the prison, the conglomeration of cell blocks beyond the control wing. They descended more stairs, a precarious manoeuvre in the complete darkness that surrounded them. Finally, Sithon could hear individual voices out of the crowd noise.

Break down the doors! We're trapped!
Find someone with more weapons!

He came to a door, on the left at the bottom of a stairwell, where blue glowing orb lights dashed by or paused for a moment and circled in mid-air before moving further away. Sithon remembered such lights from the night of Djarro's capture. Normally, they looked faint, like the glow of a cloud-covered moon. After being in the dark for nearly an hour, they shone bright enough, even when seen indirectly, to leave a trail of light across Sithon's vision.

Sithon smelled too many bodies to delineate mingled together. He moved down to the door and peered out. A huge, lofty room opened before him, with slit-windows up near the ceiling showing the night sky and clusters of stars. On every storey, rows of wire mesh balconies fell back into darkened, square-mouthed cells. Bodies in motion writhed en masse on the chamber floor, milling and shouting and jostling. Sithon wondered at first if he would be able to insinuate himself in between them anywhere. They stood shoulder to shoulder, some clothed in rough cloth and some (most likely the stasis victims) naked with damp, matted fur. Those ones smelled, too, a chemical smell like the old showers at the Base.

Well, at least I won't be the only naked one. I just hope they don't notice that I'm dry.

The noise that swelled around the packed Geedar was way above the normal polite level for conversation. They whined, they yipped and they yelled to each other across the room, sending echoes everywhere. Clearly, if these Geedar were going anywhere, they had no idea where.

Zahenna shifted her weight.

"Sithon, where are we?" she drawled, "Tell those others to be quiet."

"Sorry, it's going to get worse before it gets better,"

he said, shoving his way into the crowd.

Sithon found himself being jostled back and forth, his body parts touching others in a way that made his mane bristle. When his penis brushed the tip of someone else's tail, he shivered.

Someone stuck their nose into his back and sniffed him so hard he could feel the cold air pulling on his fur. Apparently Geedar forgot their manners in jail. He turned around to face the sniffer and found a crook-backed old male, grey striped with an unruly mop of mane and a scar closing one eye. The old Geedar grinned, letting his tongue wag out, and Sithon saw he was missing many of a yellowed set of teeth. He, too, was naked. Another clotted tuft of hair covered all but the tip of his penis.

"I guess the young'uns dry faster, eh, Mejinah?"

A grizzled, but much younger female, mottled brown and grey but with the same tufty short mane, turned up her nose and said nothing. Sithon noticed that her eyes were a harsh green only slightly more earthy than Toraus's.

The old male got pushed up against Sithon as the crowd lurched forward again. He chuckled, a whistly, worn-out sort of a chuckle. Sithon felt the other Geedar's ribcage immediately.

"Sho, whatcha in for, skinny?"

Sithon replied with the truest thing that came to mind.

"I tried to escape Ferion with my father to inform on Wardan."

The old male nodded, his nose poking Sithon's

chest as he did.

"Then you've been in here longer than I have! Mejinah and I used to run a tavern in North Dune. Family business, don'tcha know. Thing was we were also the biggest civilian arms smugglers the Queen's folks had. They caught up to us a couple months ago, but not before I took fire to some of Wardan's nasties. He can't resurrect ash, hee hee! I'm Caylus, by the way."

Sithon shifted Zahenna away from someone's flailing arm.

"What's going on in here? It doesn't seem like we're going anywhere."

Caylus angled his snout to point up over Sithon's shoulder.

"Yer facin' the wrong way, is why. Look up yonder."

Sithon twisted his torso and neck around rather than trying to turn all the way around with the crowd pressing in on him. Zahenna's feet hit a tall female in the head. She growled at him, and he flattened his ears apologetically.

The room ended about fifty rows of packed Geedar away from where Sithon, Zahenna, Caylus and Mejinah were squashed together. Sithon saw something cut with horizontal lines, like a hangar door, shaking with periodic impacts. The door reached about two storeys up, cutting through the first-floor balcony.

"Ye see that, young'un? That's the last door what hasn't been cut off by t'flames."

Sithon went to snap at Caylus, tell him not to call him young'un. Then he remembered Sashi calling him Puppy and held back. He smelled smoke here, already. At least Wardan would never be able to get to Sashi to resurrect her.

"Huh," he said, still lost in his own thoughts. He should have seen Djarro in here by now. Even in this crowd, Djarro would stick out. Sithon remembered how tall his father was, how he could dwarf even the tallest of the other soldiers at the Base, soldiers who had been chosen specifically for their outstanding strength. His ruddy, striped shoulders and head would tower above the rest of them and make him obvious, even in the semi-darkness.

"Door's stuck," Caylus chattered on, perhaps to comfort himself, Sithon thought, "Guards shot out the mechanism on their retreat. We don't know if they're still in the guard towers outside, or if they took off in the desert rovers for that blasted shadow city. Ones at the front been pushin' and bangin' at it for hours, and haint been able to budge it an inch."

Sithon frowned.

"My father could help with all this. Maybe I could too, but we'd definitely need him pushing. When you were on your way up from the stasis room, did you see an unnaturally large male? He would have been with a blind Tothari in Wardan's colours."

Caylus chuckled another one of those dry chuckles, but this time, it had a slightly thoughtful tone to it, the way someone reminisces about an old friend.

"Oh yeah, that feller. Saved the spiny one when we had him surrounded. Thought he was a guard, we did. Turns out, he was the one what flipped the switch.

Guess not all of Wardan's freaks are happy where they are, either. We lost 'em once the doors threw open and the explosions started. The fire cut 'em off, I'd say. That yer Dad, young'un? Ye don't look much alike."

Sithon swayed on his feet. Rush after rush of Smart Blood pumped into his system at once, but he felt weaker for it as it reminded him of his connection to Djarro. His eyes stretched so wide in their sockets that he felt like they must be protruding out over his nose. Every sound in the wide room was separate, and even louder than before. The noise pressed in on him, and the heat, and the smoke. He began sinking to his knees, but Mejinah shoved herself forward and pushed him back upright with forceful arms.

"Enough of this," she said, clipping the ends off her words, "You fall, we trample you."

Sithon twisted around frantically, trying to find and alternate way out of the room, some way that might lead back to the stasis tank room. He realized that he could no more find his way back there, now that Zahenna had brought him here, than he could name a strange place after having been brought there drugged and bound. The point at which he struggled to find his way was the only point on a rapidly crumbling map. He began to pant, then to whine.

"Tell me the way back to where you last saw him. Please."

Mejinah frowned. The expression aged her to the level of her father, all concern and wrinkles.

"You'll burn up down there."

"I have to try. He's already done more than that

for me."

Mejinah opened her mouth again to protest, but before she could, a giant lurch of the crowd sideways, toward the door Sithon had entered by, swept her far enough away that Sithon lost her for a moment. Caylus clung to Sithon's midsection, and if Mejinah had any sense, she would cling to Caylus.

A great gout of heat and smoke billowed out of a door thrown open on the far side of the room. The wall and the circle of crowd immediately surrounding this new opening lit up with the same violent orange of the inferno that Sithon had crossed with Zahenna. Out of the doorway, more a square of brilliant emberglare than a drab opening in a metal wall, came the silhouette of a hell-beast, a larger Geedar than had ever emerged from Bleirah's pool, his mane standing up in the shadows like the spines of a great lizard. In the shadow of this gargantua's left side travelled a vaguely Geedari shape mitigated by hundreds of spines. Together, they staggered out of a descending stairwell, flame-light licking at their heels.

As everyone else pulled back, away from the heat and the creeping smell of smoke and the two creatures who had seemingly survived all of it intact, Sithon pushed with all the ferocity of his Talent against those in front of him.

Even over the shouts and confused barks filling the room, he screamed, "Djarro! Father! I'm here!"

Djarro raised his head, swivelled his stubby ears. Sithon, practically walking over the others in the crowd, yelled again and again until Djarro squinted, put his hand to his brow and, eyes widening in recognition, yanked Tyrius forward so hard that he tripped along for a few steps before falling into stride.

Where Sithon had to wrestle his way through the crowd, Geedar parted as much as possible for Djarro and Tyrius. Djarro's stride told them as much as they needed to know about what would happen to them if they got in his way. They met in a tiny clearing near Djarro's side of the room.

Sithon and Djarro stood facing each other for a second, as if each one disbelieved that the moment had finally come. Finally, Sithon gently handed Zahenna off to Tyrius, who set her on the floor. He threw his arms around Djarro's waist and buried his face in his father's fur. Even the smell of the stasis tanks faded into *his* smell, the one Sithon remembered from that day when Djarro had given him the bauble.

Djarro did him one better. He lifted Sithon up with just his two hands, like a puppy, and tossed him, for one weightless second into the air. Then he caught him in a rough hug between the bulges of his arm muscles. Sithon had never been so happy not to breathe. He rubbed his cheek up against Djarro's, and then did it again, just to be sure he really could. Djarro licked the top of his mane, making it slick over to one side.

Then Djarro laughed, that hearty, booming laugh that Sithon remembered from nights around the fire, and he could feel it resonating in his father's chest.

That sound, that feeling all but wiped away the memories of how he had gotten here, and the predictions he had made on what would happen to them now.

Almost. Djarro put Sithon down, and he felt lighter for having been lifted that way. Sithon placed one hand on Djarro's arm, and used the other to point to the door.

"Guards shot the mechanism. We have to help them get out before we all suffocate."

Djarro nodded. With Tyrius's help, he hooked Zahenna over one arm and began pushing his way forward with the other, toward the door. Sithon and Tyrius followed in the temporary path he created.

When they reached the front, Sithon saw at least twenty young, strong Geedar lined up against the door, pulling at it from the bottom. They braced themselves against the floor, the surrounding walls and each other, they heaved and strained, and Sithon could see claw marks in the metal from where they had lost their grip, so great was their effort. Teams of others slumped against the wall, glassy-eyed and panting.

Djarro's voice sounded even more gravely than usual after so long in the tank.

"Give over," he said, shoving his way in between the two middlemost Geedar.

Djarro motioned with his head for Sithon to take up the space beside him. With his tail in an apologetic position brushing his legs, Sithon moved someone else out of the way.

Sithon reached down and gripped the door when he saw Djarro's back bend. Sithon's Blood was still high from when he had feared Djarro dead, but he knew that he would need every last bit of his Talent to help the others. Unlike other times, when he had been confused over what to picture to induce more battle rage, this time he knew exactly what he wanted to see. He pictured Sashi, being chased down by Wardan in that horrible Second Skin system, her dreams turned to nightmares and Wardan himself turned into a much truer form, an ugly fiend too vicious and scarringly hideous to keep any one shape for long. A mass of sharp edges, glowing eyes and dark, gaping mouths, Wardan descended on Sashi, taking everything that she used to define herself until finally, backed into the tiniest corner of her memory, she destroyed herself rather than be obliterated by him. With all this in his mind, Sithon pulled.

The door budged, just a little, and then with further pressure from them, it lurched upward, receding into the ceiling with a squeal of broken gears. The smoke on the ceiling swirled out into the night, and Sithon smelled fresh air rushing in. Djarro kept pushing until he was the only one holding the door up, as the others were too short to reach. It was there, stretched out to his tallest, that the first volley of darts came and ripped along the side of Djarro's ribcage. Two dark slashes appeared under his armpit, making blood spray onto the ground near his feet.

"Ow," he said, rubbing a paw over the wound as another Geedar would inspect a bump to the head.

Djarro ducked out of the way of the door just in time to avoid another few darts, which instead clattered against the stone floor. Sithon moved away from the door, too, and peered out from the frame.

The door opened onto a short ramp with railings, at the bottom of which stood a group of thirty guards or so. The front row, about ten of them, held dart bows, little horizontal launchers for the wooden darts which had scraped Djarro. Behind them, the guards held a mix of glowing energy weapons and slingshots. The prison yard behind them stretched away, bare and empty, to a tall wire perimeter fence broken occasionally by the spires of the guard towers.

"Stop, prisoners," one of them yelled, his voice quavering, "Wardan will be here shortly to deal with you. Anyone caught running will be subject to execution, followed by re-anim--"

Sithon had little time to wonder what the prisoners would do before they did it. The first volley came from a white, shaggy female, a naked stasis victim.

"Take a dung bath," she hollered back, and the entire first line sunk into a mire of liquid earth that only a moment before had been hard-packed desert sand, cracked with drought. Before their heads had disappeared under the ground, three of the remaining guards' energy weapons, bright balls of crackling blue light to Sithon's eyes, flew out of their owners' hands and smashed on the ramp, their lights dissipating like clouds in the heat.

Tyrius joined in on the fun and started pulling spines from his back, dripping blood and slime, and hurling them down on the guards like spears. Emboldened, the rest of the crowd surged out of the mouth of the prison toward the remaining crew, who bolted for parts unknown.

The crowd first squashed Sithon up against the wall, then started pulling him down the ramp. Facing backwards, he watched Djarro wade after him with Zahenna over his right shoulder and Tyrius linked onto his left arm.

Sithon got shoved to the bottom of the ramp, where the crowd dispersed in a wide fan, everyone dashing for various parts of the fence or wandering around, hollering for others that they'd lost in the confusion. Djarro caught up to Sithon there, and they moved out from the pressurized burst of escapees a ways. Now that they were outside, Sithon saw that the entire back half of the prison had been eaten up by flames that licked the night sky and coloured it the same as sunset. Smoke rose into the atmosphere, blocking out many of the abundant desert stars he had seen from the ship on the way there. The prison itself was merely a blackened frame, a gridwork like the one that sometimes showed under 'Skin glitches. Stone walls fell in as their supports gave way, and windows became menacing serpent tongues of heat.

Tyrius let the wind from the fire blow his grey mane around without straightening it. Little embers blew past him on the ground and little motes in the air.

"It's the only permanent resting place, now. I'm glad I regained my eyesight in time to see it."

Tyrius angled his nose toward the ground, and lowered his ears in a gesture of mourning.

When Tyrius spoke next, his voice came out in an uncharacteristically gentle tone.

"Did you kill her, Sithon? Something tells me it wasn't you."

Sithon lowered his nose and ears, as well.

"I wasn't expecting to find someone I knew in that control room. Sashi was ready to escape too, whether in the flesh or in the flames. Wardan had..."

Sithon couldn't finish the sentence because the realization swooped down on him like one of Wardan's guard ships armed with poison bolts. Djarro grabbed him by the shoulders and shook him.

"Oy, hey, what's all this about Sashi? Spit it out, pup!"

Sithon steadied himself by looking into Djarro's solid, dependable face for a few moments. Then he took as deep a breath as possible, and spoke.

"Sashi became the Warden, the prison-mind that kept everything in order. Wardan had an override switch on her mind, to destroy her if she disobeyed or tried to leave. That means he must have the same thing on my mother."

Djarro's mouth made a straight line that still seemed like a frown, despite the tension in his lips. He closed his eyes.

"Forget about your mother." He said.

Sun and Son

Sithon kept his nose to the ground, emitting a halo of silence and inapproachability as the party found the section of fence closest to the direction of Marrow Canyon and began working on making a hole in it. Caylus and Mejinah joined them, along with the white female who made mud and at least fifty others. Sithon stayed at the front of the group with Djarro, but worked sullenly with the tools the group had managed to smuggle out, casting sidelong glances over at Djarro every few minutes to see if his demeanour had changed. His father worked away, giving orders as naturally as a tail wag, but spared no attention for Sithon. After Djarro had said those terrible words, he had left Sithon alone to think.

Sithon did think, swirling, circular thoughts that vacillated between anger, despair and deep worry.

How could he ask me to forget her? But if I don't, will he still want to be my father? I can never forget her, but I don't want to desert Djarro, either. And what if I do desert her? Who else will care about her? Who will be there to save her from whatever awful fate that Wardan has in store for her? The minute she is no longer useful... click, out with the lights. I have to save her, but will Djarro ever accept that? I just don't know...

And so his thoughts went on setting him apart

even from the work of his hands as he tore at the fence.

"Young'un!" Caylus's voice hollered, from behind him.

Sithon realized absently that it was the third or fourth time Caylus had called. He turned without saying anything in return, ears perked and eyebrows raised.

"I knew I was glad t'meetcha! You're quite handy with makin' the doors!"

Sithon nodded as politely as possible, wagged his tail a little, and went back to work... and the cycle of thoughts.

After very little time, Djarro reached forward and pushed a circular section of wire fence out of the way, just like a door on a hinge. The entire group filed out, Tyrius guarding the rear and Djarro in the lead with Zahenna still under his arm and Sithon behind him. They had topped the rise of the third dune from the prison, and Sithon started to feel the desert chill seep back into his fur, when one more Geedar caught up to them. Sithon saw her only as a blue-white blur, so fast was her stride, and so confident, as she blocked Djarro's way. She was middling tall, thin as a tree branch, and very naked, her short, fine fur making her nipples stand out in the rapidly cooling desert air.

Djarro walked around her. She came out in front of him again.

"You will tell me, this instant, why you are carrying my daughter in such a manner."

Djarro gently moved her aside on his way forward, the way he had moved the piece of fence that looked like a door.

"'Cause she's heavy," he grunted.

Up to this point, Sithon had been following along beside Djarro, at the head of the group. After the appearance of the blue-white female, Sithon began to notice a distinct silence behind them. Zahenna had said she was a princess, so if this was really her mother... and he thought he had also heard her say that Leethia was somewhere in the prison.

Following his suspicions, he glanced backward to the rest of the group. They all kneeled, their noses in the sand, in the place where the blue female had first come striding up to them. Sithon placed a hand on Djarro's arm.

"Father, look."

Djarro stood at the crest of the dune, the kneeling multitudes below him, and snorted. The blue-white female, Leethia most likely, walked up to the top of the dune beside him and took up the same position, her arms crossed and her feet planted. The glow from the prison fire blazed up one side of her, and the darkness of the night hid the other except for an outline.

Djarro lifted Zahenna up to the light so that the new female could see the burnt side of her face. Peeling skin seamed her cheek, but the scabs had fallen off sometime during their foray into the dark. Zahenna's eyes rolled, the lids fluttering to reveal the whites beneath. "We don't mean her no harm your majesty," Djarro explained, "My son there has risked his own tail more'n probably even I know to get her here. She's sick with somethin', I'm sure Sithon could tell you better what, but she's getting better now. Sleeping it off."

Leethia sniffed him up and down, very slowly.

"You're telling the truth." It was a solid statement, not a question in the least. "Nevertheless, I would prefer that you let her down. You betrayed my administration in the past, did you not?"

Djarro's brows furrowed.

"Now, how did you...?"

"I read thoughts. Natural power for a politician. I also share feelings. Right now, I'm sure you're understanding my frustration. Concentrate and I know you'll feel it."

Djarro motioned to the rest of the group to get up and walk.

"Got enough frustration of my own, thanks. Did your little trick tell you why I was in Wardan's prison? Think hard and maybe you'll intuit the answer."

The female got in between Djarro and the others. They still knelt, faces in the sand.

"They'll answer to me now, thank you. I am Leethia, Queen of Rakaria, and I won't have you giving them any more orders."

Sithon could tell from her posture that she was used to getting a reaction from revealing that name. Djarro simply dropped Zahenna onto the top of the sand dune, where she sent a little trickle of sand cascading toward Leethia. Djarro motioned for Sithon to keep moving with him. They turned their backs on Leethia.

"Wouldn't dream of it," Djarro called back, "You

can stay here all night, if you want to. Lovely stars out here."

Sithon joined in.

"Just keep a lookout for Wardan's guard ships. You'll need some cover when they get here, and I can see there's lots around."

Sithon felt foreign emotions rush into him, like wind through a mesh door screen. He recognized the stomach-clenching tension that signified frustration, and the fumbling feeling of being unable to say something properly, accompanied by memories of his first attempts at writing.

Despite knowing how terribly angry Leethia was, Sithon kept moving. She had insulted Djarro, after all the horrible things he had suffered to try and reach her in time to stop Wardan. For that, Sithon would leave the safety of the group, even if it meant less defence against whatever might befall them in the desert. She kept calling out to them with those washes of frustration. Each time, the emotion would enter feeling like an artificial body part and gradually assimilate itself using personal memories.

Sithon only stopped and turned his attention back to the dune where Leethia stood because he heard a familiar voice.

"Where am I? Mother, is that really you?"

Zahenna staggered to her feet, knees shaking and back bent. Sand striped her left side.

Leethia held out her arms, and Zahenna sank into them, clinging on to her mother despite being much taller and more muscular.

"Oh, Zahenna," Leethia exclaimed, "I thought I'd never see you again. What in the world were you doing with those two mangy brutes?"

Sithon waited. He noticed Djarro doing the same thing, a few paces down the other side of the dune with his head peeking over. Moonlight highlighted the edge of his wide nose.

Zahenna's ears perked up a little as she looked around for Sithon. When she saw him, and met his eyes, she leaned away from Leethia a little.

"Mother, why is Sithon leaving? What did you say to him?"

Leethia narrowed one eye. She tilted her head.

"He left easily enough, and of his own accord. You should have seen the way that... that mountainous creature with him had you, crooked under one arm like a rolled-up blanket! The Princess of Rakaria!"

To Sithon's shock, Zahenna pushed Leethia away, gently, but firmly. She turned away from her mother, one hand raised and one pressed to her forehead.

"After all this time... you're still playing that game," she said softly, "Pretending we still have a kingdom. Like he's still the enemy."

Zahenna pointed at Sithon, her arm trembling.

"I know you read his mind, and you've learned who he is. As usual, you only skimmed the surface, didn't you? Didn't you? And for a name, you were willing to let him leave us, leave me, to wander the desert alone. Well you missed everything, the most important part. If I am here now, it is because he carried me... *carried me* through riots and machinery and flames so that you could see me one more time."

Leethia gulped.

"Zahenna, I..."

Zahenna shook her head, denying any further commentary. Sithon's heart felt... strangely full of light. Never since he was very small indeed had anyone stopped to defend his actions, and certainly not anyone who had previously made a concerted effort to hate him. He found himself transported back in time, remembering himself holding his mother's hand as she ran to hide him from Toraus. He remembered when Vaedra used to fight back, and felt some hope that perhaps Djarro would remember too, and see reason.

Zahenna said, "I made the same mistake that you did once. I called him a filthy traitor and a liar and tried to get rid of him. But when he escaped the Death's End, he risked his life to take me with him. It's more than I would have done, even when I fancied myself a martyr."

Leethia stamped a foot, which had little effect on the sand except to dig her foot deeper into it.

"A generation back, his family was killing our family. Toraus and Mardon Flood murdered your cousins!"

Zahenna scowled at her mother. She climbed up over the Dune with her hands to the ground, then stumbled over to Sithon. When she came close to him, she smelled like blood and vomit and wet fur, but still he felt a sudden affection for her patchy face, the funny tuft of her tail, and most of all, the obstinate set of her back. He smiled at her, and held out his arm for her to lean on. She wagged her tail weakly, just at the tip.

"Sithon never killed my cousins. He deserves better than this." Zahenna said.

Leethia lowered her tail and slouched, giving out a slight *whuff* sound. She jerked her head to the right, signalling the others with their noses to the sand to move out. Tyrius stood up first, and began nudging the others with his foot to get them going.

"I can't fight you now, when every minute Wardan is gaining on us. We will continue this discussion when, and if we are able to reach Marrow Canyon. For now, although I dislike it, they stay."

Zahenna stayed leaning on Sithon's arm and continued the struggle up the next dune, without another word. Sithon liked the warmth of her arm this time, the way it pressed into the crook of his elbow and dispelled some of the clinging chill in the air. When morning came, he would likely regret any body-to-body contact, but for now Zahenna's presence beside him eased the lingering presence of Leethia's mind, anxious and eager to discourage him.

Once or twice, he felt a breeze of displeasure pass over him, making his gag reflex threaten to spasm, making his nose wrinkle. He ignored the feelings and kept going.

They travelled over dune after dune, each one relatively similar to the last, with Djarro leading Sithon and Zahenna, and followed by Leethia and the others. Tyrius still guarded the rear, keeping a low profile against the Queen's mental probes. Sithon assumed she hadn't noticed him yet, because she hadn't called him out by the time a layer of pink began to soak up into the sky along the horizon.

They stayed alert as they walked, ears swivelling constantly and noses testing the air at intervals, but throughout that miraculous night they neither heard nor saw any sign of Wardan's followers. The sky remained clear and the ground an unimpeded roll of dunes to the horizon as the smouldering remains of Takara maximum security became first a small black bump behind them, and then nothing but a spire of smoke rising into the sky.

As the pink line along the horizon turned orange, then spread, Djarro spoke to Sithon in the unusually soft tone he reserved for matters of importance.

"I may not get the chance to ask you again, so you might as well tell me here, as anyplace... what happened to you while I was in there? How did I get here? They transported me to a prison on Ferion, but that's the last I remember. This must be Rakaria. There are no deserts like this back home."

"Wardan must have moved you when he made his coup on Rakaria. I didn't know where you were until Tyrius told me. He helped me escape the *Death's End*..."

"Wait a minute," he said, sounding more like 'waidamminut', "What's a *Death's End*?"

Sithon realized that in order to explain properly, he would have to go back a lot further with his story.

"After you left, Wardan went public with his discoveries on death, and some horrible things that even I didn't know about. Turns out he had invented a way for Geedar to talk to each other, mind-to-mind, but the technology also allowed certain users to have unheard-of power over computer systems: ships, prisons, all manner of weapons, and to create their own living environments within the system."

"First he offered his mind-to-mind device, the Second Skin, to the Queen for use with civil servants. She not only refused the technology, but outlawed it as a danger to pack mentality. As usual, he had another plan lined up behind the first one. He went in secret to some of the higher officers in the armed forces, and offered them the power of resurrection. Leethia found out and tried to outlaw that technology, too, but that was just what Wardan wanted. All but a few of Leethia's generals rose up against her, and when she wouldn't concede to their demands, they stormed the palace and murdered the King. Things quickly devolved from there, becoming a series of losing battles for the Queen's supporters, who had less equipment and experience than the remainder of the armed forces. They retreated to Marrow Canyon, where they remain hidden from Wardan's followers."

Leethia's voice piped in from over Sithon's shoulder. He jumped a little, because she had crept up on them very quietly.

"We did have some weapons left," she said, "and one of them is on Sithon's elbow. We just had to bide our time. Unfortunately, just before the last strike, I was caught out in the open and taken to Takara. Used to be mine, that prison, and what a fine facility it was. Just look what *they've* done to it."

Djarro gave Leethia an incredulous, sideways glance, but said nothing. Sithon continued with his version of the story.

"Wardan did a lot more ceremonies then. He had tanks and tanks in the bottom of the hover city he built to hold them. Every week, new resurrections pledged undying loyalty to Wardan in halls as big as the one we escaped from back there, full to bursting. If someone defied him, he would run down their town with the *Death's End*'s heat jets, then revive them as his slaves. Mother he hooked into the *Death's End* itself, and that is where she stays. I was forcibly implanted with a jack so that I had to hear her, whether I chose to, or not."

"Abominable," Leethia puffed behind him.

Sithon shrugged at Leethia, as if to say, *What can I do about it now? That's how it was.*

"And that," he said, "isn't even the beginning of the story."

As Sithon recounted the rest of the story to Djarro, the sun rose as a wavering yellow disc cut off by the dunes. It rose steadily until the sky shone a clear, harsh blue and the cruel white light beamed down directly overhead. The glare from the white sand burned in Sithon's eyes. He, and everyone else around him, squinted and placed hands up to their foreheads to ward it off, when the heat wasn't taxing their limbs too badly.

The sand in that time went from warm, to hot, to

burning, the newly-healed burn blisters on Sithon's paw pads re-erupting under the skin. He panted, Djarro panted, they all panted, and he could hear his own voice growing more hoarse and ragged as he talked.

But still, he talked, because talking kept him walking, and kept his mind off of the pain in his feet and his eyes if not his burning throat. Leethia hovered around him the entire time, and he resisted the urge to brush her away. She looked thoughtful, and the occasional thoughts and questions that she posed started to sound gentler as she went along. When he described how Vaedra had left him at the end, how she had told him never to return, he heard a polite little sniffle from Leethia's quarter, but when he looked over, she directed her head the other way, ostensibly looking for ships.

"Got to keep on the lookout, you know," she said in a rather watery tone.

Caylus collapsed at what Sithon judged to be a little past noon, by the position of the burning sun. They all gathered round him as the air wavered and bent like ripples in a pond, worried for Caylus, yes, but also very glad to have an excuse to bend down and put their hands on their knees.

Caylus lay stretched out on the sand, on the downslope of a great dune. Mejinah knelt beside him.

"He's frail, and needs water. Didn't anyone in this ridiculous party think to bring water? Into the *desert* for biting at fleas?"

The white mud-maker with the fluffy tail answered.

"There weren't any water left, Mejinah. You must know that, the place was on fire."

Djarro, who had just reached the group from the front of the line, blocked out the sun as he poked his head (and shoulders and chest) over everyone else's shoulders. Mejinah, now in his shade, lowered her ears and tail to him.

"Please carry my father with us," she pleaded, "We may find help before he gets too much worse."

And so, they carried on with Caylus slung over Djarro's back. Another stop later, he carried a retching female over his bent arm, the way he had held Zahenna, pausing every once in a while to let her relieve her aching stomach.

What are we going to do when Djarro runs out of arms, Sithon thought, *tie them onto him like sand bags?*

Sithon went on walking, panting now instead of talking and watching the heat waves bend the air in front of him. It reminded him of the way that things had swirled and jumbled themselves when Vaedra came through on transmissions. He wondered if she ever thought of him now, or if that terrifying not-Toraus took up all of her time and danced her around inconvenient thoughts of an inconvenient son.

The heat waves swayed in front of him, twirling themselves into spirals in the air. Wait, were they supposed to do that? Sithon felt the familiar dizziness, the pulling downward into mental darkness that he had felt so many days on the Death's End, only this time there was no familiar voice attached to it. His mind's ears filled with sentences strung together end to end, overlapping, in many voices. Some of the voices did not sound Geedari.

Please stand by for transDeath's End will be fully operational by mid w—terrible weather we're having up hereno personnel beyond this point after dar—kiro toryaminiw portivilom jarka hisssssssssssss...

Mixed Signals

Sithon floated through a jumble of words, layer upon layer of languages, voices assailing him from every side. Time drifted into static, space into chatter. Sithon's mind thrashed in the darkness, trying to make sense of the thoughts being thrust into him but unable to keep up. Before one group of words could form a thought, it would speed off and become something completely foreign.

Underneath it all, sometimes he could hear Djarro, close enough to know that he was still out there, but not close enough to be anything but a deep-voiced rumble in the distance.

After a while, Sithon let go of trying to make sense of the voices and let himself drift, noise bouncing off him like raindrops. Eventually, the voices started to fade, until everything went silent in Sithon's Second Skin space.

Just when the last of the voice streams had faded out to a mumble like a conversation in the next room, he opened his eyes.

As everything swirled back into position, he realized that the final stream of voices he heard came from two Geedar in white wraps, standing over him in what appeared to be a dimly lit, purplish room.

"Ahh," said the female, "He's awake, and right on schedule. I saw the tech in him the minute they brought him off Sa'li's ship."

"It still could have been the heat faints," said the male. He leaned in close to Sithon's face, so that he became a brown, fuzzy-edged blur, and the next time Sithon took a breath he sniffed deeply.

"Yes, he's healthy as a tail wag other than what that implant's doing to him," the male confirmed, "How you feeling, there, Sith... Sith..."

"Sithon, Betz. It's Ferian," said the female.

Sithon felt around in the bed—the soft mattress squished around his hands, even though it felt like a stone slab beneath that. He propped himself up against, well, it was less a headboard and more a decorative carving in the wall to back the bed, and sat up. Things around him clarified as much as they really could, given the lighting.

"Are you... scientists?" Sithon asked, examining their white robes.

The female answered, "No, we're sick finders. Our Talents allow us to identify toxins and sickness in the body. My Talent allows me to see the vital organs, and the fluids that run through them, and Betz here can tell almost any sickness by smell."

"Oh, I'm not sick. But... I'm sure you knew that already."

The female put a hand under her chin, and lowered her ears.

"Yes, we know you're not poisoned in the body,

but I *am* worried about the stress on your mind. The way it functions with that thing lodged in it... it's not natural. I can see that it's disturbing all of your bodily rhythms. You'll need to see a cut-maker soon and try to remove it, especially if you want to keep travelling out of Wardan's range."

Sithon rubbed his head. He felt an ache on the side where Wardan had implanted the receiver like it was swelling, trying to overtake his skull completely.

"So that's what happened. I reached the end of Wardan's signal range."

The sick-sniffers both nodded. They had been moving to the door all the while that Sithon had been talking to them. Betz reached the door, an ovular opening that looked like it had been worn out of the wall rather than cut, and stepped aside for his partner to go first. The hallway beyond was dark, with only a faint glow diffusing from one direction. Betz faced in that direction.

He said, "You'll be fine while you're here. We've got someone with a Talent for blocking communications equipment, whether it's energy-run or mind-to-mind... anything. Keeps Wardan's probes out. You've had a guest waiting here for quite some time, so we'll let her watch you for a while. Don't get out of bed till you're ready."

Betz's words echoed in the hallway. Sithon smelled must overlaid with the old scents of many Geedar. Was this entire place made of stone? He had expected to wake up in a canyon of some kind, but the darkness, and the stale smell, and the stone everywhere seemed more like being underground.

The room seemed odd, too. Across from him a half-moon table jutted out of the rounded wall, carved directly from the rock, and beside it on either side were two chairs of much the same shape. In the corner, a stack of blankets and pillows, faded and wrinkled, slumped against the wall. A niche held several folded clothing linens that hadn't moved in a while. The ceiling of the place rounded upward in a rather uneven cone shape, and at the tip of the cone floated a blue light orb.

On the floor beside the bed, Sithon found the drinking bowl that he had hoped would be there. He lifted it up and drank, and drank until water dribbled onto the mattress beneath him.

"You shouldn't drink too much on the first go. Trust a desert native on that," Zahenna said, stepping into the doorway so that Sithon could see her painted by the soft orb light.

Sithon put the bowl down, feeling like he was losing a friend. He reached over and placed it back on the floor, where some of it sloshed onto the stone.

Zahenna came to the bed and stood over him, tall and straight and unyielding. She looked down her nose at him a little as she spoke.

"You need to answer what I am about to ask you truthfully. Can you do that?"

Sithon wiped his mouth.

"I'm not a liar. But if you want to know the truth so badly, why not just have your mother pull it out of me?"

"Because my mother can *never* know. You know what I'm talking about."

Sithon did know what she was talking about. The ordeal at the prison had blocked out their recent history for a time, but now he remembered all too well the supple rounds of her breasts as he squeezed them and the release he had felt as she rode him—and then the horrible realization that he had just done all those things with *her*, and what's more he had *liked* it. Worse had been the violated look on Zahenna's face, as though he'd just hurt her.

"Did you mean to do it?" she asked, "Did you know you were taking advantage of me?"

Sithon took a deep breath, then released it. He searched for the right way to describe what had happened, remembering the last time he had seen her on a Smart Blood high, ripping out guards' throats and mauling everyone in her path.

"I was Smart Blood raging too, and all the things that happened out there on the *Death's End*, they made me a little crazier than normal. Please believe me. If I hadn't had a Smart Blood rush, things would have turned out much differently."

Zahenna stood there for a moment, still as a post in the ground. Then she fidgeted, making pretence of smoothing her loincloth down at the edges and then rubbing the side of her face. She drew her hand back suddenly when she met the bare skin of her scar tissue.

"The fur should grow back soon," she said weakly.

Sithon said nothing, watching her stand there, for

once uncomfortable as the center of attention. She swayed back and forth, and folded her hands in front of her.

"I don't know how to discuss this with anybody, Sithon. I want to blame you so badly, but I know..."

She paused for a long time. Sithon waited.

"I remember wanting it, too. Not you, just... the act."

Sithon moved over on the bed. Zahenna sat down by him, her head in her hands. For a moment, he could hear her panting loudly, then she whined. The stress pheromone drifted off of her, growing stronger with passing time.

"Tell me how to deal with this Talent. It's robbing me of my common sense, taking away my control, my virginity, my life. I could have a pup growing inside me. What will I tell my mother then? What possible future could it have, the pup of a Princess of Rakaria and an exiled, well, whatever you are. I can't really call you a Flood, not in earnest."

Sithon tilted his head.

"I thought you were going to kill the pup if it grew."

Zahenna took a deep breath, then let it out in a painful sigh.

"I'm sorry I said that," she croaked.

Sithon did not touch her then... no, he would still fear for his hand. He did wag his tail, once, so that it thumped on the mattress, as a sign of good faith.

"I know what it's like to grow up without a father. Whatever happens to you, I'll be there."

Zahenna looked up at the ceiling.

"That's one of the things that I fear the most."

Sithon wanted to tell her to get out then, but realized that he was actually the one who should leave, if anybody. This was her space, and she could come and go in it at her leisure. But hadn't he been good to her? Hadn't he saved her life and offered to help raise any potential offspring? He turned the other way on the bed and scowled, crossing his arms.

"You really don't understand, do you?" she said, "I used to know what was right. I had been taught it since birth, it was simple and it was easy. Floods were the enemy, mother was always just, and traitors deserved to be punished with stasis or death. No exceptions. Ever since you've come along, it's like that sense I had, of what was truly right, doesn't work anymore. And yet it still nags at me: "Remember me! It's not too late to save yourself!" I know what my heart is telling me to do, so why does it have to war with that sense of rightness? You've split me in two, Sithon, put me at a crossroads and now, I'm lost."

Sitting there, on the bed, her back bent and her face contracted with inner turmoil, Sithon felt a sudden kinship with Zahenna. He had thought her about as different from him as anyone could be, a legitimate heiress to the Elder family, strong and proud to the point of self-destruction.

Sithon realized then that her family situation, her decisions caused her just as much pain as his. Here she was, spilling out her feelings to him of all Geedar, because she could never reveal them to her own mother. Really, traitors and outcasts would probably be the only ones who could fully understand something like this, a web of problems trapping Zahenna, who was probably one step away from disownment as well.

Not for the pup, no. Females had pups young all the time, even among the nobility. Pups were not considered a dishonour, but a blessing and a sacred responsibility. A young mother who raised her pups well would be as welcome in any home as the Queen herself. No, it was the identity of the pup that would exile Zahenna from her mother's presence. The Floods had been exiled, as Sithon knew all too well, with the intention of removing the family from the gene pool. Toraus was distant kin to the Elders. They all were in the noble houses, and so killing him would break pack law. Pack could not knowingly bite pack. And so, they had left them where they would waste away from lack of nutrition, Toraus, Uncle Mardon, and Sithon's innocent mother and grandmother. Without repeal of the banishment, any pup of Sithon's would be considered Outborn in Zahenna's culture at best, a fugitive at worst. He hoped then, fervently, that Zahenna would not have to bear such a horrible blow after having already suffered so much for her mother's cause.

She said, "I'll know in a few days if I'm pregnant. It doesn't take long."

"I want to know," Sithon said firmly.

Zahenna nodded. She took another deep breath, let out another sigh, and lifted herself from the bed.

As she walked to the door, Sithon noticed that her swagger reappeared, her back and tail straightened. On the outside, at least, she was a warrior again.

Sithon caught himself admiring the curve of her rump, the flow of her tail and the way that the little tuft at the tip bounced when she walked. Sithon kind of liked that tail, odd though it was. With her red fur in full blaze, it looked like a branch on fire at the tip. He squashed the urge to consider what it might be like to take her from behind then, biting his tongue to make the thought fade.

"Mother's having a meeting later today with me, Djarro and Tyrius. Hopefully you'll be there too. It sounds important," she called to him, leaning on the doorframe.

When Sithon nodded to her, Zahenna slipped out into the hall and disappeared in the opposite direction from where the sick-finders had gone. In her absence, he remembered her smell, and where she had sat on the bed, and wished he had touched her. No, wished he had touched her all over. He caught himself in the middle of this thought, stood up out of bed and dumped the rest of the water in the drinking bowl over his head. As he shook out his fur, he thought:

Yeah, and you keep running water over yourself until the thoughts are gone. What's wrong with you? It's not Smart Blood this time, that's for sure. Look at what you've already done to her... if you really care, you'll keep your distance. That's the only way she'll ever be happy.

And yet, some part of him still wasn't so sure of

that.

Leethia's New Commission

Zahenna came back personally to lead Sithon to the place where Leethia, Djarro and Tyrius waited, a large, squarish chamber with rounded corners and barred windows that let in real sunlight and a hint of fresh air. Before seating himself on the floor, Sithon stuck his nose through the wide diamond-shaped grating and smelled the world beyond. More of that stale rock scent reached his nose, the scent of age and mildew, but also ship fuel, food and other Geedar. A small transport whizzed by, filling the room with echoes for a moment before disappearing around a crook in the canyon.

They were definitely in Marrow Canyon, then. Sithon had not had a chance to confirm their location yet, only his guesses. The rock outside was deep, light-eating purple, indeed like the marrow from the inside of a bone. Even at noonday, it folded into crags and wrinkles that held within them deep, rich darkness. If the Queen were to fly whole ships within this canyon, down far enough below the rim, no one would see. It was too wide to jump, but certainly not wide enough to let Wardan's satellite ships in for a closer look. Sithon smelled his fill and then took his place between Djarro and Tyrius in a semicircle on the floor.

Leethia loomed over Sithon, wearing an open silver robe that met in the middle to cover her breasts, and a white loincloth. She was seated on the only stool in the room, higher even than Djarro. Sithon, being directly in front of her, became her central focus.

"Geedar have always adhered to the safety of the pack," she began, "whether that pack be a family or an adopted group of fast friends. Wardan's technology destroys the pack and replaces it with a cold, artificial machine image. Why should we fly ships with our minds when our hands will do just as well? Why should we stare at another Geedar on a screen when they may just as easily be summoned to sit right beside us? Why should we communicate with one another with painful implants when we have always had the hunt-speak to communicate silently? Technology is a tool. Some tools build, and some tools break. We *only* want to build."

Sithon nodded as Leethia went along. He felt as though he had lived her words, learned the truth of them through his own experience. Leethia caught him nodding and frowned, tilting her head and raising one, haughty brow.

"What is it that you would build here, Flood? Answer me well."

Sithon checked Zahenna's body language. She stared at him, eyes wide, urging as quick an answer as possible with the forward set of her shoulders. Quickly he scanned his mind... *build? Build? What would I make for myself? Not what Vaedra made, in fact, the opposite. Yes, that's it.*

"Queen Leethia, all I want to make is a family with my father, and if I could really have anything, with my mother, too, whatever has happened to her. But I would have to get her away from the *Death's End*, and that is, in all honesty, impossible. And... I wish to beg your pardon, not for my family (they knew what they did) but for myself as a member of that family. Toraus was nearly as cruel to my mother and I as he was to your pack mates, all those years ago, and for that I vowed to be as different from him as anyone could possibly be."

Leethia still hung over him, silent and grave. She thumped her tail once against the side of the stool, which made Sithon wonder whether she was expressing displeasure, deep thought, or irritation. Certainly her expression forbade affection.

When the silence grew too anxious, Sithon said, "Search my mind, if you want to. You'll find it all there."

Leethia crossed one leg over the other, and sighed like someone who had seen far more things in life than they had ever intended to. Outside, another transport whirred by, and it stirred her short mane just a little.

She waited for the echoes of the passing vehicle to subside before saying, "I already explored these issues at length in your mind, while you looked out the window. What disturbs me about you, Sithon, is that you *are* telling the truth. I had not expected it from a Flood, and I can tell you that no one else in my service will, either. Only they do not possess my Talent for ascertaining the truth of things."

Djarro leaned over, as if to protect Sithon from the blue-white tail-thin female on the rather rickety stool.

"He can change his name. My name's as good as any." He said.

"Ah, but identities have a way of slipping out, Agent Baero. And while I may know the truth about Sithon, his identity is still dangerous to me. Even his safe passage here would be enough to alienate some of my closest advisors. You must leave Marrow Canyon by the morning, and take Agent Tyrius with you."

Sithon began to protest, but Leethia cut him off before he could do more than open his mouth.

She held up a finger.

"But, I find that despite the danger inherent in your identity, we may have interests that coincide, for this one time. I can provide you with your wish, Sithon, if only you will undertake a task for me. As Zahenna tells it, you have specialist knowledge of the workings of the *Death's End*. After our forces struck last week, the ship was disabled and stranded in the desert, where it still is, although we hear that it is approaching full repair within the next few days. You want your mother back... and I want that ship left without a controller long enough that my gathered forces can destroy it without complications. We can deal with the satellite ships—it's her that we need gone."

Sithon went cold all over. He leaned over and

placed a hand on the floor, pressing his claws against the stone.

"You want me to try and disconnect her? She could die." He said, almost to himself.

Queen Leethia stayed straight and tall on the stool, and Sithon started to realize where Zahenna got all that cold poise from.

"She most certainly will die if we launch the assault without your help. Think about what I'm offering here, Sithon—one last chance to be with your mother. If you come out of it alive, I'll also provide you and your father with transport back to Ferion and the guarantee that no agent of my government will interfere with you ever again... that is, unless we catch you on Rakarian soil."

Djarro reached around Sithon with one arm, leaning near him and speaking out of the side of his mouth, as if Leethia couldn't hear him.

"Don't do it, pup. Even with Tyrius along, it's a suicide mission, and *Her Royal Majesty* over there knows it. She wants to be rid of us. Well, let her be rid of us another way. We'll catch a freighter out of here and work our way back to Ferion."

"Oh yes, that will work well," Leethia snapped, "Find, by some miraculous chance, a neutral freighter crew and whisk yourself offworld with Wardan's agents tagging along behind, and make no mistake, I won't be long after him. There's also the matter of that thing in Sithon's head. Who do you expect to remove it so that he can remain conscious for more than ten seconds at a time? The native wildlife? I hardly think so. If he agrees to my terms, he will be taken to Lower Dune with Zahenna to the cut-maker to have the job done properly. There is another signal blocker there, protecting the town, who can keep him safe in the meantime."

Leethia raised her nose, crossed her arms and curled one lip, as if disgusted by Djarro's sheer lack of mental logic. Sithon thought some more, trying to listen to her words rather than her attitude and evaluate the best course of action. That tender, swollen feeling in his head hadn't gone away since he had been struck by the end of the transmissions. He could only imagine what it might feel like once they got out of orbit, or worse, around strange machinery and communications equipment. It felt like it had heated up back there during the bombardment of signals... what would prevent it from burning a hole right through his head, frying the most important parts of his brain? He had never even seen a cut-maker, the Talented ones who could supposedly remove things from bodies, cut them open while they were still alive and play with what was inside... he supposed it was something like the more gruesome parts of Wardan's work, only a lot more helpful to the recipient. At any rate, he had never met one during his time either on Ferion or Rakaria, and he assumed that if Wardan could have found one, or more, they would immediately have been forced into his employ. No, only a Queen probably had cut-makers at her disposal in these times of war, and the only way for Sithon to exist independently of Wardan was to have the jack taken out.

Sithon shook his head.

He said, "No, father, she's right. I have to have the jack taken out. I have to go."

Djarro stood up. His figure cast a wide shadow on Queen Leethia.

"Please, for mercy's sake show the pup some pity. Have you any idea what he's already been through? And you're a mother," he said the last word with utmost contempt.

Leethia narrowed her eyes at the sudden darkness.

"I am a mother. I take care of my own. The only question you need to answer is whether or not you will take care of yours."

Djarro stuck out his chin, the muscles in his neck flexing.

"There was never a question in my mind," he growled. Leethia folded her hands on her lap and leaned around Djarro to address Tyrius. Djarro went over to one of the windows and gazed moodily out until the meeting was done.

"Then there is no more to be said on the matter. And you, Agent Tyrius?"

Tyrius leaned back, and scratched his nose scales, and yawned. If the yawn was artifice, Sithon found it impressively well-practised.

"What's in it for me?"

"I don't kill you on the spot."

"Try it."

"Try *me*. If I'm not afraid of the brute over there

what chance do you have?"

Tyrius made eye contact with Leethia for several seconds, a practised lazy gaze to her serious raised eyebrows, and then broke gaze, signalling acquiescence.

"Count on me. Not because of the threats, mind you, but because you're so likeable."

Leethia got up from her stool and went toward the hall. As she left, she replied,

"And you're going on this mission because you're not. Now that we have a party, I'll be summoning our second-in-command of the fleet, Sali Sky to come and fill you in on the plan, as far as we have thought it through."

When Leethia's footsteps had faded off down the hall, and her smell faded from the room. Tyrius sprang up from his place. Sithon stood up to face him.

"Tyrius, what are you..."

Tyrius wrenched two large spines from his back and shoved his way past Sithon. He backed toward the door, brandishing them with one over his shoulder, like a spear, and one facing upward, like a knife. He panted.

"You'll get one apology from me, and one only. It's not the mission, puppies, it's the company. Sithon, remember JASIMOTH. It's all you need."

With that, he dashed out the door. Sithon heard an outcry from the guards at the door, but soon the screams of one overpowered the commands of the other. Sithon raced out into the hallway, Djarro and Zahenna close behind. To his left, a hallway went a short distance before opening out onto some sort of wooden scaffold attached to the side of the gorge. A guard lay clutching his right leg, which had been pierced through the thigh by one of Tyrius's spines. The other guard crouched down by him, trying to dress the wound.

"Don't you come any closer," the guard yelled, holding up his free hand, which was stained with his fellow's blood.

Two more Geedar came on them from the other way, and Sithon knew one of them immediately by smell. The queen shoved past them with a tall, masculine-looking female in close pursuit. Sithon assumed that this must be Sali, the second of the fleet. Sali's face, although creased with concern and more than a little wear (the fur on top of her nose was blasted nigh off by prevailing winds filled with desert sand) was young, probably only a little older than Zahenna. Sali's first action, once she had properly surveyed the situation, was to yell.

"Let's get after him. He could be going for the docking bay!" She shot off down the hallway, passed where it opened onto the outside of the canyon, and disappeared around the corner.

Leethia grabbed Zahenna's wrist. She pointed at Djarro and Sithon emphatically enough that Djarro moved back to avoid being pierced by her claw.

"Did they do this?"

Zahenna shook her head, her mouth wide open.

"Come on, then," Leethia said as she yanked Zahenna along behind her toward the door.

Djarro and Sithon followed the two females. The guard stayed silent this time, most likely due to the ambiguity of the Queen's orders.

Sithon felt like he swayed on his feet the moment he hit the wooden scaffolding outside. The path along the edge of the canyon snaked away in all directions, up, down, in and out of the rock face, all of the boardwalks held up by single diagonally angled beams spaced too far apart for Sithon's liking. Railing lined most of the paths, but Sithon doubted the efficacy of a single railing at waist height. Trying not to look down, he followed Djarro, listening to the loud creaks and groans from the walkway as Djarro's feet pounded into it.

Djarro and Sithon spotted the Queen and Zahenna hurrying down one of the walkways sloping deeper down into the canyon. They followed, trying to keep up. Normally, even catching up would be simple, but other Geedar were walking along the narrow boardwalks at the same time. Not only did Djarro, huge and unwieldy at the best of times, have to try and squeeze by these individuals before he and Sithon could pass, but they were usually also already off-balance and flabbergasted from being shoved out of the way by both the Queen and the crown princess seconds before.

A young female holding a wide bowl of grain tried to hold her charge closer as Djarro muscled by. Djarro squeezed himself against the wall, but in his haste he still managed to clip the edge of the pup's bowl with his elbow, sending it flying down into the canyon. Sithon looked back momentarily to see her leaning over the railing where the bowl had fallen, ears and tail drooping. He then jarred his toe on an uneven board, which sent him back to thinking about his trajectory rather quickly.

Djarro ground to a halt at a place where the path seemed to cut off and head into nowhere. He held out both arms to keep Sithon behind him.

"It's a staircase here, and they're almost at the bottom. Careful not to trip, 'cause it's a long way down."

Djarro started down a flight of stairs, narrow and slanted in places, that dropped steeply down to a long platform with a cave behind it, far below. Sithon had no choice but to look down now, or lose his footing. The canyon below them stretched down and down, until darkness claimed the walls for obscurity. The stairs shook as Djarro rumbled down them. Sithon clung to the railing, as if the flimsy thing would do any good if a stair cracked underneath him.

Leethia and Zahenna, a blue-white and red blob, respectively, reached the landing at the bottom of the stairs just in time to meet a scattered mob on their way up, in some considerable state of panic from the yips and yowls Sithon picked up on the wind. First one Geedar started running up the stairs, then another behind them, and soon Djarro and Sithon were being shoved out of the way, toward the railings this time. Sithon swayed backward, out over the pit.

Djarro reached back and linked arms with Sithon,

pulling him upright again.

"I'll anchor you, pup. Just keep pressing on, and we'll get there."

"Remind me to thank Tyrius for all of this if we ever catch him." Sithon grunted.

Sithon counted the last ten, then the last two steps one by one as they neared the bottom. The crowd fighting its way up the stairs had thinned quite a bit, but Sithon still longed for the solidity of the rock plateau. He was fairly certain that wood scaffolding was not usually designed with Djarro in mind.

The smell of the others led them toward the large cave, but before they could enter the shadow of the overhang, easily as wide as the great room in Takara Prison, a great roar of engines echoed out through the cave and along the canyon walls. Sand drifted down on them from above, dislodged from a rock shelf somewhere by the rumble that now shook the plateau.

All of a sudden, the roar grew much louder and a great white disc of a ship, smaller than the Pwarnaa but faster and sleeker shot out of the cave mouth toward Sithon and Djarro. Sithon flattened himself on the ground, and he watched as Djarro did the same. The heat of the engines and the wave of wind that succeeded the ship whipped at Sithon's mane and made his clothes flap about him for a second like erratic fabric arms before settling back on his body.

The white ship became a black blot on the noonday sun, then disappeared over the edge of the canyon. Sithon stood up when Djarro did.

"Eh, pup, your reflexes have improved. I woulda had to shove you down at one time," Djarro said jovially, hands on his hips.

All Sithon let out was a little 'heh', incredulous and shocked at the same time.

Djarro can keep that weird sense of humour about danger.

Sali came running out of the cave practically in the ship's air-wake. She stopped at the edge of the platform, barked at where the ship had been, and then howled in frustration.

"Coward! I won't let you get away," Sali hollered at the sky.

Zahenna got to Sali first, and led her away from the edge with one arm around her shoulders. Leethia arrived soon after that. Sithon and Djarro began walking over to join the group. In the meantime, Sithon was close enough to hear their conversation.

Leethia waved her arms up and down.

"He'll get us spotted! Ships are only supposed to leave under cover of nightfall! Sali, call for the snipers! Get them to shoot him down before he can escape to give our position to Wardan!"

Sali spoke in a soft, defeated voice now. "He doesn't work for Wardan, Majesty. He works for my uncle. And he didn't leave to betray us. He left because of me. Let him get shot down by Wardan's ships. He's not worth the effort to us."

Leethia's ears perked up, and her eyebrow raised in her characteristic warning glance.

"You know him?"

"I've been after him for four years. Let's go back inside."

As Sithon reached the group, he could smell the stress rising off each and every one of the females, but Sali's smell above all shone like a beacon to his nose.

I wonder what she's hiding... and why the Queen is letting it pass?

He would know soon enough why Leethia was not in a mood to quibble. The Queen pointed a finger back in the direction of the cave.

"No, Sali. Get back in the cave and prepare the *Permafrost* for launch. We can't hold the trip to Lower Dune back any longer after this incident. Before long, the commanders will hear about this little scene and I'll have enough questions to answer about who I've been bringing into the stronghold. I can't have *them* hanging about as well."

Djarro held out his hands, palms up, and tilted his head.

"You can't mean for us to still complete this mission the way we planned it. Without Tyrius's experience and the extra help he would provide us in a fight, we're doomed."

Leethia bared her teeth.

"I'm through bargaining with you, Agent Baero. If you go now, you might live, whatever you say. If you stay here, there's really no chance for you."

Djarro roared, a sound that echoed in the crags like the deep boom of thunder.

"The Bugbats take you *and* your precious administration. If I were Zahenna, I would stay at Lower

Dune and work as a mate-for-hire rather than deal with you again."

With that, Djarro allowed Sali to lead him away, stomping all the while. Zahenna cast a horrified glance at Sithon.

Mate-for-hire? She mouthed, grimacing.

Zahenna stayed by Sithon, looking behind her every few seconds until Leethia turned around and headed back up the long stairway alone. Then she waited until Sali's attention was turned elsewhere, and mouthed:

I'm coming with you.

She then put both hands on her mouth and rolled her eyes toward Sali.

Sithon nodded. Then, not allowing himself to over-think the motion beforehand, he threw his arms around Zahenna and drew her into a hug.

Flood Waters Rising

The Cut-Maker

The village looked like a pile of burned-out driftwood from the air. Sithon watched it from a distance through one of the wide windscreens at the front of Sali's ship, the *Permafrost*, as it grew from a pile of ash lying under the wide evening sun to a cluster of black tinder piles to its final form, a collection of blocky, dark wood buildings gathered around a single, hard-packed lane. It was that time of day, between the light and the dark, when everything looked more indistinct than usual, tricking Sithon's eyes into distorting distances and sizes.

They would have gotten there within an hour of departure, but Sali's instincts, and later her instruments warned her of approaching enemy ships soon after their departure. Stating her lack of surprise after Tyrius's noisy and sudden noonday departure and muttering under her breath about the Queen's tail-biting stubbornness, Sali steered them beneath the shadow of a nearby butte to wait out the brightest of the afternoon.

Sithon had retired to a small bunk room then, alone. As he flopped on the mattress, a white pad inset into the floor, he remembered another such bunk, from what seemed like a very long time ago indeed. How much he had cared for his mother that first night in the Burrow... enough to brave the limits of Djarro's good nature and the unknown terrors of Wardan's lab. He had loved her enough to risk having his head bitten off by the Mettoa, loved her enough to push Wardan past the point of wanting him dead.

But she had sent him away... told him to never come back. For the first time since the previous night, Sithon let his mind drift, let her words ring in his ears again. He knew that tone. She had meant it. Perhaps she would even be the one to kill them on their return. And yet, another part of him insisted, she had saved them from a certain, excruciating death in Wardan's ambush. Surely that proved that some part of her still loved him and wanted to protect him.

But Djarro... she would still resent Djarro. Sleep crept up on Sithon, but he fought it, anger and resentment tensing his muscles against any oncoming rest. How dare the Queen force him into this position and risk everything he had fought so long to gain? But, deep down he knew. He still remembered every blow Toraus had ever dealt him after three years of being rid of the old mange, and he doubted that he would ever be able to forget them despite his desires to the contrary. How much more must Leethia hate Toraus, who had deprived her of the love of so many family members? Sithon had been close to killing Toraus once. Wouldn't he have taken revenge if it had been offered?

No, no he wouldn't. He never would have gone

through with the thing, bite it, because Vaedra loved Toraus. He realized now that her soul was weak, sick like her body, but the source of the sickness, the claw of Toraus's cruelty jammed through it had also, perversely become the lynchpin on which her identity rested. Laying there, he suddenly understood why she spent all of her time in the Second Skin making Torauses. Without him to order her life, she would simply cease to be.

But it had to be different. She had to be able to come out of it.

I could have changed my name to Baero and fled the planet back at the gorge. We could have made it. It wouldn't have been pleasant, but I've never had that many choices to make that were. But I just couldn't resist the idea that even after all of this, we could reverse some of what Wardan has done.

And yet, he thought of Djarro, how quietly he had come along after the Queen had insulted him, for Sithon's sake. To keep him safe. There on the platform, Djarro had taken yet another blow to protect *him*. And now Zahenna had added herself into the mix, another potential sacrifice to Sithon's single-minded determination to keep Vaedra safe. He had been happy for the help at first, but how much could one more Geedar on such a mission really help, regardless of the strength of her Talent?

After a while Sithon had given up on the cot and headed for the control room. There he had stayed as the ship rose into the air again, and the others chatted behind him. The cycle of thoughts stayed, underlying everything. Now they disembarked at the glorified woodpile the Queen's supporters called Lower Dune, the orange light casting long shadows and making Sithon sway a little on his feet as he walked toward the main street with Sali and the others. The buildings here were built in an odd way that Sithon had never seen before, out of interlocking split logs that stuck out at the corners. The buildings were mostly square, with low porches running around the entire outside of them. In places, roofs had been built on the porches to make sheds or mud rooms. Mud room was a bad expression, though. Sithon didn't think that Lower Dune probably saw much mud, ever. Some of the nicer places (although nice was certainly relative) boasted rusty roofs of metal with channels bent into them for the rain.

They reached the end of the street, and Sithon noticed a number of puppies tousling over a ball of rags in one of the alleys between the buildings, chasing one another and biting at it to try and gain possession. Farther down the street, he could hear someone hammering on a piece of wood.

Other townsfolk reclined on their porches or travelled between houses, paying visits.

"Is this some sort of festival day or something?" Sithon asked Zahenna.

"It's the desert way," she replied, "It's too hot in the day to do much of anything, so they sleep then and do their chores at sundown. Inner Rakarians are practically nocturnal—when they're not confined to dark caves all day, that is."

They continued on in silence until they neared the end of the street. The hammering Sithon had heard earlier grew louder, but when they started to get close to the source, it stopped.

"Young'un!" Called a voice as rickety as the buildings.

Caylus hobbled over to them from the shadow of probably the best-kept building Sithon had seen yet in town (still relative, though) with not one but four panels of metal sheeting coming together to make a peaked roof. A sign propped up by the door declared it to be the "Royal Rakarian Pub and Last-chance Fuel Station, C. and M. Peppercorn, proprietors."

Mejinah leaned out of the door with the good-natured lethargy of someone recovering from a very trying day.

"You and your friends come on in. Our stores are all gone, but we've got beds still," Caylus said.

"Sorry," said Sali, before anyone but her had the chance to answer, "We're headed out to Darius's place."

Caylus placed a knobbly hand on Sithon's arm, keeping him back for a moment. Sithon leaned down to hear him.

"The cut-maker, eh? You try and stay in one piece. We like you better that way."

Sithon replied with a confidence he didn't entirely feel, "Don't worry. Any way I come out is better than how I'm going in."

Sali led them down to the end of the only street in town, past a double row of dusty gardens filled with a scrub-like vegetable Sithon had never seen before.

A female in coarse wraps knelt along one of the rows, uprooting a few of the larger plants, which had bulbous roots like sweet-root.

Behind her, a grouping of three town shacks had been fused together by common roofing and little connecting boardwalks. They formed a semicircle around the garden on the right-hand side of the path. The area in between the garden and the shacks formed a makeshift courtyard with a small round rock garden and an open-backed transport like those the guards used on the *Death's End* parked alongside the leftmost building. Like everything else in Lower Dune, the char-marks stretching along the visible side of the vehicle attested to the fact that it had seen better days.

A question occurred to Sithon just then.

"If this is Lower Dune, where is Upper Dune?"

"It was the first thing Wardan burnt after the capital city," Sali grunted.

Sali put one foot up on the front porch of the middle shack and knocked on the dry slats that made up the door. The door shook in its frame as she did.

When the door swung outward, Sali stepped back off the porch into the courtyard. A young, stout female with red fur-- not orange like Zahenna's, but rich and dark, stepped out onto the porch. She held out her arms to Sali, but both Sali and Zahenna piled into them, reaching around her in a group hug.

"Sydney," Zahenna sighed, "I thought I'd never see you again."

Sithon saw Sydney's face surface from the sea of arms around her. She had an uncommonly short muzzle, wide eyes and a mane that hung around her cheeks in wisps at the front. She closed her eyes, as if from deep satisfaction. When she opened them, Sydney wore a smile on her face. She wagged her tail.

"Come on in, all of you. I'll show you what there is to see."

The females followed Sydney into the shack first, followed by Djarro, who had to turn sideways and duck to angle himself through the door. Sithon came last, and shut the door behind him.

Inside, the walls were all whitewashed, and well-measured cupboards lined the majority of the room. A sling made of long poles and an animal skin hung from the ceiling from straps. Sithon noticed that the floor was cool, and smooth under his feet. He stood on shiny blue tiles.

The only unpleasant part about the room was that they all seemed to be standing shoulder-to-shoulder in it. Sydney jostled her way in between Sali and Zahenna. She tilted her head up to look Djarro in the eye.

"So, which one of you is Djarro and which one is Sithon? The report we got from Marrow Canyon was kind of... brisk."

"Djarro, Sithon," Djarro grunted, pointing with his thumb at both of them in turn.

Sydney opened her mouth and raised her finger for a moment in silence.

"...ah," she said, then, taking one hand of Zahenna's and one of Sali's, "It is really, really good to have you both here again. You wouldn't believe how lonely it is with just *Darius* for company. I should probably take you to him now, though. He's seen you come in."

The whitewashed room had three doors—the one Sithon had entered through, and one on either side of him, which Sithon assumed led to the boardwalks between the shacks. Sydney shouldered the right-hand door open when it stuck in the frame. It jiggled outward, squealing all the way, and slammed into the outer wall.

A sudden burst of sun and a wave of heat greeted them out on the boardwalk. Sand slid between Sithon's paw pads and the dry wood as he walked along behind the rest. He tried running his hand along the rope that was strung along the pathway between roof supports, but the coarse fibre stung his fingers so he kept his hands to himself.

Sydney held the door for them to enter a much darker space than the last shack. Where the cabinet shack had been painted a sterile white, this room was painted flat black, and a gum-like substance had been pressed into the cracks between the half-timbers, Sithon guessed to block out the light. This seemed to be the biggest of the shacks.

Everyone stood inside of it and by Sithon's estimation, the room could probably hold another party of identical description comfortably.

Blue light globes drifted about the ceiling like translucent eggs floating on water, meandering with the air currents because the flat roof left them nowhere to gather. In the gloomy half-light Sithon could see two bunks stacked on the wall, both with their blankets left rumpled.

Well, I guess that means Sydney just works here, unless they have some very strange customs in these parts.

Control panels covered the rest of the walls, stretching from the head of the bunks at the back of the room all the way to the doorframe. Tucked into the left hand wall, in the furthest corner of the room was a large heap of pillows made of coarse and beaten material. Sithon heard the sound of air sucking into a vent, and the fur on his tail pulled. He yanked himself away from the scent identifier, now extended out from its socket in the nearest panel on a padded arm.

"Hey, are you joking me? This is Wardan's technology."

"What's going on here?" Djarro boomed, "Who do you work for?"

Sydney held her hands out, palms outward.

"Please, don't be frightened. We're on the Queen's side, I swear." She then looked up at the ceiling, speaking through her teeth. "Darius... this would be a good time to help me out..."

A laugh came from the pile of pillows, squeaky and slurred, like the subject was in a dream state. A small, thin figure, definitely Geedari but with more the proportions of an older pup than a full-grown adult heaved itself up from the pillows, swayed once, then reached for the back of its neck. A wet click, and then Sithon saw a wire and Second Skin jack fall to the ground. Sithon raised his hackles to Sydney, getting within a tail's width of her face.

"He's a Second Skin user! I'm telling you right now, you'd better be the cut maker because I'd cut my tail off before I'd have Wardan's machines used on me again."

An exasperated little noise issued from the short figure in the corner. He (Sithon assumed it was a he, because its voice was mature despite its stature) rubbed his forehead as if trying to find a way to communicate in a lower language. The little Geedar turned around to face them, and Sithon saw that he (definitely a he now) had a much older face than his small body would normally indicate.

"I can see why you're upset, but tell me this: how do you expect to remove something as complex as a brain implant without the original equipment used to put it in?"

His voice sounded adolescent, caught between registers. Sithon crossed his arms.

"I'd have thought you would have found the way by now, if you're any sort of a scientist."

"Ha," said the little Geedar, "Wardan's the only Geedar *ever* to go by that name. He invented it. He also invented the systems that control us. I just use them. The difference is, I'm not using the systems to kill Geedar. I'm trying to use Wardan's tech to save them."

Sithon narrowed his eyes, saying, "And how did you learn to use it in the first place?"

The little one shrugged. Sithon noticed that he had tufty, gold and fawn fur that went in every direction. When he smiled, he actually had quite a winning set of jagged teeth.

"Stealing" he said, and laughed.

Sithon laughed too, in spite of himself, and he saw Djarro grinning beside him. Zahenna, Sali and Sydney seemed accustomed to this wit. They merely smiled politely. The little Geedar clambered over his pillow pile and approached Sithon. He held out a hand before he even reached the middle of the room. Sithon took the hand without much difficulty, but he had to lean down to sniff necks.

"I'm Darius," the little Geedar said when he pulled back, "Pleased to meet you. Now if you don't mind, could you crouch so I can have a look at your head?"

Sithon looked at Djarro for reassurance, still unsure of this miniature Geedar who seemed a little too familiar with Wardan, even if his story did make sense. Djarro motioned for Sithon to do as he was asked, and so Sithon crouched, letting Darius's bony little fingers trace their way through the fur behind his ear and under his mane.

"I'm Sithon, by the way," he supplied.

Darius stopped touching his scalp.

"I know who you are. I have eyes set up around the compound. Well, it looks like we're lucky... it's in the usual spot, and I can deal with it. This is never an easy cut, though. We've had some Geedar wake up without memories, or worse, with memories of things that never happened. Some of them see things that aren't there."

"There are lots of memories I'd be glad to lose," Sithon said.

"It's never those ones."

Sithon stood up. He remained silent, even though he could think of at least five possible questions just then. Darius walked over to Sali next. He took her hand, at which Sali tensed up but stayed still. Her expression betrayed a little embarrassment.

"Sali my dear, would you mind taking Djarro over to the Royal Rakarian? I hear they've nearly got the mess cleaned up from the raid, and they'll have food and clean beds for you. I need some time alone with the patients to discuss the treatment."

Sali said, "Are you cutting today?" Sithon noticed that she always seemed to use as few words a possible. He wondered if she ever really had conversations, the way she cut Geedar off. Her mane was short and brush-like except at the front, and her face was made up of almost as many right angles as Djarro's, although the features were smaller and more female.

"That's up to the patients, but if possible, yes, I want to act today," Darius said.

Sali nodded, and placed her arm around Djarro's.

Djarro allowed himself to be led out the door, but not before saying, "Use your best judgement, son. I'll be waiting across the way if you need me."

The door snapped shut behind them, and Djarro's heavy footsteps creaked off down the boardwalk. Sithon's attention turned back to the room, where he and Zahenna now faced Sydney and Darius, who stood side-by-side.

"The Sick Finders sent me reports on the location of your parasite, Zahenna," Darius said, "I'll have to go by their directions because I really have no way, yet, of seeing it for myself until I make a cut. Your operation is actually more complicated than his. I have to kill the parasite once I've opened up your body cavity because once it feels threatened, it will try to burrow deeper in. Luckily, we have Sydney's Talent to help out with that."

Zahenna grinned. Sithon wondered how she could grin in such a circumstance, but then again, she had grinned in worse.

"Yes," Zahenna said, "One touch in the right place and it ought to curl right up and expire."

Sithon tilted his head at Zahenna and the others.

Sydney held out her hand toward him, and in the gloom the tips of her fingers glowed red like embers.

She said, "I'd demonstrate what I can really do, but we have to be so careful around all this dried wood. I accidentally burned down a shed and the townsfolk were furious."

Darius leaned toward Sithon a little, saying, "Don't let her fool you. She's very, very useful around here. Without her, I'd need gadgets to do everything... sterilize the tools, stop up cuts, weld pieces together on the transport... but she can do it all with a pinch of her fingers!"

Sydney laughed a little.

"Well, I'll keep my fingers to myself for now."

Sithon did not laugh with them. The urge to laugh had eluded him for a while now.

"Uh-huh," he said, "And what's your power, Darius old friend? Just tech?"

Darius replied, "Well, in a way my Talent does control the tech, yes. You see, some Geedar have Talents that allow them to keep our ships, lights and other appliances going by producing and storing their energy. I, on the other hand, manipulate that energy. I can reverse or direct its flow, and drain it out of someone's body entirely. If you allow me to make the cut on you, I will use my Talent to drain your energy down to a low level so that you remain asleep and as pain-free as possible while I work."

Sithon looked Darius up and down one more time. The smell coming off of him smelled calm, eager to please, but not too much. In other words, he smelled fairly honest. Sithon admitted to himself that he liked Darius's smile, and doubted that any friend of Zahenna's would willingly work for an enemy agent. Besides, the Queen would have noticed if the patients she had sent to Darius had gone missing even once. The tech still bothered him, but Darius's earlier argument made sense. He didn't remember much about the operation that gave him the head jack, because Wardan had put tranquilizers into his food to get him there, but he did vaguely remember the outline of some of the instruments... they had looked like many-legged metal bugs with clamps for heads and giant, detached thoraxes that compressed and then inflated suddenly. He had also seen a lot of his own blood that day, being carefully siphoned off by a clear tube. Whatever was in his head, it would need Wardan's tools to come out again.

Sithon moved to the door. Sydney started to try and convince him to come back, but when he stopped, so did she. She dropped her hands to her sides again.

"Show me the where you make the cuts," Sithon said, swinging the door open.

Darius took the opportunity on the way over to explain more about the operations, and Sithon listened, evaluating every claim as best he could. Darius said that Sithon and Zahenna would be laid out together, unconscious, and Darius would then perform the cuts one by one. Darius was very interested in the recovery times of Smart Blood carriers, but his interest didn't seem self-serving like Wardan's. He seemed genuinely concerned with how to treat patients better. After the operation, Darius would board them both at the Royal Rakarian with visits three times a day until they recovered, which he estimated would take about three days.

Darius had to open a special scent-lock on the cut-room door. This door, heavier than the others, puffed open with the breaking of a seal to keep the desert air out. Inside, the room looked almost identical to Wardan's labs back at the Burrow, complete with a stasis tank in the corner, cupboards and counters lining the walls and those bright overhead lights that swung down on cords. The counters were littered with strange metal instruments, but nowhere were the jars of dead body parts floating in that smelly liquid. Instead, Darius had shelves full of carved models of body parts in wood, stone and even glastik, and unfurled scrolls depicting different species, their parts and functions all labelled. In the center of the room stood two of Wardan's operating slabs, the carapaces of their pedestals rough and bent at the bottom from being salvaged at some point or other. The restraint straps had been ripped away, with only their beaten leather stumps remaining to attest to their prior existence.

Sithon went to one of the counters and picked up an instrument, turning it around in his hands. Darius let him do it.

"What is this for?" he asked, never taking his eyes off of the thing he held.

"Sithon..." Zahenna protested, as though Sithon had just peed in someone's garden.

But Darius answered him. Sithon asked about the body parts on some of the shelves, and Darius told him about those, too. Sydney and Zahenna sat on one of the cut-making slabs as Sithon and Darius rounded the room, discussing and exchanging information.

Finally, Sithon was satisfied. Wardan never would have allowed him to even touch one instrument, let alone answer all of his questions. Darius smiled at Sithon the entire time, as though imparting this knowledge was a pleasure.

"Thank you, Darius. I've never been told any of this, even though this equipment was probably used on me many times," he said.

Darius slapped him on the lower back.

"Hey, I'm just glad someone asks. I never get to talk to anyone who's interested in this stuff... besides you, Sydney my dear." He said, for a quick save as Sydney prepared a glare for him.

Sithon left Darius then, and went over to sit on

the other slab, to the left of Zahenna and Sydney.

"I'll have the operation today," Sithon said.

Zahenna responded with, "We both will."

Darius centered them on the slabs, and placed folded-up sheets beneath their heads and feet. Sithon looked at the ceiling as he readied his instruments, and endured patiently as Sydney used a sharp metal edge to shave behind his left ear and scrubbed his entire head, mane and all, with a bitter smelling solution soaked into a rag. She discarded that rag after using it on him, and picked up another from a stack beneath the slab. Sydney dipped it in a jar full of the bitter stuff and started on Zahenna's stomach.

Darius stood between them and closed his eyes.

"Sithon, Zahenna, I want you to take deep breaths and think of something pleasant as I put you to sleep. It will make the transition much easier when you wake up. Just let the feeling of sleepiness take you, and trust me. You'll both wake up healthier than ever."

Sithon noticed a sudden motion over to his left. Zahenna had stretched her hand out to him, her arm tense and stiff as the half-timbers that held the room together. For once, with her head turned to him, he could see fear straining her normally graceful face. Sithon reached his own hand out and took hers, their arms linked between the slabs in a shallow u. As he felt his breathing deepen, and his eyes close to nothing but exhaustion and blackness, he still felt her hand until the very end when their fingers slipped away from each other, too slack to hold on any more. After that, so quick was his slip into the realm of numbness and rest that he never felt his hand hitting the side of the table after it fell from hers.

Burning Ground

On the first day, Sithon woke up blind. Everything around him sounded like it was underwater, and far away. Soon the sun began to peep through the white haze over his eyes, and smells ran in and out of his nose like those pups he had seen the night before playing in the alley: must and linens and the desert breeze which he assumed was responsible for the periodic clunking from above that filled his stuffy ears with reverberations that stabbed his brain. He also smelled his father, and sometimes heard a deep rough voice that could only be Djarro's, but as for figuring out the words, Sithon was still lost in a long and frustrating headache.

Morning turned to evening, and Sithon began to see rough shapes around him. He made out the white square beneath him that must be his bed, and another similar bed beside him with an orange someone lying in it that almost had to be Zahenna. Behind them, light poured through a small window near the ceiling. Near when night had settled in, and only the moon lit the room, Djarro crept in one last time. Sithon rested on his pillow and watched Djarro settle down on his knees. The floor vibrated as Djarro adjusted his position. Sithon could see the stripes on Djarro's back now, and the shadows over his eyes, as though he were painted, but only partially.

"Oh, Sithon, I wish you could hear me. That little orange feller says the cut was successful, but you heard 'im about what could happen afterwards... If Wardan cost you your mind, I'll tear his throat out myself, even if I have to go alone."

Sithon tested a finger, and realized that it still worked. He had forgotten the risk of losing his memory at all. Well, it hadn't happened, obviously. He moved his hand over slightly on the bed spread, feeling sensory input there for the first time that day in the sheet's coolness and texture, and put his fingers over Djarro's.

He succeeded in speaking, too, but what must have been the hoarsest of whispers to Djarro clanged in his ears like a fire alarm.

"I remember you," he said.

Djarro held Sithon's limp hand up to his cheek and rubbed against it. It was then, with his ears feeling like they had seas rushing about in them, that Sithon first heard his father cry.

The next day, Sithon awoke to Zahenna's voice. Much of the ocean had drained from his ears and remained on the pillow, a sticky yellow-orange splat. Mejinah came and took the pillow away, and brought another. He thanked her and lay back down.

He and Zahenna had been laid up in a large addition to the back of the Royal Rakarian, with the one small window he had seen and four beds, two on each side of the room. It was separated from the main building by a short set of steps leading into the main room, which served as a dining hall, tavern, and in this case a bed on the floor for all of the other travellers. Other than the grey roof, the rounded bumps of half-timber that made up the walls, and Zahenna, there wasn't much going on in the room in terms of things to look at.

Sydney sat on the other side of Zahenna's bed from Sithon, and it seemed that they had been up and talking for some time. Zahenna had to be propped upright, and Sithon saw a deep, angry slash across her exposed belly stitched up with a thin leather thong. He felt behind his ear for the same stitching, and a bolt of pain raced across his entire head, eye sockets and all. The burning pain, the feeling of having a coal lodged in his head was gone, though, and only a normal, if severe, headache remained.

He listened to Zahenna and Sydney's conversation without really listening to it—not that he couldn't hear this time, but it was more that they discussed Geedar and places that he had never been to, activities that he had never even heard of before, let alone done. They reminisced about the ice fields and rock desert to the North (apparently Sali's home country, because she strode up from downstairs when they mentioned it and stayed until the topic had long passed) and some sort of sport involving grabbing a bone and jumping through hoops with it in your mouth which they had clearly played many times when the Queen had still been in power. It became clear to him that Zahenna and Sydney had spent years and years together before this. As they started in on a particularly stirring account of a diplomatic trip to someplace south of the desert called 'Little Woods', Sithon finally interrupted them.

"Okay," he said, addressing Zahenna, "Was she your servant before?"

Zahenna flattened her ears and opened her mouth, annoyed. Sydney answered, polite as usual.

"No, Sithon, I'm royal, too. So is Sali, although you might not believe it of her."

At this Sali yelled something very rude from the other room involving tails and where to stick them. Sydney blinked twice, looking a little shocked, then continued.

"Sali's family and mine are steward rulers under Queen Leethia, and our families have ruled everything before, in their turn. We were here in Inner Rakaria when Wardan struck, and our families went into hiding. Unable to reach them, we were forced to stay here. Sali went into hiding by... well, she didn't really go into hiding, rather she just became a bounty hunter and killed everyone who came after her, but I chose to hide here, with Darius, where I could do some good for the sick and wounded."

Sithon let out a little 'whuff' of surprise, then said, "There's princesses everywhere you turn around here! And I thought, in Zahenna's case, the name was ironic!"

After that he lay down and let their conversation flow over him, foreign as it was, because at least he knew why it was foreign now.

As the sun was setting, Darius came to check up on them. After confirming that their recoveries were proceeding as planned, he left with the parting advice that perhaps, now that the day had cooled off and the gritty wind had died down a bit, they should take some fresh air.

And so, with Sydney leading Zahenna and Sali leading Sithon, they both stepped out onto the porch, which Mejinah had newly swept of sand, and settled down on a pair of sling chairs that had been set out for them.

They watched the sun set, neither of them saying anything, but Sithon knew that at least for his part, he was glad of the company. He wondered if she would take his hand again, but she stayed still, hands on her lap, eyes almost closed. Sithon noticed, as he watched the sky and Zahenna, back and forth between them, that Zahenna was the colour of the sunset, that she was beautiful.

After the sun had diminished to a white line on the horizon and the first of the stars began to peek out, Sithon let his mind drift, his eyes close. If he could stay here with her, with Djarro, he would do so. But even in that moment of stillness a part of his mind, even without the implant pulled him back to that black city that blocked out the sun, to the doors that crushed traitors and the ever-present rumble of engines beneath. Vaedra was still there, still alive, even beneath the weight of so much metal and darkness, and he had to go to her as soon as he was well, before the dread ship could roar to life again and undo all that he, Tyrius and Zahenna had done for the citizens of Rakaria.

He went to bed uneasy that night, wandering between fantasies of Zahenna and the impossible life he had envisioned out there on the porch, and nightmares of Vaedra, of them all burning to ashes in the Queen's assault, too late to save her.

Sithon slept in the next morning. He woke up feeling almost fit, except for the occasional dizzy spell that made him wobble on his feet and brought Sydney running with a helpful elbow.

That evening, he insisted on spending sunset on the porch again. Zahenna joined him soon after he settled himself in his chair. Looking into that sunset again, the glow like the light on her mane on a sunny day, he broke the silence.

"You know, it's almost like we're a pack... a pack of Smart Blood carriers. We all understand each other's fits, but we stick together."

Zahenna rolled her head towards him.

"I would have done better not to have understood it," she said, with a rueful grin.

"No, no," Sithon continued, "I know you hate it, but no matter why you understand, you still do. I don't think anyone could understand me better than someone who shares the same Talent. It's like we're... we're..."

Zahenna was on her feet faster than Sithon thought possible, given how lethargic she had seemed a minute before.

"Don't even say it, Sithon. Better yet, don't even think it!" She growled as she slammed the door shut behind her. He heard her heavy footsteps tromping up the stairs to their room.

Sithon rubbed his face, hard, with both hands. He sighed and stayed put, not really wanting to deal with her right away and rather enjoying the soothing thought that the sunset was still the colour of her hair, and he could look at that all he wanted.

"Sounds like yer got more turmoil in yer life than just the war, Young'un."

The voice came from down the side of the house. Sithon peered over the side of the porch.

"Caylus? Where are you?"

Caylus hoisted himself up through the slats on the side of the porch. He arched over backwards, causing a chorus of audible pops from his spine.

"Heh, still got some spring left in me," he said, "I was just out fer my evenin' constertutional and I thought I'd come see yeh."

Sithon waved a hand over the other chair, inviting Caylus to sit down. Caylus hovered his rear over the seat for a moment, tail up, then plopped himself down all at once without bending his knees. Once in the chair, he let his legs gradually bend down so that his feet touched the ground.

"So, how'd you lose the Tothari feller you had with you back at Takara? I thought he'd be here for sure." Caylus asked after studying the sunset for a bit.

"He took off at Marrow Canyon because of some unfinished business with Sali. It was pretty spectacular, too... he managed to steal one of the Queen's ships."

"Heh heh! I think that one might be a Kattari-Rah. Thought so when I saw him back at Takara. Got more horns on 'im than a reggular Tothari, that's for sure." Caylus said, leaning over to Sithon in a conspiratory pose.

"How many horns do regular Tothari have?"

"Oh, I see 'em when they wander in here sometimes, at the southernmost o' their territory, and they usually have a few on the shoulders, the nose, the arms, maybe... but that Tyrius, he was covered. Rah for sure, he is!"

A group of pups chased one another down the street, hopping over each other whenever they met. An older female called out to them not to go past the town limits. Sithon said, "What is that? Is he some sort of outcast?"

"The best sort of outcast there is," Caylus answered, "They train 'em up, one for every clan, with everything the Tothari have... wisdom, fightin' skill, healin', then they send 'em out into the world to work for who'll have 'em. When they grow too old to continue, they're honour bound to return to the tribe and bring their treasure with 'em. Not all of 'em return, but the ones that do bring wondrous things home with 'em. Queen's mercy on yeh if yeh run into one during his time at fightin', though... they only serve themselves and the tribe."

Sithon said, "He said something to me, before he left. I couldn't quite make it out. He only said it once.

Sounded like... Jasimoth? Have you ever met anybody by that name? I think they might be important."

Caylus's eyes glittered in the waning light of dusk. He grabbed Sithon's wrist, and came toward him.

"Oh, Young'un," he said, drawing out the words, "Sounds like you've got a nasty choice to make. It's not a name... it stands for the words of an old Tothari proverb."

"Yeah, he was pretty fond of those," Sithon said, rolling his eyes.

"No, no! Listen: J-A-S-I-M-O-T-H... Just Actions Seldom Initiate the Magic Of Tothari Healers. They use it to mean that healing and peace should be the business of this life, not left to the afterlife. A Geedar who drowns in the ocean to fetch a female's wrap-top is not a hero, but a fool who wasted his life on a well meaning vision taken too far. The 'Rah must've seen that yer on a path to destruction, young 'un. Ye'd best leave off it before yeh lose too much to count."

Sithon stood up.

"No, he would know why I can't turn back. It must be a password... sounds like something Wardan would use. I'm going to get some rest and think about it a little longer."

Actually, I'm going to go inside and try to forget this ever happened. Trust Tyrius not to know when a thing is impossible. I can't believe he didn't give me anything to use against Wardan!

He would have gone on fuming over Tyrius's betrayal for most of the night, had he not heard the screams from down the road, followed by an explosive burst of heat and orange light.

"Fire," Caylus crowed, leaping out of his chair and throwing up his arms, "Everybody out o' th'building before it spreads!"

Djarro and Mejinah piled out first, as they had been playing a game at a table near the door. Sali was next: she had been standing guard on the bedroom.

When those three had come out, they all went down the steps and looked down the only street in town to see a spire of flame engulfing a shack. Townsfolk fled the scene, grabbing their pups up into their arms on the way.

"Oh no... where's Sydney? Has she had another accident?" Caylus called out.

Zahenna came out of the pub, Sydney by her side. They stepped down onto the street with everyone else, Sydney gazing at the roaring flames with her mouth wide open.

"I've been inside for an hour," she said, "It couldn't have been me. What in the world..."

Sithon saw a shadow in behind the waves of heat bending the air around the house. Then he saw two shadows. A slinking, furtive one of servile posture and an unkempt monster with drool dripping from his chin. He'd know those figures anywhere, just from the way they moved when they were enjoying their victims' anguish.

"It's them," Sithon said.

"The Kids," Added Zahenna.

"Now what're they doin' here?" Djarro growled.

Sithon saw the other figure he was looking for,

across the street from the blaze. As Geedar fled, Slash snatched a small pup, perhaps a year and a half old, who lagged behind the others, stumbling on his pudgy little legs. Slash held the little male up by the scruff of his neck and grinned a most nasty grin at it. The little pup howled loudly enough at that to be heard down the street. Most of the fleeing folk stopped and pricked up their ears at the sound. Except for the howling, and the roaring of the fire the street was silent.

"Oh no," Caylus said, hobbling forward a few steps as if he wanted to go help the pup himself, "That's the Kiaro's youngest!"

Mejinah placed a firm hand on Caylus's shoulder, holding him back.

It was then that Sithon moved over to Sydney.

"Can you make flame, just from your hands?" He asked her.

She hesitated. "Yes..."

"Then if you want to save the town, you have to get closer and burn the three of them, while they're all together. If you don't, there's a good chance none of us will see tomorrow."

Sydney drew back from him. Her face became creased with disgust.

"I won't use my Talent to kill... I swore it, Sithon. You don't know what it's like to have a fire Talent... *everyone* thinks that you'll destroy them," she said.

Sithon started to raise his voice and had to force himself to stay quiet.

"So, you'll let the town burn because you're scared of what others think?"

Sydney bared her teeth, and action that Sithon would have thought foreign to her earlier in the day.

"Find some other way to fight them and don't you dare blame this on me," she snarled, "You're not being fair."

Sithon pointed down the road. Slash had, by this time, climbed up onto the roof of one of the shacks across the street from the fire. Slash and Hack menaced away any townsfolk brave enough to try to come after him for the pup's sake with swift bites and an energy knife.

"Neither will they, Sydney," Sithon whispered.

Slash swung the puppy out over the edge of the roof, with the little Geedar still hanging by the scruff of his neck. The pup yowled as he swung back and forth. Slash straightened his back and puffed out his chest, as though he were the very definition of civility. Sithon could see in the firelight that Slash's throat made an unnatural concave across the front, and the fur there was missing. When he talked, his voice was no longer the smooth purr of the rich criminal, but an audible struggle with words characterized by a squeak on the upper end and a phlegmy rumble on the lower. Sithon grinned, despite himself.

My work.

"Geedar of Lower Dune," he began, obviously fancying himself an orator, "Tell us where the cut-maker is, or I'll kill this pup in not just one, but a variety of ways. Refuse me once, and I bite off his fingers. Refuse me again, and I'll toss him into the air and use him for target practise with my energy gun. After that, well, he'll be in my large, drooling brother's court... and his jaws."

Sydney grabbed Sithon's arm and squeezed tight. Sithon had been purposefully ignoring her, but he leaned down to hear her anyway. Her whisper was so urgent that it tickled his whiskers.

"Darius is still jacked in!"

It may have been only a whisper, but everyone around heard. Sydney slunk toward the three huts, and beckoned for them to follow. Zahenna went first, followed by Sali. Djarro and Sithon came along behind them. Caylus motioned to Sithon, in the hunt speak. He nodded toward Mejinah and planted his feet.

We'll stay here to keep up appearances.

Sithon nodded. He assumed that if Slash had noticed them in the first place, collected as they were in the shadows at the other end of the street, he would have abandoned the pup right away and come after them. As it was, he hoped Caylus and Mejinah would be enough distraction if Slash *did* happen to look that way.

As they slunk through the shadows in the relative obscurity of the darkened end of the street, Sithon felt his tail start to migrate between his legs. If Slash looked the wrong way now, or caught the movement out of the corner of his eye, Darius would be ripped from the Second Skin without fully exiting the system and be slaughtered, blind and helpless and probably hung from his own eaves as an example. Lower Dune has already been targeted once for rebel activity. He wouldn't be surprised if the Kids planned to burn the whole town this time.

They managed to scuttle behind the shelter of the last building on the main street without being noticeably pursued. Sithon could still hear Slash's voice echoing down the empty street.

"Oh, I don't know if I believe that. You're going to have to try harder. Tell me where the occupants of that ship went that's parked on the edge of town." he said with that mocking tone that made Sithon want to murder him... again. The pup gave another yowl as Slash did something else to frighten it. Sithon hoped that the poor little thing still had all its fingers.

They scampered across the garden patches, scuffing up dirt and a couple of plants as they went, and reached the door. Sydney let them into the large shack on the right, closing the door slowly behind them so it wouldn't creak or slam like the first time Sithon had been there.

"We'll all get on the transport and ride out into the desert," she whispered as she fiddled with things on the panels to unhook Darius, "And when all this is done we can come back and Sali can--"

"Oh, no," Sithon said, cutting her off, "I'm through running from them. So are Djarro and Zahenna."

Darius fluttered his eyes and looked around him. He tilted his head in the inquisitive. Djarro filled him in.

"Wardan's goons. Other end of town. Get on, then."

Darius 'got on then' quite quickly, for someone

who had recently been in a waking dream state. He rubbed his eyes as Sali escorted him out the door. Djarro followed the two of them, alone because no one else would fit through the door with him, then Sithon, Zahenna and Sydney as a group.

Slash came strolling around the building, flanked by Stab and Hack, the puppy still held high over his head. A mob of townsfolk followed him, no doubt for the pup's sake. Stab grabbed the energy gun out of Slash's loincloth, and levelled it at the mob.

"Stay back," she called, "Or Hack gets the puppy now."

The crowd shuffled back until they reached Caylus's front porch, where they peered uneasily into the darkness to try and get a glimpse of the Kiaro's youngest, who by this time hung limp and whimpering from Slash's hand.

Slash's expression turned from a grin of sadistic pleasure to a strained mixture of hate and anxiety when he saw them all, standing together in the moonlight. The other two stopped up short in the middle of the garden when Slash halted them. Hack growled, and glared at Slash with teeth bared. His eyes had been re-fitted to the burned-out trench Sithon's energy knife had left in his face, but they bulged out of it with barely any socket left to support them. Sithon watched him blink and it was more of a whole eyebrow exercise.

Sithon checked on Sydney and Zahenna. Sydney reached over and took Zahenna's hand. Slash remained silent. He tossed the pup sideways into the dust, where it skidded into the shadow of the nearest building. They all lunged toward the party in unison, without hunt-speak commands at all. Hack barked and snarled, drool strands sailing out of the corners of his mouth as they ran.

Before even Djarro could react to the Kids, Zahenna shoved her way to the front of the group.

"Sali, protect the pup!" she yelled.

Zahenna cupped her hands in front of her, palms outward, and flame raced from her red and radiating hands. Heat strong enough to make Sithon feel like he would choke if he didn't pant billowed around them, making him ill with the intensity of it. Djarro and Darius shielded their eyes, but Sali's eyes were already closed. She held up a hand and hummed a steady note over the sudden roar of the flames.

Zahenna's flame stream flowed out from her hands in a rotating column, then exploded out over everything within reach. Sithon's stomach clenched up even more when he looked where the pup had been and saw the nearest house engulfed in a cloud of flame.

Slash, being the first of the Kids, ran into the flame without stopping. He disintegrated as Sithon watched, turning from Geedar to skeleton to outline of ash. Sithon never saw his mocking face again, except in the odd nightmare. Stab tried to flee, but the edge of the flame stream caught her tail and moved upward. Zahenna's flame raged up her tail and over the rest of her body. She fell where she last stepped before catching fire, the flames coalescing over the shape of her, then creeping back into nothing but rising smoke wisps and the outline of a body. Hack was the last. He fell, too, but being larger he had enough time to drag himself closer to them by a miniscule amount, and roar with a sound that echoed over everything. Hack's roar rung in Sithon's ears until Zahenna lowered her hands, fingertips still glowing, and collapsed into Djarro's knees.

Flood Waters Rising

The Lost Cause

Zahenna's glowing fingertips brushed Djarro's leg as she fell. Djarro hissed and jumped back, then rubbed his shin. Almost as soon as she fell, Zahenna caught herself, arms behind her, and struggled to her feet. Sithon could see her body trembling like someone with a fever. She hugged herself.

Before anyone could inquire, she said, "I'm fine, just a little drained. Check the pup."

Sithon's mouth crept open as he surveyed the charred wreckage, not because of the horrific damage that Zahenna had done to the garden, whose root vegetables didn't exist anymore, or the nearest shack and half of the next, which remained only as substantial piles of ash at the foundations, but because the pudgy little pup sat on top of the wreckage, whatever there was that could actually be called wreckage. He sat clinging to a half-moon shaped section of board which had apparently remained untouched during the blast, one paw fisted up in his mouth, eyes opened almost as wide as Hack's had been without sockets.

Not one hair on the fan of his fuzzy little tail had been singed. In fact, he seemed rather... wet. A white, icy stuff had piled itself up on his snout. As Sithon watched, it melted off into the pup's fur and became streams of water. The water struck the burning ground below the pup and hissed back up as steam. Sali hurried over to the pup before he could slide off of the log. She stepped on blackened patches of ground that still smoked, her feet sending up more steam with every step. She held out her arms to the puppy and after a moment of hesitation, he slid into her grasp and allowed himself to be cradled against Sali's shoulder.

"I'll take the pup back to his parents, and put out the slow fire down the way," she said.

Sali walked over the rest of the burnt-out garden, leaving the same steamy footprints behind her. A male and a female, both middle-aged, rushed out from the crowd to greet her once she cleared the ground Zahenna had charred—the Kiaros. The female was only about three quarters of Sali's size, but she nearly knocked Sali over as she rushed to hold her pup again. As she pressed the pup to her cheek, Sithon heard Mrs. Kiaro let out a wail of happiness and pent-up worry.

Sydney had moved up beside Sithon to watch everything after Sali had gone for the pup. Sithon put a hand on her shoulder, and smiled at her.

"Thank you, Sydney."

Sydney did Sithon one better and hugged him. Her arms wrapped tight around his chest, but not too tight. Just right.

"I'm sure I don't know what you're talking about, Sithon," she said, "This is your goodbye hug."

Sydney let go of Sithon and inclined her head toward Zahenna and Djarro. Djarro had already climbed up onto the back of the transport, with Zahenna seated, still shivering and hugging herself on the edge of the platform. He started the hover engines, and the thing coughed loudly once before lifting itself a barely safe distance off the ground.

"Er, I guess these things weren't meant to carry me," Djarro said, "But we ought to still be able to take it a fair ways. Hop on, Sithon."

"Sali won't be gone for long... hurry," Zahenna added, teeth chattering.

Sithon looked at Sydney with his ears perked and his head tilted. Sydney held out both hands and gestured toward the vehicle.

"Someone had to give him the key," Darius said, "*Go.*"

Sithon jogged over to the transport and hopped up onto the back edge, to sit with Zahenna. Their combined weight almost made up for the front lurch Djarro put on the vehicle's floatation. He grabbed the control *stick* (thankfully not a glove like the one Tyrius had operated before, or Djarro's hand never would have fit) and tested the throttle. After one jerky stop-start, Djarro pulled them out of the little courtyard and away from Darius and Sydney. Sithon waved to them and wagged his tail until the vehicle swung across Lower Dune's main street and behind a building on the other side, blocking them from view. Sithon wondered why he had to meet so many friends just as he was most likely about to die, why they couldn't have come earlier and spared him all of this. He wondered if there were friends in the world who could replace family, if he could have surrounded himself with Geedar who would eventually dull the memory of his mother, of the shadow looming behind her in Toraus's guise rather than going on this one, last push to calm his mind.

When they reached the edge of town, Djarro pushed the throttle forward, speeding them out over the dunes. Up one dune, Sithon could see the town from up above, the rusty metal roofs and the smoke rising off the buildings at the end of the street. Up the next dune, the town started to blur together in the dark, become a jagged mound of boards in the distance. Over a few more dunes, and Lower Dune looked to Sithon like just another one. Well, his new friends were far behind him now, and soon they would be in Wardan's territory, far away from anyone who could take them off-world.

Except, not all of their new friends had stayed put at Lower Dune, it seemed. Zahenna leaned against the wall of the transport bed, eyes closed, but Sithon saw a tall figure approaching, faster than their overburdened hover by double. It started out small, only visible on the close side of dunes, a dark stick of a Geedar travelling forward while standing up perfectly straight. It came up on them, faster and faster until Sithon recognized the taut muscles and grey fur.

"Djarro, Sithon said over the roar of the wind, "I think Sali might have come after us, and she's gaining."

"I can't make this thing go any faster," Djarro replied, "We'll just have to let her catch up and deal with her from there."

As Sali sped closer, Sithon could see her bared teeth, the way that her eyes, depite her ice Talent, glared like they would spit fire. She kept her head down, her ears flat, and Sithon knew she didn't just do it to avoid wind resistance. She stood on a small, white disc that carried her along at a terrific speed. When she got close enough to the vehicle that Sithon thought she would crash into the tail end, she swung her arm, the one with the control glove, out to the right and circled around to the front of them, where she stopped.

Djarro wrenched the throttle backward. Sithon thought the stick would rip out of its casement, or the hover would buck backward and toss them out, but it did neither. The hover stopped abruptly, throwing up a cloud of sand which rained down around them. Zahenna knocked her head against the bed wall and straightened up with a curse.

Sithon caught Zahenna's attention and motioned toward the front of the vehicle with his nose. Zahenna stretched out her neck and peered over the front console. Sithon got onto his knees to see over as well. Sali had her non-control hand out, palm facing them. Little flakes of the icy stuff from before drifted down off of her palm. Out here, with the night chill setting in, the flakes managed to touch the ground before disappearing.

"Zahenna," Sali said, "You can come with me willingly, or I can freeze the vehicle."

Zahenna stayed put. She tossed back her mane.

"Don't pull my tail. I think we're about evenly matched at this point. Sithon will die if I don't go."

Sali scoffed, "No, you'll die *with* Sithon. You're the heir to the throne of Rakaria. Show some responsibility."

Zahenna got off the transport then. Sithon had to shift his weight to prevent the thing from lurching to one side. She stood to one side of the vehicle, facing Sally down with her ears back.

"I know my responsibility. He saved my life." she said, baring her teeth.

The volume of the exchange increased.

"You're a princess!"

"No, Sali, none of us are! What's a princess without a kingdom? *Nothing*, that's what. Nothing but what she says and does, the same as anyone else," Zahenna said, putting her hand on the side of the vehicle, "If I don't do this, I won't be anything I can be happy with, much less a princess."

"He's a Flood!"

"He could be the father of my baby!" Zahenna blurted out, then clapped her hands over her nose with a sudden intake of breath.

Sali pushed her head forward, broadcasting incredulity from every muscle.

Djarro's alarm pheromone filled the air.

"How could you..." Djarro hissed.

Sithon cringed.

"You did it too!"

"That ain't a defense, pup."

Back out in front of the vehicle Sali nodded, eyes

narrowed.

"Well, well, fine mess you've gotten yourself into now, eh, Zahenna? I was supposed to be taking care of you! And what am I supposed to tell the Queen?"

"Don't tell her, please," Zahenna said, "You can't."

"I can, and will."

"I thought you wanted me to stay a princess. I won't if mother finds out. I'll end up with him in a shack somewhere on Ferion, if I'm lucky."

Sali crossed her arms, thereby lowering the icy palm that she had levelled at them earlier. Zahenna relaxed a little, let her voice die down a bit after that.

"If you turn out to be pregnant, how do you expect to hide the pup from the Queen?"

Zahenna's voice quavered.

"I don't know," she said, "But I need you to buy me some more time. Let me help him. Tell the Queen I threatened you, or drugged you. Just *let me go.*"

Sali snorted.

"She'll never believe any of that. She can probe my mind, remember? And even if she couldn't, I've tracked trained soldiers and spies over day-lengths of wild terrain. It will be my career lost more likely than yours."

Zahenna shook her head in frustration. Her voice rose again.

"Didn't I always look out for you? It was me who taught you how to get along in court when you came out of the North, half feral and ready to bite anyone that put a hand out to you. We are *friends*, Sali. No matter where I end up being at the end of this, palace, shack or hole in the ground, you'll have my gratitude and whatever aid and companionship I can give you."

Sali pointed her nose off to the horizon. She stayed there for a few seconds, letting the situation soak in the silence of the mid-desert.

"Wardan's bound to figure out what happened to his dearest henchmen, and soon. The citizens of Lower Dune will need me, and the Permafrost, to protect them from the assault. I'd better go back and call in Leethia's ground troops for support."

She swung her little travelling dot around Zahenna's side of the hover. She stopped in front of Zahenna for just a moment, her posture stiff and stern as ever.

"I'll be circling south of Leethia's assault until I find you. I *will* find you," she said.

Zahenna nodded.

"One way or the other, you'll find me."

Zahenna got back on the bed of the hover as Sali pulled away on her dot. When the two hovers moved away from each other at top speed, Sali disappeared into the night faster than the little flashing stars that fell in arcs around the center of the planet at certain times of the year.

Zahenna watched Sali leave and stared at the horizon long after her friend had melded with it. Her hand rested on the floor, by Sithon. He placed his hand over hers. She let him.

"How are you feeling?" he asked, almost not wanting to know the answer.

Zahenna's eyes broke contact with the horizon. Instead, she looked at her knees. Sithon notice that the scar tissue from the energy burn on her face had settled up, leaving a section of black skin with three stripes to it, like a claw mark, running down from underneath her eye. To Sithon, her scars, her nicked ears, her tuft of a tail made her look different, otherworldly. Beautiful. They made him remember where she had got them, and the bravery she had shown in every instance.

"I've stopped shivering. The fire Talent takes a lot of energy out of you at that level, I guess. I've never seen Sydney use it that way," Zahenna replied.

"Zahenna," he began, stopped, began again, "you may never love me, and I understand why. But for me, friends have been hard to come by, and you're one of the best."

Sithon felt his tail want to creep between his legs, despite the fact that he was sitting on it. After the incident on the porch, he wondered what she would do. Zahenna entwined her fingers with Sithon's. The sensation made a tingle go up his arm.

"Sali is right, you know. If we win this fight, I have responsibilities. Rakaria will need leaders."

Up front, Djarro snorted.

"I thought the reason we were all in this mess is because Rakaria had too many leaders... or Geedar who'd fancy themselves as such," he said, then added, "I'm including the Queen in that lot."

Zahenna flattened her ears, pursed her lips and said nothing. Sithon didn't know whether to answer Djarro or stay silent to avoid offending Zahenna. Djarro made up his mind for him.

"We oughta be there about an hour before dawn. Let's hope the Queen's got some distractions on by then or we'll have a whole lot o' friends there to greet us."

"Sali and the other air commanders will keep them distracted as best they can," Zahenna replied. Sithon watched his father for a while, standing there with the wind jostling his brushy, cropped mane. Every once in a while, Djarro would carefully steer them around the apex of a dune, his tongue coming out of his mouth a little when he did. Sithon eventually sat up a little, and watched out in front of them. He wondered if he would be able to see the *Death's End* when they got close enough, but even the night sky was only, ultimately a dark blue. The black forest of spires and turrets, hanging wires and antennae stood out against it even with the sky at its darkest point.

When Sithon felt the old, familiar dread of that haunted skeleton of metal and mind, he had to say,

"I'm sorry, Djarro. I never wanted to come back here, least of all with you."

Djarro's response was unhesitant.

"You made the best decision that you could. I don't think anyone wanted you to keep that thing screamin' away in your head."

"And... I know you want to give your mother one last chance. Just promise me one thing."

Sithon perked up his ears.

Can I promise anything right now?

Still Sithon said, "I can try."

"Let her go," Djarro said, "If it comes down to you

or her, let her go. She would want you to live."
"JASIMOTH," Sithon said under his breath.
"What's that, pup?"
"Nothing."

Flood Waters Rising

Vaedra

The first ship flew over them during that part of the night when the stars are brightest and the sky blackest... the hour before dawn. A sleek, smooth grey cruiser, it looked like Leethia had been storing it in an airlocked container until now, from the time before Wardan's insurrection.

Zahenna followed it with her nose moving in a wide arc, from behind them out to the front. She smiled with her mouth open, letting her tongue poke out a little. For the first time since meeting her, Sithon thought he could see mirth sparkling in her brown eyes.

"They changed the plan!" he said to her.

Zahenna smiled wider, saying, "I know. It's mother. She may have been willing to expend you two, but she won't let me enter the ship without a fighting chance. I think I may have saved us... if we can get to Vaedra in time."

Sithon smoothed back his mane, momentarily uncomfortable. She played a brutal game, this one, and as far as he could tell, she'd been doing it since she was a pup. He remembered how afraid he had been of her during the crash, when she had threatened him from the holding tube. After getting to know her, he realized that she had been telling the truth back there. She really was dangerous; she really did get what she wanted, whatever that might be. To get here, on this transport, she had manipulated a Queen... a mind-reading Queen, at that. She had wanted to save them, so she had saved them. Sithon also realized what this would likely cost Zahenna, though, with or without the existence of an out-born pup. To do what Leethia had done, to send the ships in hours early, Leethia would have had to tell her administrators why. Sithon couldn't think how she could manoeuvre around it, at any rate. In order to scapegoat Sithon and Djarro as kidnappers, she would need Sali's testimony.

Two more ships flew over, making the hover sway from side to side. Djarro jerked at the control stick to get them back on course, and keep them from sliding backward down the side of the dune they were climbing. The two ships followed the same course as the first, and were just as sleek and new-looking.

"Where is Leethia getting *those*?" Sithon asked Zahenna, who was still grinning, watching them.

"We still had some stockpiles Wardan didn't know about... mother just knew better than to exhaust them before we knew we could have a good crack at him. She's gambling now, though. If we don't do our part, that will be all of mother's reserve force at risk, and worse, identified for tracking."

As they topped the next dune, explosions echoed across the desert waste. Tongues of flame licked off the skin of *Death's End*—they had succeeded in landing an opening salvo, but Wardan's satellite ships pursued the smaller, more manoeuvrable fighter ships with the inexorable speed of a large predator with momentum on its side. Of the four ships, two remained. The *Pwarnaa* had likely been lost when Sashi blew the generators at Takara—if it wasn't out of commission, it was certainly still in repair. The next biggest ship, *Voiceless Victory*, was missing as well. Sithon remembered that it had been the main cargo ship for Wardan's operation during the repairs. Judging by that, it could have been halfway around the planet collecting goods from the nearest sympathetic supplier. That left the two biggest, *Nikira's Bane* and *Flood Vengeance*, patrolling the sky above their crippled mother while more ships coming from all directions assailed them.

It wasn't long before Sithon, Djarro and Zahenna got close enough to feel the rumble in the ground from the engines and from the frequent energy bursts that burned the sides of every ship in the vicinity. Drifting in as metal giants dodged and swooped in the sky not so very far above them, they entered the perimeter of the great, black mass that was the *Death's End*. Djarro stopped the hover at the long ridge of sand marking the place where the ship had crashed, nose first, into the desert. Sithon slipped off the back of the vehicle, keeping his hand on its side for the familiarity of the sensation as he beheld that horrible place again. He didn't want the light to shine on *Death's End* again—not as a working ship, anyway. Here in the darkest time of night, the time of despair, was where it belonged.

The wall of the downed ship loomed black above them, shining here and there where the metal had been worn down by sand. They had come in east of the hole which Sithon and the others had escaped from before. Here, protected stairwells and deep channels with catwalks and heavy chains between them reached over and around a sloping section of the ship which angled outward with the general sweep of the *Death's End*'s tail fin.

Sithon ducked a little as an explosion erupted on the roof above them, showering debris down onto the ground.

A shard of metal rolled near Djarro, a curl of smoke trailing out behind it. Leethia's fighters dropped a succession of explosives, trailing down the ship. Further down the perimeter a swarm of them surrounded *Flood Vengeance*, harrying the larger ship while its turrets swivelled everywhere to keep up with them. An intense energy shot connected with one of the fighters, sending it sailing to the ground with a huge, black hole in its side. As dawn lined the horizon with pink glow, Sithon saw black clouds gathering from both the East and the West, Wardan and Leethia's forces facing each other down, waiting to do battle. They needed to get into the ship, and quickly—the activity going on above them was merely an opening skirmish to the final battle. Once that battle was joined, what chance would they have on the ground against weapons from the sky, encased in armor? Sithon pointed to where the blast had gone off near them.

He said, "Let's see if we can outrun the guards to

that blast hole. From there we can..."

The wind changed directions, and Sithon smelled something funny on it. Djarro and Zahenna smelled it too, from the perk of their ears. He smelled company, lots of it, trying to stay calm, keep their pheromones low for an ambush.

Before Sithon could act on what his senses told him, Geedar popped out everywhere: along the walled stairways, in the crevices, even shimmying on their stomachs toward the edge of the curved roof. Every one of them held a slingshot, filled with a round ammunition that Sithon didn't recognize. They looked like little grey seed pods with a flashing sensor on one side.

A row of guards jogged out of the nearest crevice and surrounded Sithon and the others from behind. They held tubular energy net launchers.

Sithon felt the shimmer in his blood flash within him. He watched as Zahenna's fingers started to glow ever so slightly pink. Djarro hunched over, growling and brandishing his claws.

"Don't move," someone called from the top of the ship, "Don't... move. The sharpshooters have head-poppers trained on you."

Head-poppers? Djarro mouthed to Sithon. The figure standing on the roof, a captain by the bauble attached to his tabard, decided that was too much movement. He motioned to one of the sharpshooters, who let the payload of his slingshot hit the ground between Sithon and Djarro. The section of the pod with the red flashing sensor stuck to the ground. It beeped twice, then exploded, throwing up a blinding fountain of sand.

Sithon and Zahenna coughed as sand entered their noses and mouths. Djarro just stood there, clearing his throat after a while.

"That's a head-popper. One more wrong move and the name can tell you what you need to know," said the captain, a grizzled young male with more crooked angles in his frame than Caylus. He had a chunk out of one leg, and an arm that was a different colour from the rest of him. At least once, possibly twice a resurrection, Sithon thought.

"I take it that your master knew we were coming," Sithon called up to the captain like he'd just come for a friendly visit.

The captain barked, "Get moving! You can see how long you last boring Wardan with your stupid questions."

Sithon cast a glance over to Djarro and Zahenna. Zahenna's fingertips had returned to their normal colour, although she looked rather disappointed about it. She gave an almost imperceptible shrug, as if to say, *Well, we wanted to get into the control center didn't we?* Djarro looked rather less impressed, but still he put his hands behind his head and his tail between his legs. The captain began commanding the guard like a fussy shopkeep re-arranging the merchandise.

"All right, all right, big one at the front, where we can see you. Then the female, then the scrawny one. That's it, get around 'em, not too close though. Get the cuffs on 'em, shooters, stay aimed..."

After cuffing them, the guards opened a sealed door in the side of the ship which had previously been invisible due to some well-placed panelling. The guards then led them, with some shoving and cursing, into what Sithon recognized as the lab wing. With the ship's nose buried in the sand, the whole place tilted at an odd angle. Nasty, rotting smells assailed them from behind clumsy metal doors above, and shelves full of horrible pieces of things grinned at them from behind darkened windows below. Sithon felt his stomach begin to knot up.

There are some things you can never get used to.

When another explosion hit near them, one of the above-doors swung open, hitting Djarro squarely in the nose. He cried out, but could not wipe the blood that Sithon smelled trickling from him. The guards prodded Djarro to keep going, and he growled in a way that would convince most Geedar of their impending bloody death. He still kept moving, though, with a furtive look at the ceiling. The last blast had rocked the frame of the place so hard that Sithon had half expected it to fall down on them, too.

Eventually they reached the long set of staircases leading to the command center behind the atrium. Sithon instinctively turned toward it, thinking that Wardan would undoubtedly be up that way. He found himself shoved back in line, a stinging low-current energy buzz shoved into his ribcage at the end of a wand.

Instead of taking them to the administrative complex, the guards herded them along on the bottom floor, toward the mid-ship hangar bays. The hallways they followed now had increasingly less wall lining them, and increasingly more wire, tubing and cage panelling. In his mind, Sithon kept track of where they were in relation to Vaedra. From here, she would be back the way they had come, second floor and through the security doors...

Sithon found himself entering a room so huge, the doors on the far wall looked too small to fit through. The ceiling, striped with skylights was dingy and made of that peaked corrugated metal that the residents of Lower Dune had been so fond of. Everywhere was scuffed, everywhere were crates bearing Wardan's smoke insignia piled on top of one another and in some cases, looking like they had fallen over. Hanging from the ceiling were a succession of crane arms, some holding rotary saws, some shaped like hands, all hanging from a central track like the one that Vaedra's bucket thing had moved on. Sithon assumed that this was the repair bay for Wardan's ships, although his limited privileges on board the *Death's End* had never allowed him to actually see it. What he could see, however, was the lightening grey of the sky outside which brought them ever closer to being squashed in the workings of Wardan's mad ship.

The guards prodded the three of them onto a darker rectangle of flooring. Sithon could see Wardan's floor-length, white robe billowing around him as he hopped down off a stack of boxes. Not even the trace of a grin graced Wardan's face. He threw up a hand to someone on the wall.

"Flip the switch," Wardan called.

The floor underneath them disappeared, or rather, dropped too quickly for them to stay fully on it. Sithon hit the floor at the bottom with an elbow-crunching thud, whacking the back of his head for good measure. Zahenna screamed on the way down, and favoured one leg standing up.

"I never thought I'd *miss* Smart Blood," she groaned.

Wardan now leaned over the lip of the hole, far above them. He had trapped them in a maintenance pit, just a bit too high for any of them to jump out of. Sithon couldn't see any handholds on the smooth walls. What he did see was the ring of sharpshooters, still trained on them from above.

"Thanks for bringing back my transport," Wardan said, his voice made all the more irritating by the echoes, "It's not that I don't have more, It's just that I didn't know who *took* it." His face remained flat, unemotional.

Sithon flicked an ear.

"It's a trade. You get the transport, we get the Kids."

Wardan started to breathe harder, and his mask of indifference began to twitch away, in the lips, the eyes... Sithon continued. If he died, at least he had pissed Wardan off one more time before then, and done a good job of it.

"What was that Slash was always calling me? Dung heap? Well, now he's an ash heap. How are you going to resurrect him, Wardan? Mix him with mud and make a sculpture?"

Wardan screeched through his teeth and started to pace. The whole pit rung with the sound, rough and frustrated.

"I should have blasted you to pieces on the way here, but no, I wanted to look into your eyes as the head-poppers hurtled toward you. I wanted to lick your combined blood and brains from my lips and most of all, I wanted to personally hack your corpses to bits afterward. They were my family! My only family!"

"Vaedra was supposed to be your family," Sithon called back, "Where is she now, Wardan? Disconnected? Have you gotten tired of her nagging and decided to deal with her like you did with Sashi?"

Wardan looked around and above himself, a little nervously if Sithon wasn't mistaken.

I know why he didn't blow us up on the way here... mother wouldn't let him. Her main consciousness is probably managing the battle and doesn't yet know we're here.

Wardan's response confirmed Sithon's suspicions.

"I'm through with your questions... it was bad enough having to listen to you whine *before*. I'm sick of waiting for you to die. Captain?"

Wardan raised his arm in the air—Sithon knew that when he dropped it, the sharpshooters would send the explosives singing on the air toward them, bringing nothing but a red haze and then a brief consciousness of being in several pieces before winking out like a dead star. Wardan's hand did not drop, however, instead it crumpled in toward his midsection, fingers curling.

Wardan's eyes went wide and unfocussed. He hunched over, begging with his body.

"Vaedra... *Vaedra*! Please stop screaming I was just holding them here please..." Wardan finished this sentence and then speech devolved into heavy breathing with pathetic little moans on the exhalations. Wardan danced dangerously close to the rim of the pit.

Somewhere far above, Sithon heard the whine of the saws starting up. Two of the maintenance arms rattled along the ceiling tracks, through the middle of the guards lining either side of the pit. The air became awash with the smell of blood. Half a guard tumbled into the pit opposite from Sithon, and Djarro and Zahenna hopped away from it, with its dead, staring eyes. Cries and moans filled the air, from those who had managed to duck out of the way a bit. The saw arms came back and slashed through their cries for mercy.

Wardan half-watched the slaughter, still begging.

"Stop it, stop this now! Vaedra, you have to be reasonable about this..."

The two saw arms swung around the pit and cut Wardan's escape routes off. They backed him toward the edge, one reluctant step at a time.

Vaedra came in over the loudspeakers now.

"You swore not to hurt him! I took you at your word," she cried.

Wardan snarled, "You let him escape, and look what he did! I had no choice!"

The saws moved closer to Wardan, so that he was

standing so close to the edge of the pit that Sithon could see the underside of his tail.

"Then neither do I. Goodbye, Wardan."

Wardan swung out his arm then, and Sithon saw that he held a small control pad in it, with a switch. He yelled as loudly as he could, knowing all the while that his voice would never sway Wardan from was he was about to do.

"No, you outborn bastard, no!" Sithon bellowed.

Wardan pressed his thumb to the switch and flipped it over. The saws stopped, the lights in the room flickered and went out. Vaedra uttered one last scream that entered Sithon's bones and shook, a scream that penetrated the walls, the wires and the gears holding *Death's End* together. The scream held on as a solid, horrible note. When the sound ended, it turned into a jumble of deep motor noises, like things hitting the side of a moving cart. Wardan still stood at the lip of the pit, walled in by the stilled blades. He held his hands to his ears as Vaedra screamed, and twisted violently from side to side. He moved his foot further back and his ankle twisted, collapsed underneath him and sent him tumbling end over end into the pit.

Wardan landed head first. His neck jerked awkwardly to one side with a resounding crack. After that, the rest of his body flopped over to one side, limp and useless. Wardan's glasses remained on his face, but skewed and cracked. Blood poured from his muzzle onto his lolling tongue as he struggled to breathe.

Without even glancing at the others, Sithon ran

forward and stood over Wardan. Sithon raised his leg to kick him in the throat, but Wardan's body stilled before he could.

Sithon kicked the corpse, over and over, in the nose, in the chest, but it did no good. Wardan was beyond pain, and Sithon was still very much in the thick of it. He fell to his knees and wept.

Flood Waters Rising

One Step Too Far

JASIMOTH

Sithon remained on the floor, in a haze, while Djarro and Zahenna carefully stepped around him. Wardan's blood soaked into the fur on Sithon's knees, and he let it. He listened to Djarro and Zahenna's voices behind him, even as streams of hot tears rolled from his eyes, down his neck and into his chest ruff.

He heard Zahenna first.

"I think I might be able to heat the bar between these cuffs enough that it breaks. Djarro, come here... no, lean down. I can't reach it with you standing up. That's it."

"Don't burn me, now... ah! That's better," Djarro said, "Feels good to swing my arms around again."

Zahenna again.

"Ok, now push the release on mine."

Sithon heard the clang of a pair of restraints hitting the floor. He stayed kneeling, eyes welling until everything went bent and watery. He didn't blink, barely breathed, didn't know if he could move anymore.

The softness of Zahenna's hands brushed against his as she released the catch on his restraints. His arms flopped down to his sides, fingers curled and knuckles resting on the floor.

"Should we try to move him?" Zahenna asked, as if he was not there.

"We'll need him," Djarro replied, and then, "Sithon? Just get up and help us, this once, and we'll be outta here. This maintenance bay opens on the South of the wreckage: I saw the door on the way in."

"She's been unplugged," Sithon croaked, "Wardan managed to escape us again. He can't bring himself back, can he?"

Djarro said softly, "No, I don't reckon he can, pup. But we gotta get outta here, before one side or t'other decides to flatten our exit route. Get off your knees and come help us. I think we can climb our way out of here if we tie our clothing strips together."

Sithon remained slumped, still and weeping.

"Come on, pup," Djarro said, "We're still here, and we need you."

Suddenly, a switch clicked over in Sithon's head very much as it had in Wardan's hand. He felt an overwhelming energy jolt through him, a fervour like he'd never felt before. He felt wild, not from Smart Blood, but from his own restlessness. He ran his fingers through his mane, and pulled.

She could still be alive too... he thought. Until now I had been thinking of her like she was dead. Brain dead, perhaps, but not really dead! I have to get to her before this place is destroyed... I could still have her for months, maybe even years after this!

Sithon stood up, knees aching but otherwise filled with zealous determination and that almost unnatural energy coursing through his veins, and said, "You're right Djarro... Vaedra could still be alive. I can't just sit here. I have to get to her and bring her with us!"

Djarro, in the middle of unwrapping his loincloth, stopped unwrapping.

"Think about what you're planning, pup! You don't know what's happened to the rest of the ship. I think she'd want you to leave her rather than live like she is now."

Sithon ripped his loincloth off with a single, careless tug.

"You don't know her," he said, voice sharp, "We could have her for longer, father, just us. We'll take her with us when we go."

Djarro held out his hand for Sithon's loincloth, scowling, stubby ears flattened, but saying nothing. His brows protruded over his eyes and darkened them, like they were made of low-hanging cloud.

When they had tied the makeshift clothes-rope together, Djarro tied one end into a loop and hooked it onto one of the saw arms after several unsuccessful throws. Sithon insisted on being the one to test the rope, his motivation being his impatient drive to get to the top of the rope first. The others let him because he was light, and had Smart Blood on his side should he fall.

Sithon shimmied up the rope without much problem, feeling satisfaction like scratching an itch in the middle of his back with every pull he made up the wall. He shuffled from foot to foot while Zahenna climbed. He also looked nervously out the window every once in a while for any sign that the battle had drifted over their way.

He held out a hand and hoisted Zahenna up when she reached the top. She dropped his hand immediately afterward and moved away from him about a tail-length. They both leaned over the edge to watch Djarro climb—he had agreed to go last, lest he break the rope and strand them all in the pit.

The saw arm creaked as Djarro put his full weight on the rope. He braced his feet against the wall as he climbed to redistribute some of the weight. The rope seemed to be holding. Sithon felt a little relief for Djarro, but none whatsoever about Vaedra. He continued to fidget, getting his hands wringing now as well.

Djarro got about halfway up the side of the pit, with the rope creaking but holding steady, before the whole, wide room began going dark, the skylights filling with a jagged wall of darkness.

Sithon recognized the gun turrets on that ship from that evening he, Tyrius and Zahenna had spent fleeing across the *Death's End*'s back—*Nikira's Bane* fell from the sky, flames and smoke erupting from its nose.

"Djarro," Sithon called, "Hurry!"

Djarro pulled as hard as he could manage on the rope, muscles straining to pull him up in half the time. Sithon saw the tops of his ears over the lip, and felt a moment of relief.

Everything shook, and with a deafening roar the maintenance bay wall to Sithon's left crashed in, panelling and glastik splinters flying everywhere. Djarro's rope slackened, slipped off the arm and onto the teeth of the saw, and snapped at the loop. Djarro lost his balance but managed to grab hold of the edge of the pit with one hand.

His other hand soon appeared over the lip, as well. To Sithon's great relief, Djarro hoisted himself up so that his waist was level with the edge, then swung a leg over and climbed out.

Djarro surveyed the damage on the left wall. The rounded, black edge of *Nikira's Bane* held up what remained of the wall, but fire licked at the ceiling tiles. Something exploded on top of the ship. After the fireball cleared, most of that part of the ceiling was missing. Pieces of burnt ceiling tile clattered around them, smelling noxious.

"This place ain't gonna hold much longer," Djarro said, motioning toward the long doors at the end of the bay, "Let's get out and catch Sali while we still can."

Sithon looked back the way they had come. No smoke filtered in from under the door, and the wall looked intact except for a few burn marks. He still felt that antsy pull in his chest, that fear-based desperation.

"You and Zahenna get to a safe place. I came here to save my mother, and that's what I'm going to do," he said, although he couldn't help letting a little shake enter his voice.

"Oh no you're not," Djarro said. He advanced on Sithon, his enormous arms at the ready to grab him.

Sithon stood his ground.

"Just try it, Djarro!" Sithon yelled. He immediately regretted it, but still didn't know what else he could have said.

Djarro stopped. He closed his eyes for second, as though he had just gotten a nasty cut.

"All right, pup," he said, "Go. I won't stop you. But she's not your only family. I'm waiting here for you as long as I can. After that... just remember that I always loved you, and I'm happy that we got to know each other, even if the time was shorter than I'd hoped."

Zahenna said, "I'll stay with you, Djarro. I don't trust Sali not to leave once she has me."

Sithon whined. Vaedra was somewhere back the way they came, probably suffering. She needed him. But Djarro and Zahenna needed him, too. They needed him to convince them to leave and find safety.

He closed his eyes, so that he didn't have to see them standing there, Zahenna's hand on Djarro's crossed arm, watching him go and wondering if they would ever see him again. Sithon turned and ran, and ran out the door, through corridors blazing with heat but not yet on fire. When he reached the stairs to the command center he ran up those too, past bodies slumped against railings and slicks of blood on the landings. The guards outside Vaedra's command center had been slammed to death in the door. Sithon leapt over their bodies.

He could hear her then, screaming and screaming, but not in words. She wailed so constantly that Sithon wondered how she was taking in air. He heard half words in the screams, bits of names and rounded sounds, but nothing coherent.

Vaedra's chamber was circular, like Sashi's, only this chamber had glastik windows as thick as a snout which looked in on the chair. Wardan had wanted all of the employees of the *Death's End* to be able to see what they were capable of, if only Wardan granted them the technology to do so. The wide sliding door to the chamber was right in front of Sithon's entrance point. He went to the key pad and pressed every button he could think of to turn it on, several times quickly, but nothing happened. He hooked his fingers in between the two halves of the door and pulled as hard as he could. His Smart Blood flowed, and then ebbed, but when Sithon let go of the door he found that the metal had not even bent.

The ship rocked with another impact, as large as the one caused by *Nikira's Bane*, but closer to the command center. A piece of metal sheeting fell from the ceiling and scored Sithon's arm. He cried out, but his voice was lost in Vaedra's shrieks.

Sithon ran to the one of the glastik windows, hoping that it had been cracked by the impact. He saw no cracks in the window. Instead, Vaedra lay before him, completely broken.

She lay on her back, tossing over to each side. Cuts and bruises covered her arms and legs from impacts with the trailing wire ends and lab debris on the floor, and as Sithon watched, she added a new one, smashing her hand into a piece of vial near her.

Sithon pounded on the glass.

"Mother!" he hollered, "Mother! Can you hear me?"

Vaedra looked toward the sound, her eyes blank and unfocussed. For a moment, Sithon thought perhaps she would say something. Even a mash-up of his name with Toraus's name would bring him comfort. Instead, Vaedra's eyes rolled back into her head. She arched her back as a spasm gripped her, and the gibberish shot from her mouth with even greater intensity. Sithon's stomach ached as he noticed that she had soiled herself at several points in the room. Sithon looked up, where he knew, if he followed the path around the room, he would find an air vent that could possibly still lead him to Vaedra. Another impact jolt from behind the command center interrupted his thinking, ending its fury with the entire area being on a greater tilt than before.

Vaedra's eyes still looked at him, but Sithon knew that they weren't really seeing him. Memories flooded back to him, from that night when Toraus had died. Back at the beginning of all of this mess, when he had only had a mother. Vaedra had been wildly, uncontrollably bent on bringing Toraus back, on having him for herself and ignoring Sithon's wishes.

Sithon pressed his palms to his face. He realized now that despite all of Djarro's teaching, he was a Flood, forever and always. Only a Flood would chase after his brain-dead mother out of some madness for family unity, just as his mother had obsessed over Toraus and Toraus, in his day had been the most fervent of all, preferring to kill all those different from him rather than destroy his picture of the family lineage. Vaedra would never be Vaedra now, any more than the Toraus Vaedra had created in Second Skin would act like the Old Mange.

He had to leave her. Tyrius had known all along that it would come to this, that he needed passwords less than he needed protection from his own family madness. He dashed for the door, leaving Vaedra's cracked voice behind and hoping with all his heart that Djarro and Zahenna were still there, and could forgive him.

Flood Waters Rising

Epilogue: I Found Her at the End of the Road

Sithon woke up to the rain pattering on the roof of Flood Waters. Every morning, no matter what the weather, he woke up disoriented, wondering first where Vaedra was, and why Toraus was not hollering for him when he had slept in until the sun was high. Then, as more memories came back, he wondered where his cold metal bed had gone to, if all that had ever really happened to him.

Then he would roll over, and see Djarro's barrel chest wrapped in all their blankets (he pulled them all around himself at night, but Sithon was used to the damp anyway) and remember the rest. It was only a temporary stop over, they had fixed the holes in the roof of the last standing outbuilding with timber they had bought from the nearest village, and Toraus was long dead. Sithon had entered the main body of the ruins with Djarro only once, and the proceeds of that search lay in the corner, covered in animal skins. Of the paintings of his grandmother that Sithon had once cherished, three remained undestroyed by the leaking roof. Sithon would keep them with him now, no matter what, as a reminder that they were all together now, and perhaps, in that other place, under Darna's care, they could be happy.

Zahenna... Sithon remembered the last time he

had seen her. Her hair had glowed in the new morning light, as she boarded that ship taking her back to Marrow Canyon and her mother. He supposed he would never see her again, even if she did have their child. Especially if she had their child. Remembering her was another one of those things he had done every day. Her, and Vaedra, and Sashi... Sithon remembered, Djarro hunted, and they both spent most of their days in silence.

Sithon rolled to his feet and stretched his back. The dirt floor here seemed to collect stones, and no matter how much he scratched at his sleeping place at night a pebble would always lodge somewhere.

The chinks in the walls of the small, square building allowed for unusual visitors. Climbing vines twined their way through the stones, slowly breaking down the flat slabs that made up the building with their relentless roots. Small blue flowers grew in bunches on them this time of year, and clusters hung from the ceiling and around the doors and windows, where the most light had typically come in before Sithon and Djarro had fixed things. Sithon wrapped his loincloth around him, then grabbed two handfuls of blossoms. He then headed out into the rain.

He followed a path he had flattened for himself through the thick brush, down parallel to the old invisible barrier and out into a clearing with three piles of rocks carefully stacked in the middle. The first one had been for Toraus. The other two were for Vaedra and Sashi. Sithon wished he had something to place on the rock piles that had belonged to either of them, but neither of them had left anything. He wondered if anyone but he and Djarro remembered them at all. He placed the blue flowers on Vaedra's grave, then Sashi's. He knew that Vaedra would not want to lie anywhere except by Toraus's side.

As the rain soaked into Sithon's fur, he bowed his head. He kneeled down before the graves. After a while he began to shiver, but did not move. After the sun went down, he would head back to the outbuilding again, wet and miserable. Djarro would start a fire and try to cheer him up with stories of his childhood. They would fall asleep after a while and start all over again.

Sithon kneeled there, bent over and very tired and let his mind wander, although it never wandered very far from familiar themes.

He heard movement at the edge of the clearing, and spun around, landing on his bottom in the process. Vaedra had died once in this clearing, and the overhanging trees which darkened its edges lent it an eerie, other-worldly quality. It made Sithon edgy, if not graceful.

Only Djarro stepped out of the trees. Sithon tilted his head. Djarro had never visited this place, not even to lay the gravestones. Djarro stepped forward into the gloomy overcast light, two bunches of delicate red bell flowers clutched in his giant hands. He bowed his head as he approached first Vaedra, then Sashi's grave and laid flowers on each. He then dropped to one knee, and then clumsily shuffled down onto the other one.

"I dried enough game to last us a while," Djarro said, "Thought I might have more business here."

Sithon replied, "You once told me about a place where the Geedar live in peace, as a pack. Tomorrow, we set off to find it."

More movement, this time from the opposite side of the clearing, toward the old Base, now abandoned. Something moved in between the trees, quickly, as if trying to avoid detection. It walked upright. Sithon stood up, ready to dash toward it. Djarro Got up more slowly, laying a hand on his back.

"Steady now," he whispered, "Stay calm."

It flitted closer. Sithon thought he saw an orange tail slide behind a large tree, smooth with a distinctive tuft at the end. It couldn't be... but Sithon needed it to be her. He leapt over the gravestones, barking his shin on Sashi's, and made for the woods. He reached the treeline and sniffed the air, and it smelled like her. He pushed further into the dark and damp of the underbrush, taking large steps and calling out.

"Zahenna? Zahenna! Come out, I know it's you."

"Come on, pup" Djarro called to Sithon from behind the graves, "Did Darius cut out your good sense? Gebback here!"

"You really should get back there, Sithon," Zahenna said, appearing around the edge of a tree behind him, "Djarro worries about you."

Sithon approached her, sniffed her, tilted his head at her.

"Are you... really here?"

She laughed a little.

"Well, take me over to Djarro and see if he can see me. I think you'll find that he can."

Sithon's head still remained at an angle.

"Why?" The question was simple, but he wondered if she could answer it without a good meal, a captive audience and a roaring fire.

Zahenna smelled of stress then. Sithon had never smelled it on her before.

"A long story... and a short one. I won't be dropping off any pups with you, that much I know."

Sithon started back toward Djarro, and he could hear Zahenna following him. Although he started out ahead, she ran to catch up with him.

"Sithon?"

"Yes?"

"Is there somewhere we can be alone, later?"

"Yes."

"Do you remember what I said about my decision? If we survived the battle?"

Sithon felt a rush sweep from the tip of his toes to the roots of his mane.

"Yes..." he said.

Zahenna turned him to look at her. She brushed her cheek against his, firmly and openly.

"I've made my decision," she said.

THE END

Flood Waters Rising

Appendix: Glossary of Terms

Bleirah's Pool: (See Page 16) In common Geedari mythology, Bleirah is a goddess who filled a pool from which all knowable life sprang. Bleirah's Pool is used as an expression of surprise at the infinite variety and unexpected turns inherent in life, as well as being a euphemism for female genitalia.

Null: (See page 84) A derogatory slang word for a Geedar born without a Talent. Talentless Geedar are fairly common, and are not necessarily ostracized for not having gifts, although finding a career may be a little more tricky for them if they are not all that intelligent. In the revolution, many Talentless Geedar sided with Wardan because he promised to use technology to give them the Talents they were denied at birth.

Flood Waters Rising

Thank You For Reading With Pop Seagull Publishing!

If you enjoyed this book, then you'll love our fantasy short story collection...

Monsters and Mist

Five original short stories by Elizabeth Hirst, collected for the first time into one convenient volume!

Available Now on Smashwords and CreateSpace

For exclusive content, updates and fun, connect with us online at:

Twitter: @PopSeagullPub
Website: http://www.popseagullpublishing.com
Blog: http://popseagullpublishing.wordpress.com/
Smashwords: http://www.smashwords.com/profile/view/popseagullpublishing

Flood Waters Rising

About the Author

Elizabeth Hirst lives in Oakville, Ontario, Canada with her Husband, her best friend, three fish and a lizard named Creep. She has published work in Alien Skin Magazine (http://www.alienskinmag.com/) the Mystic Signals 3 Anthology (http://www.loreleisignal.com) and is a former creative writer for Hitgrab Inc, creators of the MouseHunt and Levynlight Facebook apps. http://www.hitgrab.com/. In addition to her efforts as a writer and publisher, Elizabeth is training to be a professional animator at Sheridan College.

Photo by Sheena Callighen, 2010

Made in the USA
Charleston, SC
29 March 2012